The Ship Finding God

D. Krauss

Second Edition April 2022
by Indies United Publishing House, LLC

ISBN 978-1-64456-432-5   [paperback]
ISBN 978-1-64456-433-2   [ePub]
Library of Congress Control Number: 2022931043

Book design by *Caryatid Design*
Cover design by *Damonza*

INDIES UNITED PUBLISHING HOUSE, LLC
P.O. BOX 3071
QUINCY, IL 62305-3071
www.indiesunited.net

To Sky. This is where we go.

~

Thanks, Angela!

God is not what you imagine or what you think you understand. If you understand you have failed.
~Saint Augustine

Once one has seen God, what is the remedy?
~Sylvia Plath

The Story So Far...

Otto Boteman suffers a massive heart attack and wakes up in what he thinks is Heaven except God is nowhere to be found, so he joins a bunch of misfits building a rocket to look for Him. In the midst of battle, the rocket takes off. Otto and the crew are immediately shanghaied to the Pearly Gates where St. Peter charges them with a mission that just might end the war between good and evil, just might. Encountering worlds of hopelessness, a hostile star fleet, dimensional barriers, Dis, the Fallen, and a creature from nightmare, the crew is reduced one by one until only Otto is left. He crash-lands the ship on a blue planet, where a dog from his childhood leads him to a distant light.

Chapter I

Rainbow Bridge

Otto sat on the rough porch of the cabin, a pipe in one hand, a scotch in the other, and watched the sunset glow on the mountains to the ... east, let's call it. After all, that's where the suns rose each morning and he'd spent his entire time on Earth calling that location 'east,' so, why change? For all he knew, it could be southwest – depending on polar locations and magnetic fields and whatnot – but he had no compass, no maps, and no astronomers around to help him figure it out.

"Marc," he whispered, "where are you?"

Cha Cha, sprawled comfortably next to him, raised her head in inquiry. "Friend of mine," Otto explained. "Smart guy. Would come in handy about now."

Cha Cha wagged a tail enthusiastically, gave a short *woof*! and laid her head back down on the floor, contented. The other dogs – Sugarfoot, Clio, Pierre, Fritz, Snuffy – echoed the *woof* and then returned to scratching and panting and other doggie pastimes, except Fritz, who went to his hind legs and put an expectant paw on the side of the rocker, looking at Otto with a quizzical expression.

Otto chuckled. "You always were an empathic little bugger, weren't you?" he said and slapped his chest carefully with the pipe-laden hand. Fritz easily cleared the armrest and squirmed happily onto Otto's lap. "Agile, too," Otto noted and Fritz looked up at him, smiling. The other dogs immediately voiced whines of protest. "You'll get your turns," Otto assured and, after a little grousing, the dogs resumed individual business while Otto considered the efficacy of lap-hosting Cha Cha and Sugarfoot and Snuffy, who were twenty-thirty pounds each.

Oh well, you made the promise.

He scratched Fritz behind the ear, a hazardous proposition while holding a pipe, prompting the dog to adopt his silly face. A silly dog, a miniature party poodle, black and white like a harlequin, smaller than usual but probably the smartest and most fun-loving of the currently assembled group. Otto got him one winter when Sherry and he were living in upstate New York. She had seen an ad for newly born poodle puppies and said, "Oh! Let's go see!" because her sister had a poodle and Sherry wanted one of her own so, in the middle of an Adirondack blizzard, Otto drove thirty miles into the hinterlands around West Chazy, hopelessly lost and firmly convinced their frozen bodies would turn up in the spring. Then a small porch light loomed out of the snow.

About fifteen puppies in the litter, all black or all white, except for this one, a combination. The owner, obviously from a line of first cousins, shook his head and said, "Ya dun't want at 'un. He's da runt," implying that many genetic illnesses would plague it (conditions the owner probably knew intimately) and Otto had no doubt the runt was destined for a burlap sack and a boot off a local bridge. But it ran right up to them yipping and wanting to play and was funny and bold and Sherry and Otto looked at each other with a mutual accord and back into the snowstorm all three of them went, spending the next fifteen years traveling the world together until Otto finally had to put him down, cancer turning this fun-loving crazy poodle into a bag of pain.

And here he was.

Here all of them were: Sugarfoot, the first dog Otto owned, a motley mix of terrier and hound who had crawled under the fence one day when Otto was ten and stayed for a couple of years until crawling right back out; Clio, the German Shepherd mix Dad brought home from work and which spent its relatively short life running like a madwoman through the fields and woods of southern Alabama; Cha Cha, Otto's best-remembered childhood dog, an exuberant, smart, and protective collie mix who was hit by a truck; Pierre, actually Mom's dog, a rat terrier, frisky and fun and abandoned by Mom when she took up with different men to make her widowhood easier and, by default, became Otto's; and Snuffy, Otto's favorite dog from adulthood, a Spitz mix with a ridiculous curly tail, socially inept, did not know how to play but really, really wanted to and won, by that, permanent endearment because Otto had more sympathy for him than any other dog.

"What are you all doing here?" he whispered.

Because dogs don't go to Heaven.

They don't. Dogs have no souls and that was, by rights, necessary because humans ate animals and if an animal had a soul, then that's cannibalism. Granted, dogs are generally not on most menus (except as a delicacy in certain Asian markets. Otto remembered the Korean waitress in Kunsan laughing at him as he eyed his bulgogi with some suspicion. "Trust me," she said, "you could not afford dog."), but, still, there's a principle here. Perhaps, owing to the special relationship between mankind and dogs, an exception was made and they were granted souls. They certainly acted soulful. Especially here, in the Afterlife.

Rainbow Bridge.

When Otto had to put Snuffy down, he received a little card from the vet a few days later. It described Rainbow Bridge, a place where all the pets of your life gather and play and romp while awaiting your arrival, and then you get to play and romp with them at the foot of the bridge until … until you hear the call and you step on the bridge and your dogs and cats and parakeets and hamsters all line up at its base and bay and bark and tweet and whatever hamsters do, whistle or something like that, a farewell as you mount to …

Heaven.

Is this the Rainbow Bridge? If so, where is the landing?

"Where?" Otto whispered.

Fritz cocked his head in concern, and then gazed towards the distant mountains. Otto followed. The peaks changed color, the multi-hued, multi-sunned (well, two suns) light casting its palette across the crevasses and outcrops. Lovely. Bright canary and soft lilac twined with scarlets and blacks. Nothing Picasso or Gaitonde ever did with color and line and pleasing blends of geometry and shade could compete. But it certainly wasn't a Rainbow Bridge. Or Bifröst.

Or Heaven.

Otto drew on the pipe then said to Fritz, "Seems Hallmark, and the Bible, are a bit inaccurate."

A bit.

Oh, not in terms of comfort. This Afterlife had that, in spades. Take this present situation: Otto on the rough-hewn porch of a one-room cabin, which was exactly the kind of place he had long fantasized running away to, surrounded by dogs and sipping scotch while wreathed in pipe smoke (a Burley, Otto guessed. Ferdinand would know) …

Ferdinand, where are you?

… enjoying a fabulous sunset(s), soon to be followed by an even more fabulous dance of evening stars and nebulae and comet wheeling above and beyond the peaks until the moons, two moons (forming a matching set with the suns), silver and blue and always full, rose in the … south, let's call it … and bathed this world in cobalt and platinum but yet, the stars soared ever brighter as comets stitched a night sky that was never quite night.

Heavenly, all right. But not the expected venue.

Which was … what? Golden thrones and marble steps and crowds of angels throwing crowns at the Father's feet and that whole 'no more tears, no more pain, the old things are washed away' stuff. That's what he'd expected. Well, if he had to be more accurate, been *conditioned* to expect, at least. Certainly not a city – or City – as big as Jupiter with shops and restaurants and …

Claudia

… but no God, no Father, so take a leisurely trip across deserts and join a crew and launch a duct-taped rocket across a universe of dark and horror and end up here. Alone. Confused. Bereft.

A bit inaccurate, all right.

He drew a slow, luxurious puff. Nothing he expected but everything he wanted, at least in terms of peace and well-being. A quiet place in a beautiful locale, surrounded by the unconditional love of known dogs – isn't that Heaven? Isn't that exactly what the Bible promised, at least in negation, because there were no more tears here? No more trouble.

And no answers.

To so many questions.

Such as, why no Father? In that fabulous City of diversion and joy hosting billions and billions of lovely people (including Carl Sagan. Had that on good authority from Virgil), there was no Father, no Son, no Holy Spirit. No Allah or Zeus, either, for that matter. Evidence for one or all of them, yes, definitely, because, Someone was imposing a different physics but the actual Beings, in the Flesh, so to speak? Nope.

And why, in this Afterlife, in any Afterlife for that matter, is there struggle, downright war, against and alongside various beings who could be angels ("Faction," Latchemondy had said) or demons or superhumans or a branch so far above humanity it dismissed existence itself? Struggle and war were supposed to be absent. Death was supposed to be absent, too, but it was here. He'd seen Machine Gun Kelly die. Or go 'poof'!

Claudia didn't go poof. She really did die.

Lots of things weren't what they were supposed to be: Pearly Gates far less than advertised; Saint Peter more shill than saint, a thought that should get him a lightning bolt enema in a real Heaven. But in a real Heaven, no one gets lost. And Claudia and Marc and Ferdinand and everyone else, everyone, became lost. Dark worlds, winged demons, rivers of forgetfulness. Dark suns.

What Akiko became.

So, I gotta ask, Father, what is this Afterlife?

And why have You abandoned me?

Otto sat quietly for a moment, then shooed Fritz off his lap and stood and walked to the side of the porch as the dogs stirred and wriggled about him, sure another evening of fetch and play was in the offing. He stopped at the end and stared at the hills that gradually rose behind the cabin. He could not see the scattered chunks of twisted and burnt metal sprawled across the grasslands fronting them. Never mind that; a pinwheel galaxy, pulsing in violet and diamond, unveiled above the peaks clamoring for his attention. Don't worry, it said, be happy. We've got much better things than the wreckage of a silly old ship. Why, look at this! Just look! The dogs danced on the grass beside the porch's drop-off and smiled and panted and made little runs up the ridge. C'mon! Play with us! Don't worry! Be happy! Everything is fine.

Otto put the pipe down on the window ledge, polished off the whiskey, went inside and to bed.

Chapter II

The Lotos-Eaters

Otto woke with sunlight(s) streaming into his eyes and dog tongues washing his face. "Stop," he said and the dogs withdrew, rejoicing and baying and jumping about the little cot that was Otto's bed because it is day, day, and there are fields to run and rabbits (maybe. Otto hadn't seen any yet) to chase and the heat(s) and light(s) of two suns to absorb and relish.

He rolled over and sat up, the cot creaking under his weight. No wonder. It was made of branches stripped of their bark and lashed together with, apparently, those same bark strips, exactly the type of cot that a pioneer or mountain man or sodbuster would have fashioned on plains or ledges or grasslands and set inside the one-room log cabin he'd previously fashioned in the middle of the great emptiness. Yes, log cabin, uneven and off-balance and mortared with mud but secure and warm.

Otto liked it. If he had been a nineteenth-century kind of guy, this would be the house he'd've built. And this grassland valley between soaring mountains is where he'd've sited it.

Funny, that.

Otto shook his head and stretched and reviewed the past eight hours of sleep for any dreams but no, none. And that wasn't due to the instant forgetfulness that waking often caused; he'd simply had no dreams. Period. Something, or Someone, was blocking them. Back in the City, back on the ship, he'd dreamed. Good dreams, odd dreams, including ones of a golden Claudia, but not here.

Why not?

Dunno, so he'd tried to discover why not. He'd stayed awake for a couple of nights straight to see if sheer exhaustion fixed it, but that didn't work because he didn't get sleepy. He'd remained as robust and energetic and wakeful for those forty-eight or so hours as if he was back in the City or on the ship. Apparently, the urge to sleep remained as much a personal choice here as it was in those places, even when Amelia ...

Lost in Dis.

... had imposed a sleep regimen as a survival tactic. But when he chose to sleep in the City and on the ship, he'd dreamed. Wondrous dreams. Some of a golden Claudia.

Why not here?

Maybe because the memory of a golden Claudia had to fade, to dissipate, because she was gone, forever gone, forever beyond his grasp. This rough cabin in a fabulous valley was his personal heaven, the destination of his soul after a life well-lived, while hers was ... what? A marble palace by a wine-dark sea? An olive grove in the shadows of cloud-wreathed volcanos? Do we impose on each other's heavens?

Probably not.

At any rate, he finally gave up and chose to sleep because staying up all night revealed nothing except that the night sky moved in what Otto considered an earth-like progress, from east to west, at an earth-like pace of twelve hours, more or less. An uneventful twelve hours.

Sleep it away, then. All of it.

That he could sleep at will probably meant that both the universal translator and healing capacity also remained intact, although he'd had no opportunity to test either. The dogs communicated in standard doggy ways. Too bad. Otto would love to hear their opinion of humans (if not so much of him personally). Bet they don't regard us as the benevolent creatures we imagine ourselves to be; instead, they know us as capricious and cruel gods, one moment a blessing, the other, a curse. After generations of dealing with us, no other conclusion was possible.

As for the healing, Otto figured he could smash his thumb with a brick or something and see what happened, or burn himself making breakfast.

Speaking of which ...

He stood, the coarse-but-comfortable percale sheets falling away from the, yes, goose-down mattress, the dogs in one voice baying their eagerness because the capricious god stirs into action. "Okay, okay," he said and, in the middle of a squirming dog scrum, reached the door and pulled up the latch. The scrum bounded away, almost taking him with it, doggy toenails scrabbling across log porch and down log steps and off and away, dog pack screaming joyously at the freedom of plain and grass and distant sunlit mountains.

Sun(s)lit.

Otto stared at the two suns, both having cleared the eastern peaks: the small, intense yellow one posted to the upper left of the larger mauve one. They generated late spring or early summer heat, warming and enjoyable but not debilitating, and the light was bright but not dazzling. Exactly the kind of dual-star system he would personally enjoy.

Ain't that funny?

Otto frowned.

The dogs whirled and pranced and mock-fought all over the length of the front grasslands, ranging to the far incline that began about five football fields away in the direction of the mountains, and then tornadoing back to the porch itself. Otto laughed. We capricious gods are amused by the sheer simplicity of lesser beings. The pack yelled at him, "Come play! Come play!" not in actual words but obvious from their antics.

Otto waved them off. "You guys want bacon, doncha?" and he went inside as a chorus of "Bacon! Bacon!", translation of the happy yelps of happy dogs, followed.

Otto went to the big wood stove and opened the firebox

and, waddya know, coals still lit, and fetched a couple of pieces of already-split-and-dried firewood out of a right handy rough container and threw them in and they caught almost immediately and the stove was heating up quite properly.

He grabbed a big iron skillet hanging from the wall and greased it up with a right handy little can of Crisco (nice touch, Lord) and opened the cabinet above the stove and peeled off several strips from the big side of bacon hanging there and grabbed some eggs from the little shelf next to the cabinet and, moments later, the kitchen sizzled and steamed and filled with breakfast perfume.

"How 'bout some French toast?" Otto asked himself. "Why, capital idea, old bean!" he answered himself and hied to the same cabinet and pulled out great loaves of thick, perfect sourdough bread and ceramic bowls in which to mix egg and, yes, a pitcher of cool and unspoiled milk and don't forget the cinnamon and lordy, lordy, look at all this.

Yes, Lord, look at all this.

Otto stared at the perfect breakfast in the perfect kitchen of the perfect log cabin. Right above the bed was a cupboard from which he could pull out any book he wanted, any movie he wanted, any board game. Not food or anything food related; that was reserved for the kitchen cabinet. The cupboard dispensed stuff. Didn't matter what kind of stuff or how many books or movies or games or jackets or jeans or cigars or bottles of whiskey he sought, they were all in there. All. The cupboard was standard-sized, rather short, with one of the log walls of the cabin itself backing it, but that didn't matter. The cupboard produced anything. Everything. Cornucopia without end, amen.

There was a sixty-inch TV screen that appeared on the opposite wall whenever he wanted to watch one of the DVDs he pulled from the Magic Cupboard, or whenever he simply wanted to watch anything. Didn't need the DVDs, actually; all the movies and shows he could ever want to watch were available on any channel he selected, often without naming them. Thrillers, horror, Marvel, whatever, showed up, depending on his mood. Had a stereo, too, a Yamaha amp with Marantz speakers, just like he had in the eighties, with all the music he could ever fancy appearing on a side table whenever the mood took him.

Exactly like his condo in the City.

Otto stepped back and watched the bacon and French toast cook. He could walk outside and play with the dogs for a few days and then come back to a still-cooking breakfast. Intent was the catalyst here. He'd have to take some deliberate action to burn it, like throw more wood in the stove or throw the food directly in the fire. But, eggs in a pan on the stove, his intent was breakfast and we shall have that.

"Ready!" he called out of the door and threw several portions of bacon and toast into the various dog bowls along the kitchen floor and put the remainder — exactly enough for himself — in a nice porcelain Amish bowl and sat down at the rough-hewn table and chair (same stripped-branch motif as the bed) as the dogs rollicked through the door to their bowls with *woofs*! and *arfs*! and hijinks. Otto watched them. This was all so pleasant. All so perfect.

All so completely meaningless.

Chapter III

The Stars My Destination

Sunset.

Er, sunsets.

Otto sat quietly in a rather tasteful canvas director's chair (the label read 'Gold Medal') placed next to a tasteful outdoor table (Pangean by Byer) set in the middle of a raised, well-made patio of smooth stone pavers on top of the ridge behind the cabin. No label, but tasteful. A Celestron NexStar 8 telescope rested on the table, poised for action. It had a label, which is how Otto knew what it was.

He'd found it in the Never-Ending Cupboard a few nights ago. He'd been rummaging around in there for grins, saw a black case in the back, pulled it out and, behold! Telescope. Quite delightful. Otto had a penchant for telescopes, throughout his mortal life occasionally owning one and, even less occasionally, taking it outside and casting around the sky, aiming at the obvious targets like the moon and Venus and whatever else showed through the streetlight-fogged skies. He'd wanted to be an astronomer when he was a kid, but a poor facility for math squelched that. Poorer motivation left his occasional telescopes rusting in the garage after the initial thrill had passed.

But those had been $60 Sears specials and this one, well. Hot stuff. A Cassegrain, if he remembered his telescope styles correctly, quite portable and easy to haul up a ridge and throw on top of tastefully made tables. It was quite powerful, too, had an 8-inch mirror which, again, if he was remembering things correctly, was no slouch. And he *had* to remember things correctly because there'd been no manual in the case. Eyepieces, yeah, twenty of them, ranging in power all the way up to 200x and settled in recesses along one side of the black case, and lots and lots of filters of various sorts stacked in other recesses, but no instructions on how to use or configure or even coordinate among them. And Otto, being an instruction manual kind of guy, was a bit lost.

"Marc," he said to the telescope, "I could stand your help about now."

Apparently this was Something to be Figured Out and, really, what else did he have to do but sit here and figure it out? No problem with basic functions: that big slot on the top of the scope held an eyepiece, and the big knob next to the big slot was a focus ring. As for the filters, who the hell knows?

Otto supposed he could go back to the Magic Cupboard and root about until he found a notebook in which to record filter/eyepiece combinations until he figured out what went with what. And then he could use said notebook to record everything he saw through the eyepiece.

Which was what, exactly?

Otto leaned back, gazing at the darkening skies … well, dark in relation to sunlit(s) because, hoo boy, a lot of bright shiny stuff up there! Already the giant pinwheel galaxy rose behind the two moons positioning above the alps, but that was nothing. Gas trails, glowing red and green, raced across the sky with comets intertwined. An occasional meteor storm sparkled amid star clusters, little groups of diamonds scattered all over the place.

Target rich environment. He could randomly point the scope and look. But, what would he be looking *at*? "Marc, I could stand your help about now."

Because, Marc, what should I be looking *for*?

Otto stared at the telescope. It did not have a computerized star finder attached, which meant that if he wanted to find something familiar, say, the City, he was on his own, because he had no idea where in the cosmos he was. He didn't know if this planet was part of the dark road, part of the immortal universe, the mortal one, or someplace else entirely. If he wanted to chart the galaxies and clusters and nebulae he saw and then name them, he could, as he did for the constellations he watched fly by his condo balcony in the City, dubbing them such things as the Inside Out Man, the Dervish, whatever. Only, those constellations never came back. These remained.

Remained, exactly, where?

Who knows? Based on the apocalyptic stretching he'd experienced (again) when the surviving crew had escaped the Fallen by crashing through the dark road, he could very well be near the City. But that depended on where, exactly, they'd been pointing the ship while conducting said crashing maneuver. He could very well be six or seven more universes distant than he assumed. You know what happens when you assume.

"You ass," he muttered.

Cha Cha, sitting at his feet among the pile of other dogs, stirred and whined, placing a concerned muzzle on his knee. Otto chuckled. "Not you," he said, and patted the dog affectionately. "Me. And Marc. And all the rest of us dunderheaded mortals trying to make sense of the universe. We're a collective group of asses."

Because none of this made any sense. At all.

If it was God's intention that Otto's Afterlife consist of a much-dreamed-about rough cabin set in a picturesque and peaceful valley populated with all of his dogs, then why the rigmarole? The City, Frank Vaughn, the Suits, the train, Out, Doc Holliday, the battle of Star City, the Pearly Gates ...

Claudia's death.

A wave of sadness washed over him, something Cha Cha must have sensed because the muzzle was now pressing frantically at his palm, but Otto refused consolation.

He looked at the telescope. Could he locate the Milky Way galaxy with it and then trace a path along those whirly stars until he found that obscure, mediocre arm where the Earth spun? Probably. Put eye to eyepiece right now and there, right there, whirly stars and arms ... but how would he know? What does the Milky Way galaxy look like from another vantage point?

"See," he explained to the telescope, "it does me little good to use you if I have no idea what I'm seeing. It's all just lovely colors."

Lovely colors.

Otto frowned and leaned back and scanned the heavens. Yes, the colors were quite fetching, and were right there. Didn't need a telescope to enjoy them.

So, why give me one?

Otto considered. Slowly, he stood and, slowly, took a 360 look about him. Perhaps you have a telescope because there were better targets than elusive galaxies and fleeting comets. That ruined city nestled in a crevasse of the alps, for instance.

Otto fumbled with the knobs until he figured out how to change altitude and dropped it until he judged the telescope was level with the alps and then squinted through the spotter. An upside-down mountain. Okay, general target acquisition. Now, where's that city? Otto leaned around the telescope and peered at the far alps. It was a bit too dark now to pick out features, but if he was remembering the landscape correctly, then the city's ruins lay somewhere in the middle of the middle peak, so, fool around with other knobs and raise and lower and cant sideways and take lots of looks through the spotter ...

There. I think.

The moon(s) shadows murked up everything, but this looked like the right area so, get a low-powered lens, slap it in the receptacle and, voilà.

A city.

Or, more accurately, what was left of one.

Otto wasn't sure if it was the light, the lens, or the condition of the place, but it didn't look so much like a city as a series of fallen-over rocks. Could be more of God's "No straight lines in nature, huh?" joke that Otto had encountered when he and Amelia and Virgil ...

You guys still alive?

... had found the canal on Dis.

But the canal had turned out to *be* a canal, so the fallen rocks over there might be a fallen city. Hopefully, not a city of the Fallen. He shuddered, remembering the battle on the ship. Maybe he could resolve the image with a more powerful lens, so he traded a few in and out but, nothing doing. Not enough light.

Hey, how 'bout the filters? He traded a few in and out and experimented with combinations but, no help. The best view was the low power one so put it back in and let's sees what we can sees.

He stared through the lens, trying to make out details. Hmm. Not a lot but, if he had to categorize the place, it was a series of fallen rocks that looked suspiciously like a medieval town, replete with wall and keep. A rather foreboding one, at that. Now, what in the blue blazes were fallen rocks that look very much like a twelfth-century chateau and village doing in the middle of a mountain here in his private Heaven?

Yes, okay, he did have a penchant for twelfth-century towns. He'd thoroughly enjoyed an afternoon spent in Ulm while doing something-or-other for the government back in the early 90s. But, twelfth-century towns weren't something on his must-have list, like a Playstation. Hear that, Lord? Along with some games?

Check the Magic Cupboard.

So, back to the question. Obviously, God had put it there for a reason. Or not. It could be nothing more than the inadvertent result of God's physics, sort of like the Firsts and the dark road and the City itself. This town is all that is left of whatever beings crawled out of the primordial mud hereabouts and discovered agriculture and built cities and died of the plague, like in some Irish legend.

Or God put it here for a reason. Something interesting to get him out of this funk, mayhap?

He squinted, looking for something interesting like movement or light, but couldn't see anything. The moon shadows were too deep, allowing a tantalizing glimpse of towers and walls but not much more. One thing for certain, the place was dead.

We should go check it out sometime.

Otto raised the elevation of the scope and looked through the lens and yeah, yeah, star fields and gas clouds, all lovely and pulsing. Whoop de doo. He lowered the scope and swung it around to the hills, messing with the elevation until he was sure the angle was right and peered through the lens.

There. The wreckage of the ship.

The moons illuminated the lumps of metal rather well and Otto easily identified sections of the fuselage, an engine nacelle, and portions of what had to be the bridge because of the control panels attached to it. Wonder why the engine room wasn't lit up like a bright green flare? Maybe the dilithium crystals got buried under tons of torn-up earth and ship. He was surprised they didn't blow up on impact, crack this planet in half. Blast him into atoms. Then he'd see God.

Maybe.

Otto slowly turned the scope through the wreck site, pleased that the light was bright enough to show the details. He identified a couple of crew couches fallen together like an "A" without the crossbar. There was even a space suit draped over some chunks of bulkhead. Lots of cool stuff.

We should go check it out sometime.

Like, now.

He thought about it. Darkness held no special problems here in his personal heaven. He was sure there were some nifty flashlights and hiking shoes waiting for him in the Magic Cupboard. But, hey, it's not like you're in a hurry or anything."

Otto stepped back from the scope and peered at the distant hills. "Boys and girls," he said to the lounging dogs, "tomorrow, we're going on an expedition."

Chapter IV

All Summer In A Day

What does one need for an expedition conducted across one's personal Heaven?

Not much, Otto had concluded. That's why the only thing he'd pulled out of the cabinet this morning was breakfast. If something else proved necessary, it should manifest itself somewhere along the way. Them's the rules.

He stood on the porch and watched the suns rise, halfway tempted to break out the telescope and scrutinize the medieval city in the light(s) of day, but not right now. One wreckage at a time. He patted his overly filled stomach (bacon and eggs and buttermilk biscuits. Max calories for a hike), whistled up the dogs, all of whom came bounding over the knoll in frenzied joy, and stepped off.

A breeze, light and playful, cooled and freshened. Perfect. Thank you, Lord. The spongy grass comforted; thank you, Lord. The dogs bounced in and out of reach, somehow locating rubber balls and Frisbees and sticks (look at that: necessary things manifesting themselves already), which they brought to him and which he threw and which they brought back for more throwing.

This was all quite lovely, wasn't it?

Otto grabbed a big red Frisbee right out of Snuffy's

mouth, whipped it, and laughed as the socially inept klutz looked at him in bewilderment and then at the other dogs streaking after the rapidly diminishing disk (man, good throw).

"Well?" Otto said, "Go get it!"

Snuffy did a double-take and, with a *woof*! plunged after the others. Otto laughed and laughed as the dog reached the scrum and blew right through the middle into a six-dog tug-of-war going on the top of that knoll, their growls audible and Otto sat down in the middle of the lovely field and laughed and laughed some more.

He was ten again. Again.

The dogs came rushing back, most of them attached to the Frisbee, their momentum bowling Otto over and he wrestled among them, tossing dogs about and then seizing the Frisbee and flinging it one way and a racquetball another, Fritz and Pierre hot on its tail. Dog crowds assaulted him and then rushed away in additional pursuits and Otto ran from knoll to knoll, hiding, but the dogs found him and crowed their pleasure and urged him to throw more objects and Otto did and hid and dogs ran and searched.

He collapsed on top of another knoll, giggling, and looked up. The suns were straight overhead.

Ah, so what? It's okay. It's all okay.

He lay back on the spongy grass, hands clasped behind his head, smiling at the apogee, time simply a suggestion because, when you're ten years old, a minute is an hour, an hour a year. The dogs trotted up, singly and in pairs, panting and smiling as dogs do, and distributed themselves about him, satisfaction beaming off them in waves. A moment of childhood, when everything is perfect, magical, right.

God — he had first discovered Him in a moment like this. Or vice versa. He'd been living in Alabama, Dad assigned to a helicopter unit on Ft. Rucker, training for the Vietnam missions that would, eventually, take his life and plunge Otto into a dismal world of abandonment and pain. But, that was months away and he was on a country hillside in a hot August watching the clouds build and build as they did in Alabama skies, intent on reaching critical mass and then relieving themselves in thunder and power. The clouds sculpted and shifted and faces peeked out of them, then not, and animals, then not, and Otto knew Someone was behind them, laughing while wielding a loop tool and armature and Otto wanted to know Him.

Otto sat up and gazed back at the cabin set against the distant alps. About two miles away, two miles he'd never noticed as he'd gone a-skipping over these Elysian fields having a lovely time in this lovely setting on a lovely day.

Dude, what are you doing?

Well, he was being ten. But he wasn't ten. He was seventy-something; at least, he was when he collapsed against the steering wheel and woke up in the City. And just as in the City, he was rushing from one pleasure to another, the wondrous shops replaced by field and Frisbee and dogs willing to play, the hypno-sky by the suns above but mesmerizing all the same.

You forget your purpose.

You forget God.

Otto looked straight up. "I am not forgetting You," he said to the blue, deep sky behind the suns. "I'm not," he said to the dogs, all lined up and waiting. They nodded as one. Otto stood. "Let's get this show on the road," he said, and stepped off.

The dogs fell in and Otto led across hill and dale, the fall and rise of the land acting as a guide. The dogs ran back and forth and Otto occasionally threw something for their pleasure but kept up the march and the dogs kept up, knowing, as dogs do, there was a destination. The time passed and the suns headed towards the horizon and more hills and ridges traversed and, about an hour before sunset, Otto stood above the shipwreck.

A lot farther than I thought.

Otto frowned and looked back towards the cabin. Lost to view. But, when Cha Cha woke him out of the wreckage a week (a year, a century?) ago, hadn't he seen the gleam of light from its distant window? Maybe light was more discernible in the dark, or it traveled in odd ways here, revealing itself in a manner that daylight prevented. Still, it hadn't taken as long to reach the cabin as it did to come back here. Perhaps he'd gone the long way around, the dogs careening him off-course. But he could see the wreckage from the back of the cabin through the telescope, which implied straight lines, sight and otherwise. Made no sense.

What did?

He chuckled and, minutes later, was on the edge of the wreckage.

The dogs had followed him down and sniffed about, curious. He speculated whether they were picking up the odor of dilithium crystals, the scent of the Fallen, the other crew members ...

Claudia's lingering perfume.

Otto slapped a part of a hull sticking out of the dirt next to him. Handholds ran all over it and he wondered if this was the same place that he and Bulsrobe had clambered while examining the FEEPS. Might even be the exact spot where the meteor storm had blasted Bulsrobe and Seth and the Widow Wyncke and the rest down the dark road. Which, intent on rescue, the ship had followed. To Dis. And the Fallen.

Otto shuddered and stepped past the hull, then stopped, puzzled. Odd. The wreckage was almost symmetrically dispersed around the hollow where it now rested. The big pieces — mostly hull and bulkheads — enclosed the perimeter, concentric circles of wreckage spiraled to the middle where a lot of crap piled a la a burial mound. Looked like Stonehenge.

"Or a crop circle," Otto muttered.

He followed the first line of wreckage, the dogs trailing as Otto examined the hull pieces stuck in the ground like croquet hoops. Apparently, the ship had hit fairly hard. He remembered it tumbling end over end before breaking apart and leaving him, still strapped in the pilot seat, upright and unharmed in the middle of the hollow. He had no doubt that he'd been equally torn apart during the crash, but the Afterlife's healing powers had slapped him back together. He supposed.

Let's verify that.

He ran his hand across a particularly sharp part of hull,

wincing as it cut deep, and then watching with some amusement (and relief) as the gusher of blood stopped almost immediately and the flesh knitted

"That's good," he said to the startled dogs, "See, if I fall off a cliff or something, I'll be okay. Eventually."

That left only the universal translator in doubt. To test it, he needed a Hottentot to trot up and engage him in conversation. When one didn't, he continued through the wreck spiral, noting that the size of the pieces diminished in a balanced manner as he moved towards the center. Feng shui. Or art. Ship Falling in Mud. Un-Winged Lack of Victory.

The Pity.

Otto frowned, placing the fully healed hand on an amazingly intact locker standing upright on the first drift of the next wreckage spiral. This was art, all right, a monument, but to what?

The valiant human spirit?

No.

"To our hubris," he whispered.

City not good enough for you? So you build a rocket to find God and complain to Him about it?

See what happens.

No, no, that's not it.

St. Peter himself had urged them on. Latchemondy had, too, supplying them with fuel that never ran out and a merry little jolly boat unmerrily named The Charon to scout out locations on the way. It wasn't arrogance, a questioning of God; it was an urge to find God, stand before the Throne and look into His Face and say, "Father."

"Father," he whispered to the suns, the largest one now touching the western hills. No answer. He didn't expect one. He didn't expect a lot of things on that crazy trip across the universes, like the crew incrementally disappearing (some of them in cruel manners) or the ship smashing into what turned out to be his personal heaven. But, above all, he did not expect to fail.

"And I haven't," he said to the sun(s) with defiance. Simply because the ship was gone didn't mean the mission was.

Otto raised a fist and shouted, "I WILL find You!" to the sun(s) and the sky and the Somebody making art out of ship wreckage. He turned to the dogs, all sitting before him, expectant. "I will," he reiterated.

Which meant he'd have to rebuild the ship.

Otto laughed, genuinely amused, the dogs picking up on it and adding their barks of doggy joy. Him, rebuild the ship? He couldn't figure out the relationship between nail and hammer, a defect highly amusing to his wife and appreciated by numerous over-charging contractors. So how did he intend to slap another rocket together?

"What else do you have to do?"

Amelia had said that to him back at Star City. He'd been standing at the bottom of the crew ladder, Amelia in the crew door above him, the ship already in pre-launch sequence and about to take off without him and he'd mourned and groused that it would take a long time to build another ship and that was her response. And then Claudia swept him into the ship and on this journey and now here he was with dogs and cabin and twelfth-century ruins and nothing else to do.

Might as well get started.

He passed the locker and immediately bumped into a dangling sleeve of the pressure suit he'd seen through the scope earlier. He chuckled and pulled it off the bulkhead, examining it for damage. Nary a tear; the goldfish bowl helmet attached, and still whole.

"Gonna need this," he said and carefully laid it across an upright crew couch sitting nearby. Never know when you have to go outside and clean the retros, er, the FEEPS, the Field Effect Electric Propulsion Subsytems that rocket builder Konstantin should not have had any idea about but, here they were. The dogs examined the suit as Otto rummaged around. He'd need some tools. A wrench. A screwdriver. An oxyacetylene torch and a containment system for dilithium crystals. Don't forget a radar scope.

He stopped and scrutinized the ground. All that stuff's probably buried under twenty feet of rubble. Take him about a year to dig it all out even if he stayed with it night and day unless the Magic Cupboard produced a steam shovel. Figure an additional year or two figuring out how to use everything, then another year or ten piecing together a ship that would (a) actually work, (b) launch without exploding, and (c) maneuver in space (better study up on those FEEPs). All that time, romping with the dogs, eating great meals, and exploring twelfth-century ruins.

An entertaining hundred or so years.

He laughed. At *least* a hundred years, given his level of stupidity. But, what else did he have to do?

All right, give yourself a little bit of credit: maybe fifty years. After all, he didn't need a full-sized shuttle, just a one-man ship. Or, maybe one man and one dog.

"Who wants to go?" he asked the pack. They immediately stopped their suit inspection and danced around him, barking. He could almost hear, "Take me! Take me!" Chuckling, he play-fought with them and gauged the sun(s) off to the west for how much daylight remained.

Not much. The big sun was about halfway down, the smaller one already touching the horizon, the light from both turning red and casting across the wreckage.

Where something gleamed.

Otto gaped at it. All of the scattered wreckage glowed in one color or another of yellow to red under the setting suns, but this particular spot was bright. White bright, almost like an arc light. Quite a sight. Right?

Knock it off.

Could be the dilithium crystals. Let's go see.

He made as much of a beeline as the wreckage allowed, picking his way through while keeping the gleam in sight. Funny that it remained bright while the surrounding metal dulled under the dulling suns. So it had to be the crystals, but shouldn't those be green? Maybe the ship's impact had altered them and they were reaching critical mass: crack the planet and launch him into space without the benefit of ship or suit.

Now, wouldn't that be fun?

The gleaming spot was purt near the middle of the crop circle. Otto detoured around a couple of bulkheads and suddenly on top of it ... and suddenly puzzled. It looked like a blade. A blade attached to a long pole.

A halberd.

Taccola's halberd, to be exact. At least, he figured it was Tac's. No one else had wielded one during the fight with the Fallen.

"How 'bout that?" Otto said. Of all the things he didn't expect to find, this was right up there. And of all the things he didn't *need* to find, this was way up there. He needed screwdrivers, not medieval weapons. What was it doing here? It should be buried under tons of ship and rock, not sitting here pristine and gleaming in the sunsets.

"Gee," he said to the dogs, "how unnecessary." He looked around, expecting to find the pipe wrench he'd used during the Fallen fight or the Contender he'd used to stop Akiko, but nope, only shreds of metal and crew couch and bales of twisted wire. And one perfectly intact halberd.

Why?

Otto sighed. You should know by now, bub, that asking the reason for things was pointless. Accept that, for some inexplicable purpose, God had decided to offer up a halberd. A Big Mac would have been better, but Otto supposed he could pull one out of the kitchen cabinet. He supposed he could have pulled a halberd out of the Magic Cupboard, if inclined to own one, but he wasn't. He had no use for a halberd, except maybe as a wall decoration.

And yet, here's a halberd.

Pierre walked up to it, stiff-legged and suspicious, and gave it a sniff. He growled and backed away, hiding behind Otto's legs.

"Know how you feel," Otto said, reaching down to pat him, "Tac was a jerk." Or is. Depending on his current status. Which is: not here.

Despite the jerkdom, Otto wouldn't be upset if the little jerk suddenly popped out of the ground or a locker or something; at least, until the first time Tac acted like a jerk. Then Otto'd stab him with the halberd.

The other dogs lined up behind Pierre, showing the same displeasure and Otto had to laugh.

"You guys are great judges of character."

He reached down and grabbed the halberd by the middle ...

... and blew through the air, his skin and hair frying like he'd been hit by lightning.

"*Augh!*" he yelped as he slammed hard into an inconvenient piece of bulkhead and then slid down it, his nerves sparking and burnt. Somewhere, the dogs screamed in pain and he tried to get up, tried to reach them, but a whirlwind descended, knocking him to the ground.

Unconscious.

Chapter V

The Long Rain

His face was wet.

"Stop it, Cha Cha," Otto said and made a feeble effort to push the dog away, but his hands met neither fur nor an enthusiastic tongue licking him awake. Or, at least, he didn't *think* no fur or tongue – sparks of electricity arced from little finger to elbow, which might explain why he was physically unable to feel a frantic dog trying to wake him up.

Or maybe because no frantic dog was there.

He opened his eyes and saw nothing. Not an absence of dog, but nothing. At all.

"Great," he whispered, "I'm blind."

A flash of lightning proved otherwise, the massive bolt dazzling him as it danced across the sky and disappeared.

Ah, a thunderstorm.

He was wet because it was raining. And rather hard.

A peal of thunder followed the bolt, then another bolt and more thunder and the rain became a downpour. He was soaked. In his personal heaven.

"I didn't ask for a thunderstorm," he spluttered. "Didn't ask for the Fallen or Dis, either, and how'd that work out?"

Should probably get out of the rain.

Blinking out the wet, Otto peered around, trying to locate

some shelter. A couple of hull pieces a few yards away leaned against each other in a passable lean-to.

Let's go.

Otto flapped hands at the mud puddle he sat in but he didn't have complete control yet. With concentration and much effort, he pushed himself to a standing position but sparks of electricity flew from knee to little toe, throwing off his balance; he leaned against the bulkhead, waiting for it to pass. Felt the same as when he'd touched Akiko's Sword of Eternity, which had also blasted him across the room. But, last he checked, Tac's halberd wasn't part of the Firsts' weaponry. Tac wasn't one of the Firsts, either.

Was he?

"Nothing surprises me at this point," he muttered and tested his legs. Okay, back in control. He took a step, maintained balance, congratulated himself, took another step and, finally got under the hull pieces. Good, at least he wasn't getting wet. Or wetter.

His hands and arms worked better now and he braced against the metal pieces and pulled himself around where he could see out. "Cha Cha!" he called, "Cha Cha, come here!"

Nothing.

"Clio! Snuffy! Come on," and he whistled but the only response was another fork of lightning and its subsequent thunder. He went through the list of dogs several times, clapping and whistling, but not one showed up.

"Went home," he concluded. "Ran home," he clarified as another peal of thunder rolled across the wreck site. With tails tucked and looks of sheer terror on their faces because dogs don't do thunderstorms. Probably all scrambling to get under the cot right now, snapping and pushing at each other, with nary a thought of their beloved master out here on his own.

Ingrates.

Otto chuckled. Okay, let's head home and drag them all outside and dry them off and laugh at them for being such big chickens. Otto peered at the solid curtain of rain outside the lean-to. Sure, let's do that. After the weather clears.

It didn't.

After what felt like a half-hour, Otto figured this was going to be an all-night rain. Maybe all day.

Well, isn't that friggin' lovely.

Stuck under an accidental A-frame in the middle of a junkyard with rain pouring down. At least the little electric sparks running all over his body were about gone. Now he was merely wet and cold …

Cold.

Hey. I'm cold. Actually cold.

And he hurt. Real hurt. Real pain. His arms, his back, his legs, as if he'd been run over by a truck or something.

What's this? There's been more than enough time for the universal healing power to kick in and fix the residual effects of the electric halberd.

But, it hadn't.

"Oh no," he breathed. Back on the ship, the farther they got away from the City, the more things went wrong. The translator acted up. It took longer to recover from injuries. Discomfort increased. Like right now. He was shivering and soaked and his feet and even his ankles felt they were in a big puddle …

Oh no.

A flash of lightning revealed the problem: the water was rising, and fast.

Of course.

He was at the bottom of a knoll and the downpour was filling it up. Boy, was it filling it up. At this rate, he'd be neck-deep in the next few minutes and in danger of entering the kind of hopeless situation Latchemondy had said would defeat reconstitution. And with the healing powers fizzling right now …

"Gotta go," he said to the lean-to, and leaned out.

Immediately, the water was up to his knees and tugging at him. A current. That meant the water flowed into a depression, and a deep one, given the strength of it. So, best to get out of it before he got swept off his feet. Slogging along, Otto waded around the lean-to, keeping his balance with a hand on the metal.

Man, is this hard!

He was already gasping for air by the time he cleared the lean-to.

Gasping for air. Like a seventy-something old man. Which he was.

More evidence of the rapidly failing health powers. More

urgent, then, that he get to safety. The last bolt had revealed a small rise to the left and Otto sloshed through the water, making for it. He was about three sloshes that way when he hooked his feet around something hard and pitched forward, right on his face, right in the mud. Spluttering, he pushed up and angrily grabbed at whatever was tangling his legs …

And got a searing, sharp pain in his right hand.

"*Augh!*" he screamed and yanked his hand out of the mud as another bolt of lightning flashed the scene. His hand was covered with muddy blood. And missing its little finger.

"What! What?" he yelled as he grabbed the hand and squeezed the area below the wound, attempting to staunch the geyser of blood and the waves of pain and shock.

"What?" he repeated. "Is there a shark in there or something?" And he kicked viciously at the puddle, levering a long object out of it …

The halberd.

Otto stared at it as bolt after bolt turned the area to day.

Man, did Tac have it in for me, or what?

Gingerly, he pushed the halberd with his toe, bracing for another blast of psionic energy or whatever, but nothing. It rolled a bit. That's all. Good. No longer a magic wand, but still sharp as crap.

His hand throbbed and the spasms came back but not electric ones, wound ones, and Otto squeezed harder, trying to stop the blood and pain. Too bad he couldn't stop the water, which lapped around his hips.

"This is ridiculous," he said, and, with much difficulty and not a few screams of pain, worked his shirt off and wrapped it tightly around his hand, ending with an unsightly bulge where his little finger used to be. Water had reached his belly button and he kicked out, seeking purchase. The halberd rose out of the mud and draped across his ankles.

Wow. Someone really, REALLY, wanted him to have this.

"Okay, okay," he said, irritably, and pulled it to him with his good hand and used it as a pole to stand up, carefully avoiding the blade because

"You know, like to keep the rest of my fingers,"

and probed the water with it as he went along. He found a rise and followed it; good thing, because the water was reaching for his chest. But the rise kept pace and, after what felt like a couple of days, he gained ground, the water lowering as he moved along. After a couple of more days, he reached the flood-free top, gasping, winded, heart pounding and threatening to explode with the effort.

What the hell?

He leaned against the halberd, wheezing, the blade end above his head. His hand burned and he wondered how much of that was the amputation or mud-induced gangrene.

Okay, healing power, anytime you're ready, get my air back. And my finger.

Anytime you're ready.

The rain continued, so did the lightning, and so did time, but his hand was on fire and he was cold and getting colder and his legs were shaking and he was so tired.

So. Tired.

A wave of exhaustion swept over him, buckling his knees.

Oh my God, feels like I haven't slept in weeks. Months.

Since he'd woken facedown on a cobblestoned street in the City. Years ago.

He slipped down the halberd, curling into himself, rain and mud be damned, and fell instantly asleep.

Chapter VI

That Is, Of Course,
Unless The Horse Is The Famous ...

Eyes, hard and judging, examined him from some great, cold distance. Pitiless. Shadows reeled about it.

Something moved.

"*Yap!*" Otto squealed and jerked and bolted out of the dream and sat up blinking, a raging headache splitting his head in half, but nothing compared to the headache in his hand. He looked at it. The shirt-bandage was blood-soaked and crusty and half-off, the stump of his scabbed-over little finger poking through. So, against expectations, he didn't get a new one overnight.

Which means the universal healing power is officially kaput.

Great.

He looked up. He was facing the distant hills, the land rolling away to a misty horizon. Daytime, but clouds covered the sky, gray and spent and uneven. Dreary. And disconcerting. There hadn't been an overcast day here since he'd arrived. Even more disconcerting: a lake, right in front of him, gray and dreary and uneven with objects poking out of it here and there. It took him a while to realize those were pieces of the shipwreck tall enough to break the surface, which meant there was little chance he would salvage anything out of there today. Or tomorrow or anytime, unless the lake receded.

Something velvet and wet suddenly nuzzled his ear.

"*Yap!*" again as he slapped at it with, naturally, the injured hand so, "*Ow!*" as the wound seared him. While squeezing the little finger and rolling around screaming, he managed to slip down the hill and into the lake up to his belly button, with that dang halberd jammed against his back. The stick end, thank God.

"Cha Cha!" he yelled, "will you stop?" and he turned to push the dog away.

But it wasn't a dog. It was a horse. Or, at least, a horse's leg.

"What the heck?" Startled, Otto followed the leg up to a big horse face that dipped into his, big horse lips nuzzling him.

"*Pfht!*" he spluttered and pushed and the horse face reared back and Otto squinted.

Yep, a horse.

Well, that was unexpected. "What are you doing here?" Otto asked it.

The horse cocked its head, let out a long, merry neigh, and then kicked mud right in Otto's face.

"*Ack!*" He flapped around which, of course, caused more searing pain from his injured hand and he howled as he wiped mud out of his eyes with the unseared hand. "Very funny, horse," he snapped. "Reminds me of another very funny horse ..."

He stopped. "Flicka?"

The horse neighed joyously again and kicked more mud at him.

"Yep, Flicka," Otto spluttered as he wiped his eyes again. When they were clear, he stared at the horse.

Talk about unexpected. And suspicious.

"To repeat, what are you doing here ... no, better question, *how* are you here?" Really, how?

The last time he saw Flicka was at the launch gantry when he vaulted out of the saddle and then scrambled up the ladder (at Claudia's urging) while the ship's engines rumbled ominously.

"You shouldn't have survived take-off. You shouldn't have

survived the battle. So, okay, apparently, you did, but you shouldn't be here, you should be back in Out running around with Kenny and the gang. We're at least two universes away from Out ... or one away and one back, I don't know. So, how are you here? How did you *get* here?"

Flicka gave him a what-a-stupid-question look.

And it was. Otto had never received any satisfactory explanation for any of the perplexing and impossible events that had happened to him since dying in the car. Bromides from Latchemondy and Ian and even Claudia, that was about it. Best conclusion he reached from all that and all this was that all of this, from the City to the lake in front of him, was the product of his very active but coma-drugged brain working overtime as his stroke-ravaged body tried to recover in whichever ICU he'd ended up after dying — or nearly dying — in the car. But even that, as logical as it was, didn't explain things like a prank-playing horse, unless he was channeling Mr. Ed. Lots of scenarios like that — from Kenny the barbarian to Prester John — evaded explanation. Otto concluded that the best thing to do was let it ride, until something — anything — made some actual sense. This didn't, so let it ride.

Otto waved at the horse. "Forget it. Help me up."

Flicka turned sideways and Otto noted the horse sported the same Mongol saddle he'd ridden during the battle of Star City. He grasped the stirrup with his good hand and, struggling, pulled himself up.

"Oh, man," he gasped, resting against the saddle, "do I hurt."

Boy, did he.

Mostly the hand, which felt like pulsing lava, but the headache dividing his vision into fours and fives, offered stiff competition. His back, his legs, and his shoulders were all victims of an eighteen-wheeler slamming into them at sixty mph. Repeatedly. And he couldn't breathe.

"Yep. Definitely back to being seventy," he wheezed.

Flicka gave him a sympathetic nudge.

"Thanks," Otto said, "but I really need the universal healing power to click back on. You know how to do that?"

Flicka repeated the what-a-stupid-question look.

"Didn't think so."

He peered across the saddle. The gray clouds continued past the horizon, the knolls rolling under them. A hint of the foothills to the right indicated the alps, which meant he was facing the cabin. At any moment, he expected the dogs to splash through the ponds and puddles dotting the landscape here and there and converge on him. But, nothing.

Where were the dogs?

Otto looked at Flicka. "So, if you're here, does that mean Jakto's here, too? Kenny? Pashtun?" He paused. "Claudia?"

Flicka didn't bother looking at him.

"Okay. Then, can you get me to the cabin? I could stand a Tylenol."

Flicka nickered softly and tossed her head and Otto grasped the top of the saddle but Flicka pulled away.

"Hold still," he groused and grabbed the saddle again but she moved again, splashing in the water. "What?" he said, irritated.

The horse nosed the water, pawing at something. Otto looked.

The halberd.

Otto shook his head. "Forget it. That thing's dangerous." He held up the wrapped hand as confirmation. "And I'm not a big fan of its former owner."

Flicka moved away from him, continuing to paw at the halberd. She even got a nose under it and flicked it in his direction, then looked at him expectantly.

"Dammit," he muttered and made another attempt to mount but she shook him off.

"All right! All right!" he shouted and reached down with his good hand, gingerly grasping the halberd's pole but no Taser effect, so he pulled it to him. "What am I supposed to do, hold it like a lance or something?" he asked the horse. Which was not without precedent: after all, he'd jousted a few Vikings off the wall during Kenny's mock attack on the fjord.

While riding Flicka, come to think of it.

She looked back, her eyes resting on the stirrup. Otto followed her gaze. A leather pocket lay next to the stirrup; it looked about the right size to hold the halberd's shaft. With much difficulty, he hoisted it in place and was somewhat surprised when it stayed upright.

"Now, no funny business," he warned and, with even more difficulty and a complete lack of grace, pulled himself into the saddle, sat up and was instantly dizzy and sick to his stomach, lurched, and caught himself on the saddle horn.

"I think I'm going to barf," he said to Flicka, who looked back at him in some alarm, but he held off.

"Take me home," he whispered, "Please."

Gently, carefully, Flicka trotted away.

Chapter VII

Stop, Drop, And Roll

Otto lay in the cot. He wasn't exactly sure how he got in it but did have half-memories of pitching in the saddle for what he'd swear were days, crawling up the cabin's steps and across the floor and hoisting over the side and falling immediately into blessed sleep. For what he'd swear were days.

He stared at the rough ceiling. What's with all this sleep? It used to be a simple Afterlife recreation pursued for the heck of it. Now, though, it was downright necessary. Vital. Like it was for any seriously injured mortal back in the world of the living. And boy was he seriously injured. And hungry. And thirsty.

Was he regaining consciousness?

Otto considered. Maybe he was slowly rising through the layers of coma. Any moment now, he'd hear the beeping of monitors and the wheezing of some machine breathing for him, distant announcements over a hospital intercom and the hurried steps of nurses and doctors down hallways. "How are we today?" some bright, breezy RN flapping into the room.

"No change." Sherry, haggard and beaten, voice sorrowed, her overnight (over a week? Over a month?) vigil still unrewarded, wondering when Otto would emerge from this deep, horrid unconsciousness.

Sherry, wait until I tell you this dream. You won't begrudge me the time.

He stirred and felt a stab of pain up his arm. He held up the injured hand, sans shirt-bandage, and looked around until he spotted the bloody cloth wadded up on the floor.

Must have worked it off while thrashing around in the bed.

He examined the finger. Ugh. Getting worse.

It was an angry red now, the color of infection.

One good thing about waking from this coma, I can get the finger fixed.

'Course, my finger won't need fixing when I wake up.

He chuckled and carefully dropped the hand and waited for overhead banks of neon lights to appear and doctors' faces to hover worriedly in and out of his vision and a lot of stupid questions that he did not want to answer because all he wanted to say was, "Sherry, you won't believe the dream I had."

Dressed in organdy, I held your hand.

How could she believe? He didn't.

Because, when people die, they do not end up facedown on a cobblestoned street in a City that defies all logic. And they did not join a bunch of misfits on some half-baked voyage across the stars to find God. No. When we die, actually die, we wake up in a golden Throne Room with the benevolent Face of God bent towards us, compassionate, welcoming. Cross the river and rest under the shade of the tree.

If none of that happens, then you're, obviously, not dead.

So, wake up.

Wakeupwakeupwakeup …

Otto braced, expecting sight and hearing to clear under those anticipated banks of neon lights and doctors' faces and then massive disorientation as he came back to reality, followed by a sense of relief that he was, indeed, alive, and then despair as he wondered how damaged he was. Would he be able to walk? Drive? Talk? Because it'd be tragic if he couldn't tell this tale.

Even more tragic: forgetting this entire, wondrous dream altogether.

"Oh, no," he whispered, "no, no, no. I'm not forgetting this." Lose Ferdinand and Kenny and Unathi and William Godwin? The pursuit through the streets of the City, the Suits attacking the library, the gunfight on the train.

Claudia.

Otto gritted his teeth, willing everything into memory. Stay there. Be alive and present and ready for the telling or the writing or Morse code eyeblinks — whatever means left to his battered, diminished body. Most dreams become fragments on waking, mere colors or dreads, a vivid image or two but without context, baffling, and there was a serious danger the same thing would happen to this one. He'd thrash awake and, as doctors and nurses and Sherry restrained him, he'd lose the details, a wonderful, fabulous, mind-blowing dream … *pfhht*, gone, all that's left of it a residual sense of wonder. But whenever Otto had been shocked awake by things like an unexpected alarm or a terror-filled nightmare, he remembered everything …

So, shock yourself awake.

Otto raised the injured hand and drove it, gangrenous stump first, into the cabin wall behind his head.

Some levels of agony are so intense they don't elicit a scream, not even a grunt, only nausea and breathlessness as tidal waves of pain wash over and through, turning blood to rusty iron and concentrating all of the senses onto the mere half-inch or so of throbbing, raging horror at the end of what was left of a finger. His head spun, his stomach heaved and bile flooded his mouth as his hand exploded like a grenade.

"Oh," was all he managed to say.

He did not emerge screaming out of a coma and into a world of antiseptic smells and IVs as hands pushed him back down onto the bed, Otto shouting, "I've got to tell you this dream!" over and over. No, he was still on the cot in the cabin and experiencing pain at a level rarely before experienced, which required an appropriate response. He leaned over and vomited onto the rough-hewn floor.

Several times, in fact.

"Oh, man," he said, weakly. "What a mess. And no nurse to clean it up."

Which meant he was still in a coma. Or, that he was actually dead, having been actually dead ever since the heart attack and was, after a very bizarre rocket ride, laid up in a cabin in his personal heaven. Which was disturbing because, right now, he was sick and injured and feeling very, very far from heaven.

How can he be mortal if he is dead? One sort of offset the other, didn't it? Or did one imply the other, having to be mortal to be dead? And if he was mortal, it was a bit unfair to now reside in a Heaven filled with Suits and Fallen and Firsts and hosts of other things far from mortal and infinitely more powerful than he, and infinitely hostile.

"Can't survive those guys," he told the piles of vomit now stinking up the cabin.

At least, not from bed.

Gingerly, Otto got up, avoiding the vomit landmines he had laid for himself. Shuffling over to the kitchen sink, he pumped the water handle (a quaint and amusing feature when he first got here but now, quite annoying) and ran cold water over the finger, gasping at the pain. Need to put on another bandage before slopping up the vomit, so Otto walked over to the cabinet and opened it ...

Empty.

He blinked. No side of bacon, no sourdough bread, no sourdough anything. Not even a sourdough wound dressing.

"What the heck?" he said to the empty space.

Holding his dripping hand, he carefully made his way back to the bed and opened the Magic Cupboard and, yep, empty.

"Now isn't this a fine kettle of fish?" he said.

A kettle of fish would actually be good because now he had no supplies. He had nothing.

Obviously need to reboot this thing. Let's see. Control alt delete, wait until the Magic Cupboard re-cycles and starts spewing out bandages and mops. Okay, where's the keyboard? The on/off switch? The plug?

No idea.

Otto watched the Magic Cupboard for a moment and closed it, counted to thirty, opened it.

Nope, nothing.

Tried that a couple of more times, even ran his hand over the outside looking for an indentation or switch and, really, this is ridiculous.

Now what?

Otto shrugged. The answer is obvious: when facing a rather hopeless situation, drop back twenty and punt.

He pulled the sheet off the cot and tore part of it into a dressing, a hazardous undertaking with one hand and his teeth. Would have made a pretty funny YouTube video. One-handed wrapping of his little finger with more teeth assistance would have made another funny video, but he wasn't laughing. This was serious crap. Bandage was nice, but he needed to treat the finger with iodine or something and there was nothing to be had.

One problem at a time, bud.

Satisfied that the dressing would stay in place, Otto hazardously tore more of the sheet into rags and did a half-decent job of wiping up the vomit. Carefully balancing the messy sheets and former shirt to avoid contact with the finger, he dumped them in the sink and washed them out.

Whew.

At least the vomit stink lessened. To the point he could now eat something.

Eat what?

Otto checked the cabinet again but still nothing. Halfheartedly, he reached up with his good hand to the little shelf and flapped about and, whoa, waddyaknow. Some eggs hiding in the back with a half-empty jar of salsa (Made in New York City?) and a can of refried beans. When all you've got is lemons ... he grabbed the big iron skillet hanging from the wall and greased it up with the handy little can of Crisco, opened up the fire box on the stove.

Coals were out.

"Great," Otto whispered and scrambled around the shelf again and found a little box of matches. He threw some wood shavings into the firebox and went through three matches before he got enough of a spark and then blew that into a flame and eventually had enough heat to cook. All with one hand. He broke the eggs one-handed — a skill he'd had for years — into the skillet, struggled with a can opener and dumped in the beans (not all of them because he couldn't hold the can to scrape it out) and threw the salsa on top. Looked a lot like the vomit he had cleaned up, but it sure smelled good.

All right. Breakfast will be ready soon. Now, let's see about some other things.

A shirt, for one. He went back to the Magic Cupboard but still nothing so he pulled a thin red cotton blanket he'd never used off the bottom of the cot and wrapped it around himself in a sloppy semblance of a toga, managing to tie off the ends so they actually held together. He looked down at himself. "A drunken Roman," he concluded, and headed back to the stove. He checked breakfast, which was progressing nicely, and then stepped through the door and onto the porch.

Still gray, still cloudy, but it had lifted to the point he could see the alps now. The light dimmed so it must be late afternoon. Man, he'd slept, hadn't he? Why hadn't the dogs woken him?

"Cha Cha!" he called, then whistled, "C'mere, girl!" and squinted across the land but nothing moved. He called for the other dogs. Same nothing.

"Where'd y'all go?" he wondered aloud.

A sound to his left made him turn, hopeful. Flicka was at the end of the porch, looking at him.

"At least you're still here," Otto said. He went down the steps and Flicka came around and nuzzled him.

"Yeah," he stroked Flicka's forehead, "I miss the dogs, too."

Maybe the doggy version of the Rainbow Bridge had come for them, a doggy Heimdall taking them away to Snausage Heaven for an eternity of cat chasing, and fireplugs.

"That'd be nice," he said to Flicka. "So, what's the horsy version of Heaven? Hayfields and heated barns?"

Flicka looked at him, snorted, and turned her head towards the alps. Otto followed her gaze. A stream of sunset broke through the clouds, a red and orange spotlight falling on the medieval ruins, clarifying them. Broken towers and cracked walls flared in stark relief, as well as a series of giant stone steps ascending from a platform to where a gate used to be. He'd never noticed those details before. He'd never noticed the sunset falling so brightly on the ruins before, either.

Must have something to do with the clouds.

The place looked really, really old. "Twelfth century, all right," Otto said, "but BC."

Flicka took a couple of steps towards the alps, gazing intently at the ruins.

"What do you see?" Otto asked. He wasn't sure if horses had good eyesight, but something sure had her attention. "Is it the dogs?"

Flicka merely swooshed her tail as another burst of sunset illuminated the place, bringing with it a sudden burst of warmth ...

Warmth?

Otto whirled. The cabin was on fire.

"Crap!" Otto yelped and leaped through the door, immediately leaping back as the flames reached for him, scorching his face.

"Crap! Crap! Crap!" he yelled again and desperately pushed at the door, trying to find a way in to put out the fire.

How?

He paused. Good question. The entire kitchen was engulfed. The only available water was the kitchen sink. There wasn't an outside spigot to which he could stroll over and hook up a hose and leisurely spray the fire down.

One-handed, I might add. But I gotta do something ...

He looked wildly around for a shovel or a bucket of sand or even a fire alarm to pull, but nothing.

He thought of pulling the toga-blanket off and beating at the flames but the fire doubled, roaring as it bit into the rest of the log cabin, lashing at him from the doorway. He stepped back, shading his face from the heat, almost losing his balance. The fire doubled again, driving him off the porch and down on the ground and farther back, heat pulses forcing him to a safer distance where he watched the cabin wrap itself in flame.

Took about twenty minutes to become nothing but ash and smoke.

Otto, by that time, was sitting on the grass, idly playing with a weed, while Flicka stood over him, still gazing at the alps. It was night now, and the coaled-over cabin was the only illumination because the clouds still covered the sky. A couple of bright spots up there marked the moons, but they didn't provide enough light to see. Not that there was anything to see anymore.

"Another fine kettle," Otto muttered at the weed and absently squeezed the wrapped finger, which burned with as much intensity as the cabin coals. Flicka nickered a bit and Otto patted the upper part of a close leg. "Yeah, I know," he said, "stupid to complain when I'm the one who set the fire."

One of his endearing traits: he didn't blame others for his

screw-ups.

He sighed, watching the coals flare and redden then flare again. Weariness set in, how much of that was due to injury and growing mortality, or the recent loss of so many things, he did not know. He should flop over and go back to sleep and see to all this when the daylight returned. At least the grass was soft and bug-free. He looked down, suspicious. Was it?

Flicka nickered again and shifted rather dangerously and the last thing Otto needed was a horse stepping on him so he rolled over and pulled himself up the length of the stirrups. Poor horse, all this time still saddled, halberd and all.

"Want me to take this off?" he asked as he patted the seat.

The horse shook her head and snorted and flipped her mane at the alps. Otto looked.

A light.

He rubbed his eyes, not sure whether it wasn't some vision artifact, spots caused by his staring at the flames. But, no, there was a definite light in the far-off ruins, in one of the upper levels, maybe in a tower window. It flickered like a torch, and then was gone.

"What was that?" Otto asked.

No answer. Like Flicka was going to say something. The horse remained still and Otto squinted at the distant ruins and knew he needed to jump in the saddle and kick Flicka into a gallop and race across dark fields and hills and up scree and platform and steps and into the castle and see who—or what—that light was.

But the weariness rose like a volcano, numbing him, and he slid down the stirrup and curled into a ball and fell asleep.

Chapter VIII

Yea, Though I Walk ...

Otto sat in the saddle and watched smoke wafting here and there from the cabin remains. Too bad that side of bacon wasn't poking through the ashes; he could stand a BLT. Heck, at this point he'd settle for a handful of half-raw mystery meat. Handful of raw oats.

"Got anything?" he asked Flicka and slapped the saddlebags hanging either side of the halberd.

The horse glanced at him then turned back to the distant castle. One-track mind, this horse. Flicka had stared at it ever since Otto woke up, stirred, groaned, waited for the stiffness and pain to subside to the point he could move and sit up. And then gangway to the remains of the cabin, barely parting the toga in time before assaulted by a good five-to-ten minute urination, the first of its necessary kind since he'd arrived in this weird Afterlife. Before, it was recreation, like sleep.

"If that doesn't prove I'm back to being human, nothing does," he muttered, and worried whether he would also have to download soon. No toilet paper. And no toilet.

How embarrassing.

But, no such urge. He made his clumsy way back to the horse, head pounding and even thirstier than yesterday, and stared at the cabin ashes for a long five minutes, willing that side of bacon to emerge. At least a singed BLT but, nothing. He milled around until he figured it was pointless, then made his clumsy way into the saddle, Flicka not moving the whole time, fixed on the ruins the whole time. Otto followed her gaze, expecting to see a flickering light in a tower window, but no. Maybe it was too bright, clouds notwithstanding, and, since the cabin was gone and there wasn't anything more to do here, maybe he should check it out.

After breakfast.

Otto lifted one of the saddle bag flaps and gingerly probed inside with his good hand. Way things were going, wouldn't surprise him to brush Freddie Kreuger's razor blades and lose a couple more unwary fingers. He did feel something, but it wasn't sharp. It was flat and rough like a stick of cardboard.

What is this, a bookmark? Suspicious, he pulled it out.

A stick of jerky.

"You're kidding, right?" Otto asked the horse, who ignored him. Otto regarded it for a moment, wondering if bookmark was a better use. But better than nothing, he reckoned, and pulled off a section with his teeth and chewed on it for the next ten minutes. Tough, gamey, but it had a pleasing, if unidentifiable, flavor.

Not beef. Hmm. This was a Mongol saddle and a Mongol horse so the jerky was something Mongols like. Camel. Or horse.

"Cousin of yours?" Otto asked Flicka but the horse didn't respond and Otto shrugged and bit off more and had to admit, as thin as it was, the jerky was rather satisfying.

And salty.

"Man," Otto said, choking down another piece, "I could stand a Pepsi." Or a beer, or anything cold and satisfying, for that matter, to chase this horse-salt tablet.

He rummaged around in the saddlebags for a Budweiser but all it contained was more jerky. He brushed against a leather loop hanging off the saddle, grabbed it, and pulled up a skin bag covered with black, coarse hair with a stopper on the end.

"Don't remember having this when we charged Star City," he told Flicka but, heck, didn't know about the jerky, either. It wasn't as if he examined the saddle before the fight began. Too busy.

He pulled out the stopper and cautiously sniffed.

"*Whew!*" he retched and almost threw the bag away because, man, rank! Like spoiled milk.

Another one or two suspicious sniffs and then a suspicious taste test.

"*Yuck!*" Yep, spoiled milk, but not all that bad. Akin to buttermilk, and, while he was no buttermilk fan, he must do something about the salt caking his throat so ...

Otto upended the bag and gulped the smelly stuff down, surprised he didn't vomit. Surprised he didn't drain it, too, he was that thirsty. Wisely, he stopped guzzling, re-corked it and re-looped the bag. Never know when he'd find the next bag-o'-swill.

"Horse jerky and mare's milk," Otto said, affectionately patting Flicka's neck. "You must be nervous."

The horse didn't acknowledge him, remained staring at the distant ruins.

"What are you looking at, man?" Otto lined up the horse's gaze and aimed along it like a sniper rifle but saw nothing. Nothing that should attract such equine interest, anyway. Were horses like cats and could see ghosts? "Can you?"

No response. Otto let a decent five minutes go by for Flicka to respond but she didn't and he suspected she would not. He was going to have to find out for himself.

"Okay, okay," Otto groused and looked once more at the smoking cabin.

Nope, no bacon.

"Let's go, then," he said, and gently kicked Flicka in the ribs.

They were off. It took Otto a few moments to settle into the rhythm, and he placed his good hand on the halberd's shaft to steady himself.

"Like riding a bike," he concluded after a moment and let Flicka have her head. The overcast was brighter, so it must be getting close to noon.

Gray, why are the clouds gray? With the combined colors of the suns, shouldn't they be purple or yellow or something?

Maybe because his mood was gray.

They were on a long slow incline terminating on top of a ridge. The surrounding land was fairly flat and uninteresting and Otto was soon bored out of his mind. Too bad he didn't have a

Sony tablet or something, could watch YouTube if he could get a signal. He strained at the horizon, hoping to locate a microwave tower.

Nope. Oh well. Let's brood, then.

Been a very interesting couple of days, hasn't it?

Yes, indeedy. And without going through all the quite familiar details, the big, overriding question is, why? What could possibly be the reason for stripping him of his immortality, his cabin, his food, and his dogs?

"Cha Cha!" he called but no response, not even the Booming Voice of the Almighty echoing over the lands, "Because, Otto, it is My Will! Darest Thou Question?"

Well, yeah.

"See, Lord," Otto spoke to the emptiness, "Your Will or no, none of this is making any sense. And you know us humans, Lord, we need explanations. Reasons. Answers." He paused. "Okay?"

Silence.

There you go. There's your answer.

They rode for what had to be hours, and Otto gradually turned numb. Except for his little finger; that continued to throb and flare and Otto should have checked it but, really, why, what could he do, pour some mare's milk over it?

Hmm. Tastes vinegary, so maybe has an antiseptic quality. Or maybe it would hasten the gangrene, so let's not.

He went into a trance until they reached the top of the ridge where the shift in Flicka's gait shook him out of it and he opened his eyes …

And gasped.

"Whoa!" he called out and Flicka did, almost upending Otto. The horse looked back at him, annoyance clear on her face, but Otto waved his good hand at their front. "Look at this!" he said.

A battlefield.

Or the remains of one.

The slope before him stretched down to another valley before rising again to an opposite knoll, over which the ruins of the castle and its towers loomed. Skeletons, rusted piles of metal and other unrecognizable objects lay all over the place, covering what Otto figured was about two to three miles of ground, with giant boulders strewn across it all like accents.

"Wow," he whistled.

Carefully, he had Flicka pick her way down the slope, a trip of about a half-hour until they reached the bottom and he pulled the reins to stop, Flicka registering more annoyance.

"Why don't you hold your horses?" Otto said with his own measure of annoyance, a comment that should have been funny, except he was too unnerved. Grunting, he slid off the saddle, using the halberd shaft to keep upright, and looked.

Good God.

Disjointed skeletons, a skull here, a femur there, sets of ribs ranging from human-sized to horse-sized, some piled but most lying singly. No weapons that he could see, swords or spears or halberds, not even an M-16. Maybe they accounted for the piles of rusted metal, but those looked more like fused armour than anything. The bones stretched out of sight in all directions, over the top of the next ridge. Otto did quick calculations: if ten or fifteen bones constituted the basic frame of one person ... angel ... Suit ... whatever, then there had to be hundreds of thousands of bodies here.

"Good God," he whispered.

He stooped and carefully tapped what looked like a leg bone near his feet. It dissolved into dust.

Otto arched brows. "Been here a while, hey?" He straightened. How long did bones lie around before they became dust? A year? Ten? "Ten thousand?" he asked.

A breeze picked up, a mournful one, cold and bereft, and Otto shivered, more from the eeriness than the sudden chill.

"Stay here," he said to Flicka and, using the halberd as a walking stick, stepped along a natural fall. Every bone he touched immediately turned to dust and gathered in the breeze and was gone. He stopped before an almost intact skull and stared at it. Looked human. Not that he was an expert or anything, but he'd been to enough autopsies to get a general sense of proper human anatomy.

'Course, Suits looked human enough, except for the elongated faces, but that should show up in the skull. Right?

He shrugged and noted a pile of bones that had to be a horse of some kind and stepped towards it to get a closer look.

Not a horse. A dinosaur.

"You've got to be kidding me," Otto whispered to the strange breeze, and squatted next to the pile, careful not to touch it.

Long snout, scimitar teeth, big pits for the nose … yep, a dinosaur of some kind. Probably a tyrannosaur, albeit a small one. Allosaurus? Maybe.

So, what happened here, a battle between dinosaurs and men?

"Shades of *One Million Years BC*," he said and immediately looked around, expecting Raquel Welch to skip over the ridge in a fur bikini.

No such luck.

All that moved was the grass under the breeze. He looked back at the dinosaur pile.

Maybe men hadn't fought the dinosaurs but rode them into battle, like some kind of war horse. So to speak.

Against whom?

Otto gazed at the distant castle set in the mountainside.

Against whoever was living in there, obviously. Otto turned and surveyed the extent of the field. If the big stones scattered here and there were projectiles, then they'd been fired from the castle at the dinosaur-riding enemy … assuming they'd been riding dinosaurs.

He could be all wrong and the dinosaurs *were* the enemy and the human remains mixed among them were soldiers from the castle, and the great stones weren't ammunition at all but what remained of the castle's outer perimeter of defense, where both forces had met in a terrific battle.

Whatever. Point is, there'd been one terrific battle.

"Who won?" he asked the breeze, but no answer. From what he could see, it looked like no one did. He stared at the castle.

Well, one way to find out.

He turned and stumped back to Flicka, heedless of the bones, the horse pawing the ground with impatience.

"All right, all right," he said irritably as he drew near, "Can't a guy do a little bit of sightseeing?"

She neighed in disagreement and flicked her mane at him and Otto tsked and set the halberd in place and grasped the saddle to haul himself up …

"Otto!"

"*Ack!*" he yelped in shock and terror and tumbled off the stirrup, catching himself on the ground with his bad hand. "*Ow!*" he screamed, grabbing his hand as he was enveloped by a cloud of bone dust.

"Otto!" the voice yelled again. "Don't go!"

Waving the dust out of the way, Otto grabbed the halberd with his good hand and yanked it out of its holster, tucking the length under his arm. Comforting to have a weapon, although he didn't know how effective he would be wielding it one-handed.

"Who's there?" he called.

"You mustn't go!" the voice again, a man's, carried at a distance, and Otto whirled in its direction, halberd as ready as he could get it. He peered. A figure stood about two football fields down the fall he'd traversed.

"Who are you?" Otto yelled.

"Don't go any farther!" The figure took on a pleading aspect. "Go back to the cabin, instead!"

An inflection in the voice sounded familiar and Otto frowned, concentrating. Couldn't place it.

"Cabin's not there anymore!"

The figure advanced, hands held out, imploring. "Nevertheless," the man said, "you must go back there. You will be all right!"

What!

He will be all right?

Otto was struck. That was something practically everyone in the City had said to him when he was running around the streets trying to make sense of the place. And one particular person in the City had said that to him in exactly the same deep, rich burr this guy had …

Otto gasped.

"Ian!"

Chapter IX

Starring James Spader

Otto stepped forward and shook the halberd at the fast-approaching Scot.

"That's far enough!" he growled.

Ian stopped, his look changing quickly from surprise to perplexed as he eyeballed the wavering blade. "Otto!" he pleaded. "I am not your enemy!"

"Yeah?" Otto pointed the halberd at Ian's face. "You and that crazy horse of yours tried to kill me!" He looked back at Flicka, who was standing off, wary. "No offense," he said.

Flicka shook her head in a none-taken response.

Ian raised placating hands. "We were not trying to kill you," he said, "We were trying to save you."

"Funny way of showing it," Otto snapped. "Your freakin' horse almost stomped me into hamburger." Another look back at Flicka. "Again, no offense."

Flicka stared at him like he was crazy.

Ian took a step towards him. "Admittedly, George's response was a bit excessive. But, given events, you may have to admit he wasn't excessive enough."

"Back off!" Otto warned and threatened him with the halberd again. Ian made a hasty retreat.

So, Otto noted, he's afraid of this thing. Good.

"And what events are you referring to?"

"This!" Ian waved his arms about. "Your entire, foolish journey across the heavens. And your equally foolish effort to reach that!" Ian pointed at the distant castle.

Flicka rumbled an angry response and Otto shushed her.

"Why is it foolish?" he asked. "What's in there?"

Ian visibly shivered, visibly paled. "Something evil," he whispered.

The hackles rose on Otto's neck and he could swear there was distant, demonic laughter in the hollows of the castle stones. He turned and stared at the ruins.

"What?"

Ian's gesture took in the surrounding bone piles. "You see all this, and have to ask?"

Otto steamed. "Yes, I have to ask!" he roared, shaking the halberd angrily. "This doesn't tell me a blasted thing! Except it's a battlefield." He paused. "Right?"

Ian raised an eyebrow. "Of course it is," he said in a what-are-you, stupid? tone. "Don't you know one when you see one?"

"Yes," Otto said between clenched teeth, "but who fought here? And what's in the castle?"

Ian looked at the bone piles mournfully. "Forces. The same ones that have fought each other in all the places of this universe, in one form or another, since ... since ..." and he looked up, taking in the castle, the expression on his face a blend of horror and exultation.

Otto fumed. Well, isn't that friggin' cryptic? And you know what else is cryptic? "Ian, what the hell are you doing here?"

Ian looked downright offended. "I think that should be rather obvious, Otto. I am here to warn you."

"Got that much, Ian, so, let me clarify. *How'd* you get here?"

Ian laughed. "All the miracles of this Heaven, and you ask?"

Otto let out a long, exasperated breath.

"Look, I am damned tired of all this answering a question with a question kay-rap. And don't tell me this is Heaven." Otto shifted the halberd into a better grip. "Because I'm seeing very little evidence of that."

"Then, Otto," Ian said, "come with me to a place that has all the evidence you need."

Dramatic pause.

"Come back to the City."

Otto started. "You have a way of getting back to the City?"

Ian smiled. "Where do you think I came from?"

"Geez! Stop answering me with questions!" Otto shouted. "Give me a straight-up answer, man!"

Ian stood quietly, then nodded. "You're right. I'm being an ass. And, in answer to your question, yes, I do have the means to get both you and me back to the City. Through a ... portal. Best word I have for it." He pointed down the fall. "It's that way, about a mile."

Otto squinted along Ian's point, expecting to see ... what? The Star Gate? But there was only the flat, featureless land diminishing to a gray distance.

"A portal. Which leads back to the City. With a snap of the fingers and a few incantations, I'll bet." He frowned. "Riddle me this ... if you've got a portal between worlds, then why did we need a ship to leave the City?"

"You didn't. You had absolutely no reason to leave the City. I tried to tell you that."

"So you did." Otto's eyes narrowed. "Ian, are you still an agent?"

He held his breath, expecting the Scot to dissolve into dust and blow away in the breeze, as he had back in the City when Otto had asked him the same question, an event prompting the murderous attack by Ian's horse, George. And Otto's subsequent rescue by Unathi, in a DeLorean, no less. And everything since.

But Ian remained Ian. Or, whatever he was now. A downright animated whatever he was now, in fact.

"Yes!" The Scot waved hands in exasperation. "I'm an agent! Of common sense! And common sense tells you this stupid journey is now over and it is time to come home!" and he pointed insistently back down the fall.

Hmm. Go back to the City. Restore his immortality. Get his little finger back. Ease into the condo and catch up on HBO. Spend evenings at Grendel's quaffing Irish ale and singing Celtic drinking songs, then stroll over to Godwin's and buy a couple of books — maybe the original Masoretic texts or an ARC of *The Adventures of Tom Sawyer* — then off to one of Ferdinand's stores for a fine cigar and a bottle of wine and then into a nearby library to laugh at Madelyn Murray O'Hair and her very bad life choices, maybe a train trip to Out for a three-day card game with Doc Holliday and Machine Gun Kelly so they could tell him how the heck they survived the Suits' attack. Then, after saying 'hi!' to Moy Jin and Pashtun, three days back and a cheese Danish at Frank Vaughn's little pastry place where maybe Frank, himself, will show up and tell Otto, with great calmness this time, how Frank's mother beat him to death because he forgot his report card on the last day of school, and, finally, home, settle on the balcony, a wave at Deng Xiaoping across the way, and watch the rushing stars …

All without Ferdinand. And Marc.

And Claudia.

Or God.

Otto eyed him. "Come home. With you. With someone who once tried to kill me. Through a portal that until, moments ago, didn't exist."

His own dramatic pause.

"Common sense tells me that's a very bad idea."

"To be fair," Ian responded, coolly, "It wasn't me that tried to kill you, but George."

"Ye-e-e-s." Otto said. "You were too busy trying to pull your various dust motes back together. Good job on that, by the way. Who helped you?"

Ian said nothing, simply stared at him.

"And who's running the portal, Ian?"

Ian still said nothing, and a distinct air of menace settled between them. Flicka suddenly walked up and stood next to Otto, breathing hard, combat on her.

"What's going on?" he whispered to her.

In answer, Flicka shrieked and launched at Ian.

"Crap!" Otto yelled, thrown off-balance by the horse's rush. He spun about, jamming the halberd shaft into the ground to keep upright and refocused.

Flicka reared up, hooves flailing at Ian, who had stepped back and ducked into a crouch. He reached into his coat and pulled out a long shimmering blade …

That looked extraordinarily like Akiko's Sword of Eternity.

"No!" Otto yelped and pushed off, bringing the halberd up and charging, finger be damned.

Flicka leaped frantically to the side to avoid Ian's blade and, in three giant steps, Otto got under her hooves and drove the halberd past the blade and into Ian's chest.

Ian dissolved, sword and all.

No shock, no bolts of lightning throwing Otto across the field, only a sudden rain of what looked like sugar around the halberd blade, all of it falling into a pile.

Otto withdrew the blade and, gingerly, probed the sugar, fully expecting a flash of lightning and a sudden transport to the world of black suns and thousand-eyed monsters, but nothing. Flicka had, in the meantime, gathered herself and walked up to him, nickering gently into his ear.

"You're welcome," he said, and sifted through the sugar, but even the sword was gone. "The Firsts," he whispered. He looked at the horse. "How did you know?"

Flicka blinked at him and then snorted, perturbed.

Otto raised eyebrows. "What? Could you smell them or something?"

The horse turned in a huff and gazed at the looming castle.

"What'd I say?" Otto asked, bewildered. "I'm not making fun of your nose or anything, you know."

Flicka remained motionless and Otto waved a hand in dismissal and then turned back to the sugar pile. So, the Firsts had found him, at a moment when he was mortal and wounded and easy to dispatch, and instead of sending the Akiko-thing to put an end to him, they sent Ian.

The real Ian. Same incomprehensible accent. Same expansive way of talking. Same sugar pile (well, it was more like dust back in the City, but that's quibbling). And trying to persuade him to go back to the City.

Why?

Could have easily left him here alone to die from gangrene or starvation or old age ... well, older age. It's not like he presented much of a threat.

Did he?

Back on the ship, right before the beautiful Akiko had turned into a monster of the black suns, wielding a magic sword that dissipated whoever it struck into so many pain-filled molecules, sending their souls into screaming orbits around the black worlds with thousand-eyed monsters as company, she'd said, "We shall have no such weapons."

"We" being the Firsts, and "weapon" being Otto. Or, humans in general. He had no idea what she'd meant. Still didn't, but suspected the poor mud creatures she held in such disdain had a quality absent in the rest of creation, even among the Firsts. Something that could undo them.

Flicka shifted and Otto turned and the horse looked at him and stamped impatiently.

"I'm guessing whatever's up there doesn't want us to show up, does it?" he asked. "Otherwise, why was Ian trying to keep us from going?" Flicka nickered an assent.

Otto stared at the ruins. Clouds thickened above the ramparts and Otto swore a light flickered momentarily in a window.

"Let's go introduce ourselves," he said, and mounted.

Chapter X

Along With Some Orcs And Trolls

One thing the short but effective battle with Ian had proved, Otto needed a better method for handling the halberd. He'd almost dropped the thing when charging the guy, his little-finger stump providing no purchase. Fortunately, adrenaline had kept his grip but he shouldn't rely on that, especially if the First living in that castle (or whatever was living in that castle) slapped his little-finger stump. He'd drop the halberd and jump around like a sissy. And end up orbiting black-sunned planets.

No thanks.

So, while Flicka carefully picked her way across the bones and stones and metal, Otto carefully unwrapped the sheet bandage, shook it out to get rid of as much of the crusted blood as he could, and then examined the finger, which pulsed and throbbed in protest of this treatment. The pain, though, was a little more tolerable and the red color hadn't advanced, so maybe it was healing.

Yeah, right.

He was probably just getting used to it.

Otto cut a strip of material from the sheet with the halberd blade and re-wrapped the finger tighter this time, then used the rest of the strip to fashion a kind of looping handhold on the shaft. Now he could wrap his arm around the halberd to hold it steady, like a sniper with a rifle strap. The sheet wasn't the best of materials for this purpose and he considered using a strip of his toga-blanket, instead, but why mess with success? Besides, the toga was the only thing keeping him warm.

Because it was getting noticeably colder.

Otto peered at the sky and shivered. Still overcast, the clouds darker, but not from impending rain, from the impending sunset. The breeze remained but there was a bite to it now and Otto wondered if the next round of weather was coming in frozen.

Wouldn't that be lovely?

He stared at the castle. Despite looming over the battlefield, it looked no closer than it did when they'd resumed the journey about an hour ago. Maybe it was like a distant peak, so big it looked close but was actually miles away. Which meant the castle was huge, which meant whatever was living in there required a larger than normal living space.

"Great," he muttered, "Who's in there, Smaug?"

Flicka's ears pricked back at his question and he patted her gently on the neck. Good ole Flicka. Back in Out, she'd been quite the practical joker: throwing his hat around, loosening the saddle so it fell off when he tried to mount, and riding under low-hanging branches to knock him on his rear-end. Not that there were any trees around here to pull off that particular prank, but there weren't any in the desert they'd rode across during Kenny's raid on the Vikings, either, and she'd still managed to find a few. Otto looked around, expecting any moment for one of those non-existent trees to materialize and Flicka to accelerate and *whoomp!* Otto on his butt.

But, no trees. No anything, only piles of bones and stones stretching in all directions. The next valley was probably as bone-strewn.

"Helluva battle," he concluded. With a helluva lot of participants. And they'd been unsuccessful.

What made him think he would be successful?

Otto considered. If several combat divisions of angels and dinosaurs couldn't overcome the thing in the castle, then his own chances appeared mighty slim. Except, the battle had been a few years (decades, millennia) ago, evidenced by the dusty skulls, and maybe the castle's landlord had enfeebled since then. The castle's state of disrepair so indicated. Besides, Otto was human. Humans tended to do well against Firsts.

"At great cost," Lydia whispered in his ear.

He gasped and looked wildly around, his jerky movements prompting Flicka to shy and Otto had to pull on the reins while shouting "Take it easy!" to get her back under control. Finally, the horse held, looking back at him with some alarm. Otto ignored her and stared about, trying to locate Lydia, but he couldn't see her among the lengthening shadows. Didn't mean anything; if Ian could show up out of the blue, so could she.

Or anyone, for that matter.

Like Claudia.

He stilled and quartered the area like a hunter seeking its prey, but nothing moved. No golden-haired beauty wafted across the stones and bones, smiling her sun-like smile at him, arms reaching out in greeting. No Afro-haired Lydia, either, leaping on the back of the Akiko-thing and strangling it as Otto reached for the monster's Forever Sword, his touch sending a jolt of lightning straight into both Lydia and him and then the Akiko-thing had grabbed her ... and, well, that was the end of Lydia.

"At great cost," he acknowledged her ghost.

Ghost.

Kind of a funny word to use in this here Afterlife, but he couldn't think of a better one to describe the spirit of someone recently departed, even if they were already departed, once they became departed. Again. Into what? Another Afterlife? One that actually contained God? Or were there layers and layers of Afterlives, each one harder and harder to reach, requiring more and more struggle, more and more pain?

Otto gazed across the valley. The guys and gals who once belonged to all these bones, what happened to them? Where did whatever had animated them − soul or spirit or alma or *nu shuma* − get off to? If his recent contact with the Firsts was any judge, they all floated among the black sun worlds, millions of weird souls screaming in agony as the thousand-mouthed giants ate them. But, during the moment he'd floated among the black suns himself, he hadn't seen millions of weird souls screaming in agony, only the giants.

And they were eating planets, not people. Maybe the millions of weird souls had never left. Maybe they were still here.

A valley of ghosts.

Otto frowned, noting that another degree of darkness had settled across the landscape.

"I don't want to spend an evening out here, old girl," he said to Flicka. "Got a feeling it might not be very pleasant. So." He pointed at the distant castle. "Think we can make the Dragon King's stronghold before nightfall?"

In answer, Flicka stepped over a pile of ghost bones and broke into a trot, jolting Otto as she beelined towards the hill. Otto gripped the saddle, shrugged, and eyed the darkening sky, wondering whether they'd beat sunset.

They didn't.

By the time Flicka topped a rise that Otto guessed fronted the big platform, it was full-on night. Not that he could tell; it was pitch black out here. And colder. The breeze had picked up and was eagerly exploring the gaps in his toga, but Otto didn't dare adjust it for fear of throwing Flicka off her rhythm. Doubted that he could; she kept going with no hesitation.

"Have you got night vision or something?" he asked, but she ignored him and Otto huddled against her neck, carefully snaking a piece of jerky out of the pack from time to time. Thank God he didn't feel another urge to urinate because he didn't want to stop. He was too scared.

Scared.

He could honestly say this was the most scared he'd been since waking in the City. And there had been plenty of scary moments: the Suit pursuit; the Suit battle; heck, even the launch of the ship. Not to mention the meteor shower along the dark road and the Fallen and the Akiko-thing. All downright terrifying. This, though, was magnitudes scarier.

Because something palpable, something in the dark, moved about with an ugly purpose. Not anything Otto could hear or even see but it was here, all the same. Its eyes, hard and judging, scrutinized him from some great, cold distance. Pitiless. Shadows reeling about it.

And he was defenseless before it. He was mortal and wounded and wielded a flimsy blade at the end of a flimsy stick to fight what he instinctively knew was something entirely different from the other horrors he'd encountered thus far. And he felt no assurance, heard no still small voice telling him it would be all right.

It wouldn't be all right. When the thing in the dark manifested, it would eat his soul.

Flicka lurched to a halt.

Oh no! It's here! Otto cringed and wanted to shout, "Run!" to Flicka but all he could manage was a Lisa Simpson "*Eep!*".

Panic will do that.

Flicka nickered softly, not exactly a panic-filled response, and Otto squinted along the horse's neck, trying to see.

And did.

A soft, grayish-blue light was creeping across the front of him. Otto held his breath, expecting glowing eyes and bared fangs to materialize but no; the fuzzy and indistinct landscape quickly gained detail. Otto looked up and saw two bright patches in the clouds.

Ah.

The moons had found a couple of thin spots in the overcast.

How fortuitous.

The valley floor behind him also gained detail, and Otto saw the bones gleaming in cobalt, the great stones in flecked gray and black. Nothing moved down there. No ghosts. No black thing.

Otto peered. He and Flicka were on a flat piece of ground, the top of the rise, Otto figured. The light strengthened and more of the surroundings became clearer. As they did, Otto whistled softly.

Flicka had parked them at the bottom of the platform. And, boy, was it big.

"Could land a 737 here. A couple of them," he whispered.

Flicka nickered in agreement. Two low walls bordered the platform, running along its sides. Medieval guard rails, Otto guessed.

The platform rose at a steep angle hiding the other side. Above it loomed a massive gateway made of giant stones similar to those littering the battlefield. The gate arched over a smashed double portcullis, both sides hanging at precarious angles, as if their hinges had rusted away. Above the gate, gigantic battlements stretched in both directions, towers flanking each end. It looked like the battlements continued around, no doubt encircling a village and blocking his view of it. The keep towered above everything. If medieval urban planning held true, it was probably in the dead center of the village, about three or four football fields away from the gate.

Otto followed the line of the keep upwards. The moons had strengthened or the clouds had thinned, whatever, and the cobalt glow lit the stonework, revealing a series of deep cracks up and down. How the keep remained upright, Otto couldn't figure. The top was crenelated above an arched window. That had to be where the owner of the flickering light dwelled. Otto stared at it for a full minute, but the window remained shadowed.

"Come on," he said and Flicka stepped onto the platform.

Otto craned up the keep as they advanced, frowning at the rook-like top.

Bit worrisome, that. One good archer up there could end this journey fairly quick. Better yet, one good catapult launching one of those giant stones.

The tower stayed in full view as they ascended and Otto braced, prepared to launch himself off Flicka should a bow — or a catapult sling — show itself. Hope such a leap didn't mean a tumble down the mountainside. He glanced at the platform nervously, but it was so wide he'd have to put in extra effort to fall off it.

Flicka had a hard time with the steep angle. Otto wondered what the friction coefficient was between iron horseshoes and stone walkways. Did Flicka even have horseshoes? He had no intention of leaning out of the saddle to find out. Might unbalance her right off the side.

Somehow, though, she kept moving in a more or less straight line and, after what had to be an hour, the platform levelled and they were facing the massive stone stairs leading up the mountain to the shattered gate.

"Finally," he said. Flicka gave him a dirty look. "Not you," he said. "I meant we're here. And I don't necessarily want to be."

Not at all. Don't want to meet whatever's schlepping around in there. Don't want to get eaten. Perhaps we should call this off.

He gripped the halberd shaft and leaned forward, considering the wisdom of flight over fight.

"Okay," he sighed, as wisdom fled, "let's get this over with."

He readied for Flicka to head up the steps.

She didn't.

Otto chuckled. "I know how you feel." He did. And sympathized. "But," he continued, "during my very interesting life — and, come to think of it, this very interesting Afterlife — I learned it's always best to go straight at things. Especially when it's something you absolutely, positively, categorically don't want to do. So," and he kicked Flicka gently in the ribs, "let's go straight at it."

Flicka didn't move.

"C'mon, girl," Otto urged, "let's go. We have to see what's in there." He held up a placating hand. "Granted, I don't know any more than you *why* we have to see what's in there, but we do. So ..." another kick.

Flicka shuffled a bit, snorted, and looked back at him with some irritation.

"What?" Otto asked.

The horse flipped her mane and pawed the platform, extending her nose and staring at the bottom of the steps.

"What?" Otto repeated and followed the horse's gaze.

Even in this better light, it was hard to make out detail, but there was something, or more accurately, nothing ... a dark line, a shadow.

Otto stared but couldn't make it out.

"What is that?" he asked Flicka, "A dip in the platform?"

The horse remained intent on it, which meant he'd have to dismount and look.

Oh, joy.

Painfully, carefully, dragging the halberd along with him, he did.

Nope, not a dip. A floor break. About ten feet wide.

"Wonderful," Otto muttered and looked over the edge. He'd never been afraid of heights, always thought of them as a chance for an alternate perspective so never had a problem leaning over cliffs or out of tall trees. But this thing was bottomless. Black. Forever.

A fall into eternity.

Dizziness hit him and he lurched dangerously over the gap,

yanking himself back by jamming the halberd into the platform and driving away from the opening.

Whew.

Carefully, Otto approached the edge again and gauged the distance between the fragmented end of the platform and the fragmented first step. No way he could leap that. Maybe he could pole vault it with the halberd.

Riiight.

Like he'd ever pole-vaulted anything wider than a sidewalk crack, and that when he was six. With an umbrella. Besides, his finger was messed up. Maybe if Flicka got a running start ... he looked back at her and raised inquiring eyebrows.

She looked at him like he was crazy.

"All right," he sighed, and looked around. One good thing, the guard walls still connected to the other side. But how well? Otto wasn't sure they'd hold under his weight, much less Flicka's. He wasn't sure she could even get up there. Even if she did, the guard walls had rounded tops, which meant there was no way Flicka could keep a grip on them. So much for all the easy solutions. Looked like the only way across was by shinny.

"Wonderful," he repeated, and walked over to the right side.

The wall had worn smooth; after millions of years, what'd you expect? This meant the end still attached to the steps over there should be equally worn, hanging on by mere thread or whatever is the concrete equivalent. Otto pushed on the wall but it didn't give.

Hmm. Maybe it was solid enough.

He leaned his full weight on it with both hands, but, again, no movement. Using the halberd to assist, Otto straddled the wall, his feet clearing the platform, and bounced up and down. The wall held.

Flicka was still in the same location, watching him.

"Think it'll be okay," he called to her. "Wanna give it a try?"

Flicka gave him another are-you-crazy? look.

"Okay, fine," Otto said and peered across the way. "Maybe when I get over there, I can find something to make a ramp."

Behind him, Flicka snorted, the horsey equivalent of, "Uh huh."

Otto threw out hands, a somewhat precarious move given his

position.

"What? I don't want to leave you behind. You've been excellent since you showed up. Didn't throw my hat once." He paused. "You ARE supposed to go with me, right?"

He turned, another precarious move, to get Flicka's answer. The horse stood there mildly, patiently, but silently, not even a wink and a nod and Otto realized it was a pointless question. What was Flicka going to do, suddenly speak? Turn into Balaam's ass, which would be a downgrade despite the vocal abilities? Not that the Great Magical Genie running this place couldn't pull it off, but he doubted very much that it would.

Life's a mystery.

Apparently, so is the Afterlife.

Get on with it.

He scrutinized the opposite side. Seemed okay. Seemed. He pushed but his feet were too high off the platform to gain traction. Otto looked back at Flicka. "Little help?"

The horse slowly walked over and placed her forehead against his back and gave him a hard nudge.

"Whoa!" he yelped as he almost fell off, "Wait a minute!" Otto lifted the halberd and held it widthways like a wirewalker's pole, centering its weight.

That's more stable. "Let's try that again," he said and Flicka pushed and he threw the halberd forward with both hands as a counter and, this time, Otto stayed upright.

In this manner, Otto slid along the wall, stopping every three feet or so to check the connection to the other side. It wasn't the fastest way to proceed but was the safest and, before he knew it, Otto was over the gap.

Which was a problem.

Flicka, obviously, couldn't help anymore. One more step and she'd tumble off. And he'd already seen the result of trying to push himself along. He frowned.

How to continue?

Maybe he could tightrope walk, using the halberd as an actual balance pole, but talk about a stupid idea.

Better to crawl along the top of the wall, but the halberd would be an encumbrance.

So, toss it.

Otto stared at it. Had it already served its purpose? It'd been a handy cane and walking stick, and a handy Ian-sticker. But, now, it was in the way, so time for it to go. Otto shifted in preparation for heaving it over the side but, hold on, let's not be hasty. Perhaps it still had a use. Like protecting him from whatever lived in the keep.

"Prefer a shotgun," he said and waited for the halberd to morph into a .12 pump with a strap for carrying it over his shoulder, but it stayed a halberd.

"Okay," Otto said, and wondered what to do.

Well, it had kept him stable while Flicka pushed him, so maybe he could use it as a lever.

"I'm going to try something," he said to the horse. "Best you stay back. You're too close to the edge and your weight, with mine, might be enough to collapse it."

A slow clop of hooves as Flicka moved away and he glanced at her to assure she was far enough. Satisfied, he wrapped his arm through the makeshift sheet handle until his bad hand was tight against the shaft, and then rested the bottom of the shaft on top of the wall between his legs. Angling the halberd forward, he pulled down on the handle while bracing the bottom with his other hand. Lots of leverage doing that, and he pulled himself easily along the wall. Rinse, repeat, and, about ten minutes later, he was halfway over.

Point of no return, this.

Catching his breath, Otto looked down.

Woo wee, vertigo.

Hastily, he fixed eyes on the opposite wall until it subsided. Man, where'd that come from? Must be a combination of the blackness and stupidity.

"Dunno about this," he said.

At a shuffling behind him, he looked back at Flicka, who had advanced a step or two towards the edge. "You think I should go on, or come back and find another way across?"

Flicka vigorously shook her mane and gave a full-out neigh, staring obviously at the opposite side.

Otto shrugged. "Okay, if you say so. But, if I fall, I don't want you giving me any crap."

Flicka snorted a promise to give him lots of crap. Carefully,

Otto reset the halberd shaft and pushed.

The wall collapsed.

An instant so surprising that Otto was actually suspended in air for a half-second as the stones fell away. But only for a second as gravity took over. As relentless here as on Earth.

"*Augh!*" he yelled, plunging among giant concrete pieces into the Crevasse of Eternity. Flicka shrieked as the rest of the platform also collapsed, taking her along with it, the two of them falling down and down and down and doomed to bounce off the rock walls forever and ever and Otto screamed and screamed.

And jolted to a halt.

The concrete slabs kept going, smashing into the rocks, immediately lost to view as forever swallowed them, the sounds of their collisions continuing long after they disappeared. So did Flicka, tumbling head over heels smashing into the rocks, saddle and stirrups and bags flying off her, the entire group of horse-and-tackle disappearing from view as her neighs of terror echoed and re-echoed.

"Flicka!" Otto shrieked, his echoes joining hers.

But just his echoes. He remained in position. Gasping, Otto looked up to see why.

A little finger of the wall was still attached to the opposite mountainside, the halberd's pommel hooked around it. His bad hand was still wrapped through the sheet which was wrapped around the shaft.

That's why.

With a yell, Otto grabbed the shaft with his good hand, hanging on for dear life. That motion put him in a dangerous side-to-side swing and, any moment now, the pommel was going to swing right off the wall finger and send him right after Flicka. With a death grip on the shaft, Otto closed his eyes, willing the halberd to stop. Gradually, torturously, it slowed and, after a moment, he opened his eyes and looked up. The pommel was tight against the wall.

Relief flooded through him, but he didn't relax. No telling how long the wall protrusion or his grip would hold, especially since the bad hand was going numb quickly.

So let's take advantage of this, shall we?

He peered up the length of the shaft, but climbing it wasn't an option because there was nothing for him to climb to. The protrusion was barely wide enough to hold the pommel, much less him. He looked at the opposite wall. There were some shelves over there, not very wide, but, if he could reach them, he could get out of here.

"Another fine kettle of fish," he whispered, and cautiously reached out with his foot, but the shaft canted and he hastily pulled back. The shelf was too far away.

So, what now?

Let go?

He looked down, into black eternity.

"Flicka!" he called.

If the horse responded, then maybe it wasn't that deep. Maybe he could survive the fall, like she had.

Silence.

"Forget it," he whispered.

Swing over.

Otto almost laughed out loud. He'd just got himself to stop swinging, remember? But, short of someone coming along and tossing him a rope ... Otto waited a respectable moment of time for someone — Ian, say — to come along and offer said rope. Perhaps some incentive:

"Ian! I'll go back to the City with you! I will!"

No rope appeared.

Otto tsked. "Swing it is, then."

He peered at the opposite wall and then up the halberd's shaft. It was hard to tell in this light but it looked like the pommel sufficiently overlapped the protrusion for him reach the other side without it slipping off. Looked like.

One way to find out.

Breathing deep and hard to calm himself, he twitched his feet. Gently, gently and slow. At first, all he was doing was jerking around like some kind of idiot puppet but, slowly, the halberd began to swing. He pushed his ankles a little harder and the swing widened.

"Take it easy," he commanded himself, afraid he would get a little too enthusiastic and end up swinging the pommel right off. Patiently, he worked it and, soon, his feet were arcing closer and closer to the wall. On his swing back to the platform side, he decided to go for it and extended both legs hard for one last big push and he was Tarzan on the vine and almost there! Almost there!

The protrusion broke.

Otto flew almost horizontal, the last part of the swing giving him enough velocity to hit the opposite wall, but only his feet and lower legs landed on a shelf while the rest of him, led by the halberd, was pitching down the crevasse. If he let go of the shaft he might stand a chance, but the wrapped hand, now completely numb, held.

Desperate times demand desperate measures.

With a strength he did not know he had, Otto swung the halberd up and over his head and right into the shelf's wall.

Krang!!

The sound of metal against rock was like a bad comic book effect as he toppled over ... and then he wasn't toppling; instead, he was hanging halfway over the edge, gripping the halberd shaft so tight he was sure it would snap.

Must have jammed the blade into something.

Otto considered a "woo-hoo!" but that might be a bit premature. After all, he was still unbalanced and rather close to pitching headfirst into the Endless Cave of Death.

Let's remedy that.

Carefully, good-hand-over-bad, Otto hoisted himself along the shaft, sure the blade would un-jam at any moment, but, no, it remained. Minutes later, he was standing on the rock shelf, his back and legs planted firmly against the wall. Gasping and panting, he disentangled his bad hand from the sheet, getting an immediate rush of pins and needles as blood found its way back.

"*Ow*!" he said as the pins and needles discovered the bad finger and highlighted it. He grabbed at the bandage to tighten it and, when the rush of fever and agony subsided enough, stared at the halberd.

Yep.

The blade was stuck between two boulders.

"Thank you," he said, and patted the shaft affectionately with his good hand.

The halberd flipped up and over, falling down the crevasse.

Otto watched it disappear into the dark below, the sound of

metal clanging against rock still audible long after it was gone.

Guess it had served its purpose.

Like Flicka.

Otto squatted on the edge. "Flicka!" he called. "Can you hear me?" Nothing, so he called out a few more times, but no whinny, no nicker, not even a hoof weakly striking rock. Maybe she was too hurt to respond. Maybe she was waiting for him to climb down and render aid.

Maybe she was still falling.

He stood as tall as possible and stared into the cobalt sky.

"Would You do that?" Otto asked God. "Would you let a fun-loving horse who showed up here unannounced — which had to be Your doing — and was a big help giving me a ride and food and protecting me from whatever that Ian thing was, a dumb animal who has no idea what's going on, no idea of the issues involved here ... would You let that horse tumble through the dark forever? You would let that happen? You would?"

Because a just God would not do that.

A just God.

Seen any recent evidence of Justness, Otto, old boy?

He stared at the roiling, death-blue clouds for a while.

"Why are You doing this?" he whispered to them.

No answer.

What. A. Surprise.

Chapter XI

Torch Song

Otto had no idea how long it took him to scale the wall. Time was not the measure; pain and exhaustion were. He didn't know the ratio between escalating pain and minutes required per level of escalation but, by the time he grasped the bottom of the first step's base—the (broken) platform where this all kicked off—and, wearily, hauled himself up and over, he was a single and throughgoing meat bag of pain.

That's measure enough.

Between the flaring finger stump and the bruised and battered rest of him, a couple of days in a hospital bed would be lovely.

As long as that included a morphine drip.

But, no rest for the weary. Or the wounded. Especially in this Afterlife.

Otto stretched full out on the platform remnant, little more than a just-wide-enough ledge, letting the injured hand dangle over the edge. Not a good idea: the odor of gangrene wafting from the pinky stump would probably attract the interest of passing vultures. Or passing dragons, which'd take a nice bite of him before moving on. That actually might be a good thing; the whole hand was in dire need of amputation, or felt like it was, anyway. Slowly, he pulled it back and scrutinized the bandage. Sopping with blood now.

What'd you expect after a twenty-foot rock wall climb?

Otto sat up and replaced hand-dangling with feet-dangling. Might as well give the dragon a better choice of meat. And there *was* a dragon around here somewhere because, Holy Hannah, whatever was using these steps was big. Or whatever *had* used them. The layers of dust and grime indicated nothing had passed this way in centuries. He brushed at the crap covering his pants, but all that did was smear it. He tsked at the mess.

"What will the Dragon King think?" he said.

He pulled his legs underneath him and pushed up, precariously close to the edge but, hey, fall into eternal darkness, get eaten by a dragon, what's the diff?

The light was still the same, although Otto had expected the moons to set by now. Maybe they were hanging around to see how this would go. And, judging by the size of the step, not very well. Otto's head was inches short of the top, so this step was at least six-and-a-half feet tall. Dragon-sized.

Otto bounced up and down to get glimpses over the edge, but all he could see was another step waiting for him. One of several more, for that matter, ascending the side of the mountain to the tower and the wrecked portcullis.

Seven, eight, nine ... he stopped counting.

Essentially, he had several mini-mountain climbs ahead of him. He blew out a big breath.

"This is gonna be fun."

He stared at the top of the step ...

Then turned and sat back down, letting his feet dangle over the edge.

"I ain't Edmund friggin' Hillary, ya know," he told the Crevasse of Eternity, "and I've done all the climbing I'm going to do for one Afterlife. Unless you want to send a Sherpa my way." He waited.

No Sherpa appeared.

Otto drummed his feet slowly on the rock wall. Perhaps the vibrations would stir the Whyte Wyrm out of its slumber, slithering up to see what all the fuss was about.

"No fuss," Otto called down, "it's just me. No one important. Tasty snack, though." And he drummed a little louder to get the Wyrm moving. Maybe if he timed it right, he could leap onto its head and ride it up the steps like an elevator. "'Cause I ain't climbing nuthin'. Hear me?"

Ride it up the steps like an elevator.

Hmm.

The Dragon King, being a King, had some kind of wait staff: guys to cut the lawn, cut the hair, and cut up the virgins for nightly sacrifice, and they weren't climbing these particular steps daily ... unless they were also dragons and trotted up and down like it was nothing.

Let's assume they're people-sized, like the skeletons down in the valley. Maybe the skeletons are the wait staff, or were. Or the dinosaurs are. Were. They had to get in and out somehow

So, with no mechanical lift of any kind immediately apparent, how did non-Wyrms get in and out? Was there a back way in, a servant's entrance? Probably, and it was probably at the bottom of the crevasse which meant he had climbed in the wrong direction.

"Typical," Otto groused and he squinted down the hole, hoping to spot a door or something, but no. He rocked to his feet and cast about, half expecting to spot a lobby with an elevator bank, but of course not.

"You bring me Ian, but not Otis?" he complained to the crevasse. "Tsk, tsk."

Well, let's follow the logic. Shrimpy humans have to get castle access somewhere and, if it's not at the bottom of the bottomless pit then it's around here. Somewhere. He stepped over to the side, half-sure this was pointless but ya never know, and examined the wall next to the first step.

And found a series of normal-sized steps cut into it.

"Well, well," he said. So, Smaug the Merciless had some mercy on his minions, did he?

Carefully, Otto put out a foot and tested the nearest of the small steps. Solid as the giant ones. Holding onto the wall, he swung over, settled on the human-sized steps, bounced a bit to ensure they were, indeed, solid, and ascended.

"Told ya I wasn't going to climb," he said smugly to the moons.

But, essentially, he did because, Holy Hannah, were there a lot of steps. Didn't know exactly how many because he didn't bother to count but one of the benefits of working for the Dragon King had to be the daily cardio. He was exhausted by the time he reached the portcullis.

"Could stand a bit of that healing power about now," he said as he leaned against one of the rusty lattices "Or an aspirin. And a cup of coffee."

Mmm. Coffee. Wonder if this place has a Dunkin' Donuts. Otto stared through the gate.

No, it didn't.

Dreary, and that was being diplomatic. A stone road curved slightly from the gate and down a small slope to, yep, a village. As glimpsed through the telescope and as expected. Vegetation broke the road in several places, some of it yards across, downright hedges. The buildings were broken, too; that is, the ones he could make out in the silver-blue light. All of them had at least one wall crumbling into dust and ruin.

Dresden, a week after the bombing. This was the decay of ages, though, not high explosives.

He watched for a few minutes but nothing moved and no light glowed. No lamps. No torches. Not even a 7-Eleven.

"Looks like no one's home," he said.

Which was good. He wasn't sure he wanted to meet the minions of a dragon, unless it was Danerys Targareon. But she wasn't exactly a minion; she was the mother of dragons. Minions would be less photogenic.

Cautiously, Otto squeezedinto the small gap between a couple of the grates that had formed a skinny 'A' when they fell from the top but were still riveted together at their heads, both held in place by the grilles still attached to the stonework, one of those forming the crossbar about halfway down. There was barely enough room for him to shuffle through toe to heel, and he did an odd bunny-hop under the gate.

Better check your twelve, bud, before stepping under an obvious ambush site. He squinted.

A brass plaque, surprisingly bright, hung on the upper lintel. Maybe the overhang had protected it from the weather all these centuries.

How likely was that? Not very.

More likely, it was new and, therefore, an indication of recent maintenance, which was an indication of minions still kicking around. Alarmed, Otto braced for a horde of Valyrian-steel-swingin' dragon slaves, but nothing moved.

He went back to the plaque, almost rupturing an eyeball trying to read it, but it was too dark for him to make out details. Too bad he didn't have a flashlight. More out of habit than hope, he slapped at his pants pockets but knew there was nothing unless God had left him another box of Frenchie cigarettes and a Ronson like the one in that ridiculous Platan admiral uniform ...

Wait. What's this?

He reached tentative fingers and pulled out a box of matches.

"How the devil ...?" Oh, right.

When he lit the stove that ultimately lit the cabin, he'd used these matches. Must have put them in his pocket and, in the subsequent excitement, forgot about them. Absent-mindedness sometimes leads to pleasant surprises, like finding ten dollars in the laundry.

Otto opened the box. Okay, about a dozen matches, good. He pulled one out and struck it and held it up to the plaque but it was too far away to catch the feeble light. Needed a bigger match.

Or a torch.

Otto looked around and spotted a scraggly bush right outside the gate. He bunny-hopped through and checked it out. A few prospective branches stuck out from underneath and Otto grabbed one and pulled it but it was too short. He grabbed three more that had other defects, such as too thin or too sticky with some kind of sap, before he found one thick and long enough to serve.

Okay. Now, what do you know about torches?

Well ... nothing.

All that he remembered came from movies like *Indiana Jones*, in which torches were readily available and already lit. They all had some kind of cloth top that burned forever. Otto looked at the stick and then at the bandage on his hand. Nope. Need that. He then looked at the toga. Could wrap it around the stick and then light it with the match, but then all he'd have was a shish-ka-blanket that would turn to ash in about two minutes.

Irritated, Otto wiped some of the sap from his hands onto the toga. Maybe torches were actually a Hollywood invention and had never been used by a real human at any time in history. If he wanted to read the plaque, he would have to wait for sunrise. He'd have to wait for sunrise to explore the rest of the village, for that matter. Maybe he'd find a nice stash of Duracell batteries and Eveready flashlights in one of the buildings, but, until he did, might as well hunker down for the evening.

So, let's start a fire, get warm, and get some sleep.

Otto gathered up some more sticks and debris and built them into a pile of tinder underneath the gate. Except for sap drippings here and there, the stuff was bone dry, which was odd, given the last few days of weather. But at least it'll make a good fire so let's not question. Otto struck a match and lit a corner of some dry grass, watching as it immediately smoldered and coaled up its length. That's not promising. Getting down on all fours, he blew at the ember. It brightened and crept up the stalks but didn't flame, and Otto was sure it would go out when it reached the first bit of sap ...

The sap flared into bright, intense flame.

Surprised, Otto sat back. Well, that's nice. It'll burn itself out pretty quick, though.

But it didn't.

If anything, the sap burned even hotter and brighter. Other drops of sap next to it smoked and also burst into flame. Five minutes later, all of it was still burning.

Volatile stuff, this sap.

Otto grabbed the long stick out of the pile and went to the bush and rubbed an end of it through the leaves until the top three or four inches were sap-coated. He brought it back to the fire and stuck it into the flames. The sap flared and brightened.

"Look at that," he said, wonderingly. "Must be a creosote bush. Or a kerosene one."

Still not sure, Otto leaned the torch against the gate and sat back and watched to see how long it would burn. Ten minutes later, it was still brightly lit.

"Waddya know," he said and went back to the kerosene bush and collected seven or eight good torch candidates. He coated an end of each in the bush's sap and, carefully, set them through his pants belt until he looked like some kid carrying a bunch of toy swords. Even more carefully, he picked up the burning torch, ensuring he didn't get too close to his spares. Wouldn't do to ignite them. He'd get hot foot. Or hot something.

Stepping back through the gate, Otto held the torch up high, towards the plaque. It was way up there but the torch was bright enough to see definite letters inscribed on it. Holding the light as steady as possible, he traced the lines.

"That's a V," he said, after a minute. "Definitely a V." An ornate one. Obviously someone around here has a gift for calligraphy.

He kept reading. "So, V ... something. V ... oh, an O." He squinted harder. "It's V, O, something. Something ... ah! An S! ..." and he paused. "An S," he whispered, "Vos."

And he knew what the plaque said.

Vos Teneo.

Which Virgil had translated as, "You know," as the poet read the words off a strikingly identical plaque hanging over the entrance to the city of Dis. The city of ...

The Fallen.

Gasping, Otto almost lost his balance as he hastily backed through the gate, the torch held before him like a weapon.

The Fallen! Here!

He shook the torch back and forth, the whoosh of it cutting the air as a warning.

And as a beacon, you idiot, the light a marker to which the Fallen, gray locks flying, will swarm, bursting out of the ruins screaming their unearthly call of triumph and murder, their feathered bat wings slapping the air as they drew their swords and dove straight for him.

Silence.

Cautious, Otto peered at the sky, sure a squadron of Fallen was up there spiraling into attack formation. Nothing but silver-and-blue tinted clouds. He turned towards the village, expecting an army of Fallen to come rushing at him, talons outstretched as in the tunnels under Dis, but the road was empty.

Suspicious, Otto worked his way back to the gate, but no Fallen showed. Nothing showed. The village was dead.

Come to think of it, so was he.

At that, he chuckled, and the tension broke.

Otto took in a deep breath. He looked up, right at the plaque.

"All right," he said to it. "Let's go see what I know."

Chapter XII

Didn't Get A Harumph Out Of That Guy

Thirty minutes later, he still didn't know anything.

It had taken him at least ten minutes to reach the first two buildings set across the road from each other, and he'd explored them both. That had taken no more than an additional ten minutes because there was nothing in them. Nothing. At all. No busted-up furniture, no piles of debris consisting of picture frames and old clothes and dishes and such, not even a mural, just walls and floors and windows on the two or three sides of the buildings still standing. No idea what the buildings were for.

Potemkin village?

Otto stood in the street between the two buildings and considered. This might be the fake Rock Ridge that Sheriff Bart and the Waco Kid set up in the desert to distract Hedley LaMarr's thugs. His eyes drifted to the keep.

Distract from whatever lives up there, perhaps?

Right this very moment, the Fallen version of the Waco Kid was aiming a pistol at the dynamite and the place would go up and the next thing Otto knew, he'd be fighting Dom Deluise. That would be different. Otto raised the torch in anticipation but no Dom.

Let's go.

Otto trudged up the road, keeping a wary eye on the rest of the buildings in case Mongo showed up. Or dinosaurs. The torch was doing gangbusters, throwing out a ring of light about ten feet around. The wreckage and walls caught the light rather well and Otto was sure he'd spot the beady eyes of any Fallen waiting there in ambush moments before they came rushing out and eviscerated him. He hoped the Fallen were flammable because setting them on fire was about his only chance.

The road wound through the village, cutting into the buildings at one place and then cutting out at another, like Edgar Allen Poe's version of the Yellow Brick Road. It was midnight dreary and broken and dust-covered and scary as crap. Otto looked around nervously. If a raven flew out, he'd die of a heart attack. Again. But no raven. No pigeons. No life at all.

How old is this place?

Otto figured two thousand years or so, given the style of everything, but that didn't make any sense. Besides the obviously broken walls, the place was in too good a shape for the kind of weather they were experiencing.

Well, the weather in the last few days, anyway.

Otto gazed at the clouds. Those hadn't showed up until he'd paid a visit to the shipwreck; before that, all bright skies and sunlight. But that might be coincidence. The ship may have crashed during the last two weeks of summer or something, and this cloudy, gray, graveyard weather was the norm.

"Hey," Otto said to one crumbling wall he passed, "why don't you let Marc out so he can explain the weather here? I mean, if you can find Ian, finding Marc should be easy."

No one emerged.

Speaking of weather …

It was getting even colder. Otto shivered and stopped to tighten the toga, a hazardous proposition given the extra torches. Maybe he ought to light one and carry it around like a space heater because the wind had picked up and there was ice in it now.

Man, it feels cold enough to …

Snow.

It started slowly, sharp needles against his face that he first thought was rain. But, when he held out his hand, the rain was little solid barbs of ice, quickly followed by giant flakes of snow.

"Well, this is just friggin' lovely," he said and pulled the toga up and around his head, dropping a couple of torches in the process.

By the time he reached down to pick them up, there was already a half-inch of snow covering the road. He looked around. A half-inch covering everything. Gray skies, wrecked buildings, stone road, all covered in gray snow.

What ambiance.

The wind was blowing the snow directly into his face. He turned away and the wind followed him.

Naturally.

The torch hissed and the light cut severely and Otto was sure a few more minutes of this and the torch would go out.

Gimme shelter.

Stumbling against the wind, Otto lurched towards the next building but the roof was gone and snow was filling it. Snow was filling everything, like the rain had filled shipwreck valley.

"What's with this place?" Otto yelped. "You couldn't drown me, so now you're gonna freeze me?" Might.

There was no windbreak or overhang or something good enough to keep the snow out, at least, nothing he could see …

A light.

More of a flicker in the dark than anything and, no it wasn't the torch because that was down to half strength and blowing the other way. Otto peered hard through the wind. The light came from …

There!

Another flicker. Otto slipped around the corner of the building and braced against the wind, straining hard to locate the source. At that moment, a break in the clouds and the wind and snow and, clear as day, for one blink, he saw the keep. With a light flickering in the top window.

Like a lighthouse.

The snow covered his ankles but Otto pushed through, pointing the sizzling torch right at the keep like a compass needle to keep his bearings. Hard to do because his line of travel took him over rubble and right up to shattered buildings, which necessitated a detour. After fifteen minutes or so of this, Otto had lost his bearings, aided by the snow transforming into a blizzard

"Why are you doing this to me?" Otto asked the sideways snow, lashing him into a corner of a broken wall. The torch guttered and Otto knew there was no relighting it. The snow and wind were too intense to risk a match. He risked a look around the corner but got a face full of snow for his trouble. Rubbing his eyes clear, he burrowed deeper into the corner until at least the wind was cut.

Actually a relief. Funny how a tiny improvement in one's condition feels like a lottery win.

This particular wall jigsawed down to a big opening in the building, and Otto slid along it until he stumbled across some loose stones and into a relatively covered area. At least he was no longer snow-pummeled, although the cold still came at him. Shivering, Otto stepped into the middle of the room and raised the torch, now back to full-on brightness.

"Man," Otto said, admiring it, "pretty good stuff." He frowned.

Yes, it's pretty good stuff, isn't it?

The sap was like a dab of never-ending petroleum jelly, put a little in a carburetor and drive 500 miles. Unlimited energy from a shrub.

How … miraculous.

"Where's a Holiday Inn bush when you need it?" Otto groused to the walls.

The immediate response was a drop in the temperature. Otto brought the torch dangerously close to his chest to get warm, pushing it hastily away when the toga smoked.

Holding the torch high, mainly to keep from self-immolation, Otto looked around. Empty building, like the first two, with nothing indicating the building's purpose. A window set in the opposite wall was surprisingly free of snow and wind. Must be at the right angle. Otto walked over to take a look outside. No need for stealth; the torch announced to all and sundry that he was in here.

The blizzard pushed hard but the visibility was rather decent. A series of other buildings, some of them intact, staggered across from each other, resembling a shopping district with what looked like a walkway between them. Not that he could see the walk; there had to be ten inches of snow covering everything by now. But the line of it was apparent and Otto followed it along to what looked like a distant wall.

He squinted. No, not a wall, a … gate. In a wall. With a drawbridge connecting it to the walkway. And beyond the drawbridge …

The keep.

Blessing the unconscious sense of direction that somehow got him into the right house and right window, Otto craned his eyes upward but the sill blocked the top of the keep.

Thing must be massive.

But, now he had a beeline and it might be a good idea to get across that drawbridge before it turned into a snowbank. Otto was about to turn around and head out of the broken wall but, hey dude, beeline. Sticking his head out of the window (into another faceful of blizzard), he judged it to be a five-foot drop to the ground. Ankle-twisting distance, but the snow should soften it.

Should.

He straddled the window, keeping the torch inside the building to preserve it as long as possible, and put his bad hand down on the sill to vault over when he felt indentations in the wood. Pulling the torch closer, he examined the sill and, yes, there, something carved.

A pentagram.

"What the hell?" Otto breathed. He pulled back into the room and squatted, setting the torch so the light fell obliquely across the sill.

Yep. Definitely a pentagram.

"Devil worshippers," Otto whispered and stood and looked around, expecting to see an altar with an upside-down cross and a basin to catch the virgin's blood in some corner, but nothing.

So, the villagers were Satanists. No wonder the dino-riders had attacked them.

And lost.

Chilled more by that thought than the weather, Otto stared back out of the window at the distant keep. Whatever the dino-riders came for had lived in there. Or might still be living in there, if the light at the top was any indication.

You sure you wanna do this?

"Nope," he said and went out of the window.

Chapter XIII

Relativity

As if it knew his intentions, the snow aimed right at Otto and tripled its onslaught, driving him off line and almost into another building. Despite that, he kept his balance and view of the drawbridge, although the torch went out. No big problem. In the odd way of snowstorms, the light remained blue and diffuse and sufficient for him to see. Now, if he could keep the snow out of his eyes.

His feet were blocks of ice, the Nikes absolutely no good in this kind of weather.

Should have put on the Timberlakes for the trip to the rocket wreck. But, hey, who knew all this would happen?

From getting Tasered by a halberd to burning down the cabin, and now slogging his way through a blinding snowstorm dressed for a pick-up game of Roman pelota.

The snow had obliterated the walkway and he stayed on it by checking his level; whenever he hit rough going or imbalance, he knew he had veered off-course so moved back until things smoothed. After about, oh, seven or eight days of this, Otto finally slogged through the gate, which was nothing more than a gap in the shoulder-high stone wall, and arrived at the base of the drawbridge.

Big, it was.

Otto eye-measured it as best as he could in the very angry snowstorm and figured a couple of tanks could drive across it side by side. Which begged the question as to what needed such a massive means of crossing the moat.

A legion of Roman soldiers?

A mid-sized dragon?

A mid-sized devil?

Otto anchored himself against a post sticking out of the ground and leaned over the edge of the moat filling with snow.

So probably empty of water and therefore not teeming with alligators or eels.

But any moat designed to protect dragon demons probably had some kind of noxious elements in it.

Best not to fall off the drawbridge and find out what those were.

Otto braced against the wind and moved to the center and gingerly tapped the edge of the drawbridge with a frozen foot. Seemed solid enough, but it could be as old as the valley bones and one good step would turn it into dust and there'd Otto be, tumbling into a snow-filled moat of noxious elements.

Quickly, he jumped on the drawbridge and, just as quickly, back, prepared to flee into a nearby building should things collapse, but not even a vibration.

All right.

Otto stepped on the bridge, bounced a little bit but felt no yield.

He shrugged. "In for a penny," he said and boldly strode across.

Took a minute, even though the drawbridge was long enough to accommodate an emergency F-16 landing. Amazing how a sense of unease motivates your feet, frozen or no. He scampered across the end and under an overhanging gate in record time, and faced two massive doors. Shod in metal. With no doorknobs. Or keyholes.

"Wonderful," Otto said, and peered along the doors' expanse. Big, dragon-demon big. And etched and sculpted but the light was gone so he couldn't see what was depicted. Probably the demon-dragon munching on dino-riders. And trespassers.

At least he was out of the wind and snow. In fact, it was

downright calm here and Otto considered lighting the torch but it was a decent bet the sap was all used up by now, if it wasn't saturated by the snow.

Don't want to waste a match so try a new torch.

Otto pulled one of the spares out of his belt and scrutinized it. Sap was still intact and the wood was dry, or, at least, dry-ish.

So, here goes.

Otto fished the matchbox out, struck one, and held it to the new torch's sap and, yepper, ignited. Blinded for a moment, he accidentally laid the old torch next to the lit one and, holy frijole, it also lit.

Two-fisted torching.

Otto hefted both torches and examined the doors. Pictographs, hieroglyphics, whichever term applied, all over them, akin to the Assyrian reliefs found on walls in the Iraqi desert, rows and rows of armoured soldiers presenting swords, tightly packed, the right-side-door guys facing the left ones, like the angel army at the Pearly Gates. Otto expected them to break into, "*Awk*! *Do*! *Hekel*! *Do*!" – or whatever those guys had been shouting – at any second. The gap between the facing soldiers rose the entire height of the doors to what looked like a throne at the top that straddled both doors, the seam evenly dividing it.

It was too far away for Otto to make out much detail, but it could pass for a standard Hollywood prop, big back and arms with what appeared to be wings spread like a canopy overhead. No one sitting on the throne, no emblems inscribed, but definitely the king's seat.

So let's go see who the king was. Or is.

Great idea. How?

Otto stared at the doors. Obviously there was a trick to this thing, but Otto had never been good with puzzles and it was cold out here and he wanted to get inside so he had to do something. So he did.

He knocked.

It was like ringing a bell, tolls of struck metal reverberated around the gate and down the drawbridge and, no doubt, throughout the entire keep, waking the demon-dragon and its attendees, all of them grabbing axes and flayers and trooping down the stairs to greet the visitor.

"Stop it! Stop it! Stop it!" Otto fiercely whispered at the doors and frantically placed his torch-laden hands on the doors to dampen the bell tolls …

And the doors slowly swung open.

Otto leaped back, holding the torches like weapons, ready to meet the onslaught of dragon and orcs, but it was dark and still, only the sound of rushing wind and snow behind him.

Wary, Otto held the torches out to light the portal, but didn't see beady eyes and scaly tails arrayed there. An arched stone roof disappeared beyond the range of the torches, the stone walls supporting it doing the same, except for a giant staircase on the left, right inside the door.

Where do these stairs go?

"They go up," he replied in his best Bill Murray and chuckled and stepped through the portal.

They did, indeed. Massive stone steps rising then disappearing around a corner, a rusted metal banister running with them. Obviously, this was the way to the top of the keep. He took one long look down the hallway, but nothing moved and there was nothing of note. There may be another set of metal doors at the other end, but waste of time to look. Whatever wanted to eat him was waiting at the top of these stairs.

So, let's save some time and go be dinner.

He stepped up, keeping one torch ahead and one behind, both in defense more than illumination. The strange blue snow-light continued in here, although there were no windows or arrow slits or any wall openings convenient for shooting at dino-riders, at least that he could see. The stairs were almost as wide as the drawbridge.

Room to swish tails, Otto figured, and gripped the torches tighter. Which was a laugh. Dragons ate fire for breakfast. And ate knights. And seventy-year-old bad-handed idiots.

Bare walls, no pictures, no sculptures, not even a torch holder, only the banister which Otto, wisely, avoided. Didn't need to touch it and have its clanging tell Smaug he was on his way. Smaug could probably smell the torch sap, anyway, and was already donning a bib.

It was still cold but, absent of wind and snow, felt warmer. His feet thawed, which was unfortunate.

"Ouch! Ouch! Ouch!" Otto whimpered as he danced from shoe to shoe, trying to get the pins and needles under control. After about a minute, he could feel his toes again.

After about another twenty minutes, Otto hummed, "The Long and Winding Road," because, man, this staircase was both. He'd never been a good judge of heights, but he guessed the top of the keep must be, at best, eight or ten stories. So far, he'd traversed more than eight to ten flights of stairs, but he'd have to, right?

It would be at least two flights per story, right?

At least.

After twenty flights, though, Otto grew suspicious. These were flights too far, so what was going on? Was he in an Escher painting or something? To someone outside the frame, he appeared and disappeared along several disconnected stairways, climbing forever as eternal life turned out to be nothing but a mounting of steps in a futile effort to discover the end.

And then he discovered the end.

Clearing the last few steps while muttering about how ridiculous this was, Otto turned onto a landing and face-to-face with another metal-shod door, half the size of the first, but still impressive.

"Must be the place," Otto said and held both torches up to see.

This door was also etched, but no soldiers to be seen; the wing-shaded throne in the middle of it, that's all. Still empty.

"Let's see why," Otto said, and pushed on the door.

It didn't move.

Otto blinked and pushed again, but the doors stood firm.

"I am NOT going back downstairs!" he declared to the doors and pushed harder but they remained unyielding. He stepped back and scrutinized the doors, but, like downstairs, no knobs or keyholes he could see.

Crap.

He'd have to find the secret panel. Otto set the torches in the different corners of the door, checking first to see if they were in danger of setting something on fire — no — and ran his good hand over the metal. Nothing apparent. He focused on the throne, tracing it with his fingers, at least, as far as he could reach. Given the size of everything, the secret panel was probably well over Otto's head. He stepped back.

"All right," Otto placed his hands akimbo, "what do I do?"

Silence.

Otto threw his arms out and bellowed, "Open sesame!"

Nothing.

Otto blew out a breath in exasperation. "This is stupid," he said.

He stared at the two doors for a moment and then walked right up to them.

"Hey!" he yelled, "You in there! Open the damn door!"

Which was immediately followed by the distinctive sound of a door unlatching.

"Uh oh," he gulped and took a frantic step back, scrambling at the torches and raising them in combat position.

No dragon flew out and, after a minute, Otto cautiously approached and pushed. The door slowly swung open and Otto braced again but no orcs. No flying monkeys, either. He stepped through.

A long hallway ran some distance, illuminated by a line of lit torches set in the walls, giving the place an eerie reddish cast. The walls were made of the same metal as the doors, and similar etchings covered them up and out of sight. They looked like battle scenes: the same soldiers from the front doors beating the crap out of each other with swords and clubs and axes, but no one got hurt.

Maybe they were nerf weapons.

Otto craned at the roof, but the torchlight obscured it. Probably more etchings up there, or ten-foot bats staring at him hungrily. Uneasy, Otto looked down the hall, which stopped abruptly and opened into a room that glowed, probably with more torches, the detail lost in the distance.

Gonna have to walk down there and take a look, I guess.

By the way, who lit the torches?

Frowning, Otto crept down the hall, checking the floor and the walls for a tripwire and the resulting arrows or big rocks or claymore mines, but all he saw was the continuous battle engraved on the walls. A never-ending battle, with the opposing sides indistinguishable, the objectives unclear, the war waging on and on.

There is nothing but the war. Unnerving.

Otto finally reached the end of the hallway, sure rank upon rank of soldiers stood opposite the threshold and would give him just enough time to say, "Crap," before falling on him the moment he stepped through.

So, he stepped through, torches ready ...

And whistled.

Because, wow. Just wow.

"Is this a hall, or is this a hall?" he said admiringly.

Fit for a king. Or kings. First, it was huge. Gargantuan. Godzillian. A couple of football games could run simultaneously in here without interfering with each other, cheerleaders included. And marching bands. Second, the gold. Everything was gold, the roof, the walls, the floor ... that is, what floor was visible under the massive, inch-thick carpets, all of them depicting all kinds of scenes from all kinds of a mythology Otto did not know: odd-looking creatures entwined among grape arbors and rivers, attended by what could very well be Firsts, except these looked happy.

And that was merely the first nave inside the first set of piers; it looked like additional naves and aisles stretched to the right and left, probably with their own sets of piers. Acres-wide murals, set off from each other by marble framing, illustrated the ceiling. They looked like more of those mythological scenes. Acres-long golden candelabras, suspended by golden chains under each mural, stretching rhythmically into the distance, supplemented the torches. A red hue tinted everything almost to purple, quite pleasant. And quite disturbing.

Because, who lit all these candles?

"Somebody pretty tall," Otto said and stared down the way, looking for the dragon. All he saw was the nave disappearing in the distance, gold and purple and lights blurring into obscurity. He headed that way, pausing at the first set of piers and looking both ways ready to fight, but no one, or ones, stood there, only more piers and light and naves, at least six deep on either side, all of them running in the same direction he was going.

Where his host waited, expectant. And hungry.

Okay.

Otto broke into a brisk trot, torches out and ready, head on a swivel, watching for soldiers or dwarves or whatever. He made good time because he was good and tired of all this silliness and wanted answers to lots and lots of things.

The size of this place, for example. How did a regular-looking keep contain such monstrous rooms? There was no size relationship between the keep he had struggled to reach in the middle of a friggin' snowstorm and the one he was striding across right now. No relationship at all. Somewhere along the line, he'd walked into another dimension or something, probably at the last set of doors.

The cold, his hand, and torches, for other examples. The standard for this Afterlife was the City, where nothing like missing fingers and freezing temperatures happened. Stuff did happen in other places, like Dis, but not to this degree. Some temporary exhaustion, such as he and Virgil and Amelia experienced when they hiked to the gates of Dis from the river banks, but no floods and blizzards and cutting a finger off with a halberd as a bridge collapses and your horse falls, forever and ever

And, frankly, Otto had had enough.

E. Nough. End it.

"End it!" Otto bellowed as he cleared the last set of piers and beheld the throne placed against a gold wall, the wings spread across the top of it, the soldiers of perpetual battle etched in gold rows on gold walls on either side of it.

And the being, dressed in black robes, sitting on it, regarding him.

Responding, in a voice of thunder, "I will."

Chapter XIV

Reaper, Grim Or Otherwise

"Uhm." Otto, chary, took a step back. "Let's not do anything hasty, okay?"

Eyes of brass shining from under a black hood regarded him. "Did you not ask for it to end?" said the voice of thunders.

"Yeah, I did, but, uh, I think I was speaking metaphorically. Or something like that. So, let's be sure we understand each other, dragon," Otto hefted the torches threateningly. "You make a move, you got a fight on your hands."

No doubt a very short one, but a fight, nonetheless.

The brass eyes blinked. "I am not a dragon. And I do not want to fight." A pause. "There has been too much of that." The creature, formerly known as a dragon, made a slow significant gaze at the etched soldiers on the wall behind him.

"Okay. Good. We have accord," Otto said cautiously, although he lowered the torches. "So, if you're not a dragon, what are you?"

"As you. The Created."

"By God?"

The once-was-dragon cocked its head in a curious-dog manner. "Who else?"

"Establishing bona fides, that's all. Because, well, it has been a long, strange trip."

"Indeed," the thunder rolled across the floor. "I have watched your travels. The struggle across the lands of joy, your flight across the heavens, your time of peace." Brass Eyes inclined its head. "And now you are here."

Otto held up a hand, er, torch. "Hold on," he said, "You could see me? I don't mean right here, I know you can do that, but everywhere I've been?"

The what-could-still-be-a dragon nodded.

"How? Wait!" A halting torch. "Wrong question. Why?"

The dragon-in-disguise considered that for a moment. "I am drawn to ... futility."

Otto laughed. "You and me both, bub. *Por ejemplo*, I've been considering the futility of crashing a rocket into the side of a planet and swinging across chasms on a halberd. A halberd, mind you! In the middle of a blizzard, no less, and climbing the dark tower to walk into Henry the VIII's, the IX's and X's, for that matter, rec room only to have a Jawa tell me how entertained he's been by all this." He took a breath. "You are a 'he,' right?"

"For our purposes," the thunder.

"Okay. Where are my dogs?"

The Jawa brought up hands, or what Otto figured were hands, although they were long and spindly and wrapped in the same black material as the cloak, and rested its — his — shrouded chin on them. "Where you left them."

Oh no.

Otto shook his head. "This is going to be another one of those cryptic conversations, isn't it? I mean, I'll ask you a question and you'll give me the Bhagavad Gita, or Herman Hesse, or Latchemondy." Otto arched an eyebrow. "You know Mr. Latchemondy?"

Nod.

"Figures. You two probably went to the same school." Otto paused, his mind whirling through the possibilities. Many subjects to choose from, such as never-ending piers on top of a keep that should not be able to contain even a fraction of a room this size, and sudden blizzards and mortality, and valleys full of dusty bones and dinosaurs, and a war that went on forever.

And the location of God.

But a good investigator always starts with the basics. "Who are you?" Otto asked.

Eyes shone brighter and the hood rumbled, "I am not named."

"Really? You must have had rather cruel parents. When they called you to dinner, what did they shout? 'Hey, you in the hood, soup's on!' Something like that?"

The hood tilted a bit in some annoyance, and the thunder repeated, "I am not named. But," it continued, "if you must, you may call me …" a pause "Worthless."

Otto started. "Wow," he said. "You DID have cruel parents. What'd they do to you, man? Why would you call yourself that?"

"I do not."

This was getting weirder and sadder and Otto wondered whether he should give Cloak Boy a hug or something. "I'll meet you halfway and call you 'Worth.' Deal?" Otto asked.

The hood tilted in assent.

"All right," Otto said. "So, Worth, tell me," and Otto swept the torches out, "what do you do for a living? Are you Lord of All You Survey? Or do you just sweep up around here?"

The brass eyes flashed in anger and Otto concluded that snarkiness might not be the best of tactics to use on a creature that considered itself worthless. Could prompt a lashing out.

"Sorry," Otto quickly said, "I'm a bit of a smartass."

With a thunder of agreement, Worth slowly lowered his hands to the throne rests. "I am … a watcher, for lack of a better term. I am of no benefit in that, but it is my task."

"Whew," Otto said, "You should consider Xanax, Worth, because you are bringing me right down. And you don't look like a Watcher. They're tall and bald and wear nice bright robes."

Confused flash of the brass eyes.

"Okay, okay, sorry. *Marvel* reference. So, what are you watching?"

An incline of the head. "Futility."

Otto's temper flared. "Look," Otto pointed a threatening torch at the robe, "I don't want to hear that anymore. You want to call it futility, then fine, Worth, ease mine." Dramatic pause. "Where's God?"

"Where you left Him."

Otto was incredulous. "Where I left Him? Left Him? I didn't leave anybody! All I left was …"

The City.

Otto's temper suddenly flatlined. He thought for a moment, then framed another, quite devastating question.

"You mean that God is in the City?"

The brass eyes regarded him almost sorrowfully.

"The City," Otto whispered, "You're saying He's there. Been there all this time, then. So, why … why didn't He reveal Himself?"

The thunder was gentle. "He revealed Himself to you at every moment, every turn. In every one of your sorrows and pains, He stood there imploring you, and you would not see because you would see God as you would see God, in your image, in your imaginings. You would not see Him as He Is."

Otto threw hands, er, torches, out. "And what is that, Worth? What is He?"

"He … Is."

The sense of it came crashing down on Otto like a stone bridge into a crevasse of forever. In summary: there is no throne room, there is no location for God because Is, simply, Is.

"He's here," Otto said.

Worth nodded.

"And He's in the City."

Another nod.

"But … then … this is … all this …"

And the sense of something else came crashing down.

"It's. Futile."

Worth said nothing.

The strength went out of Otto's legs and slowly, like an edifice of strength and power losing its very mortar, he sank to the floor, dropping the torches to either side.

"No," he breathed.

The thunder of Worth's voice had rain in it. "There is nothing more tragic than the end of childhood. When we shed our dreams, our notions, and we no longer see through a glass darkly, we are done. Done with fighting. Done with war."

Worth turned and looked at the soldiers fighting the forever battle on and on throughout the room. "It is the end of all we think we are. It is heartbreaking."

Heartbreaking.

Oh, yes, that it was, and more. Far more.

It was earth shattering. All illusions gone. All this adventuring had been for nothing. He'd lost Claudia for nothing. He would have found God anyway, there, right there, in the City, among the billions and billions of happy souls who had already found Him. He'd have met Claudia at Grendel's like he did but, instead of jettisoning her body out an airlock, he'd be hoisting a few ales with her right now. What's worse, it's not as though he was ignorant of this; a few of those happy souls had tried to warn him, had told him not to go on a stupid rocket trip ...

Do not go on a stupid rocket trip.

Otto's eyes narrowed. "You sent Ian," he said, "Back there in the valley of skulls."

The brass eyes dimmed somewhat and Worth nodded.

Suspicion crept up Otto's spine.

"Hmm. Funny, that. He didn't seem overly fond of you."

Worth nodded again. "There are enmities across the Creations. One does not know nor understand the other, and there are fears. But if you keep the image of the Is firmly, hold it in mind, then you see all the spokes of the wheel. And there is one hub." Worth dropped his head. Humbly, it seemed.

Something rang untrue about that, but Otto couldn't quite place it.

"A hub, you say ... that implies a central point. A place. From where everything springs."

He paused. "Say God's Throne. Which I'm looking for, by the way."

Worth chuckled, the sound of far-off cannons. "I know. And it is your futility because you seek a place that is every place. You follow what you conceive and do not see that you have already found it."

Already found it.

Otto saw, clearly in his mind, Claudia and a hoisted mug of ale.

Worth shifted and then slowly stood, a tall, gaunt, specter in black ... very much like every caricature of death Otto had ever seen. All he lacked was a scythe.

Bit disturbing, that.

Worth looked at Otto for a moment and then held out beseeching, spindly, cloth-wrapped hands. "Console yourself with this, mortal, that you had so much of the love of God in you, you were moved to make true your childhood, your innocence. This earns you reward; not one that you can touch, but one within yourself. No one else will know of it, but it is there, in the mud of you."

Mud?

Hadn't some other strange creature recently referred to him as mud?

Otto sat up, staring at Worth the Death Cartoon. "Can I try a word out on you? It's ameno ... amino acid, ah me-o mio, down at the bayou ..."

"*Amenominakanushi*," said in quiet thunder.

"Yeah, that." Otto cocked an eyebrow. "Care to comment?"

Worth stood taller, if that were possible, and the brass eyes burned. "They are Other, Unsanctioned, the Orphaned," thunder rumbled around the room. "They are not of you, not from you, not part of you."

"Yeah?" Otto cocked another eyebrow. "They were very much a part of the crew. One of them, at least. And they are very intent on keeping us from finding God. Friends of yours?"

"They are NOT!"

The thunder almost blew out Otto's hearing and he gasped, slapping hands over his ears.

"They are somewhere else, a chaos! Chaos! The cloth draped on the wings of the oak!" And Worth whirled and held up talons at the wings spread above the throne.

Otto gaped at him. "What the HELL are you talking about? Yggdrasil? You mean *that* oak? So where am I, then? Valhalla?"

Silence.

Worth, a much quieter and calmer Worth, turned to him and bowed his head. Not humbly.

Sadly.

"They hinder. They annoy. They are ... afterthought."

"Would you start making some sense? Please?" Otto shouted and in frustration slammed his hands, including the bad one, against the floor.

"*Ow!*" he yelped and grabbed the bad hand and blew on it fiercely, like he was six years old or something. "Dammit!" He grimaced as the finger stump throbbed. "Stop screwing around! Just tell me what they are. Demons? Devils? Is that why there's a pentagram in one of the windows back in the village?"

Worth was downright surprised by that. "In a window?" the thunder queried.

"Yeah," Otto examined the fingerlet for any renewed signs of bleeding. "One facing ..."

And he stopped.

Facing the keep.

"You, Worth," Otto said, looking up, "Facing you. Why is that?"

Worth was standing ... no, he was not. He was floating. An inch or so but floating, nonetheless, in front of the throne. The brass eyes glowed with ice and a terrible, terrible intent.

Otto's blood stopped.

"It is ... pitfall," Worth said. The thunder was bereft and lost and angry.

"What's pitfall?" Otto whispered, terror overpowering him. "The pentagram?"

"It is the Five, a recess in earth's broad ways." Worth oscillated from side to side. "I am out of nothing."

Ex nihilo.

The phrase echoed darkly in Otto's mind, a sudden translation into the Latin, as if the universal translator had kicked in, in reverse, taking the English he heard Worthless speaking and making it ancient ...

Like the word, 'Worthless' ...

... which is, which is ...

... in the old tongues, the words of pre-history, the language of recording ...

"Belial," Otto breathed.

A moment of shocked silence. Then Worthless threw off his cloak.

And Otto beheld nightmare.

Chapter XV

A Rose By Any Other Name

What stood from the throne was at least three times the size of Worthless the Death Cartoon. It was no longer black; it was red, a deep, violent, burning red. No longer spindly, either; it had become a gigantic, grotesquely muscled creature with arms the size of battleships, a square head riddled with massive protuberances that might be horns but looked more like tumors. The brass eyes, about the only connection to the old Worth, remained, but six or seven times bigger and brassier.

And the thunder.

"You NAME me?" Belial roared.

Otto didn't know thunder could do that.

"You do NOT name me!" Belial roared again and pointed a worm-crawling, misshapen hoof of a hand at Otto.

Hoo boy.

On reflex, Otto grabbed the torches and jumped to his feet, assuming a samurai fighting stance. Not that a red-skinned, gigantic, hoof-handed monster would be intimidated by a couple of oversized matchsticks, but you go with what you've got. Guy seemed more upset about his name than anything …

Oh, right.

If Otto recalled his teenaged delving into witchcraft lore accurately, to know the name of something is to gain power over it. Because of that, lots of pagan peoples like the Celts and Teutons and Amalekites hid their real names. Lots of ancient stories covered frantic efforts by one entity to discern the name of another. Rumpelstiltskin, for instance.

"Rumpelstiltskin!" Otto shouted at the monster.

Belial lowered his massive, tumor-laden head and stared at Otto. "You mock?"

"No." Otto waved the torches. "I'm not. I'm throwing things out, h stick. Like, weren't you the one who actually told me your name? Albeit, in English?"

"I was not this," and Belial made an appreciative sweep of his hands down the tumorous, muscle-slabbed body he now possessed.

"True," Otto agreed, "and I'm real different before I shave, but the name's the same."

"It is," Belial nodded. And smiled. A ghastly, fang-laden slash of a smile with teeth heading in every direction, rotted meat hanging off several of them and something alive and grubby peeking out and screaming something unintelligible. "You are Otto Boteman, son of John Boteman and Jean Castle, son of Garrick Boteman who was once Boatermann, and daughter of Lyric Castle of the moors ..."

As Belial went down his genealogy, all Otto could think was, Hey, that's right, Grampa's name was Lyric. How cool. Wish I had been named Lyric.

And he was. And then he was Roger Castle, and GoForth Castle, and John the Boat Man, and Odoacer and Walafrihd ...

And he had been Named.

Belial made a gesture. Otto turned to stone.

Not literally; in the figurative sense, in the sense that he could not move at all, as if someone had dumped a few truckloads of cement all over him. He was still breathing, but it was through a straw, the torches still up and threatening but he could not move them, could not step, could not escape.

"What's …. happening?" he squeaked through the straw.

A rumble began low in Belial's throat, something that might be a chuckle except Otto didn't think the thing had an actual sense of humor. "I have your names, mortal. All you are and have ever been. You exist at my say."

Lovely sentiment, that, and was probably the theory behind all those pagan attempts to gain someone's name. But, instinctively, Otto knew it was wrong.

"No," he squeaked.

"Yes." Belial licked his teeth with a tongue made of serpent. "It will be a pleasure to flay the flesh from your bones, mortal."

What's with the consonance? Otto thought. But this wasn't the time for a grammar discussion. Had to break the grip of this spell, first. Be grammatically correct afterwards.

"Not true," he hissed.

"It is not?" Belial lifted his massive hoof-hands from which barbed, twisted claws slowly emerged. "You will soon see." And the monster stepped off the dais, eyes brassy with joy and murder.

Ordinarily, Otto would have loved to correct the monster about the specific truth he referred to: not the pending fun of flaying his flesh (consonance reigns supreme), but Belial's previous statement that he, Otto, existed at Belial's say. But Otto didn't have the breath for it. Nor the time.

"I …" he wheezed, "… am!"

And was no longer stone.

Instantaneous release messes with one's balance and Otto almost fell into a heap, but that would not be wise because Belial, having seven-league strides, would be on him before he recovered, so Otto windmilled backwards, inadvertently waving the torches like an airplane marshaller.

Belial stopped.

Whew, thank God, because Belial was close enough to step on him.

Maybe Otto's sudden mobility had surprised the demon. Let's surprise him a little more, say with a show of defiance?

"Okay, Worthless Boy," Otto taunted, "Flay time's over!"

Which was funny, despite the situation.

Belial towered above him, the eyes volcanos. "You are mistaken," Belial rumbled, "It is the way of this. It is the outcome. You are mortal and flesh; I am eternal and spirit. One cannot stand before the other."

"Wait. Are you actually trying to talk me into a flaying?"

Such temerity.

Belial inclined his tumor head. "You are an intelligent creature. You cannot help but know this will happen. It is inevitable."

Otto's temper stoked.

"Well, thanks for the compliment, Worthless, but inevitabilities? Aren't." Otto adjusted the torches to put as much flame and stick between him and googly teeth as possible. "Running away is a viable alternative to flaying, ya know."

"But, it is known!" Belial sounded almost perplexed, "I have your name. I smell the sin of you, the recompense demanded. It is my right!" and with a bellow of sheer power, Belial raised both hoof-hands and brought them down like freight trains going off a bridge.

Whoom!

Otto barely evaded the double blow, skipping backwards in barely enough time, but the force and vibration threw him off-balance and he tumbled onto his backside, torch-laden hands splayed to catch him. Somehow he hung onto the torches, but that was from sheer terror, not agility.

Because what faced him was beyond terror.

Belial crouched between massive arms, head thrust at Otto, his face a mask of gleeful rage, eyes pits of lava swirling with hate and lust and hunger, his teeth bared and the grubs and worms among them gnashing their own teeth. The monster's breath was sulfur and corruption, its skin the inscribed parchment of the damned.

"Get away from me!" Otto shrieked and kicked out with both feet, connecting square with the monster's nose.

It was like kicking a bag of maggots, but Belial reacted, like a kid on the playground getting a nose punch.

So, it can be hurt.

Otto rocked forward and thrust the torches at Belial's eyes. The monster frantically tilted backwards and Otto took that opportunity to back-roll over his left shoulder, regaining his feet and some distance.

"Get back!" Otto shoved the torches at Belial again. "Get the hell away from me! You have no rights on me, man!"

All eight or nine feet of pit-demon rose to the ceiling and squared its shoulders. "My right to you is my existence." Belial rumbled. "You have not paid."

"Paid what?" Otto waved the torches around and cast a desperate eye about the room. Had to be an exit door around here somewhere.

A hoof point. "The offense of you. I have found it in your line. The offense remains. It is in you."

Despite the need to get out of there as fast as he could, Otto's curiosity piqued. "What offense? Did Walafrihd steal a horse or something? Warrant's still valid?"

"You make jokes, human?" Belial raised a hoof in emphasis. "It is your failure. You are found wanting and there is to be judgment. It is why you are delivered to me." And the eyes glowed brighter.

Delivered?

"Came here pretty much on my own accord, bub," Otto snapped as he swung the torches like nunchakus. "Had a nice thing going back there in the valley, you know, before I decided to take a hike …"

Otto paused.

Hmm. Maybe Worthless was on to something. None of this mess began until Otto went traipsing over to the shipwreck. Flood, fire, a surprise horse, an even more surprising Ian, a couple of collapsed bridges and a snowstorm later, here he was.

Almost as though he'd been driven here.

Almost.

Otto furiously shook his head. "Nope, nope, nope! That ain't it. You putting a lantern in the upstairs window got me here. That's not delivery. That's bait."

"And yet," Belial looked down his nightmare nose at Otto, "if you were humble and grateful and rejoiced in the gifts of God, you would not have come. It is futility."

"Still on that, huh?" Otto said but as deflection because Belial, without moving, had struck him. Hard.

One could make a rather strong case that Otto was, indeed, an ungrateful snot. By turning his back on the City and his condo and free HBO, by engaging in a weird war with the Suits and scrambling into the rocket and careening across the universe fighting Horace's old men and the Fallen and then turning his back on the dogs, Otto had set these things in motion. None of this would have happened if he had stayed home, maybe opened up a business with Ferdinand selling cigars and wine, spent his evenings quaffing the finest of pilsners from Claudia's collection, sang songs, told tales, rejoiced in the grace of God.

And be satisfied with it.

Otto lowered the torches. A lot of people in the City had told him that God was right there: Ian, of course; Rousseau; even Pashtun, although that guy'd been quite an enthusiastic participant in the charge on Star City. Billions of others in the City believed it. Had done so for thousands of years. Why else had it taken about the entire length of human existence to gather up the minimum number of people necessary to crew a rocket designed to look for Him?

Even Konstantin, the rocket's builder, didn't want to go; he only wanted to build the dang thing.

And the thirty people (well, thirty-one) who'd finally taken off, what were they but some of humanity's biggest malcontents? Amelia Earhart, Taccola, Sacajawea ... yeah, great people in their own right, but not exactly ones to remain satisfied with the status quo. And he was among them, so maybe he was downright incapable of seeing how wrong and stupid it was to blast off from a perfectly good Afterlife and go merrily poking his big fat nose into things that simply weren't his concern.

The need to know.

The most important operating principle governing access to classified information: do you need to know?

Soldiers did not need to know why the general was marching them in a rainstorm down a crappy hill to assault trenches and barbed wire; salute smartly, yell "Yes sir!" and just do it. The general had his plans and if he went around briefing everybody to satisfy their curiosity, then the enemy would have them, too. And the soldiers die on barbed wire.

And the war is lost.

And if a bunch of mewling humans shot themselves off into space because they were too stupid to know what was good for them, thereby sending shock waves throughout the universes and stirring the Firsts and the Fallen and demons like Belial to come pouring through once-impassable gaps, then, without intending to, without knowing they had done so, they usurped the General's plan.

And the war is lost.

Otto looked at Belial, the demon returning his regard as an expression of grim satisfaction slowly spread across its features.

"You know," he rumbled.

Vos Teneo.

It went through him like an electric shock and Otto gasped.

Yes, he DID know. But not what Belial implied.

Furious, Otto took a dangerous and reckless step forward.

"Listen, you freakin' horror movie reject!" Otto shook the torches at him. "I KNOW, all right! I *know* full well what a scumbag me, my ancestors, and pretty much everyone else who ever lived, was. And is. But I also know that you and the rest of the craphead Fallen and Firsts and demons and dragons and whatever the hell else is running around this place have absolutely no say in our judgment. Not one iota!"

Dramatic pause, and dramatic stance with the torches lifted high.

"Only God does!"

At this point, Otto expected Belial, undone by the truth, to collapse into ash or get swallowed up by the Jumanji board or something. But he didn't.

Instead, he smiled. "In that, you err," he thundered.

And charged.

With a roar of ten thousand damned souls and the power of earthquake, Belial stomped one dinosaur foot after the other right at him.

"Crap!" Otto yelped and dove for the side, a nearby pier the only thing saving him from being squished into marshmallow. The pier didn't fare so well, shuddering under the impact and losing half its structure. Otto covered his head and went fetal to escape the rain of cement. Frantically pushing out of it, he picked up the torches on a dead run and beelined for the next pier, ducking behind it ...

KaRAMM!

The top of this pier exploded as Belial's hoof-fist smashed through it, raining even more cement on top of Otto. Scrambling along the floor, Otto switched around the pier and was on Belial's blind side, but not for long. The monster's brass eyes tilted into view, and another fist crashed through the pier, knocking the rest of it out of the way, the ceiling above it sagging in response.

Belial grinned at him.

"Not the brightest of ideas to bring the roof down, you know!"

Otto shouted as he backpedaled.

"It matters nothing to me," Belial rumbled, and took a step over the wreckage.

Otto kept backpedaling but, unless there were an infinite number of piers he could use as barricades, this wouldn't end well.

Need to do something else, like, oh, finding an exit. Finding a transporter to beam me up, Scotty. Getting an eagle to pick him off Saruman's tower. Absent those, then stopping Belial.

"And just how, exactly, do I stop a ten-foot demon?" he muttered to himself while gauging his next escape route. "Need a wizard's staff and a pointy hat."

Or a pentagram.

Otto stopped. A pentagram. Like the one carved in the window sill. A symbol used to keep demons at bay.

Otto reversed his motion and ran towards the monster. Belial, puzzled, watched his approach.

"You shall not pass!" Otto yelled and drew a pentagram in the air with a torch.

Belial jerked like he had been slapped.

"You mean, this works?" Otto said in wonder, and drew another one in the air, amazed when Belial staggered back like he'd been punched.

"How 'bout that?" he said and now it was sparkler wars, drawing the five-pointed figure with the lit torches and driving the monster back to the throne. Belial covered his eyes and whimpered at each torch pass, stepping farther and farther back.

"Aha!" Otto yelled in his best Errol Flynn and dropped into fighting stance, torches at the ready, and whipped another air pentagram in Belial's face ...

And flew through the air, head and body ringing from Belial's backhand.

The course of his flight took him across the edge of the last shattered pier at the perfect angle and height to score his back along the top of it and then somersault him to the floor. That might actually have saved him from a broken neck.

It didn't save him from a broken nose as he landed face first.

Wow. Did that hurt.

Otto rolled to a sitting position and clamped hands over his profusely bleeding nose. Yep, by the way it was wiggling, broken.

All the street fights he'd been in, all the karate tournaments, Otto had never broken his nose. Fingers, toes, the side of his head, yep, but never the schnoz. Good thing, because he'd have quit the martial arts right away.

"*Ow, ow, ow!*" Otto chanted as he pushed the cartilage back and forth in an attempt to get it back in place so he could get his air back. He was inhaling pretty much all blood right now, which can't be good for the lungs. His vision tripled and smeared with tears and he took a moment out of resetting the nose to wipe his eyes and screw his vision back.

Belial stood in the last place Otto had left him … er, from where Belial had propelled him. The torches on the floor bracketed the monster. Belial looked at them and then raised his eyes to where Otto sat.

"You did not close your star," it rumbled smugly.

"What?" Otto said, but it came out "Vwa?"

"I didn't connect the dots? Okay, next time." Otto doubted Belial understood his nose-choked words, but probably got the sentiment.

Belial regarded him and Otto braced.

Three giant steps and the thing will be eating my liver. Or flaying my skin, whatever its pleasure.

Otto waited for the attack so he could move one way or the other, but knew it was pointless. He didn't have enough energy left to move one way or the other. This was going to be bad. Unfortunately, it wasn't going to be quick.

Belial lowered his head and glared at Otto, then looked at both torches flanking the most direct path …

And gingerly began sliding to its left, giving the torch there a wide berth.

What the hey? Wacha doin', Worthless? Come straight at me, dude, and this is over. What, you scared of fire or something …

Fire.

Not pentagrams. Nor airgrams.

Fire.

With a flexibility born of desperation, Otto leaped to his feet and whipped the remaining torches out of his belt. Holding them to either side, he made straight for the burning torches and passed them through the flames as he swept past, the unlit torches igniting and flaring like giant Roman candles. Otto skidded to a stop and thrust the handfuls of torches at the monster.

Belial turned to face the new threat but shied away, keeping his distance.

"Close the symbol, my eye!" Otto snarled. "Nice deflection there, chief. But it's these!" And he snapped the torches at the demon again. "What, remind you of a future appointment? In some rather large lake?" Another snap of the torches.

Belial reacted but then caught himself and took a step forward, staring down at Otto, his eyes glowing with their own fire. "They will not last," he rumbled.

"Really?" Otto waved the torches. "I hear that Lake will be around for eternity. With you doing laps in it."

Belial shrugged. "There are futures, and there are other futures. Those," and he pointed at the torches, "have certain futures." He paused. "They will burn out."

"Maybe," Otto said, "but I'll be long gone by then."

"Will you?" Belial's smile was cruel. "Do you know the way out?"

The demon made expansive gestures around him. "Can you find the door? And, if you do, I will follow. Wherever you go, however far."

The eyes glowed with hunger. The talons re-emerged.

Chills run down Otto's back. Worthless had a point. Several of them, to be exact, all on the end of those mangled hoof-hands. He looked around wildly, trying to spot a way out, but nothing was apparent. And, even if there was a red *Exit* sign conveniently placed within view, how was he going to outrun this thing? He couldn't. He had to keep it here while he made his escape. How?

Otto looked at the torches. Why, with fire, of course.

Otto thrust the torches into the rug at his feet. In seconds, it caught and, seconds later, a river of flames licked eagerly along the fibers straight to where Belial stood.

"What are you doing?" the monster roared.

"Giving you something to deal with," Otto said, and reached out to both sides, setting the banners hanging from the piers alight. Those things must have been made of pressed gasoline or something because they downright exploded, roaring to inferno levels in seconds and racing up the piers ...

And setting the ceiling on fire.

"Uh oh," Otto said.

He watched, fascinated, as the flames leaped from buttress to bulwark to balustrade, each exploding like a Black Cat on the Fourth of July, raining down sparks and embers that settled into more rugs and tapestries and ignited them, in turn.

"You FOOL!" Belial screamed, holding massive arms over his head to ward off the embers while dancing around the pools of fire advancing on him. "You have killed us both!" and Belial roared and bounced and shuffled from pier to pier, trying to escape the flames.

He couldn't.

Couldn't.

"Maybe me. Definitely you," Otto said and threw the torches, one to each side of the screaming monster, the others in a 360 around Otto's position as protection. He and Belial were encircled by fire.

Backing up to the pier, Otto snatched up one of the original torches and held it in front. Not that he needed to bother, Belial was raging and foaming at the fire surrounding him, beating at it with the hooves and cloven feet, screaming in pain as each swipe blistered his skin.

A foretaste of what's to come, Otto guessed.

There was a deeper rumble which Otto first took to be Belial's bellyaching (good consonance, that), but then the floor shook and he had to crouch to keep his balance. Even Belial stopped his thrashing about and looked around, trying to locate the source.

Great, Otto thought, several of Belial's buddies are running to his rescue. They'll be dining on Otto-kabobs in the next few minutes.

Otto braced, ready to meet the first Cthulhu-like horror that burst into the room seeking human meat …

The roof collapsed.

With a roar of timber and flame, the center of it peeled down like a banana skin all the way to the floor and settled gently across it, a burning walkway. Otto leaped aside, but a section of the roof slapped his back and seared his shoulders.

"Augh!" he screamed. But that was nothing compared to Belial's.

"AHHHROOOO!" A bellow of pain and death and judgment burst from the firestorm, skewering Otto with ice and loss, such loss.

Staggered, Otto fell back, barely managing to keep his feet as the firewalk bounced and settled around him, the black hole that had suddenly opened in his heart a worse thing than burning.

To live with the certainty of such judgment ... no wonder Belial was in a bad mood.

At that moment, a giant hoof-hand burst through the flame wall in front of Otto, the talons splayed along its ends, snapping and whipping at him.

"Augh!" again, but this time in terror, not pain, and he stabbed instinctively at it with the torch.

And saw ...

Forever.

Not only the black suns of the Firsts, but suns of ice, suns of fusion paired with suns of lost souls and the unborn, suns of evil and good, all paired, all dancing about themselves, all encircled by planets of cold and emptiness and light and fullness in a whirl, a DNA molecule set in an ether of soot and water and oozing black masses and plasmas of green glowing fire.

Suns. Sons.

Otto screamed. Belial screamed. The wonder. The terror.

Belial shook off the torch and Otto fell backwards over a part of the pier as the hoof retreated and the fire swiped at Otto's legs, burning him. He screamed again from pain. Bereft, his nerves flaring, his soul whirling, he scrambled backwards into a miraculously clear area.

And saw stars.

Not the suns. Sons. Real stars.

He blinked hard, clearing his eyes, trying to make sense of it.

Oh. Yes, the roof, having collapsed, now revealed the night sky.

Otto followed the path of stars down and saw them clearly through the far wall, which had, apparently, collapsed into the firewalk.

The exit sign.

Otto rolled to his feet, hard to do, his leg muscles cramped and tightened, and he figured they were burned to the point of almost uselessness. So this was going to be a run of pure adrenaline.

He ran, from pure adrenaline.

Giant sections of flaming roof crashed in front of him and behind and beside him and he held the toga-blanket to ward off embers and put his head down and charged for the stars.

Flares blasted at him from all sides, sometimes driving him off target but he bore through and pushed back and then he was at the edge of the wall and there were stars and mountains and he leaped, sure that he would be a flaming star for the thirty or forty stories straight down to the boulders ...

And fell right into a snowbank.

Cooling. Cold. Soothing.

Otto, sure he was making a sizzling sound, rolled deeper into the snow, almost crying with the sheer relief of it. He settled his back into the welcoming, healing snow, and looked back.

Belial stood in the wall rift, all of him burning, a flame monster, his mouth an "O" of agony, the creatures in his skewed teeth imitating his throes. The brass eyes molten lakes of sorrow, the monster reached its talon hooves to its face and tore at the fire eating him alive, the skin falling off in chunks to reveal a horror.

A horror.

Corruption and rot and death and emptiness, so much emptiness. Lost. Eyes of brass overseeing a valley of emptiness, a conscious decision to turn its back on hope and joy and be alone. Forever.

Belial screamed. And screamed again.

And went supernova.

A blinding explosion of pure white pain and loneliness and void pulsed across the land and blasted through Otto like X-rays and gamma rays and Otto screamed and was lost and empty.

And gone.

Chapter XVI

Dark They Were, And Golden Eyed

The cold.

It heals.

Not really, Otto decided; it numbs, and a lack of pain does not mean healing. It did make moving around a lot easier, though.

So, let's move.

Otto propped on his elbows and stared at the keep, no longer the gigantic multi-story monstrosity it had been when Otto first climbed the stairs but now an old, medieval ruin, a shrunken black finger against the stars, small and bleak.

Did the fire do that, or did the cleansing of its demon?

Perhaps evil is larger in our minds than in actuality.

That's a lovely thought, Otto decided and wiggled his legs deeper into the snow. He could not feel them anymore, but numb was preferable to burning.

So let's ice-soak them a while longer.

He looked back at the keep. How it had managed to remain standing after Belial blew up, Otto couldn't figure. Energy like that should have levelled the place, and all of the surrounding mountains. And Otto. But, here they all — and he — were, safe and sound and freezing to death. Not in keeping with the physics that he knew: when something goes nova, space for at least a light year in all directions is fairly obliterated. Maybe not quite a light year, maybe just a mile or two, yet everything was still here, a strong indicator that Belial had not gone nova despite appearances; heck, had not even exploded in any standard sense, the way, say, ten feet of dynamite should have.

Was Belial, instead, ten feet of conflict, the judgment awaiting him and his defiance of it balanced within his red, tumor-laden body, inexorably incompatible and volatile and dangerous but intact until the moment a mud creature sets him on fire?

We mud creatures are a lot more dangerous than we suppose.

Another lovely thought.

The keep was cold and lightless.

Dang. You'd think exploding demons would leave some trace, some afterglow laced through the stone, giving off enough heat that some guy lying in the nearby snow could at least crawl over and warm up a bit.

But, no. Nothing. The only light came from the stars.

Otto looked up. At least the cloud cover was gone. As were the moons. Well, that's new. First time he'd seen a moonless sky here. First time he'd seen weather, too. Otto wondered, again, if more time had passed than he realized and he was witnessing the seasons change.

Probably.

It had been at least several weeks — if not months — since he'd crashed the ship and followed Cha Cha to the cabin where he had spent idle days and idle nights upon idle days and nights. He wasn't sure how big this planet was nor the distance from the sun(s), but it looked and felt Earth-like, so one could assume things like orbits and tilts were roughly comparable. Roughly.

But what if it wasn't? What if this was a much larger planet with a much longer orbit?

"Winter is coming," Otto whispered in his best John Snow.

Heck, winter was here. And might stay here for ten or twenty months or however long it took to reach spring.

"Great," Otto said. "If I had known that, I would have stayed at the cabin."

Hmm.

As had occurred to him during his *tête-à-tête* with Belial, none of this silliness happened until he went back to the shipwreck. He'd had spring and dogs and moons forever and a day ... until the day he skipped off to the valley. He'd *not* had snow and Ian and dismembered fingers. Visiting the wreck was a tripwire of some kind, setting the planet into motion, setting many things into motion.

F'rinstance, his mortality.

And, boy, was he feeling mortal right now. Well, feeling numb, which was a sensation Otto had never enjoyed but Novocain was better than the dentist drill. And the pain of a seventy-five percent burned body was magnitudes above that so, thanks, snow and ice. Snow and ice had a downside, though, like hypothermia and losing toes and the rest of his fingers. Probably should get out of the snow and ice, then.

Slowly, Otto willed arms to move and elbows to set and knees to follow and, in a clumsy and quite laughable stagger, got to his feet. Conflicting waves of numbness and agony battered him. His lower back and both legs were without feeling, while his nose, chest, and arms were on fire. Maybe he should plunge headfirst into the snow until everything went numb.

Right. Plan on never getting up again, if you do.

Otto carefully rotated his neck to check his range of motion and not bad, not bad. He flexed his shoulders in an attempt to crack his back but all he got for that were nerve endings screaming up and down his spine, so stop it. He then tested the other major joints, gaining control of them one by one.

Okay, reasonably able to move, so time to get moving.

Where?

Otto glanced at the keep but nope, uh uh, ain't going back in there, no way, no how. One of the more intact buildings in the village, yeah, that's the ticket, maybe the one with the pentagram window. All right.

Where?

He paused. The pentagram should be on the same side as the drawbridge, which should be somewhere 'round front, because he was now in the back.

Right? Or had Belial blown him out of a side window?

For all he knew, the drawbridge had shriveled into a two by four and he'd never find the dang thing.

So, let's take a bird's eye view: the keep had been east of the cabin, so the front of it would be west of where he was now. I think. But where's west? Where's north, for that matter?

He squinted at the sky. Sure could use a compass about now, or some moon(s)rise. Then he'd know where south was. Hey, look, there's the Big Dipper...

The ... what?

Shock more intense than fried nerve endings ran through Otto and he rubbed his eyes hard, something his broken nose simply did not appreciate, and looked again and, yes, Big Dipper. And, there, that kite-looking thing, Boötes. So straight overhead must be ...

Cygnus.

The summer night sky above his house in Virginia.

"No way!" he gasped and stared at the patterns. "No way!" he reiterated. "I'm not seeing it right. It's just asterisms, I'm configuring them in a way I expect."

Yeah, that's it.

Then explain the Summer Triangle up there linking it all together, chief.

He couldn't.

"What. The. Hell. Is. Going. On?" he whispered.

This made absolutely no sense. Summer skies in the dead of winter? Earth summer skies at that, on a world with double suns and moons and comets and galaxies?

Maybe he was waking up.

Could be. The nurses might have wheeled his comatose self onto a balcony and this was what he was seeing. 'Course a balcony indicated a rather high-end hospital and Otto doubted his insurance would cover that. More likely, he was out of the hospital and in his own backyard, strapped in a wheelchair and drooling on his shirt.

Boy, won't Sherry be surprised when he stands up and yells, "The Big Dipper!"

Okay, let's do that.

Any time now...

The keep and its grounds stretched before him. His backyard did not. The Dipper and Boötes remained. The comets and galaxies and moons didn't come back.

What. The. Hell. Is. Going. On?

A wind had picked up in the last few moments and it was a knife through the toga, which had not fared well during his run-through-fire. He shivered.

Okay, let us grant that this is a rather bewildering situation requiring much rumination, but getting out of the snow and cold has a higher priority. Shelter now, ruminate later.

Otto stumbled through the ankle-deep snow, which should have been harder-going except it was light and powdery, a rather marked change from earlier. Another benefit of ridding the local area of its resident evil: the snow improved.

It took about thirty minutes for Otto to get around the keep and into the village. He wasn't sure if he was on the drawbridge side or not but, who cares, there's buildings, the nearest one about fifty yards off. Shouldn't lose too many of his toes between here and there.

Hunching against the wind, he reached the closest wall in about ten minutes but, forget it; all that was left of this place was the wall. The next building across wasn't much better and building number three, next to that, didn't even have a wall, only a slumped roof.

"C'mon, man," Otto said, "third time's supposed to be a charm."

Fourth was.

Or, at least, the fourth had walls and roof and a relatively intact set of windows and doors. Utterly lacking in charm, though. Otto, so cold by now he could barely clear the threshold, shoved the door open enough to gain entry.

Gonna flop right down on whatever kind of floor this place had — stone or wood or manure — and go right to sleep.

Which, if he remembered correctly his first aid training about the process of freezing to death, meant he was never going to wake up. Which, given context, was hilarious.

With some effort, he pushed the door shut, cutting off the wind, and immediately felt warmer but knew it was mere contrast — the place, itself, was still cold. And empty. No furniture, no rugs, no tapestries, nothing he could use to start a fire, if he could. Otto was sure he still had the matches somewhere, but his frozen and burned fingers probably lacked the dexterity to strike one.

Let's settle for being out of the wind, then, okay, Bucky?

Otto leaned against the doorjamb and, slowly, carefully, slid down it. His back was numb enough that he could do so without screaming, as long as he kept his shoulders still, but, already, he could feel pins and needles vibrating up and down his legs. One of the disadvantages of shelter: he now gets to feel how injured he actually is.

It came in waves as his circulation returned and the burns and bruises asserted themselves into a perfect storm of sheer agony, with a trough of relief followed by a bigger and bigger wave. The bruises stayed mostly undertone, except for his nose, which was a big bass drum pounding his head to mush.

Certain pains had never bothered Otto. Cuts, for one. Given his general clumsiness, they were almost an occupational hazard. He'd zap a finger with a razor blade − "*Ow!*" — apply a tourniquet (well, Band-Aid) and iodine − "*Ow!*" − and he was good. He'd broken his toes so many times − mostly from walking into things, not from something cool like kumite − he set and taped them himself, no doctor required.

But headaches …

"*Ow! Ow! OW!*" Otto expressed his displeasure at what his nose was doing to his head. Could use an Anacin, but he doubted there was a bottle or two of that lying around this place. He could rub the two acupuncture points on both hands that relieved the pressure of a headache, but they'd probably been burned away. Besides, he didn't have the fingers to rub them; at least, not without sloughing off the skin.

Really needed that Anacin.

Really needed help.

Because there was no way he was getting out of this building alive. Or, at least, what passed for life in this universe. If he did not freeze to death in the next hour or two, then he would die from sepsis and starvation and this damned headache sometime the following day.

"Father," he whispered.

Powerful word, that.

It and its alternatives − daddy, dad − was the name of that big and vibrant and powerful man, the strongest on Earth, the most fun one on Earth, who swept Otto up one-handed and swung him onto his shoulders, the nylon of Daddy's flight suit so slippery and soft under Otto's legs and they were charging through the yard with Cha Cha in pursuit and he was terrified and exhilarated because this was scary but Daddy had him, Daddy had him. And when he collapsed in some miserable corner because his little girlfriend was now walking around with that Tommy guy, it was Dad who sat down next to him and gave him a Pepsi and told him stories of his own heartaches and losses until Otto felt better, felt assured, felt like he'd be all right.

And then Daddy's helicopter went down on some nameless Vietnamese hill and Daddy was gone and Mom disappeared soon after (even when she was in the same room) and, from that time on, Otto had to heal his own hurts.

Barely tolerated in grampaw's house to the point it was preferable to stay out of it, cold and alone on some dark street, Otto walked alone, lost, but places to stay and food and the occasional pat on the back showed up from unexpected quarters so that he ended up graduating from high school fairly intact and, years later, found that Father, that big and vibrant and powerful Being, on a cold, snow blown runway in Asia. It was as if He knew Otto would find Him there, and had thrown him the various bones along the way, hidden, unobserved, but there all along: Daddy in the audience or on the sidelines encouraging son to keep going. The many times since, enemies to the front and back, his own demise certain, but he knew this Father well by then and he'd called, and the cavalry had arrived.

Always this presence, hovering, strong and sure and immutable and out of sight but at the corner of the eye and always in mind, a harbor, an anchor. Always there.

"Father," he said again, louder this time.

Answered by a scraping sound back towards the far part of the room – light, quick, but something. Otto, startled, peered hard but the area was steeped in shadow.

"Who's there?"

The movement stopped but Otto sensed a presence in the background, hovering, strong and sure.

Was it Latchemondy?

Maybe. The guy showed up at the oddest times.

He hoped it was the Widow Wyncke because she was at least a doctor of some kind. Or Claudia, because her tears would heal him instantly.

Heck, he'd even settle for Taccola.

The dark shape moved.

And growled.

What remaining hair on Otto's neck rose. Not a "who." A "what."

Two eyes, brassy and burning, stared at him from the other side of the room.

Oh, great, Belial, or what was left of him because this was a significantly shorter version.

Not that it mattered. In his present condition, even mini-Worthless could flay his flesh.

Another set of brass eyes took position next to the first. Then another. And another. And ...

He lost count. Ten, twelve, more, sets of eyes.

Belial's children?

The room flooded with moonlight, silvery and pure, like the moonlight of Virginia. How comforting.

Except for what it revealed.

Chapter XVII

Leader Of The Pack

All Otto could think was, "Wolves? You sent wolves?"

Because, really, wolves?

Now how in the blue blazes was that help?

The pack formed a semi-circle, heads lowered and eyes blazing in the now annoying moonlight. They growled deep in their throats, low and menacing, warning Otto.

Like he needed warning.

In the few seconds he had left in this Afterlife, Otto concluded he was experiencing a grand example of God's humor. After all, he was parboiled and roasted, which must be a fairly rare treat for wolves since they usually ate their meat raw. It was, also, a grand example of God's humbling: wanna make sure you don't get a swelled head over beating a demon there, bub, so I'm gonna feed you to the wolves.

"In my defense," Otto said, "I don't think I'm all that," and he raised a weak hand and made a grand dismissive gesture.

The pack darted back, snarling and fangs bared, which Otto understood. A man raising a hand was usually precursor to a gunshot and a dead wolf. After all, man was wolfdom's only natural enemy and some skittishness was expected.

As was the pack quickly getting over said skittishness and rending him limb from limb.

Otto braced.

But, the wolves hung back.

So, the race memory of aimed guns is strong with these guys, is it?

Might work to his advantage. Otto leaned forward and brought both hands up as if he was holding a rifle. "Git!" he ordered.

Sort of worked. The pack jumped back a bit more and registered alarm but didn't scatter. Otto had to actually fire a weapon for that effect. Still, he'd bought some time, maybe ten seconds.

One of the wolves stepped forward into the moonlight. Judging by its size and obvious attitude, this was the alpha male. Quite beautiful, it was mostly black with a silver chest and white blaze down its forehead. There were old scars running along the side of the beast so, seasoned fighter.

Great.

Otto trained his fake rifle between its eyes and gestured threateningly and the alpha backed up but then stood, obviously waiting for the flash and bang.

"Okay, Lord," he whispered, "a flashbang would be good about now. You know, lightning, thunder?"

But nothing. Of course.

Alpha, apparently satisfied that Otto was, indeed, faking it, stepped forward again. Lowering its head, Alpha examined Otto with luminous eyes that had turned green in the moonlight.

Seeking the choicest cuts, Otto figured.

Otto stared back, but not directly into Alpha's eyes. He'd read somewhere that canines considered that a challenge. Otto would like to be eaten quickly, not have to fight for the privilege.

Alpha took a couple of more steps forward, bold now. The rest of the pack whined and shivered, licking its chops, and Alpha snapped a growl over its shoulder at them. Shut up, boys, daddy's gonna get the prime rib and then you can have the hamburger. Otto lowered his gaze to Alpha's paws and turned his head to expose the side of his neck. Make it quick, will you? The sooner I get to the throne room and ask God what's the big idea here, the better.

Alpha finished his mental drawing of Otto into choice cuts

and padded forward at a rather leisurely pace. Otto wondered how bad it would hurt. Alpha stopped at Otto's feet and began sniffing his sneakers.

"Sorry," Otto said, "Haven't had time to clean them."

Alpha glanced up briefly and then returned to sneaker-sniffing. Downright embarrassing, this: his feet were apparently so pungent that a wolf pauses to savor them before tearing his throat out.

"Like I had time to take a bath," he groused.

Alpha didn't even bother looking up at that but settled on the laces, looking at the loose strings with some puzzlement, then turned and looked fully at Otto.

This is it.

Otto held his breath.

Alpha, though, returned to the laces and began nibbling them a bit.

Going to eat him from the feet up, huh? Wonderful.

Alpha pulled the strings a little harder and managed to untie one of the shoes. The moonlight played along the wolf's hide, the scars merging into a pattern akin to angel wings ...

Angel wings?

Otto blinked.

Alpha looked up at him, blinked in response, then lowered its head to Otto's ankle and, gently, carefully, licked his burned legs.

Otto wasn't too surprised. Alpha was probably getting his first taste of medium rare and wanted to check it out before digging in. But there wasn't any urgency and Alpha remained in place, gently licking.

It didn't hurt; well, Otto didn't *think* it hurt because he had lost all feeling in his legs, other than the sense of burning, so he had no idea if Alpha was reaching bone or not. Didn't look like it. Alpha seemed content with taste alone.

He heard shuffling and Otto looked up to see the rest of the pack approaching.

Okay, good, finally, a sudden rush and snarl and rip and he was done. The pack broke into two directions, settled on either side of Otto's legs, and began their own licking regimen.

Licking. Not eating.

Otto had read somewhere that dogs' tongues were actually

sanitary, that it was a good idea to let them lick wounds because their saliva held a healing enzyme. Otto had doubted that because dogs eat their own vomit, which had to leave a few species of noxious bacteria hanging around their teeth. But the article had described ancient techniques of putting a dog on a wound, and the wound healing instead of corrupting.

But that was dogs, not wolves. Otto didn't know if wolf saliva had the same qualities but wolves definitely did not have the same regard for mankind. If they were Cha Cha and his pals, then Otto would be feeling fine, would quietly lie here, dog vomit be damned, and let the dogs clean his wounds ...

Lazarus.

No, not *that* Lazarus, the other Lazarus, the one Jesus named in a parable. The beggar covered with sores laid at the rich man's gate, and the dogs would come and lick his wounds. Taken to the bosom of Abraham. Comforted.

Maybe God has sent help, after all.

Alpha disengaged from Otto's ankles and moved through the crowd, pushing them out of the way until he reached a position overlooking his chest. Alpha nosed aside the remnants of the toga and sniffed at the burns there, then resumed his gentle licking.

Slowly, Otto raised his hand and, just as gently, laid it on the scruff of Alpha's neck. The wolf looked at him and Otto figured this was a liberty too far and he'd be minus a hand in the next few seconds, but Alpha cocked his head and even rubbed against Otto's arm. Carefully plunging through the thick fur, Otto began scratching.

He scratched. The wolves licked.

Chapter XVIII

Cosplay On A Budget

Three days. And nights.

Otto drowsed through most of it. The licking soothed and the undulating fur blanket of wolf bodies pressed around him warmed, making him sleepy. He woke each time the moonlight faded and the sunlight expanded and vice versa, occasionally finding himself on his stomach and the wolves working his back.

"Thanks, guys," he'd murmur and then go back to sleep.

On the fourth exchange of light sources, the wolves were gone. And he was cold again.

But at least he wasn't burning.

Otto raised his hands, clear and bright in the sunlight, and stared at them.

Wow.

No longer the charred results of a flamethrower attack but instead, a very bad case of sunburn.

Wolf licking is a rather effective therapy.

He flexed the remaining fingers and was pleasantly surprised that he could actually touch his palms. The skin was tight and dry but everything was intact and functioning. Even the stump was clean. Otto turned his arms over and examined the forearms. Much the same, although they were tighter and he couldn't fully extend them.

Now for the acid test.

Slowly, Otto got his elbows underneath him, marveling that he was not immediately engulfed in pain, pushed up and stared down at his exposed stomach. Same condition as the hands: sunburn instead of char, but with lots of scars mixed in, some of them almost gouges.

Guess I won't be doing bathing suit ads anytime soon.

Otto worked his way up to a sitting position and looked down his legs. His jeans and sneakers were tatters — whether by fire or wolf tongue, he couldn't tell — and the sunburn motif continued all the way to his feet, as did the scarring, but worse. Guess Nike ads were out, too. But, he could move and the pain was bearable, so, go for it. He rocked forward, pulled his legs underneath, and slowly, very slowly, stood.

Oh. Wow. Did. That. Hurt!

What did he say about bearable? Waves of pain washed over him, tsunamis of it. Gasping, Otto swayed, almost losing his balance — but, man, stay up, stay up! — because it would be a real trial getting back to his feet. Closing his eyes, Otto fought the swirling vertigo and waves of spinning eyelid lights, almost tipping too far to one side — but stay up, stay up! — and, after a few moments, the spinning subsided and he was stable. To a point.

Otto opened his eyes directly at a window blazing with searingly bright sun(s). "*Ack!*" as he jerked away, his vision reduced to one big yellow spot — at least it wasn't spinning. While his vision recovered for the second time, Otto took a quick mental inventory of his other hurts, because, boy, did he have some other hurts.

In sum, it felt like someone had worked him over with a baseball bat and then set him on fire. Made losing a finger feel like a papercut. He shouldn't have made it out of the keep, much less here. He should be nothing but a lump of barbecued popsicle right now but three days with a wolf pack and lookee hyeah, fit as a fiddle … well, still breathing, at least. And standing. And mobile.

And cold. Did he mention that already?

Shivering, Otto hugged himself and looked around for a handy wolf blanket or toga or burlap bag.

Nope. Nothing.

But there *is* sunlight, as his dazzled vision confirmed, so let's put it to use.

Shuffling over, Otto canted his eyes off-center, stood full to the light and basked.

Ah. Downright hot, that.

Otto wondered at the efficacy of tanning already burned skin, but warmth was the priority now. He'd worry about skin cancer later.

The light was so bright that Otto could see nothing outside. Covering his eyes with a hand, Otto made a small opening between his fingers and peered through, adjusting until he had blocked enough of the suns' light to see.

The keep was right there, superimposed against a deep blue sky with a puffy cloud silhouetting the top. Almost picturesque, except the keep was shrunken and forlorn, dark and featureless, as though the walls were absorbing the light or something. A tower on the Gates of Mordor.

The land rolled away to either side of the keep, snow-covered and pristine in the dazzling light. Buildings stuck out of the snow here and there, abruptly ending at some indefinable line that Otto figured was the crevasse, soooo ... he must be behind the keep staring back towards the field of skulls, which lay well below his vision.

Wait a minute ...

Otto furrowed a brow. Didn't he, while seeking shelter a few days ago, walk around the *front* of the keep?

Yeah, he did.

So, if the keep was in front of him now, then he should be looking *away* from the crevasse.

Right?

Confused, Otto peered around but all he could see was the side of this building and the hint of another one to the left so he stumbled around to the door and stepped outside.

Woo, ice foot, but need to figure out some directions. Start by fixing the suns. Otto cast about and located it almost straight overhead ...

It. A sun. Singular.

Not the suns. Plural.

Otto squeezed his eyes shut and waited until all the red spots disappeared then made another quick glance through his finger sunglasses, gasping as the light punished his vision but, yes, one sun.

Where'd the other one go?

Probably the same place the galaxies and comets and nebula had.

"What's going on?"

Suns don't pick themselves up and go elsewhere, not without involving a lot of explosions or helium flashes or other stuff Marc had once unsuccessfully tried to explain to him. Which meant this planet should be a burnt little ember, much like his back, but no; there was still an intact and snow-covered world out there. The other sun was, simply, gone, leaving a bright yellow one high up there, much like the sun of home.

Like the stars of home.

Was this Earth?

If so, it was a part of Earth Otto had never visited. Maybe this was Transylvania, which was the only place he knew replete with medieval keeps and villages and battlefields strewn with skulls ... probably not; those skulls should have been cleaned up by now.

Maybe it was Transylvania a couple of million years ago, when dinosaurs ruled the earth and angels showed up to fight them, or ride them, against keeps populated by demons, a series of events not recorded in any history books Otto had ever read.

Pre-history.

Could be.

Otto considered. Pre-history was the province of myth and guesswork because there simply wasn't a lot of reporting on it, a line or two in surviving epics and scripture and the fossil records of a gigantic lizard-looking animal life scattered hither and yon. Even with such a dearth of information, though, paleontologists had managed to throw together some plausible timelines. Bombardment by comets and meteors formed ice and water and seas, and things spontaneously woke up and got legs and crawled up on land and, a few years later, here we are.

Nowhere in any of those timelines, though, was there any mention of dino-riders. No paleontologist had ever raised the possibility. At least, not for Earth.

So, this wasn't Earth. Despite the earthlike stars and sun. Had to be someplace else.

Unless the timelines were wrong.

What if all those Dino the Dinosaur skeletons out there in Montana weren't the evolutionary result of time and single cells, but something else entirely? Say, a pre-mammalian species on a pre-glacial earth, the mounts of angels, their bodies lying where they and their angel masters fell in battle against Belial and his friends. That giant meteorite all the scientists believed wiped the species out was actually artillery, or a demon igniting.

"Are you freakin' high or something?" he asked himself.

Wolf saliva must have hallucinogenic properties.

Otto chuckled. Could be.

Here he was, on the basis of no evidence, refuting the work of centuries. Because, dude, a twelfth-century villa, keep, and valley full of angel skulls wouldn't escape the notice of even the dullest explorer, much less evade the advanced technologies that archaeologists have been using lately. Heck, they'd found the outlines of Roman camps and even the resting places of Neanderthals, so there's no way highly organized structures like these would escape notice.

Unless they were buried.

Under ice and snow.

Tons of it, miles of it, like in the Arctic.

Otto thought about it for a moment and then dismissed the whole concept. Even if everything was under a glacier, it would attract notice. Weren't they finding prehistoric houses deep in the tundra out there in Greenland or something?

So, as previously concluded, this wasn't Earth, not even pre-history Earth. But it was certainly Earth-like.

Why?

Otto had no idea and, frankly, didn't care. Metaphysical questions were better tackled when one was clothed and warm and fed, Maslow's hierarchy and all that. So, let's take care of those lower-order needs first and then get back to the Great Mysteries of Life. Or Afterlife.

Otto stepped back inside and made a half-hearted search of the room in a half-hearted hope there was something here he could use but no joy. Need to expand his scavenging to other structures.

Great.

He was cold and hurting and didn't feel like slogging around in the snow but, dude, clothes. And boots. And more torches or something else that demons didn't like.

And a hamburger would be nice, too.

Was feeling a mite peckish, wasn't he? Given what he'd endured the last few days, hardly a surprise. For a mortal. But he wasn't supposed to be mortal anymore and food and drink were supposed to be optional ... speaking of drink, he could also stand a canteen or two of nice, fresh water.

One good thing about a snow-covered world, water is readily available.

Otto went back outside, squatted down, and looked at the snow suspiciously. He was fairly sure that snow was not a good remedy for thirst; it had to be melted and then boiled to kill the thingies in it anxious to deposit themselves in some unwary human's intestines.

He shrugged. "Risk it," he said, scooped a handful and swallowed some, immediately getting brain freeze. "*Ow! Ow! Ow!*" he giggled, like he was eight years old again and suffering from the effects of an orange Push-up.

He scooped another handful and held it in his mouth to melt, the water trickling down his throat.

That would do for now.

He staggered upright, his burned legs still not functioning well. Add to that frozen feet and knees and now hands and it was a wonder he didn't pitch forward. And he was back in the frigid wind.

So let's not waste any time out here or you'll end up an orange Push-up.

He slogged towards the next building but it didn't look promising because one side of the wall facing him was gone. So little chance anything inside had survived but, surprise, a pile of rags lay against a far door. Otto went through the pile, most of the rags dissolving into dust as he did, but he managed to save a couple of strips. They weren't big enough to serve as a shirt or anything but might help insulate what was left of his sneakers. He wrapped them around his feet, making several adjustments before tying them off and testing them.

"Spongy," he said, bouncing up and down until the rags flattened to the point he could keep his balance. He lifted one rag-wrapped foot, now six times bigger than it used to be, and scrutinized it. "I'm a French soldier fleeing Moscow," he said, and headed over to the next building.

It was a bit awkward waddling through the snow with rag-Nikes but, after a few waddles, Otto got the hang of it.

As good as snowshoes, these things.

The rags kept his feet dry and warm, too, so they must be waterproof, whether from age or some kind of oil infusion he had no idea and didn't care. They worked, and one doesn't look gift horses in mouths …

"Flicka?" he called, against hope that the horse was stamping impatiently on the other side of this building.

No such luck, but he did find some twine on the floor. Grabbing that, Otto went for the next building.

In this way, Otto made a circle of the village and gathered useful stuff: a long, bandage-like, thick velvety cloth that made excellent leggings; a couple of leather wraps that went over the leggings like a pair of spats; a very wide red banner with a tear in it that slipped over his head like a Templar's cloak; a couple of leather bags, flexible enough to serve as mittens; and a heavy, long, iron rod that was probably a spear shaft but would do as a walking stick.

By the time he'd finished, the sun had lowered and shadows extended to the point that some glass fragments dangling in a window of the last building became a mirror. Otto stood before it and examined himself.

"Gandalf," he said to his image, "without the pointy hat."

Otto cast about for said hat but all he found was another cloth that served as a decent hood. He draped it over his head and went back to the window and frowned.

"Not Gandalf," he concluded, "A Sith Lord. A shabbier version, anyway."

Appearance notwithstanding, he was now warm.

Or, warmer.

The temperature was dropping in time with the sun and the breeze picked up, but the clothes made it bearable. His get-up was scratchy and stuck to his burns in a couple of places and taking off this Halloween costume would, no doubt, involve a lot of screaming. But he'd do that at a hospital; that is, when he found one. Right now, he'd like to find a McDonald's, get some McNuggets and a coffee. Scavenging advances one's peckishness.

Otto stumped to the door and peered out, hoping to spot the glow of golden arches, but the only glow was that of sunset behind him ...

Illuminating Mt. Everest before him.

Otto gasped. "Where the heck did THAT come from?"

Because it wasn't there when he started collecting cast-offs. Or, maybe it was and he hadn't noticed ...

Oh, c'mon! A mountain that monstrous was noticeable for hundreds of miles in all directions.

Otto pressed his eyes with the mittens to clear them of hallucinations but, yep, mountain still there and he stepped through the door, planted the rod in the snow, leaned on it, and marveled.

"Huge" wasn't a word big enough.

The mountain ... soared. Transcended. Overwhelmed. Otto had to bend backwards to take it all in, an endless height of rock and snow, a pyramid to the moon, blazing red where the sunset stroked the snow piles, blue where it touched the rock, a symmetry of colors and elements that owned the sky and the earth. Clouds haloed it, themselves golden and crimson in the changing light and masking the top where the Throne of God had to be, *had* to be, because a mountain this size could only hold God. Or Zeus. Or Asgard.

And it had not been there an hour ago.

"What's. Going. ON?" Otto shouted at the mountain. At the sky. At the world. Because this made no sense at all. Just. No. Sense.

Unless the geography of this place had kept it hidden.

Hmm.

Otto stared at the mountain one more time, then tromped around the building and looked at the village. Okay, he was now definitely on the other side of the tower and definitely opposite the crevasse, and, yes, this made for an entirely different view. So, depending on how low the valley of the cabin and dusty skulls, there was, indeed, a good chance the mountain remained out of sight until he'd cleared the back of the village.

But the mountain *should* have been visible from the valley of the shipwreck; at least the peak if not the top half, but he didn't remember seeing it. Yeah, the alps, they'd been in view until the rains began, but this thing dwarfed them. It should have been the anchor of the system, the center point for the other peaks, which were mere foothills against it.

Maybe it was an issue of parallax ...

What is parallax, anyway?

"Marc?" he called, but no answer.

The light softened and reddened and Otto watched as the sun touched the distant horizon and the knolls where the ship and the cabin — and maybe the dogs — waited. It looked peaceful, calming. Warm, the snow merely in patches down there. If he started walking now, figured out how to get back across the collapsed bridge and then shinnied down the steps and down the ridge, he'd find everything as it once was.

A better cabin.

Maybe a cat or two to keep the dogs amused.

Flicka.

Claudia.

Otto turned to the mountain. The dying light turned into ruby lasers exploring and probing every detail, every outcrop ...

And a trail, leading out from the back of the village through a crumbling wall and gate and stretching for miles over a rise and dropping out of sight then re-appearing at the base of the mountain and winding up and around, up and around, all the way into the clouds. As the light disappeared, Otto saw a flare in the clouds surrounding the peak. A fire.

An invitation.

"Gee," Otto said to the mountain, "I wonder where I'm supposed to go next?"

Chapter XIX

You've Been Eaten By A Grue

Otto stayed in the hood house for the night. The moment the sun disappeared, a wind like a battering ram of ice came barreling through the village, turning the place sub-Arctic, and ending his plans to immediately assault the mountain trail.

Do it in the morning, in the light, in the warmth because a night hike meant freezing to death a couple of yards out of the door so, forget it.

The stars of summer — Big Dipper, Sirius, the whole schmeer — sparked brilliant in the frozen air, mocking him. Maybe it was summer on Earth. Definitely not here.

The clothes helped but a fire helped more and Otto gathered fragments of window sash and collapsed roof shingles and built a little teepee of kindling out of them, then dug through the leggings to what survived of his pockets and, glory be, matches. One strike to light the teepee, about twenty minutes of feeding and blowing to get it going and, presto, a means to survive the cold. May not survive his stomach, though.

Man, was he hungry. He'd eyed some of the window sash, wondering if he could stew it into some kind of a woody broth, but he didn't have a pot to boil it in, which meant he couldn't melt enough snow for a good, long, satisfying drink of water, either. Too bad; a good, long, satisfying drink of water has a marked effect on hunger pangs, which were signs of dehydration more than anything. He'd do better if he had something to drink than eat, because a person can go thirty days without food, but only two to three without liquids. At least, that's what survival school taught him. He'd go for a pizza, all the same.

Otto scooped snow out of the door and shuffled back to the fire and let it melt in his hands and drank it and ate the remaining snow crystals and repeated the process about twenty-thirty times, shivering the while and watching his sunburnt hands turn blue. He wasn't sure how much this snow eating was off-setting the warmth he was building up from the fire and the clothes. Eating snow to hydrate might actually lower body temperature, becoming a wash, so to speak. At least, that's what survival school taught him, but he was no longer thirsty and, after another couple of hours of fire-feeding and shivering, he was no longer freezing. Cold, yes, but beggars could not be choosers.

Each time he'd scooped snow, he'd looked up the mountain at the cloud line and the firelight dancing behind it as clear and bright and inviting as the stars.

"Fire, fire everywhere, but not a morsel to eat," he said.

Because, no doubt, whatever produced that cheerful light was big and roaring, a massive fireplace, say, stretching from wall to wall with blazing tree trunks cooking great spits of whole hogs, great cauldrons of soup hanging from tripods and boiling away, a grand banquet table on the opposite side spread with grapes and honey and roasts and Christmas goose where a giant, merry man dressed in red-and-white ermine and sporting holly wreaths on his head hoisted a horn of ale in one hand and a giant drumstick in the other while bellowing, "More drink! More food!"

Otto started awake.

It was still night and Otto sat up and stirred the coals and added more sash until it flared and warmed his hands before going out and scooping another handful of snow. He stared at the massive silhouette of mountain against the dark sky, the Dipper now replaced by Orion as morning advanced the normal cycle of constellations. At least it was now a proper winter sky for a proper winter landscape. The clouds were still there, the fire at its line also still there, whipping in and out of the vapor. So, the Mountain King's banquet continued.

Otto swallowed the snow and went back inside and curled next to the fire and back to sleep.

It was full-on morning when he woke again, the sun blazing through all the openings, the shadow of the mountain canted to one side, allowing in the light.

Thank God.

Otto rose, shivering, and stood in the doorway and took a sunbath, exposing his sides and back until the frozen dew vaporized around him, leaving him ethereal. The sun was at the mountain's right shoulder, so it must have been up for a while.

Time's a wastin'.

"Waiter!" Otto yelled to the mountain, "An omelet! And make it snappy!"

No one popped their mouth and yelled, "Very good, sir!", so probably wasn't going to get breakfast.

Bet the Mountain King had breakfast, cold goose breast and ambrosia.

If Otto hustled along, he could get on the end of it. He looked back at his own fire and thought about making a fire bundle but all he knew about them was their existence, not how to actually build one. His luck, it would ignite in his pocket and there he'd be with new burns. He doubted the wolves would show up and attend to it because that would be on him, not demons. He still had two matches, so bring some kindling, in case he found firewood along the way.

Or something flammable. Like a demon.

Because let's be clear here, bub, you're going to find something along the way, something that will help you survive, even if it took three weeks to reach the Hall of the Mountain King.

That was the overarching theme here in his personal Heaven: tools were provided. Sure, he had to take the initiative and use the tools but there they were: cabin, dogs, halberd, horse, wolves. Matches. Just had to spot the item, collect it, and put it in his pack until its use became apparent. It was a game of Zork.

A game.

Otto frowned.

A stupid game. An unnecessary game. Not even an interesting one because the 'outs' were already built in, like a wizard's staff under a rock, a laser gun on a shelf, and all he had to do was Control Key and Loot and Arm and kill the trolls and aliens. Play for a while, giggle, then stop, save, watch some TV, go to work, go out, sleep, and leisurely go back to the game every other day or so until he killed the last boss and got the epic message at the end.

What would it be at the end of this one? "Good job! You have now reached the throne room! Enjoy!"? Or, "You have touched the Holy Grail and have been dissolved into nothing. Start a new game?"

Stupid.

"This is just STUPID!" Otto shouted at the mountain. "You're just STUPID!" he shouted again while pointing at it. "Cut the crap! Just ... come and get me!"

Come and get me.

God, Father, Zeus, Whoever, stop all this Shaolin Temple Path of Enlightenment kay-rap and come and get me. Send an angel, a legion of them, heck, a '72 Dodge, something, to take me out of this freezing village and up Thy wondrous mountain where I can lay down in green clover while Your Benevolent Gaze heals my burns and my wounds and the rents and tears of a lifetime of battle while I rest.

"Let me rest," he whispered.

He listened, half expecting an answer.

Only the wind.

Otto waited for a moment, placed the spear haft in the snow, and set off.

Cold, but there was nothing like a vigorous walk to build up some heat and he was comfortable after a few hundred yards or so. Built up an appetite, too, especially when that was his starting point and Otto kept an eye out for those elusive golden arches. Knowing this place, he'd find a shuttered Gino's, instead, a sign for the Gino Giant dangling off one corner and flapping in the wind.

But even a picture of a hamburger would be delicious, so, tempt me not, Madison Avenue.

The trail through the village and out the back was discernible in the snow and the ersatz snowshoes made it easy going and, before he knew it, Otto was at the gate. He paused and looked at both sides. A low wall, with the remains of hinges where the gate itself must have hung, that's all. It was the sort of gate Otto expected on an English farm, a sheep gate of some kind. He stared at the trail as it led from the gate to the first rise of the mountain.

What kind of sheep lived on mountainsides, those big fuzzy ones that looked like giant Q-tips? More likely it was goats, bad-tempered horn-headed goats that had gone feral sometime in the last 10,000 years. Badass goats at that, with wolves and such running around.

Otto made an irritable gesture at the trail. "So," he asked, "can I count on getting butted off a cliff at some point?"

Probably.

Otto stepped through the gate and probed with the shaft and found his footing and launched. He didn't look right or left, keeping himself tilted towards the sun as much as he could. The sun was still off the mountain's right shoulder and Otto reasoned he'd have it for at least an hour before he reached the first shadow, a blue-gray finger reaching out from his left. Then figure another ten to twelve hours before he got around the first turn and into sunlight again, but there wouldn't be any sunlight again because it would be full-on dark and there he'd be, on an Arctic mountain at night with badass goats and hungry wolves.

Stupid.

Otto wondered how many thousands of years it would take before the next person, idiotic enough to blast off from the City and crash over there in the Valley of the Dogs, stumbled across his frozen-solid body sticking out of the snow. He'd be like that iceman they found splayed in the Pyrenees, a look of genuine consternation on his face. An Ottosickle. The next guy would strip him of this get up ...

Please, do. I look ridiculous.

... and add it to his own motley collection of rags and flags. Maybe he'd even find the matches and the kindling. Then leagues farther until that guy, too, fell frozen. Then thousands of years later, the next victim stumbles on both of us.

Stepping stones.

Otto paused. Was that what he was? A blaze cut on a tree? A high-water mark? Okay, humans, you've gotten this far, let's see how much farther you can go. Maybe six, eight, twenty-five more intrepid explorers later, someone crests that mountain and lo! There! God Smiling On His Throne!

Great for number twenty-five. Sort of sucks for the previous twenty-four.

Gazorbeam.

Otto almost laughed aloud as the image popped into his mind. The skeletal remains of Gazorbeam, one of the supers from *The Incredibles*, a movie Otto found downright hilarious and watched every time he found it playing on some channel. Gazorbeam, whose only function was to cut the password into the rock so Mr. Incredible could continue the mission.

Then die. And rot.

"You could've at least given me laser vision," he muttered, and plodded on.

It took less than an hour to reach the first shadow, and Otto looked back before crossing its border and yes, the sun had shifted towards the valley.

Hmm. This could be an early sunset.

Not that he would know, since he would be walking in shadow the whole time, his first clue arriving when he could no longer see the trail.

What can you do? Why, nothing.

Otto hunched forward and crossed the blue-gray line. Immediately, the sweat through his clothes turned ice cold. About twenty minutes later, an ice beard formed on his face. He wiped that off with a mitten and adjusted the hood to make a mask, imagining he now looked like a Sith ninja. A shabby one.

Plod on.

Otto didn't look around, didn't try to mark the time, just kept one eye on the trail and the other wary of any possible outcropping − or badass goat − tripping him up. The going wasn't too bad. The trail skirted the bottom of the mountain, which was so broad and flat the trail merely rose by half degrees. This much landscape to cover, the ancient trail builders could afford a leisurely approach. Otto wasn't so sure he could, though, given the freezing temperatures.

Plod on.

Every fifty feet or so, Otto broke the ice forming on the mask so he could breathe better ... and noted that he could breathe better. After the beating he'd taken these last few days, he wasn't in the best of shape to ascend the Matterhorn, but, here he was, hanging in there. Imagine how much better he'd do if he had a cheese sandwich.

Otto halted, expectant, but one didn't fall out of the sky, so off he plodded.

The shadow extended as far as he could see, the cold remained, and he kept going. Steady, no great shakes in the speed department, but the journey of a thousand miles began with one foot after another and another ... and it was suddenly afternoon. Late afternoon. Otto stopped, slightly surprised that he had fallen into hike-hypnosis so readily but c'mon, cold and hungry and intent on featureless snow, what did you expect? So now, it's decision time. The day was ending.

Keep going, or stop?

Otto stretched and closed his eyes tight to fight off the snow blindness and tilted his head up and slightly cracked his eyelids open until he was satisfied his vision was clear and looked around.

Okay, still on a trail on the side of a rocky mountain the size of Jupiter, still freezing and hungry.

The only change being the position of the sun, which was behind him off his left shoulder a few degrees above the distant knolls. Otto looked up the side of the mountain and searched the cloud line until he located the firelight and noted it was now farther off his right shoulder, so he had made some progress, six, seven miles. He looked back down the trail and ...

Yep, looks about that distance from the village gate.

... which was still discernible, as was the finger of the keep. Not bad, considering he was ill-equipped for a winter's hike.

Otto turned back towards the setting sun and looked over the valley. Not a lot of detail, rolls of land and winks of water here and there. He couldn't make out the wreck or the cabin and attributed that to distance and angle rather than the more disturbing idea that both were gone. Not something he wanted to consider right now. What he considered, instead, was turning in for the night.

Doesn't seem to be a Hampton hyeah 'bouts. Too bad; they

usually hosted an excellent breakfast bar.

Otto's stomach rumbled at that and he stood, musing.

All right. I can go on, even past dark.

The trail was flat and apparent enough he could see it in starlight, and there'd be a big moon anyway, since there had been a big one during the wolf nights. But he was mortal again and could not walk for days and nights across a tundra, inclining ever upwards, winding around and around the mountain until he was deposited at the foot of whatever castle contained the banquet hall and his waiting host, without there being some kind of deleterious effect.

Like dying.

He needed to rest. Somewhere warm.

Snow cave.

Otto knew the concept: dig a hole in the snow and slip inside all snug and bug-like and rely on body heat to keep from freezing to death. Snow is an excellent insulator; that is, when it forms the walls of a cave. Not so when the walls of said cave collapse. Otto had never built a snow cave — his survival school had been the *Reader's Digest* version — and was not sure he could do so without ending up entombed all snug and bug-like. But there didn't appear to be a lot of other options.

Sighing, Otto looked around and noted that snow was banked up to his right. Function of the incline, he supposed, and making his task a lot easier because all he had to do was dig into the side of the drift until he had a respectable cave.

Worth a shot.

Grasping the spear haft, Otto positioned it at the thickest part of the drift and poked around. The haft was good for breaking up the snowfall but he had to excavate it by hand, which he did to great effect with the mittens. In a surprisingly fast hour, he had an actual hole big enough to climb inside, which was good because it was sunset.

Otto stared at the cave and then back at the plunging sun. Already he felt the cold increasing.

"Gonna have to do," he said.

He shaped the dug-out snow around the entrance to create a windbreak and then gingerly crawled in, making small movements to ensure he did not bring the thing down. Inside, he was pleased to see he'd made the cave long enough to cover him, legs and all, and with enough height to actually turn over. He was in a comfortable position, head slightly elevated.

It ain't a Hampton, but it beats the side of the trail.

Otto wriggled into the snow, trying to shape it. Only thing missing was a mattress or evergreen boughs or something because he was right on top of the snow and that may offset any warmth from body heat.

Eh, be okay.

The ceiling was about a foot from his face and he let out a long satisfied breath right into it.

Hmm.

Otto slowly squeezed out of the cave and walked around the drift, careful not to step on it. He stopped where he guessed his head would be located and drove the spear haft until there was no resistance.

Okay, air hole, through which a passing polar bear will be happy to pull him up and through. At least somebody will get dinner.

Otto went back to the cave entrance and grabbed handfuls of snow and swallowed them, then looked up at the cloud line.

"Get a stew going, Mountain King," Otto said to the bright fire behind it. "I'll be there tomorrow." And he crawled inside.

Chapter XX

Be Sure To Leave A Mint On The Pillow

Otto didn't get there tomorrow. Not even three tomorrows later.

The fourth tomorrow after the first snow cave, Otto woke in his fourth snow cave and wondered why he even bothered. Best to pull the snow down on top of him, go right to sleep, and process into an Ottosickle because he was nowhere. Nowhere. He hadn't even cleared the first turn of the mountain yet.

And he was starving.

To. Death.

Bleary, weary, frozen and hurting, he elbowed his way out the entrance of the cave until he was back under full blue sky and mountain shadow and decided to simply lie there. It was too much effort to sit up, much less stand up. His stomach gripped and roiled, desperate to find something to cling to but all it had was snow water, and that was cramping him. And it wasn't hydrating him because he had not urinated in two days and he was going …

To. Die.

Okay. Let's die.

Otto waited to die for a while but then he got bored with it and forced himself to stand, swaying. Oh, man, what a headache, a constant, pounding, eye-blinding one that left him confused and apathetic. A lack-of-coffee headache, one he'd get about eighteen hours into a stakeout and inevitably led to very bad decisions like "let's take a little nap, shall we?" or "maybe I'll walk over to 7-Eleven and get a giant coffee" and miss the five-second drug deal and he'd have to set up again the next week.

Galling.

Maybe he should go on over to 7-Eleven.

Trembling more from weakness than the cold, Otto reached down into the snow and got himself a Big Gulp, freezing his teeth, his stomach leaping right out of his body, standing in front of him, aghast, and yelling, "Knock it off!"

"Okay, okay." Otto waved a weak hand and his stomach gave him an annoyed look and jumped right back in, still complaining.

So, we're already hallucinating, are we?

Otto couldn't fathom whether that was due to thirst or hunger or his brain melting. Or, more accurately, freezing. Snow caves, as advertised, became quite snug after a few hours, but not enough to unthaw him. And the caves weren't catered.

"All right, enough bellyaching," — got a chuckle from his stomach at that one — "let's get this show on the road."

He stabbed the spear haft into the ground and staggered a step or two before he almost pitched over from vertigo, so he stopped and rested and eyeballed the trail.

Still there. Still snow-covered. Still going up.

But at least now, he could see the point where it crested the horizon, which meant he would soon be on the other side of the mountain and have an extraordinary view of the valley down there with its strip malls filled with Taco Bells, Applebees, and Wings and Things. Even a Sheetz.

Let's hold that thought. Let's get that far before we die.

The sun stood overhead when Otto, puffing and struggling and ready to collapse, actually got that far. Hauling himself up the shoulder, he wavered at the point of the trail where it began an upward turn, and peered eagerly down.

No strip malls. Just more snow.

Otto sighed.

Not that he was surprised but it would have been nice to be pleasantly surprised. At least the view was different. Sort of. Another valley, or, more likely, a continuation of the first, disappearing in a distance of hills and knolls much the same as behind the shipwreck, except this one had a river coursing through the center of it.

Must be a purty good sized 'un to look so wide at these miles.

Otto followed it around some bends and noted a flattening in the distance and a diffuse gleam of sunlight.

An ocean.

So, we are a coastal mountain, are we? Now, where on Earth was there geography such as this? The Arctic, right? Lots of mountains, lots of snowy rivers and ocean.

But, if he was remembering his 8th-grade school larnin' properly, it was the *Antarctic* that had a giant mountain smack dab in the middle of it; a volcano, at that.

Suspiciously, Otto looked up the mountain trying to spot a steam plume but the angle was such he couldn't see the peak. Couldn't if he was standing right on top of it, either, because the clouds up there were so thick …

Hmm. Wasn't that evidence of a steam plume? How else do you get clouds up there?

Otto tried to remember his 8th-grade weather concepts but drew a blank. He gazed at the cloud mass and followed it back but he'd turned the corner and was now out of the banquet fire's line of sight.

Hope the meal is still cooking.

Not that it mattered; he'd lick the stone-cold, crusted-over pots.

There was some movement at the bottom of the cloudbank.

Otto started. Yeah, there, at the rock line …

What's that?

Otto squinted, using the cloud cover to edge the sun out and stared hard enough that tears formed, so he broke away and wiped his eyes and looked again and …

Yeah, movement. What was that? A bird?

A bird.

Otto rubbed his eyes again and reacquired and …

Yep, a bird.

… lazily circling in and out of the cloud cover …

Now, how in the blue blazes does a bird survive at that height and in this cold and what had to be some rather terrific winds? Must be a really big bird to do so. Really, really big …

Too big.

Not a bird.

A Fallen.

Otto gasped and almost fell down as the Fallen continued its lazy circling in and out of the clouds.

"Oh, man," Otto breathed and looked desperately around but there was no place to run, no place to hide. And he was definitely not in any shape to fight the thing. He could barely hold on to the spear shaft, much less heft it. If that thing wanted to come down here and eviscerate him, it could.

Easily.

But, it didn't. It floated in and out of the cloud. Out for a joy fly, he guessed. Maybe it didn't even see Otto.

Hah.

Otto watched it for a moment more and then shrugged.

Okay, so, the enemy has spotted me.

He was a red-and-brown splotch against a white background and the nearest cover was about two thousand feet straight down. Nothing he could do about that. Come what may. Otto hunched against the cloak and dug in and stepped up and began the next shelf of the trail.

At least this leg of the trip was a bit more interesting. He had a better view of river lands and ocean and had the company of the Fallen, which kept its distance but also its position.

Kind of entertaining in a way, this expectation of instant death. The Fallen will eventually get hungry enough to come down and snack on my liver and, well, that would be an exciting few seconds.

Not that the thing would get much sustenance from Otto's dehydrated husk, which was equivalent to a stick of beef jerky or something. Man, he could use a stick of beef jerky right now. Otto looked at the Fallen, hoping it read his mind and dropped him a Slim Jim. No such luck.

Okay. That's it, getting dark, time to turn in for the night. Motel 6, or, more accurately, Snow Cave 5, we'll leave the lights on.

Otto took a long last survey of the river valley, gripped the spear shaft and turned back around towards the incline ...

Where the Fallen stood.

He was too tired, too numb, too cold, and too beaten to react much.

"Of course," was all he could muster; that, and maybe gripping the haft a little tighter.

The Fallen stood about five yards away, in front of the snow overhang Otto had intended to excavate. It stared at Otto with more simple regard than anything, its pale gray eyes jutting between its pale gray-to-almost-white shoulder-length hair. Didn't look hostile. At least, it wasn't baring its fangs preparatory to driving them into Otto's neck. Wings folded, it was dressed in the standard uniform: crossed leather belts over a bare chest, gray, tight slacks of some kind, the fairy boots. And the sword.

Don't forget the sword.

They stared at each other a long enough moment for the sun to shift and the light to lessen.

"Make it quick," Otto said, closed his eyes and turned his head to allow for easier decapitation.

He heard the slow drawing of metal from the scabbard and braced.

Okay, Lord, ready or not, and in a fashion, I find utterly ridiculous after the last few month's ridiculousness, here I come.

Otto opened his eyes at a sound which wasn't the hiss of steel through air and thwack of blade against bone. No, it was the sound of digging.

Otto widened his eyes. The Fallen had its back to him, digging into the snowbank with the sword.

A bit unexpected.

Otto considered a couple of immediate possibilities. One, run away. "Where" wasn't important; as far up or down the path as quickly as his exhausted and rag-footed body could get. 'Course, the Fallen had only to unfold wings and be on him in seconds but maybe the Fallen would be so amused by his pathetic attempt it would laugh itself to death. Two, drive the spear haft right through its shoulder blades.

Ha. It is to laugh.

Otto lacked the strength to do much more than scab the thing, and would end up facing an annoyed, sword-wielding Fallen.

So, three, simply watch.

He did. Quietly. Without any speculation as to what the

Fallen was doing, although it looked suspiciously like preparing a grave.

Don't think so, though.

First, the Fallen, being the Joe Pesci of creation, would make Otto dig the grave. Second, if it were a grave, the Fallen would have already killed him by now because, really, if you're Joe Pesci, why dig a grave when your victim can do it? Third, the Fallen didn't bother with graves. They'd simply leave Otto's hollowed-out corpse by the side of the trail.

About ten minutes later, the Fallen straightened up, turned around, regarded Otto, and stepped out of the way.

A snow cave. A really nice one.

Otto blinked. The Fallen blinked back, then stepped to the edge of the trail and disappeared over the side, out of sight. Otto waited a moment to see if it came back — it didn't — then squatted and peered inside.

Yep. Roomy and deep and very nice, especially with that merry little fire dancing inside a small depression about halfway up one wall.

A fluttering behind him announced the Fallen had returned. Otto tensed for the long-expected decapitation but all the Fallen did was step past him, carrying an armful of evergreen boughs. Otto stayed in position as it went inside the cave, emerging moments later.

Otto looked.

A bed.

The Fallen stared at him and then made a welcoming gesture at the cave entrance.

"You're kidding, right?" Otto said.

The Fallen paused and made the same welcoming gesture, with a little impatience to it this time.

Otto said nothing, just sat there non-plussed. Did this thing seriously believe he was going to let himself be sealed alive inside a snow cave, albeit a real nice one? Granted, it did seem like a lot of trouble when all it had to do was throw him off the side of the mountain, but there's a principle here.

The Fallen waited a moment more, apparently lost patience, shrugged, and flew away.

Otto remained in position, halfway certain the Fallen and his buddies were laughing themselves silly behind some outcropping and would return momentarily to make him an Ottokabob. The sun touched the mountainside and the shadows fell and it was noticeably colder. Otto waited well past any kind of propriety, shrugged at where the Fallen had flown off, and climbed inside.

Four-star accommodations, these.

Warm, first of all. The fire was a large candle that looked like it would burn for days, giving off a very pleasant incense, almost like sandalwood. Reminded Otto of high school. All he needed was a doobie and a box of Ellio's pizza. The boughs were springy and fragrant and he slowly rolled over on his back and settled in and let out a long sigh of relief.

Man, that's good.

He blinked at the smooth snow ceiling as warmth seeped into him.

Perhaps now is a good time to puzzle over the Fallen's extraordinary behavior but, you know? Let's do that in the morning.

He slept.

Chapter XXI

Tantalus

Very well, in fact.

Otto hadn't woken this refreshed since ... when? A power nap in his condo in the City? No, doesn't count because waking refreshed was a benefit of the place, like HBO. Had to be sometime when he was still alive so, let's see, maybe during those three or four days he'd been right smack in the middle of the Philippine Revolution and ended up in Hawaii with the Marcos family and got relieved by Secret Service and went to the Q and fell, fully dressed and unwashed, right into a cot and did not wake up for twelve straight hours.

Yeah, that.

Otto stretched, pulling up short as his back burns registered protest, and settled for doing one limb at a time. Still toasty warm in here, the candle having burned only halfway down. Funny how so small a flame could produce so much heat. Insulating properties of snow, he guessed.

And of evergreens because, whoa, this was one comfortable bed. Maybe I should roll over and do another twelve.

Places to go, stuff to do.

Otto sighed and tested each limb again and slowly sat up, noting he was quite short of the ceiling.

Good work, Fallen.

He worked his way up to standing and, yep, still had a couple of inches clearance. Looks like the Fallen had measured him, see if he fit inside a crockpot.

Speaking of food ...

His stomach let off a rumble sufficient to start an avalanche and Otto halfway seriously braced, expecting the cave to collapse.

Chuckling, he patted his stomach and said, "Down, boy. Let me get you a drink."

He scraped at the wall but it was packed so tight he couldn't get a real handful.

Good job, Fallen.

He went outside and straight into blinding sunlight and snow. Almost noon, given the sun's position overhead, giving evidence of a twelve-hour sleep cycle; that is, if this planet's rotation was divided into twenty-four-hour-long cycles. Could be an hour and a half, which meant he'd slept even longer than twelve hours. Earth hours, that is. Squeezing his eyes tight, Otto opened them in increments until he had adjusted to the brightness.

There was a package at his feet.

Otto stared at it. A very nice package; someone had made an extra effort. A rectangle of beige paper, rather thick, almost like parchment, with both ends flattened and sealed like an envelope. Looked about the size of a brick. Looked like ...

A Meal Ready to Eat, known in military parlance as an MRE.

"No way," he said, then stooped and gingerly poked the envelope with a good finger, halfway certain it would explode and immediately yanking back but not because a fuse lit. Because the package was hot.

"*Ow!*"

Did that mean the fuse had ignited and the resultant C4 explosion was going to spray him all over the landscape? Otto gritted his teeth and waited to become so sprayed, but nothing blew. Carefully, with several accompanying yelps, Otto pulled at one of the sealed ends. It came apart easily and steam rose out of it, along with an amazing aroma of jasmine rice and soy sauce and teriyaki salmon.

Yep, an MRE. As prepared by White House chefs.

The perfume of cooked food enveloped him, short-circuiting every sense he had — except for raging, insane hunger — and Otto collapsed, almost falling back into the cave.

Oh, man!

He'd probably ingested 4-500 calories from the smell alone. Struggling back to a sitting position, Otto pulled the open packet to him, some of the rice and sauce spilling out. A fork stuck out of the end and he seized it, tines covered in bits of rice and fish and he held it up almost in worship.

"Breakfast is served!" he crowed to the air.

Who served it?

Otto stopped. Good question. He hadn't seen or heard a vendor truck pull up, but he had a pretty good idea who'd delivered. Looking up, Otto searched the cloud line and, bingo.

The Fallen was up there, drifting in and out of sight.

Otto's stomach performed backflips and high fives but Otto held position. This unbelievably wonderful meal was provided by the Fallen. Where was the last place a Fallen had offered you refreshment?

Why, on the banks of the River Lethe.

And what had been the result of accepting said Fallen's hospitality?

Ooh! Ooh! Teacher! Teacher! I know this one!

He'd lost Amelia, Virgil, the shuttle Charon. He'd nearly died of space exposure (and that while still in his City body). Most of the crew lost to the swarming Fallen, Akiko finishing off the ones they'd left, and he'd lost the ship as it plunged into the valley back there, which led to him shivering and starving over a river valley right here. And he'd lost the dogs.

All from a drink of water.

Otto worshipped the food bits on the fork.

Oh my God, it smells so good. It looks so good.

His now-screaming stomach demanded satisfaction. The teriyaki would fuel him and refresh him and strengthen him and he'd stride forth from the ice cave laughing at cold and starvation, pitching the spear haft away because it was superfluous as he, in power and joy, traversed the mountain and made his way to the Hall of the Mountain King.

Where he will serve for the rest of eternity.

A coldness crept up Otto's spine, one different from the snow and ice. The cold of lost souls.

Slowly, Otto pushed the fork into a bit of the snowbank until it was all the way in. He stared at the package for long moments, then reached back into the cave and fumbled around until he found the spear haft and pulled it out. He used that to haul himself up and stood over the still-steaming package, regarding it.

He weaved in and out of the odor, inhaling as much as he could before he pushed the package into the cave with the end of the haft. Then, driving the rod into the snow, brought the cave down on top of it.

About halfway through this, it occurred to him that maybe he should have grabbed the candle but, nah. He patted the snow down with his hands until it was nice and packed.

Okay. Should some polar bear need a snack, it can dig into the freezer.

His stomach jumped out of his body and on top of the snowbank, gaping at him in utter astonishment. "Are you nuts?" it yelled.

"No," Otto responded, "Wary."

"That was a MEAL! An actual, honest-to-God meal! You idiot!" his stomach leaned at him in outrage.

"True." In measured tones. "But I'm not interested in selling my birthright for a mess of pottage."

His stomach expressed utter contempt. "A Biblical reference. How nice. And when was the last time you actually *read* the Bible, jackass?"

Otto thought. Been awhile.

"Some things stay with you," he finally said. And he hoisted himself out of the snowpack, using the haft to keep his balance.

His stomach said a few choice things about Otto's lineage — which was funny because, dude, where exactly did you come from? — and then it jumped back inside, grumbling and rumbling the whole time. Otto didn't blame it. A stomach has a single-track mind.

A shadow fell across Otto and he looked up. The Fallen was about thirty feet above him, circling, surprise on its face. Otto waved.

"Thanks for the cave," Otto called, "Good work. The boughs and candles were an especially nice touch. And thanks for the breakfast, but I'm not feeling it." He paused. "Not at all."

The Fallen looked at him with incredulity, shook its head, and flew off. Otto grabbed a handful of snow, swallowed it, measured the trail, and set out.

Chapter XXII

Terra Incognita

Five more nights in the Fallen's snow caves. Five very comfortable nights with sandalwood candles and evergreen boughs and a wonderful MRE, fresh and steaming in its parchment package, waiting for him at the cave's entrance every morning. And every morning Otto and his stomach got into an argument as he shoved the MRE into the cave and buried it while his stomach, and the Fallen, looked at him like he was crazy. Then, he set off.

Today, the sixth of this trek, he was beginning to think both of them were right: he was crazy.

He was high up the mountain's shoulder by now, the trail remaining fairly flat and walkable but at a constant incline, a calorie-eating upward movement. Guess he'd lost about fifty pounds on this trip, his body consuming whatever reserves were stored hither and yon, including those around his stomach. Now when said stomach jumped out and berated him, it looked like an old dried-up purse. Otto had the good taste not to mention that, even though he found that amusing.

You ain't a stomach, you're a saddle.

His headache had taken on Jurassic proportions and was, even now, stalking the inside of his cranium looking for food.

So was Otto, for that matter.

"Uhm," his stomach piped up, "there's really no need to look. That bat-wing thing leaves a good meal every morning. A really, really good one. You idiot."

Otto held up a hand. "Let's not start this again, okay? I have more important things to consider, such as, evidence of insanity."

"You're talking to your stomach," said his stomach. "And your stomach is answering. You even *see* me. Case closed, your Honor."

Otto had to admit that was airtight.

He looked down the mountain. The view had gotten better and better with each switch of the trail, each crossing of a shoulder. He was now back on the shipwreck side and had a clearer idea of the geography. Definitely a coastal plain.

The river on the other side of the mountain actually touched the upper part of the shipwreck valley, which was dotted with lakes and ponds. How many of those pre-existed the thousand-year rain, Otto didn't know, but the river was the bracelet and the lakes were the necklace, jeweled and shining with the different colors of the changing light: sapphires in the morning, diamonds at noon, and rubies at sunset.

The knolls ran out of sight to a grayish horizon that glowed and burned in sunset, magnificent thunderheads rising above them and Otto concluded there must be another set of mountains below the horizon causing updraft and subsequent storms. That much of 8th-grade science he remembered.

So, best conclusion, he was on the coast of a continent very akin to Antarctica, if not actually Antarctica, which Otto was more than halfway convinced it actually was. He had no specific feature identifying it as such, but there was a feel to this place.

A loneliness.

A forgotten place of legend, known but rarely visited save for the occasional scientist or adventurous tourist or starving mortal bent on finding answers to the riddles of the universe. It was light and dark, the purity of ice and snow covering the death of rock and sand where nothing grew, nothing, as void and lifeless as the Gobi.

With air conditioning.

It was stark and beautiful, a confrontation, a fence; a place where humanity could not thrive, could only make incremental forays before the nature of it drove them away. It proved that humanity was limited to the places God allowed, while His other things, far beyond our ken, ranged the entire cosmos.

There, there be dragons.

Otto looked up. On schedule, the Fallen careened in and out of the cloud line, which was much closer now. Otto saw the Fallen's baffled expression.

He chuckled. Can't blame you, dude. I'm willing to use your very fine snow shelters, but not a morsel of your very fine cooking. Why is that, you ask? Well, I can always build my own shelter, you're just providing a convenience, so I don't feel like conditions and caveats regarding my immortal soul are involved. But I'm not sure I can overcome the effects of your solid food equivalent of the River of Forgetfulness. Could be a difference without meaning, but we humans are a stiff-necked lot, aren't we?

Yes, we are.

Otto gazed over the valley again, trying to locate the shipwreck but was unable. Fitting. Humans are blind to the vehicle of their folly. Who else but humans would reject perpetual comfort to fling themselves across the void, confronting dragons, and death, and loneliness? All because we are unsatisfied with the stock answers, with the way things seem. We want to know why.

"Why" is the most powerful question in the universe.

Which makes humans the most powerful beings in the Universe.

"Careful," Otto whispered to himself, "you're dangerously close to heresy. And no one expects the Spanish Inquisition."

Otto braced for Cardinal Ximenez, but nothing. That's because it wasn't heresy. Even God has limits, that whole "make a rock even He can't lift" meme. Humans, though, could make such a rock. They had done so, time after time. It was the power of the lesser; inherent weakness made humanity invulnerable.

Because we are Proof. It's why the Firsts sought our destruction back in the days we were mud, why the Fallen seek our oblivion in the waters of forgetfulness, why all the higher orders (of which Otto suspected there were legion) furiously opposed humanity's quest for the elusive Father, the Creator, the

Source. If we find Him, if we stand before Him and ask the most powerful question in existence — Why? — then the orders are undone. Because there is more to existence than mere existence, higher orders. And your defiance of that condemns you.

Life seeks, it does not rest.

Seek, then.

Otto bent to the haft and pulled himself along, struggling up the bank and onto the trail. It was steeper here, the view now much shorter, a close horizon over which the trail crossed and disappeared. So, he was at another shoulder and another aspect of this Antarctica of billions of years ago or billions of years from now, or, the present but sitting in a side dimension. Maybe a mix of all three. He gazed back down the mountainside one more time at the valley of shattered ships and lost crews and the end of childhood and hunched his way over the top.

Took a while. The angle was tougher and Otto had to spend most of his time watching his step. Last thing he wanted to do was tumble down a few thousand feet and start this hike all over. Because he would.

He'd have to.

Life seeks.

The sun was with him this time, since he was on the shipwreck side, and he was snow blind inside an hour.

That's fine.

It forced his concentration on where he was going, not what lay below. So he became instantly alarmed and puzzled when the light changed into something else.

Torchlight.

Otto stopped and rubbed his eyes and leaned on the haft and looked up. The cloud line was a mere thirty or forty feet away, draped like a gauzy curtain at the very bottom of a set of steps flanked by two giant torches.

The Hall of the Mountain King.

"Lucy," he whispered, "I'm home."

A wave of relief and exhaustion swept through him and he settled to his knees. Weary, so weary. The journey of a thousand miles does not end with the final step but with a sense that he'd done about all he could do and it would really be nice if a reception committee marched out about now, hoisted him onto a sedan chair and carried him, triumphant, into the Mountain King's presence. He'd get a portion from the King's table and the two of them'd quaff ale horns and throw them into the fireplace and roar nonsensical Viking phrases.

Heck, Otto would settle for the Spanish Inquisition about now.

No one came out, though, and Otto concluded this would be exactly like everything else: he'd have to do it himself, because if ya want a job done right, yadda yadda.

He examined the steps, that is, what he could see of them. The torches — giant wrought-iron contraptions of rod and basket, the flames burning from some kind of pitch attached to a center core, dancing and roaring in the wind — were placed next to the first set of steps and did an excellent job illuminating the next three or four, but not much beyond that. The cloud cover was too thick.

If he wanted to see more, he'd have to mount. The last time he'd mounted obscure steps, though, his horse had plummeted down a crevasse. Since there was no horse available, he'd be the one doing the plummeting.

Is it, then, better to stay right here?

Didn't get all dressed up for nothin', dude.

Otto blew out a very long preparatory breath while idly tracing the trail, which continued, but Otto saw where it hawked back sharply and ended at the bottom of the steps.

He could forgo the remainder and cut straight across but that seemed like cheating, so he hafted the snow and, about twenty minutes later, was there.

Still nothing much to see, despite the better angle, and Otto turned and looked back down the valley. The village, the keep, the crevasse, the valley of skulls, all fading in the fading daylight.

"Goodbye," Otto said, and mounted.

Chapter XXIII

That's One Small Step

At first, Otto expected the Fallen to swoop down and block his path, hand resting on its sword as warning, but the guy disappeared the moment Otto hove in sight of the torches. Otto supposed it had flown to the top of the stairs, waiting to receive him, offer a bottle of wine and a sack of salt, then eviscerate him and eat him — well-salted — chasing it all down with the wine. Which, given its ministrations of the last six days, was out of character, which, in itself, was uncharacteristic.

Don't worry about it.

The clouds thickened as he climbed until the torches reduced to orange spots behind him and Otto was sure he would walk right over a cliff and right to where Flicka had gone, but, quite abruptly, the clouds thinned into a merely annoying fog and Otto was at the first landing.

The only landing, that is.

Otto halted on a concrete platform flanked by two stone lions. Not the African and New York City library sort but the Chinese kind, all mythical and over-carved and both roaring and striking out with paws. Otto eyed them for a moment, expecting them to animate and eat him but they stayed stone. Before him, the landing became a plaza, a giant brazier in the middle, also lit but the flame was quieter, even though it was as bright as the torches. And behind it …

A Buddhist temple.

"Are you kidding me?" Otto said.

But, the temple didn't chuckle and say, "Hey, c'mon, having some fun here," and morph into a mead hall or castle or something. It remained Buddhist.

A simple temple, not one of those elaborate ones lording over mountaintops all over Asia. Plain, the corners curving up to a tiled roof, the front wall a pale, unadorned, blank slate with two shuttered windows set on each side of massive doors of dark, shellacked wood. A temple bell, intricately carved with ideograms that looked suspiciously Chinese but could be Elvish for all Otto knew, sat before the entrance, grayish in the mist. Must be the doorbell.

So, let's ring it.

Slowly, holding the haft more for protection than balance, Otto approached, watching for ambush, but nothing moved. The bell reminded him of those he'd seen hanging from tori gates in temple courtyards in Korea, round and brass with clappers but sometimes with a log striker suspended next to it on a cable. No such striker here, not even a clapper, so no apparent way to ring it.

Convinced this was a bad idea, Otto hit it with the haft.

A low tone, undramatic, pleasing but it hardly rang throughout the town square. Otto was wondering if he should hit it again, harder this time, when the wooden doors creaked and cracked and slowly swung open. He moved into combat stance but no one emerged. Light did, though, warm and pleasing and quite unthreatening, the very kind of peaceful light one expected from a mountaintop Buddhist retreat.

"If there's some guy in there wearing a sarong and sitting in a lotus position and ready to tell me the Meaning of Life, I'm really going to be pissed," Otto muttered. "Unless it's George Carlin. Then it'll be funny."

The mist remained, as did the cold, but he didn't feel either anymore because he felt something else: expectation.

Something awaited him. Something important. Otto didn't think it was the throne room, but it *was* a point of departure.

Wheels turned, gears lining up, machines set in motion, all requiring a key in a lock and a twist to the side.

I am the key.

"Pretty full of ourselves, aren't we?" Otto whispered to the threshold.

But, no, he wasn't and he didn't mean it in any self-important manner. It was …

Mere progression.

Things had advanced to the point where he was about to enter the mountain fastness of Daruma or somebody else of that stature. And it didn't have to be Otto who entered. It could have been any human, such as Marc, Ferd, Amelia, even Tac.

Claudia.

"Should be her," Otto whispered again.

Really, of all the people who had started this journey, she was the most deserving. She had been brutalized on behalf of God, and had been waiting for thousands of years longer than Otto had even been alive to see Him. 'Course, that required her endurance of the thousand-year rain, the slog through the valley of skulls and a little polite conversation with Belial, but she could handle it. She was a lot tougher than him.

So, why me?

Because any human would do. Any.

"Won the lottery," he concluded.

It was that simple. He had stopped at 7-Eleven to get some coffee and, on a whim, bought a Scratch-off and tossed it on the passenger seat and forgot about it and found it a couple of days later and took a nickel to it and, lookee lookee, a million dollars. Just the way things worked out.

A key is shaped from blank metal. The metal, itself, is nothing special.

Let's unlock the universe, then.

Or, let's not.

Otto dithered. The beauty of it, he could dither as long as he wanted. No one was going to come out and escort him inside.

Uh uh.

This was a goin'-of-your-own-free-will type of situation, and it was irrevocable. This was a threshold eternally crossed.

He did not think it was cosmologically momentous — the universe did not hold its breath — but something of serious import would begin.

That is, if he went inside.

Sure you want to do that?

Otto wasn't. From the moment he'd snap-decided to scramble aboard the ship at Claudia's urging, this whole adventure had been sort of a lark. Even when all the serious crap happened, like the Fallen killing most of the crew, it was only a movie: Indiana Jones, Errol Flynn swinging through the masts while the bullets flew, exciting and fun and dangerous but not quite real. It may not even *be* real. He still wasn't sure if all this was nothing more than the coma-induced ravings of a brain let loose from its inhibitions.

But if he walked into the temple, it would be a levelling up.

He did not chuckle at that. Some references applied universally, whether he became a Master Assassin seeking out the Borgia on an X-Box or became the catalyst for changing the nature of man's relationship with eternity. There is a point where everything is different, the challenges more difficult, the assurance of success less assured. Because he could fail. And if he did, so did all of mankind.

You want that kind of responsibility?

"What the hell are you talking about?" he asked himself. "Where is this coming from?"

Really, where?

No one had handed him a scroll sometime in the past few weeks showing the entrance to the Lonely Mountain, and he did not take it upon himself to waken Smaug and acquire the ring. He had died. He had woken. He had questions, so he went to ask them. He did not do so on behalf of mankind; mankind could ask its own questions.

But, you are a key. Adam took the apple. Caesar crossed the Rubicon. Washington took command of a rebel army. They were keys. Keys turn.

Otto considered the temerity of comparing himself to Caesar and Washington but acknowledged the principle. One person does something, and everything changes for everyone.

Cross that threshold over there, bucko, and everything

changes. For everyone.

How do you know that? he asked himself.

C'mon, himself snorted back.

Good answer.

Seriously, c'mon. All roads are leading up the side of a mountain and into a Buddhist temple. Do you seriously think it's going to be a side quest?

Otto wavered, wondering if he should decline the challenge. Let things be. Go back to the valley and rebuild the cabin if it wasn't already rebuilt, gather the dogs, enjoy an eternity with them. Leave the changing of the universe to someone better.

He strode across the plaza and through the doors.

Chapter XXIV

There Is No Dana Only Zuul

Warm. And bright.

Otto rose on his toes and let out a long, "Aaaaah!!"

Wow, was this nice.

Cold flowed up his spine and out of his skull, so happy to be free, gripping Otto in violent shivers as it departed. He folded into himself, closing his eyes and letting the sudden warmth permeate. His hands tingled with renewed circulation and his cheeks turned back into flesh and he was human again.

Central heating: one of the benefits of civilization.

He was still hungry, though.

Wonder if there's a White Castle anywhere close by?

Otto opened his eyes and looked but nope, no castle, no sliders, no salad bar, instead, a long golden hallway. Not completely golden; the floor consisted of pale gray stone tiles stretching to a left-hand turn and continuing around it. The right-hand wall was a series of wooden supports and cross-hatches very reminiscent of old German houses, with what looked like pale gray mud plastered in between. The left wall leading to the turn was a series of golden panels so rich and burnished, they had to be actual gold. The panels shimmered with a diffuse light, the source of which Otto could not identify. Maybe they were self-illuminating.

The panels were deeply etched, with scenes in an odd combination of Hindu and Japanese styles of such extraordinary detail that Otto had to step back to take them in.

The panel closest to him depicted a circular wave of creatures or gods so alien Otto did not know if they were beast or demon, all engaged in various activities from eating to fighting to sleeping and, yes, fornicating, all around a central point of extreme brightness that Otto realized had been painted onto the gold. It was a diffuse center point with no figures discernible inside it. Otto scrutinized the surrounding monsters.

The one below the bright spot could be a thousand-eyed First, while the four beings either side of it, engaging in what looked like a friendly wrestling match, might be the creatures whose skulls littered the Valley of the Keep. Others were clearly the same angels — or whatever — that had escorted the crew from the ship to the Pearly Gates. The genus of the remaining monsters, though, Otto had no clue. They were of a form similar to the angels, but corrupted, like mutants.

Otto involuntarily shied away from them.

He slowly walked down the first panel, fascinated by the drawings and trying to figure out what all this represented, reaching the second panel after a few minutes, which stretched down the middle portion of the hallway and was of a different character altogether. It was a landscape, still in the same Hindu/Japanese style, but richer.

Otto sensed color in the gold: blues, reds, and purples meshing into a long, long valley ringed by snow-capped mountains, the same bright spot from the first panel still the center point of this work but now distant. Clouds surrounded the bright spot and swept over the valley like a vortex in some old sci-fi movie.

There was something darkly ominous about the valley and Otto frowned, inexplicably wary.

A river ran across the scene from left to right, patches of what looked like willows here and there. Indistinct figures stood on either side of the river, regarding each other. Otto couldn't tell what they were, but they seemed more human, or humanlike, than the things in the first panel.

Otto continued his slow walk of scrutiny, following the river and trying to discern enough details about the figures to decide if they were kinsmen or not, when he abruptly reached the third, and last, panel, and an abrupt change of subject.

The City.

Otto took in the panel.

Yep, the City.

Its glorious towers of diamond and crystal and ruby all piled up, layer upon layer fading away to that same bright spot as in the other two panels, although this spot was larger, actually stretched across the entire panel and silhouetted the buildings. Roads led everywhere, and the intensity of detail was so complex that Otto could have spent several days picking out features of balcony and window and storefront and park and, eventually, his own condo.

Except there was something so starkly wrong about the place that Otto went from wary to alarmed.

The City was empty.

No one walked the streets. No one sat on balconies. No joyous parade of vehicles along the park, no Ian and George pulling their carriage along in the hopes of snagging a fare, no Ferdinand standing with great satisfaction in front of his shop of many textures. William Godwin was not polishing the windows of his extraordinary bookstore, nor was Grendel's rocking to the beat of an Irish jig. No one was there.

No one.

Otto moved back, eyes narrowing suspiciously. "What the hell is this?" he said.

A City devoid of people. Maybe it was the pre-City, what the place looked like before the first humans came strolling in some 35,000 years ago or so.

No, that's not right.

Jakto had told him the City he entered around 1200 BC was vastly different from its current incarnation, mostly stone and Assyrian type buildings, until the Romans showed up and took over City planning. Otto had the impression Jakto's City was more plain and forest with the occasional ziggurat breaking up the view than bustling metropolis. So this couldn't be the pre-City. It was of a different nature altogether.

A wish.

Otto frowned. Someone dreamed of a City empty of its

humans, and had carved a panel to reflect that.

Who, or what, wished such a thing?

"The Suits," Otto breathed and looked wildly up and down the hallway, expecting a squadron of those melon-headed Nosferatu, Brooks-Brothers-wearing crapheads to come charging around the corner and rip him apart, as they'd tried to do to him so many times in the City. And here he was without a lance. Or a halberd. But, nothing moved and he relaxed.

Maybe not Suits. They hadn't shown any hostility to humans per se, only to *certain* humans who had the temerity to reject the grace of God's City and go on a half-baked quest across the deserts to join a crew of malcontents bent on launching a half-baked rocket into the ether.

Latchemondy had called the Suits a faction, not enemy, which implied Suits believed humans had a place in eternity's hierarchy but it was limited to living and working and enjoying the City. Nowhere, and nothing, else. Humans shouldn't get up on their high horses, or on rockets, but they shouldn't be exterminated, either.

The Fallen, then? Otto wasn't sure they had the brainpower to yearn for a human-less City. They're more like drones than anything.

Which left the Firsts.

Otto stepped farther back until he was in the middle of the tile floor and could scrutinize each panel in turn.

All right, what was he looking at here? The first panel, let's call that Creation. The bright light in the middle was the Big Bang, the First Cause, the Un-moved Mover. God. From which (or from Whom), on whim sprang forth the Universe and the angels and the devils and the Firsts.

No, wait, that was wrong; devils came later. Angels and Firsts and, judging from the pictures, some other creatures that Otto had not yet had the pleasure of meeting.

He shuddered. Like to forgo that, if possible.

The second panel ... Garden of Eden? Maybe not specifically, but it did depict the emergence of the mud people, which was not a happy day on the Firsts' calendar. At least, according to Akiko.

That brings us to number three and the human apocalypse,

which, according to Akiko, was a Firsts' wet dream.

Put the entire package together and Otto reached the unhappy conclusion that this temple belonged to the Firsts, making it a rather unwelcoming place for errant mud creatures.

And him without a Contender.

Otto saw the left-hand turn off the hallway from here. It was also brightly lit, but that could be the glow of a thousand-eyed First, its mouth wide open and salivating at the prospect of some human meat. So, prudence dictated that he, quietly and forthrightly, backpedal out of this hallway and across the plaza and down the mountain and rebuild the cabin and find the dogs and Let Well Enough Alone.

Don't know anybody named Prudence. And Otto didn't take dictation.

Cautiously, Otto slipped up to the third panel, giving it one long and annoyed look.

"Bite me, Firsts," he sneered which, upon reflection, was a poor choice of words. He slid along, taking his time to reach the corner. Even more slowly, he peeked an eye around it.

And gasped.

At the solid wall of Fallen who stood there, all looking at him.

"Crap!" Otto yelled and whipped back, slamming against the third panel. He squeezed his eyes shut and braced for a thousand or so talons to reach around and strip off his skin.

But, nothing.

Otto stood like that far past the moment it became silly then opened his eyes, but no Fallen waited there, ready for dinner. He slid down the panel a bit in a laughable evasive maneuver and did another quick looksee.

Yep, wall of Fallen, still there, still looking at him.

Hastily, he pulled back and pressed against the panel, trying to make himself invisible.

I think they know you're here, bud.

Otto blew out an exasperated breath. All right, thirty seconds left, fourth down, thirty yards to go. Can't punt. He leaned off the panel and boldly walked around the corner and stopped in the middle of the hall.

"You want me, come and get me," he said to the Fallen, and

spread his arms belligerently.

They didn't. Instead, the wall of Fallen stared at him impassively. The moment stretched past the point of being sillier. Otto lowered his hands and cleared his throat. "Uhm, boys?" he said. "What are we doing here?"

A ripple in the back of the crowd became a wave and suddenly the wall parted as the Fallen stepped to either side of the hallway, forming ranks facing each other. As they unfolded, Otto saw past them to a distant chamber, a rather large one.

Large? No: *huge*, could be a nave in Belial's keep. Wonder if said demon was down there somewhere, steaming — no pun intended — and ready to flay some Otto? Otto gathered himself to flee, but nothing moved down there.

From this perspective, the far chamber resembled the Viking feast hall Otto had originally expected. It was all dark wood paneling and monster crossbeams jutting here and there, with monster torches blazing here and there as well. The center wall had some very intricate silver symbol carved in it that had to be fifteen or twenty feet across for it to be so clear. Looked like a Celtic knot.

Does that mean a druidic feast awaited him down there, honey and bread and ribs and roasts? Oh boy!

The last row of Fallen finally stepped aside and Otto eagerly craned his neck to spot the anticipated banquet table groaning under tons of food and drink and ...

No banquet table.

Not even a sideboard.

Instead, there was a chair; more accurately, a throne, tall and regal and set upon a silver dais directly underneath the silver knot, with a red upholstered high back rising to what looked like two silver spear points above the seat. And seated there ...

Some guy.

Otto peered at him, surprisingly able to make out details at this distance. White or maybe Arabic, had that skin tone, a shock of white hair over black eyebrows (which was a bit odd), and dressed in what Otto figured was some kind of royal tunic, a one-piece, also white. Sprawled in the seat, one leg draped over a throne arm, foot dangling, he gazed rather languidly down the rows of Fallen at Otto, patient and interested.

Otto was suspicious; anyone who commanded a phalanx of Fallen was probably not an immediate friend to mankind, especially someone who decorates his entranceway with friezes depicting mankind's demise. But the Fallen had not fallen on him and the guy looked benign and you're here, so ...

Otto strolled down the honor guard of Fallen towards the throne.

Neck on a swivel, he watched the Fallen carefully, ready to spring into combat should they spring on him. Not that he could do much more than kick one in the shins as they divided him into about forty pieces, but he wasn't going quietly ...

He'd get off at least one good shriek before they ripped his throat out.

The Fallen, at attention, their arms rigid by their sides and well away from their swords, stared at him as he passed but they didn't look hostile. They looked bored. Otto understood that. Standing in formation while some yahoo marched past to meet the general was probably the dullest way to spend an evening. Much rather be eviscerating.

About halfway down, Otto stopped watching the Fallen and concentrated on his host. The guy hadn't moved, his arms splayed comfortably alongside the leg draped over the throne, the other leg planted on a silver footrest, a tiny smile on his face. Nice face, lined and expressive. The guy was maybe forty-five or fifty years old, trim; he worked out. Probably had a membership at Ye Royal Planet Fitness. Several rings of various glittering jewels adorned his fingers, but he had no crown. Odd. A head of state, or head of planet, should be sporting a diadem. Maybe that nice shock of white hair was his crown. Maybe those beetle brows made wearing a real crown impossible. Maybe he should ask.

"Why aren't you wearing a crown?" Otto asked as he cleared the last set of Fallen and stood before the throne, set about six feet higher than the floor. Of course. The ole' "taller than thou" tactic.

The guy chuckled, a deep, sonorous one, and smiled perfect teeth at Otto. "Because I am not a king."

Wow. Guy should be on the radio.

"What a lovely singing voice you must have," Otto said in his best Bill Murray, and then threw his hands out. "But consider, you're sitting on a throne. You have minions" — Otto gestured at the bored Fallen — "and this qualifies as a throne room." Otto flipped "therefore ..." hands.

"Nevertheless," the guy pipe-organed, "I am no king."

"So, what, then? You're the croupier?"

The guy laughed aloud, slapping his hands together in genuine mirth. "You humans!" he crowed. "You are most amusing."

Otto raised an eyebrow. "I'm taking it, then, you are not human."

The guy shook his head. "I am not," and he turned his face. Otto saw the shape of his skull. Something was a little off, like the soldier escorts on the little moon.

"Angel," Otto whispered.

The guy said nothing, regarded Otto quietly.

"Okay," Otto said, after a moment, "Who are you, exactly?"

"My name is Helel ben Shahar," the guy said and inclined his head in greeting.

"Helel? Like halal? Are you Muslim?"

"No," he smiled. "But you may call me Abalisah, if you wish?"

"Abala ... no, that's even harder to say than Helel. Or halal. I want to roll my tongue or something and I never learned how to do that. Spanish guys thought that was hilarious. Can I call you Ben, instead?"

Another incline of the head. "If you wish."

"I wish. I guess you're Jewish, then. With that name."

Ben gave him a cutting look. "We've already established that I am not human."

"Oh, right," Otto shrugged, "Sorry. I'm a little off right now. Could stand a cup of coffee."

Ben raised a jeweled hand at one of the Fallen and it immediately bowed and left the ranks, heading down a corridor that ran left and right behind the throne.

"What?" Otto asked, "He's going for coffee?" He paused. "I'm not sure I want ..."

And Otto could say no more because the aroma of the best coffee ever brewed overwhelmed him as the Fallen appeared at his right hand brandishing a silver serving tray on which sat a lovely white porcelain cup of steamin' joe.

"Oh, my God," he breathed.

Ben inclined a hand. "Your coffee, Otto."

"How did you ... oh, never mind." Otto threw a thumb at the Fallen. "S'pose Belial briefed the help here, so I'm guessing you know all my names, down to the Neanderthals."

Ben pointed at the coffee. "Why don't you drink that and then we'll discuss it?"

Such a gracious gesture, a gracious host.

His hands trembling, Otto reached both to the cup, gently placing his palms around it. Perfectly hot. The steam rose in a cloud, like a jinn seeking its master, curling about Otto's hands and then tickling his nose.

Oh, man. Otto stared at the pure, ebony elixir of life a mere sip away, then looked at the Fallen.

And saw Virgil and Amelia standing by the river, the Fallen giving them a cup. And the blankness, after the two of them drank the waters of forgetfulness.

Otto slammed both hands on the tray, knocking it to the floor where it clattered musically − proof it was silver − the cup shattering and splashing his knees with hot, lovely coffee.

"*Ow*," Otto said.

The Fallen leaped back, at first looking surprised, then its eyes blazed and it snarled and it reached for the sword and Otto figured this was it ...

"Enough!" Ben commanded and the Fallen quailed, stepping back, fear in its eyes.

Fear.

Otto grabbed the spats wrapped around his knee and hurriedly flapped them, trying to cool the hot liquid there. "*Ow! Ow! Ow!*" he whimpered.

Ben watched him coolly. "So," he rumbled, "you refuse my hospitality once more."

"You sent the MREs, didja?" Otto blew at his coffee-soaked cloak. "No offense, but I don't accept provisions offered by your pals here," and Otto made a glance at the Fallen, who remained cowed and trembling.

Ben nodded. "I understand your caution, given the incidents

at the River and all. But I assure you, these provisions are not tainted. I offer them from my own table. If you like, I will taste test them first." And he made a magnanimous gesture.

Otto straightened up. "So, you know about the river as well as my name. Names. You're very well informed."

"I have an excellent intelligence corps," Ben said and looked at the ranks of Fallen.

"That's what they are, huh?" Otto finished dabbing at the coffee and could not help but pause to savor the perfume of it still on his fingers. "I thought they were more like drones."

Ben made a gesture of assent and Otto straightened up. "Okay, let's stop dancing. Who, exactly, are you? Exactly."

Ben gave Otto a little smile and then a long sigh. "I am the same as you, just not human. Created, as you were. And on a quest to solve the riddles of the Universe, as you are."

Otto made exaggerated looks at the throne and at the ranks of Fallen. "This is your idea of a quest?"

Ben chuckled appreciatively. "Right now, I'm on sabbatical."

Otto gave his own appreciative chuckle. "'Sabbatical.' That's good. From what?"

"Saving Creation."

Otto paused and considered that as he wiped more of the coffee on his lips and then looked at Ben. "Ya know, I haven't been running around this Afterlife as long as you. At least, that's what I'm betting. And I've got a sneakin' suspicion that every concept I ever had of the Universe and Creation and just flat-out existence is just flat-out wrong. Downright childish. But I am pretty certain of one thing." Otto paused. "The only Person who can save Creation is God."

Ben nodded, a sad look on his face. "Yes, that is what you think. And you are right, at least in your mind, because it comes from your current conception of existence. And because you have not discovered the truth yet, you cannot be held liable for your current misunderstanding."

Otto snorted. "And what truth is that, Ben, Dispenser of Wisdom?"

Ben leaned forward, the sadness a living thing on his face. "That, simply, there is no God."

Silence.

More from Otto's shock than anything. After a few moments, Otto gave an opinion. "Bullcrap."

Ben sat back, hands out, head cocked in an angle conveying, "Fine, believe what you want," the dismissal of an ignorant child. And Otto, at this moment, felt very much like an ignorant child.

"Let me clarify," Ben said, "There is no God in the way that you think of Him. Of this, I can assure you, and I advise you to consider that yes, you may be operating from several misconceptions. But," Ben raised a finger, "the understanding you need will take much explanation and you are exhausted, you are starving, you are dying of thirst and cold. Please, Otto," and there was a genuine plead in Ben's voice, "accept my hospitality. Eat some bread from my table."

Here Ben produced a loaf of what looked like sourdough French bread, broke off the crust, broke off a piece from that and put it in his own mouth and chewed and swallowed and gestured to show that he was okay, and offered the other piece to Otto.

"Don't," a voice warned in Otto's mind.

He gazed at the bread, so warm, so moist, reached out and carefully took a small piece and ate it.

He was suddenly so very, very tired, far beyond the exhaustion of the trek. A warm, euphoric blackness enveloped him and he felt strong arms gently reaching under his back and even more gently lifting him.

"Rest now," a voice said.

And he did.

Chapter XXV

Finger Bowl On The Right

He was in a bed, a nice one, crimson satin sheets and a crimson throw — with Ben's silver symbol blazoned in the middle — pulled up to his chin. The bed had a firm mattress with enough elevation at Otto's head and back to ease the pains he'd incurred during the trip up the mountain. And before. He felt clean and tingly, downright sterilized, as if he'd been freshly scrubbed and bathed.

Wonder who did that? The Fallen? Worried, Otto probed under the sheets to ensure he was still intact. He was.

The intactness check revealed he was dressed, too, and he lifted the sheets to see in what. Nice PJs, also satin, mauve instead of crimson, with the little silver symbols running all over them. Not exactly his color or style but he'd — obviously — not been consulted. One look at his mountain-climbing ensemble had, no doubt, convinced his dressers that Otto lacked taste.

"Hey," he muttered, "you work with what you got."

Otto dropped the sheets and looked up. A canopy — satin, of course, and crimson, of course — with the expected silver symbol embroidered in the middle.

Wonder what it means?

Otto threw back the sheets and sat up. Nice room. A lovely thick carpet dressed the floor, plush and pale in contrast to the heavy reds and purples of bed and PJs. Someone has some color sense, apparently. The carpet invited a plunging of toes through it, so he wheeled out of the sheets and did so. The bed was a four-poster — duh, else no canopy — made of a dark, luxurious wood, probably mahogany. Paisley print mauve drapes laid on all four corners of it, evidence of more color-coordination. A blanket folded across the foot of the bed, mauve, naturally, very thick and furry, like the blankets Otto used to buy in Korea. Probably a decoration, since the room was warm and the sheets and throw sufficient cover.

The fairly large room had a few pale upholstered footstools scattered here and there. In the wall to his right, was a dark wooden door. Set next to that was a dark wood dresser, with a giant mirror reaching halfway to the ceiling. Otto waved at himself. Wrought-iron chairs sat on either side of the dresser, the silver Celtic knot inscribed in their center bars.

Against the bed was a night table, brass and wrought iron, with a brass lamp and porcelain shade with symbols painted on it. Not Ben's knot, something Otto did not recognize but of a Celtic theme. Otto examined the lamp but could not see a switch of any kind so he had no idea how to light it. Not that he needed to. Plenty of light streamed in through two sets of French doors, one in front and the other behind him, both covered by white sheers.

Curious, Otto stood up, noting a pair of overstuffed beige slippers at the end of the bed next to one of the footstools. He walked around to them and, yep, they fit. He continued around to the front French doors and pulled the sheers aside.

"Wow," he said.

He was on the side of the mountain — or *a* mountain — overlooking the valley, or *a* valley. The mountain was brightly sunlit, the drop plunging quickly into blue shadow and rock and ice, the bottom hidden because of the angle but Otto figured it was a couple of miles straight down.

"Have a nice trip," he said. That old joke.

Looming opposite him was the razor-sharp top of a mountain ridge. It completely blocked what should have been his view of the knolls and hills rolling away from the valley ... Valley of the Shipwreck, Valley of the Skulls, whatever.

Odd.

During his travels up the big mountain to Ben's temple, there'd been no massive mountain range blocking his view of the valley … valleys, whatever. He'd circled the entire mountain at least once and never did he encounter the now very present razor-topped ridge.

Coastal plain and the previously mentioned valley(s) with their bordering knolls, yes; ridge, no.

"Hmm," Otto said. He walked over to the opposite set of French doors, parted the sheers, and looked out.

An ocean.

Way, way down a couple of miles but definitely an ocean, replete with whitecaps and a sliver of a beach. The water glittered in the sunlight as it stretched to the horizon, the waves throwing sparkles back at Otto. Icebergs floated here and there and Otto saw, far to the left, what looked like an ice sheet extending from the shore across the ocean and out of sight.

Funny, during his travels up the big mountain, the ocean had been far away. Now, here it was. Somehow, the mountain − with him on it − had taken a stroll of about twenty or thirty miles and sat down on the edge of the ocean, maybe to do some fishing. And it brought another mountain range along with it. Good thing he'd been asleep because, wow, what a ride that must have been.

Was this still Antarctica?

Otto turned the tasteful brass knobs and stepped through the French doors onto the balcony.

Definitely Antarctica because, man, was it cold!

Otto shivered as he stepped up to the wrought-iron railing and confirmed he was standing above an ocean festooned with ice sheets and bergs that stretched to the horizon and out of view. Good thing he wasn't bothered by heights because, Holy Hannah, was he up here!

He spun about and leaned against the railing and looked up, but the roof of this condo blocked most of what he could see, only parts of the mountain overhanging the balcony and some blue sky beyond it. He could not see the sun, so he must be on a north-south axis. He wondered if the ocean was north, because that meant it bordered the Straits of Magellan.

But if it was south …

What's across the south coast of Antarctica? *Is* there a south coast?

Otto straightened and turned around to look for New Zealand and was immediately eye-to-eye with a Fallen hovering a few feet off the balcony, its bat wings fully extended and fluttering in the wind, its eyes fixed on Otto.

Bit startling, that, and Otto held up a hand. "Don't worry, bub. I have no intention of jumping," he said, made a half bow and hastily stepped back through the French doors and shut them, in case the Fallen decided to follow and make a snack out of him.

Speaking of snacks ...

Otto looked around, expecting a tray of canapes positioned somewhere near the bed, but nothing.

Eh, that's fine, wasn't really hungry.

Wasn't, was he?

Otto frowned. After about two weeks of nothing but snow cones (and those without cherry syrup), he should be ravenous. But no. And that wasn't good because a starving man eventually reaches a point where he no longer feels hungry, usually the point right before dying. But he didn't feel like he was dying (which was silly, given that he was already dead). He felt pretty good, in fact.

All because of a little crust of bread?

Otto held the frown. The little piece Ben had given him shouldn't have eased his hunger this much. If anything, it should have kicked his appetite into high gear, willing to gut and barbecue a Fallen to satisfy it. That was sure some magic bread ...

Manna?

Didn't look like manna, which, based on what he'd read, was some type of white paste, like hominy, that the Israelites gathered from the morning dew.

Yech, but the stuff apparently worked as advertised.

He couldn't remember if the Israelites turned it into loaves of French sourdough bread or not, but supposed it was possible. Whatever, one little bite of it and he was no longer starving, although he did feel a mite peckish.

Could do with a cheese Danish.

Otto glanced around, hoping he'd overlooked something like a small serving cart with cheese Danishes piled on top of it, along with a carafe of that wondrous Fallen coffee. No such luck. Otto looked at the door. Perhaps a buffet waited behind it. Otto walked over and opened it. He whistled.

Nice bathroom.

Roman-bath nice because, heck, it was a Roman bath. The same gray stone tiles as Ben's temple entrance led across the floor to a sunken tile tub the size of an Olympic swimming pool, from which steam rose into the air. A pleasing scent of mint suffused the area. Benches and platforms all over the place, all draped with towels sporting Ben's Celtic symbol, and a raised seat in one corner Otto figured was a toilet. By the way, did he need to use it? Well, no, he didn't.

Dehydration?

Restoration of his immortality?

Otto looked down at his PJs. In seconds, he peeled out of them and stood there, naked, scrutinizing his legs. Still burned, but obviously healing.

Was that due to the Crust of Magic French Manna Bread, or the ministrations of the wolves?

Otto went out of the bathroom and stood in front of the dresser mirror, twisting and turning so he could examine his back.

Yes, also still burned and gouged, badly in places, gonna scar over and be a constant source of itch and stiffness ... except it wasn't.

It didn't hurt at all. Otto threw out his hand. Yes, the little finger was gone, a stump of its former self, but it was pink and covered and quite a cute little thing. No gangrene. No scab. No pain.

Otto stared at himself. He looked good for a guy with third-degree burns all over his body and a missing finger, not to mention Belial-inflicted bruises, a guy who had spent the last few weeks in sub-zero weather shivering in ice caves. And starving to death, let's not forget. He shouldn't look this good. He should look like death warmed over.

Conclusion: immortality was returning. Albeit slowly.

Otto nodded at himself, flexed his arms into a Schwarzenegger pose, and then walked back into the bath. He dipped a toe in the pool and sucked in breath.

Hot. Damn hot. But, when in Rome, or, specifically, a Roman

bath …

Otto eased himself in, laid his head on a built-in head support, and spread out.

"Comfortable?"

Otto, startled awake by the voice, yelped and splashed about, fight-or-flight kicking into action. He regained balance after a moment and looked.

Ben stood by the side of the pool, same white tunic, white hair, and black eyebrows, with a look of amusement on his face, no doubt prompted by Otto's reaction.

"I was," Otto said, "until you scared me half out of my mind."

"Sorry," Ben chuckled, "I thought you heard me come in."

"Nope." Otto shifted to hide his nakedness, wondering how modest he had to be with a non-human. "I was asleep."

In a deep, wondrous sleep, thank you very much, one devoid of dreams but filled, instead, with the sensation of heat and floating. And now, wow, did he feel good, all relaxed and loose, like he'd been given a brand new body.

New body.

Otto stood, modesty be damned, sending a small tidal wave across the pool, staring at his arms and legs and then as much of his back as he could.

The burns, the scars, were all gone.

"I came to invite you to dinner," Ben said.

"You mean breakfast." Otto was still absorbed in his miraculously scar-free self.

He stared at the pool. Healing waters?

"You have slept for two nights and one day and the better part of another," Ben said, "By the position of the sun," Ben made a vague gesture at the roof, "it is the evening meal. But I suppose, if it is your first meal upon waking, it is breakfast."

"You can call it brunch for all I care." Otto said absently, intent on his newness.

"Fine," Ben made a small bow. "Then you will accept my invitation." He paused. "Without reservation?"

Otto looked up. Ben had raised a quizzical eyebrow, quite a feat, given its mass. "No. I mean, yes, I accept. No to any reservations. As long as you guarantee my safety, that is."

Both eyebrows up now. "You mean, from my legions? Then, it is assured." And he made another small bow.

Legions?

Otto shook that away as he considered adding a caveat that Ben, himself, also assured Otto's safety from whatever he — Ben — was. He was certain that Ben could do whatever he wanted to Otto at any time he so chose, without any assistance from the Fallen and without any binding assurance, either. In fact, requiring such an assurance might be an insult so egregious that Ben reflexively sicced his legions on Otto, whose new body would last no longer to a Fallen onslaught than his old.

Maybe he should not poke the bear, so he nodded a careful assent.

"Fine," Ben said again, sounding relieved and making Otto wonder if he could have refused.

What would have happened? Nothing good, most certainly.

"I have taken the liberty," Ben continued, "of providing dinner clothes for you." He swept an arm back at the spa door. Otto saw a Fallen standing at attention next to the bed. "I do think that dinner in formal wear is so ... civilized ... don't you?"

Otto's dinners back on Earth had been mostly in jeans and a T-shirt and in front of the TV, but he had attended a fair share of dinings-out and -in during his career and had to admit there was something elevating about putting on the Ritz and supping with pals.

Ben, though, wasn't a pal.

"Sure," he said, non-committally.

"Good," Ben rubbed his hands together almost gleefully. "When you are ready, come on down." And he turned and walked out.

Down where? Otto felt like asking but, no need, the Fallen will give him directions. Or throw him out of the window so he could glance at the dining room as he plummeted past it to the valley floor.

Otto stepped out of the spa and cast a suspicious glance at the Fallen, but it stood quietly, harmlessly.

All right, take Ben at his word.

Otto moved around the other side, staying out of the Fallen's reach, and examined the clothes on the bed.

A tuxedo. How civilized.

Otto picked up the jacket. No tails, so black tie tonight. Apparently, he didn't rate white tie, but nice all the same. The tux was single-breasted with a shawl collar, satin facing, double vents, faced buttons, and cummerbund instead of a waistcoat. Matching pants, turndown shirt with studs, suspenders, and a pair of Oxfords rounded it out.

Otto chuckled to himself. In some mysterious manner, he had acquired tux expertise while alive that had never really served him until now. Funny how spurious knowledge will sometimes come in handy. Otto carefully placed the jacket and then looked at the bowtie ribbon and frowned. This was the limit of his spurious knowledge because he had no idea how to tie it. He'd always used a clip-on.

Gauche.

Wing it.

Otto dressed, starting with the silk boxers and T-shirt (white, thank God, not crimson. Nor with any silver symbols), relying on racial memory to get pleats and cuffs properly aligned and fastened. He picked up the ribbon. Okay, so, one side obviously has to go over the other ...

A clawed hand snatched the ribbon from him, somehow leaving his fingers and skin intact. The Fallen turned him around by the shoulders and whipped the ribbon around his neck.

This is it, death by bow tie.

Otto tensed in preparation for the coming fight. But the ligature didn't ligate as the talons flurried about his throat and seconds later, the Fallen stepped back. Otto explored his neck but there was no course of blood and he could still breathe so ...

Taking a quick peek at the mirror, Otto saw a perfectly tied butterfly sitting at his throat.

"Thanks," Otto said. He looked at the Fallen's talons. "Pretty deft with those things, ain'cha?"

The creature stared at him. All the better to defenestrate you, my dear.

Otto finished dressing, taking his time, then stood in front of the mirror and admired himself. "Bond," he toned, "James Bond." From a distance, anyway.

Otto turned to the silent Fallen. "You like?" and flourished his hands.

The Fallen said nothing, did nothing, so Otto went back to the mirror for a few more moments of ego-boosting, then said, "Lead on, Alphonse," and gave the Fallen a mock bow.

It strode over and opened the door next to the dresser …

"Uhm," Otto said, "that's the bath …"

And went into a hallway.

Otto, surprised, waited a few moments, then, cautiously poked through the door and stepped into a pale-carpeted and crimson-wallpapered hallway where a Roman bath had once been. The Fallen stood a few feet to his right looking back at him, impatiently.

"One day, you guys are going to have to explain how you do this," he said and followed.

The Fallen led, making a series of lefts and rights at the end of each corridor — of which there were many — until Otto was hopelessly lost. If he'd forgotten his wallet, he'd never find his way back to retrieve it. Speaking of which … Otto checked the jacket pocket but it was empty.

Of course.

It's not like he needed his driver's license or tip money. He hoped.

Otto and his escort inclined downwards and Otto got the impression again of an Escher print. Or, the Tower of Babel. Did Escher do a Tower of Babel?

As Otto was trying to remember what little art history he had ever learned, they came to a set of gigantic wooden doors, dark and heavily lacquered, with two giant brass knobs set in them. They reminded Otto of the gates of Dis, except those were metal. These had scenes of marching armies carved in them from top to bottom, the top set going left, the one below going right, alternating all the way down to the floor.

Otto stepped closer. Yep, the same guys carved on Belial's door, rows and rows of armoured soldiers, except they weren't presenting swords; their swords were sheathed, as were the banners. These guys were intent on wherever they were going.

Otto couldn't tell if this was one army on a long march and each different panel showed how far they'd gone, or several armies going different places.

"Awk Do Hekel Do," Otto whispered.

The Fallen standing beside him started and gave Otto a searching look, then reached over and turned the knobs. The doors slowly opened and Otto braced for whatever the heck was next.

He expected the same Viking-sized hall as Ben's throne room, with torches and crossbeams and banquet tables, but no. It was small, more like the intimate rooms reserved for muckity-mucks in the backs of quality restaurants.

Somewhat incongruous, given the giant doors.

Same dark wood paneling but no giant torches; Japanese lanterns, instead, the paper kind with kanji written all over them (or Elvish or Celt or something pictographic) and spreading a soft glow over the place. Ben's Celtic symbol was inscribed on each wall, but there was no other adornment. Set in the middle of the room was a table covered with a clean white tablecloth, in the middle of which stood a candelabrum suspiciously like a menorah, short candles in each stub giving off more soft glows. Two dinner settings, white china plates with a thin silver rim, several glasses of various sizes tastefully arranged about them with several smaller, silver-rimmed plates spinning out like a porcelain solar system. Crimson napkins lay rolled in the center of the plates with a constellation of silverware, from a teeny tiny fork probably used to chip shrimp out of shells, to others that could well be farm implements, spread from left to right and above, smallest to largest, and intersecting the plates and glasses. Two mahogany chairs, highly polished with crimson upholstered backrests, opposed each other.

Ben sat in the one facing Otto. "Please," he said, gesturing magnanimously, "join me."

Ben wore a tux, too, this one with a peaked lapel which, if Otto remembered his tuxedo hierarchies correctly, was more formal than his own. So, a bit of one-upmanship. Ben did carry the tux with a lot of dignity, though, as if he was born to it. Probably was, proverbial silver spoon — or whatever aliens used to eat soup — in mouth, or tooth-lined opening, or whatever his true alien self looked like.

Otto took a suspicious glance about the room and, yep, a couple of Fallen silently standing in the shadows. Bodyguards.

Or waiters.

Eh, what are you gonna do?

Otto moved to the empty chair. A Fallen intercepted him and pulled the chair out, Otto eying him the entire time but the Fallen made no more aggressive move than pushing the chair back, and then melted into the shadows.

"You have a well-trained staff," Otto observed, rather dryly.

"Indeed," Ben smiled.

"Mind telling me what, exactly, they are?"

Ben waved a hand in dismissal. "In time. First, though," and Ben clapped his hands.

A door opened in the wall to Otto's left, under the silver symbol, and a Fallen carrying what looked like a silver staff walked in, followed closely by four other Fallen, all in line, all in step. The first two Fallen carried napkin-wrapped bottles while the two in the rear bore silver-covered dishes. The baton-Fallen stopped right at the middle of the table, staring straight ahead, the line halting behind him. After a single moment, he rapped the baton on the floor and the bottle bearers performed perfect right-and-left faces and marched to the ends of the table, standing at attention. Another floor rap, and Otto's bottle bearer wheeled to the table and pulled back the napkin, then bowed so the bottle label was at his eye level.

Otto stared at it. The same Celtic symbol, this time in gold leaf. Otto glanced at the Fallen and then across the table at Ben, who was examining his own proffered bottle.

"I take it this isn't Pabst Blue Ribbon," he said.

Ben laughed. "No. It is wine."

"From ...?"

Ben smiled. "Some place very far away. But, it is excellent wine."

"Have to take your word for it, Bennie. I'm a beer man, myself."

"Noted," Ben said as the Fallen poured a small amount of red in Ben's glass. He did some kind of wine tasting ministrations with it, spitting some into a silver bowl produced by his wine-Fallen, and then nodded. Otto's Fallen poured his glass full and then stepped back.

"A toast," Ben said, raising his glass to Otto.

Otto picked up his own. "To what?"

"The course of human events," Ben replied and looked at him expectantly.

Otto held his glass level. "You know how the rest of that goes, right?"

"What do you mean?"

"Well, without exactly quoting the flowery language, it talks about the necessity of a people separating from tyranny."

Ben's smile was warm. "That is why I chose those words."

Otto considered. He did not think Ben and he were talking about the same things, but the sentiment was fine.

Otto shrugged. "Skol." He raised the glass higher, then took a sip. "Umm!" he delivered his verdict. "You're right. This is good."

Ben laughed. "Of course! Nothing but the best for you. Now," and he clapped his hands together gleefully, "let's eat!"

Chapter XXVI

Course Interrupted

The plate-Fallen fell out of line and presented their dishes, pulling off the covers with courtly gestures that should be impossible for talon-bearing, bat-winged monsters, but, done well. Otto's Fallen tilted the plate before him …

Asparagus.

Otto eyed it.

Okay, death by gaggy vegetables, then.

Otto looked at the Fallen, which had raised its eyebrows in expectation. What, did it want him to wax poetic about friggin' asparagus?

"Get real," he said to the Fallen, which stood there, quiet, waiting. For what, Otto had no idea.

At the sound of silverware on porcelain, Otto looked up to see Ben spooning the asparagus onto one of his smaller plates.

Oh. You serve yourself in this restaurant.

Otto picked up what he thought was the right fork but the Fallen frowned, so he hovered over the remaining silverware until the Fallen nodded in approval. Otto grasped it, some kind of spork-looking thing made of silver, and dished out one gaggy vegetable.

Cautiously, he tasted it.

Not bad. Had a nice texture and a vinegary taste.

"Hhm," he said and made short work of the asparagus, noting that Ben did likewise, although he'd taken quite a fair portion from the serving plate. Guy liked his dinner and appeared to know what he was doing, so Otto decided to take cues from him and heaped asparagus on his own dish.

Both Fallen stepped back, re-covering the plates. Ben finished what was left of his and nodded at the baton-Fallen, who stamped the rod. The plate-Fallen stepped back, about-faced, and left the room while the bottle-Fallen charged their wine glasses.

Ben, smiling in approval, raised his glass to Otto. "An excellent first course," he said.

Otto raised his glass in agreement. "It was. And I'm not much of a veggie guy."

Ben nodded. "The chefs can make the most unappealing foods palatable."

"And who are these chefs? Your ... legions?" Otto tilted an eyebrow at the Fallen.

Ben wiped his mouth with his napkin. "They are."

"Okay." Otto took his own napkin off the big plate and followed suit. "So, is the next course cyanide soup, then?"

Ben chuckled. "No, Otto, it is not. You have nothing to fear. I assure you, neither my legions nor I will do you any harm here."

There had to be some qualifiers in that but Otto decided it wasn't a good idea to highlight them. "Okay, take your word for it. Then, why don't you tell me what your legions exactly are?"

"Very well." Ben adjusted his napkin on his lap. "They are the same as us, part of the Created."

Followed by a pause that went on too long and Otto realized this was Ben's complete explanation. At least, without further prompting. "Dunno, Ben," he said, "You don't see a lot of guys like that on Earth. Except maybe in the Senate."

"Ha!" Ben liked that. "Yes, quite. But, of course, they are not of Earth."

"So, you know about the Senate, too." Otto toyed with the wine glass. "Can I conclude that you're pretty well-versed in all things Earth?"

Ben inclined a hand.

"Why is that?"

"Surely you have figured out by now that Earth holds a rather central position in the Universe. And, yes, I know," Ben grinned. "Stop calling you Shirley."

Otto stared at him. "Wow. You can make movie references, too." He paused. "How is that?"

A new pair of dish-Fallen marched in bearing silver tureens.

"Ah!" Ben clapped hands together, a broad smile on his face. "The next course!" Baton-Fallen did his floor rap thing and one of the tureen Fallen presented it to Otto. Thick, creamy soup with steam rising from it, infused with the savor of ...

"Potatoes?" Otto asked.

"Leeks and potatoes!" Ben exclaimed joyfully and dipped a goodly portion into one of his bowls. Otto noted which dipper and bowl Ben used, made a similar selection, and scooped his own. He then waited until Ben selected the proper spoon, grabbed his copy, and took a suspicious taste.

Man, good.

Otto raised the spoon and saluted the Fallen, then fell to.

Ben apparently thought it was good, too, because he took about three bowlfuls in the time Otto finished his one. The Fallen hovered, providing ample opportunities for Otto to refill but he kept himself to one serving. Might have to move rather fast.

"So," Otto interjected during Ben's last spoonful, "getting back to our conversation, what are the Fallen? Species wise, I mean."

Ben raised an eyebrow. "Fallen?"

"That's my word for them."

"And how did you arrive at that?" Ben asked around a mouthful.

Otto gestured at his Fallen. "Well, look at 'em. Wings and hair and stuff, but kinda nasty. Definitely not human. More like what we earthers popularly consider fallen angels."

Ben went still. Dangerously so. Alarm gripped Otto's spine, doubly so as the Fallen leaned a little towards him, eyes glowing. Might have to move rather fast.

Ben stared at him for a moment, then carefully wiped his mouth with the napkin. "'Fallen,'" he said. "Such a ... judgmental word."

Otto blinked. "Come again?"

"It implies a certain viewpoint. The problem with certain

viewpoints," Ben dabbed daintily at his fingers, "is that they are sometimes ill-formed."

"Okay," Otto said, his guard up. "Then tell me why it's wrong."

Ben shrugged. "One man's Fallen is another man's Elect. Next course!" and, hands clapping, he was Ben the Gastronome once again.

As the tureens swept away, Otto fumed. Talking to Ben was like talking to Latchemondy: a lot of circular, double-speak. Nebulous crap that could mean anything. Maybe they were brothers ...

Brothers.

"Say, Ben," Otto said, "While we're waiting for the vichyssoise or something ..."

Ben gestured at the retreating tureens. "That's what that was."

"Oh. Okay. Well, anyway, do you know a guy named Latchemondy?"

"I do."

"You guys ... pals? Colleagues?" He paused. "Related?"

Ben sat back, regarding Otto. "We are of the same Creation, but he is an apostate."

That was interesting. "Apostate, hey? Pain-in-the-tocus would be my choice of phrase because, well, don't think I've ever heard that term used for an angel."

A slight smile crossed Ben's face. "'Angel.' I guess that is the best approximation you can muster, but it is woefully inadequate."

"Well, then," Otto made a snarky hand gesture. "Here's your chance to educate me."

Ben made his own snarky hand gesture. "You've seen enough by now to understand there are many more levels of Creation than your limited mythology informs."

Limited mythology? Otto felt a pulse rise in his temple. "Gee, Ben," Otto said, "that sounds almost like an insult."

Ben's hand turned up in apology. "I did not mean it so. It is simply that humanity has suffered for millennia under misapprehensions that have caused many difficulties. Deliberately imposed misapprehensions, I might add."

"From whom?"

"I think you know."

The pulse remained. "I thought you said there was no God."

"I said," Ben fussed with some of his silverware, "that there is no God as you conceive of Him."

"Okay. So why don't you tell me about a God I *can* conceive of, and why this God you describe is interested in keeping us poor little mud creatures in a state of ignorance."

"Mud creatures?" Ben shook that off. "I do not use that term."

Otto nodded. "That's right, you haven't. It's an insult the Firsts prefer."

"Ah, them." Ben pursed his lips. "They are an arrogant bunch. Unruly. Violent." A pause. "Unnecessary."

"With you on the arrogant part, but, 'unnecessary'?"

Ben turned his palms outward. "An unfortunate aspect of uncontrolled power is that it sometimes gets away from you. You release energies and things ... form."

"I'm not following you."

Ben picked up a wine glass and a knife. "Think of it this way." He tapped the glass and a clear bell tone rang out. "You conduct an action, such as striking a glass, and there is a result, the pleasing tone. It is an unintended release because all you wanted to do was strike the glass. But, the tone, nonetheless."

"I'm still not following you."

"God releases His power without thought, creating the proto-Universe, and other things spill out. Because unreserved power cannot be contained."

Otto furrowed his brow. "Okay, wait. This proto-universe, that's the black sun place, right?"

Ben nodded.

"So, you're saying God did that deliberately but the Firsts ... kinda showed up?"

Ben nodded again.

Otto stared at him, incredulous. "Oh, come on, I'm not buying that. God controls His power and all of its results. If the Firsts exit, it's because He wanted them to."

"So you think."

"You're saying things happen out of God's control?"

"As I said, God is not the God you conceive."

Otto sat back. "That can't be," he said.

Ben said nothing, looked over as two more tray-bearing Fallen marched out of the kitchen and lined up behind Baton Boy. Slam of the baton, and Otto was presented with shrimp scampi. He grabbed whatever fork looked right and shoveled some onto his plate, not even bothering to check his actions against Ben's.

Screw him.

About his third mouthful, Otto pointed the fork at Ben. "Essentially, you're telling me that God is not God."

"As you conceive Him." Ben was relishing a forkful.

Otto waved his fork. "No. Uh uh. Won't work. God cannot be God unless He is God."

"Ah, the ontological argument," Ben nodded, pleased. "Because you conceive of God, therefore, He is the God you conceive. But, consider, he might be a lesser God."

"No. That's Zeus. Or Chuck Berry."

Ben laughed here, which earned him a point

"God is infinite and absolute."

"Yes, He Is, but that doesn't mean He controls it."

"Pfhww!" Otto responded. "Then He's not God!"

"More ontology. But existence is not a predicate."

"Huh?"

"Never mind. Point is, the conception of something does not assure its existence."

Otto canted the fork. "But, in this case, it does, because we have the proofs."

Ben arched an eyebrow. "What proofs?"

"Well, the usual stuff. You know, the existence of the Universe, the knowledge of God ..."

"... the various revelatory texts, yes, I know," Ben waved a hand to dismiss that. "But all that is PR. It is what God wants you to believe."

"So it's not true?"

"No, it's true. It's just not the entire story."

Otto stared at him for a moment. "'Not the entire story.' One that you and the Firsts and the Suits and God-knows-what-else floating around out here seem to be all briefed up on, but not us low-life mud people. Now, why would that be?"

A slow smile formed on Ben's face. "Because of your ... unpredictability."

Otto regarded him. "'Fraid you're gonna have to explain that one, Benny."

Ben sat back, his gaze rising to the ceiling. "After all this time," he said softly, to the point Otto had to strain to hear him, "the Creations are known. Their strengths, weaknesses, their predilections. There is a ... balance, for lack of a better word, and things are now static. Except for you. You are the newest Creation, and you are an unknown." He considered Otto.

Otto considered how baffled he was. "How is that a factor? We're not exactly bristling with cosmic power."

Ben smiled, "And you have an itty bitty living space."

"Oh, man," Otto could not help laughing. "Another movie reference. And you make my point. We're too small to bother with."

"Except, you have God's regard."

"That and a quarter ..."

Ben furrowed his brow and Otto smiled inwardly. So Lord of All He Sees over there isn't up to speed on all human expressions. "What I mean," Otto said, "is that regard doesn't make us powerful. Or a threat."

"On the contrary," Ben replied, "having the favor of the most powerful Being in all of Existence makes you as powerful. And quite a threat."

As Ben said that, his face ... shifted, for lack of a better word ... into a darkness that chilled Otto to the marrow, then, just as suddenly, shifted back to his affable self.

Warning sirens blew in Otto's brain and he made surreptitious glances at the Fallen to see if they were moving on him. They weren't. But there was a reflected darkness in their eyes.

Otto slowly pushed back from the table. "I think I'm done eating."

Ben showed genuine surprise. "But," he almost spluttered it, "we have four more courses!" He flipped a hand at two more Fallen who had entered. "Apple slices!"

"Still," Otto said, as he made sure he had enough room to jump in either direction, should things suddenly go awry.

Ben was crestfallen. "I have offended you," he mourned, the prospect of lost dinner a grief overcoming him. "I did not so intend." Ben looked down at his hands and Otto swore the guy was about to burst into tears.

Suddenly, he brightened, smiling and pointing a finger to the roof. "But of course! I can make it up to you! I can show you something!" Ben leaped up, almost knocking the chair over in his haste but one of the hidden Fallen jumped out of the shadows and caught it in time.

Ben gestured frantically at Otto. "Come with me!"

Fight-or-flight syndrome again kicked in.

"Where?" Otto asked as he gripped one of the knives.

Ben didn't answer but zipped over to the kitchen door and flung it open, disappearing inside. Moments later, his hand came out and made a "follow me!" gesture. Otto didn't know who was more startled, him or the Fallen, who all stared after Ben with the closest expression to "flabbergasted" they could muster.

"Okay," Otto muttered, "I'll play," and he stood and walked over, slipping the knife surreptitiously up his sleeve.

Cautiously, Otto opened the door and checked the area before entering. It was a huge kitchen, downright institutional, with rows and rows of stainless steel tables covered with what had to be hundreds of steaming pots and pans. There were at least two industrial-strength ovens set against a half wall across from him, both big enough to cook an ox. Between them was a brick pizza-oven-looking contraption that could handle all of Domino's yearly orders.

Pantries and cupboards scattered all over the place, filled to the brim with various china settings and silverware. Fallen were all over the place, too, most of them wearing stereotypical chef's clothes and all of them staring after the rapidly receding figure of Ben, who was down a hallway running past the half wall and silhouetted by what looked like a bank of floor to ceiling windows at the end.

"Come!" Ben called back and made another "follow me" gesture and disappeared in the far brightness.

The Fallen all turned to Otto, confusion and hostility roiling their faces and Otto eased back, his fingers slipping towards the hidden knife. But they made no move, so Otto cautiously slipped along the floor, gaining the hallway without incident and then hastened after Ben, quickly reaching the place where he had disappeared.

Otto faced a glassed-in corridor that ran to the left all the way out of sight. The windows overlooked the iceberg ocean, the mountainside falling away. Otto stared at the view, the whole area still brightly lit by the hidden sun. Man, the architecture of this place was downright hallucinatory because the ocean and the beach now looked farther away than from his room.

Hadn't the Fallen led him downstairs?

Escher print.

"Come on!" Ben called from far down the hallway and Otto looked and saw him wave before he resumed a trot. Otto wheeled and sped up but Ben was pulling away.

"You wanna hold up there, chief?" Otto called but, apparently, no.

The end of the hall looked about three miles away and Ben was obviously heading for it.

"Murgatroyd," Otto muttered and slowed down. He'd get there when he got there.

As the distance closed, the light at the end of the hall expanded, diffuse and soft and taking over the closer he got. A few hundred yards farther on and the light enveloped him. It was as though he'd entered a soft-glow tunnel, the floor still apparent and the hallway ceiling still visible, but the windows overlooking the ice-ocean obscured behind a gauzy curtain of brightness. It was disorienting and the only way Otto stayed upright was putting a hand on the left-hand wall.

"Come on!" Ben said, startlingly close.

Otto took a tentative step and, when he didn't topple over a cliff, stepped out with a little more boldness ...

... into a solarium.

Best word he could come up with, but it did it no justice because this was a few levels above that. It was a glass ... no, crystal ... observation room. No, observation chamber, big enough to house a couple of aircraft carriers. The floor was pure glass overhanging the mountainside, the rock and ice cliffs falling a couple of miles down to the beach fronting the ice-ocean.

Otto expected a Wile E. Coyote moment: a few seconds of

defying gravity before a slow plummet to the bottom, followed by an anvil.

But the floor held and Otto remembered to breathe and look at the rest of the windows. The mountain soared above them, still blocking the view past that direction, but the sky and ocean and cliffs and icebergs were there, spread miles and miles about him.

Ben stood about a hundred yards away, at the far point of the chamber where the crystal floor met the crystal wall, right over the ocean. He turned and, even at this distance, Otto could see the look of delight on his face.

"Come!" he gestured and went back to the view.

Making sure every step was solid, Otto eventually drew alongside. Ben gazed with great glee at a point on the horizon and Otto followed but it was ocean dissolving into haze.

"What are you looking at?" he asked.

"This!" Ben said and waved a hand.

The ice-ocean, the beach, the sky, everything, disappeared.

Chapter XXVII

The Kingdoms Of The World

A city. No, a country, an empire, centered on a palace of red and black with soaring cupolas of gold mounted on each corner.

"The Kremlin," Otto breathed. Immaterial whether it actually was; it looked like it.

The empire flowed on, to distant steppes and tundras, cold and blank and forbidding. Armies clad in green and red marched in giant squares around it, tanks corps and artillery and missile launchers interspersed among them, as wing after wing of bombers flew escort overhead. Risers lined all the routes, young people in white shirts and black pants with red scarves around their necks stood with hands outstretched in salute, singing a dirge of praise and lust, their eyes almost exploding with frenzy and rage. Grandstands lorded over all, men in great fur coats and officer hats stood in line across their lengths and grimly watched the crowds.

Villages wheeled about them in concentric circles, linked by great cities of factory and steel, cloud banks of soot and smoke cloaking everything as the red-scarved men and women, marching shoulder to shoulder in lockstep, scythed wheat fields and hauled coal and ore to the factory entrances in a continuous exercise of dump and fill, escalators flinging the tailings out for miles from miles-deep mines in which more of the red-scarved swung picks in unison.

A chant kept time, the words unintelligible, but the rhythm — that of struggle and sacrifice until death — ensured everything moved in unison.

"What is this?" Otto whispered.

The empire clouded over then faded and a bright sun seared the world, beating mercilessly on deserts of dunes and canyons across which caravans of camels and horses swayed for hundreds of miles of empty landscape and streamed in and out of gates of giant cities enclosed by great walls and minarets, all of them golden and marble and blinding in the light.

Cavalries wheeled in formation about the walls, continuously charging and dancing among themselves, scimitars flashing like diamonds. Clouds of arrows rose suddenly from the ground, arced over, and then fell like rain among the dead sands. The cavalries parted and lines of tanks and tracked vehicles swept past, all in a gull-wing formation of an endless blitzkrieg across endless dune and desert, accompanied by swept-wing fighters that dipped and cavorted in the mistrals. The cavalries flanked great masses of foot soldiers clad in kufiya and scarf and strapped with bandoliers and goose-stepping along the way as they brandished long rifles and bayonets.

The armies made for giant stone monuments scattered about the desert, pyramids and sphinxes and monoliths fronting streets of stone and marble where priests and priestesses clad in white and gold, bearing crowns of Nefertiti and Cleopatra, hoisted alabaster jars of smoking incense up to altars set between the paws of stone lions. Millions of white-clad worshippers ranged behind them bowed to the ground, a single note of music rising above them, unknowable, but known.

Desert birds, indignant, wound their shadows through it all.

A fog descended and the desert disappeared and the fog thinned and there were skyscrapers, steel and glass, row upon row upon square and lot knitted by eight and ten and twenty-lane highways spinning and climbing among it all, cars and trucks roaring to and fro day and night. Sunset blooded the windows and the vehicles.

Transport planes, dwarfing the C-5s and 17s Otto knew, rose

almost vertically from the city centers and spread out above the highways. Lightning danced from building to building, casting from one radio tower to another, each bolt a billion words and pictures constantly exchanging information and cruelty and murder. The song of tires and engines and movement, sheer movement, was anthem.

Roman legions marched shield to shield down the highway medians between the glass towers, plumed helmets bobbing in time as drawn swords beat a cadence on the shield tops, the sunset light turning their brass bosses into blood and death. A shout of exultation with each beat of the sword, a blast of trumpets in answer, and the engines and horns and wheels humming about them sounded their approval. People lined every window in every skyscraper, men and women in business suits clutching at the glass and each other, fists waving in rage, eyes black with hate and mouths open in screams of triumph, all jumping and pushing to get the better view.

Fog again.

A land of mist and valleys, silver-lit by a crescent moon, shapes of buildings outlined by lanterns hanging on roofs and walls, pagodas with torches in their courtyards stretching on to distant mountains of temple bells and jade towers and red lacquered tori gates. Mile-wide rivers flowed past hundred-story tile and marble temples, fleets of junks and rams knotted throughout and escorting gigantic aircraft carriers with upswept ramps and squadrons of red-starred fighters poised to launch. Landing craft, green and red, splayed behind the carriers, each of them jammed to the gunwales with short-helmeted green-clad soldiers peering over the edges, ready, regarding.

Hiding in the fogs were the scholars, long robed, arms hidden in great sleeves as moustaches drooped and silver hair flowed down their backs. Men in black suits and black expressions posed among them, watching the landing craft with critical eyes. Below them, whether by street height or attitude, multitudes in black pajamas, eyes empty of life and thought, awaited a single word to fly down avenue and over barrier and across waters to take, and take, and take.

"What. Is. This?" Otto breathed.

The empires flowed past him, connected now in a circle that

wheeled across Otto's sight, one taking prominence over the other but all of them having their day, as one ascended the other descended, the cycle of things, the way of things, change the names and capitals but it is all the same.

All.

"WHAT! IS! THIS!" Otto screamed.

The empires faded and the fog became brighter and dazzling and Otto had to shut his eyes tight against it, his lids reddening as the light they blocked strengthened until it reached a level and stopped. Otto carefully opened his eyes, stabs of bright light forcing them closed again and again until he adjusted. He was back in the observation chamber, the glass below and around him, and the sudden vertigo forced him into another round of eye shutting until his stomach settled and he wiped them and opened them and there was Ben, standing quietly to his left.

"The kingdoms of the world," Ben answered his earlier question.

"What world?" Otto asked. "This one?"

Ben nodded. "They are the kingdoms of history, the kingdoms of now, and of tomorrow."

Otto shook his head. "They look remarkably like the kingdoms of Earth, the ones from my history, my present, and maybe from my tomorrow."

Ben chuckled. "That's because they are Earth's."

Otto frowned. "Then what are they doing here?"

Ben looked at him. It took Otto a minute. "Wait. Are you saying we're on Earth?"

Ben didn't respond, merely smiled and gazed back out of the window. Otto pursed his lips. "So, this IS Antarctica. But that's impossible."

"Why?" Ben asked.

"Because … it's impossible. Worse than that, it's downright ridiculous. That would mean I've somehow managed to cross, not only the Universe, but the boundaries between life and death and ended up back on my home planet. Which I'm pretty sure would cause all manner of fuss. At least, according to Bernard." Otto flashed on the argument they'd had on the ship about going home. "And, besides, I doubt you could keep this mountain fortress of yours a secret. Someone would have noticed."

"Yes," Ben agreed amiably. "If there was someone around to notice."

"Yeah, okay," Otto said, "granted we do not have a huge presence here. Only McMurdo Sound, I think." Otto paused, trying to remember if that was Antarctica or the Arctic. "But satellites are all over the place and they'd have spotted you. I mean, James Arness found the flying saucer under the ice, and he wasn't even looking."

Ben chuckled. "I think the John Carpenter version is better."

"Better effects, certainly, but you gotta go with the classics. And the point stands."

"As does mine," Ben said, and took a few steps back towards the rear wall.

Otto unconsciously stepped with him and noted the glare was cut in half, the light shadowing until it was downright pleasant. Puzzled, Otto looked up expecting clouds or curtains, but neither was apparent. He eyed Ben. Nice trick.

"What point? About someone being around to notice?"

Ben nodded.

"Doesn't wash," Otto said, "If this is Earth, as you imply, then there's plenty of people running around who'd notice. Unless ..."

Ben waited, merely raising an eyebrow as Otto worked it out for himself. "...there aren't any people here. Anywhere. Is that what you mean?"

Ben flipped a there-you-go hand.

"So, what, a nuclear war? Plague? Zombie apocalypse?"

Ben chuckled. "No. Nothing like that. Such events require a human population which has developed to the point of initiating such horrors."

Otto dismissed that. "What are you talking about? We're already that far along, except for maybe zombies and, well, there is the Democrat Party."

Ben chuckled again but said nothing.

Otto chewed on it until it became clear. "We're back in time. There's no one to notice because people haven't shown up here yet. No Captain Cook. No Shackleford. No Eskimos. Right?"

Ben inclined his head. "You have it."

"So, we're time-traveling." Otto thought about that for a second, then rendered a verdict. "What a load of crap."

Ben was genuinely surprised. "Why would you say that?"

"Because it's a load of crap. Just a complete load. I'm supposed to be dead. I'm in the Afterlife, where I got chased by Nosferatus in nice suits until I jumped on a rocket and got chased by your pals over there," Otto jammed a thumb at a couple of Fallen standing quietly off to the side, "and then, next thing I know, I'm in a dustup with a big friggin' demon right out of a comic book and, now, I'm starring in a time travel epic. It's … it's …" Otto struggled to find the right word as Ben waited patiently.

And found it.

"A trope." Otto announced. "It's a trope."

Ben regarded one perfectly manicured hand. "I'm afraid I'm not following you."

"It's made up. All of this. It's made up! It's a sci-fi novel with everything thrown in, the entire kitchen sink and then some. What'll be next, wormholes? Parallel dimensions?"

"Now that you mention it …"

"Oh, STOP it!" Otto shouted, throwing his arms out in frustration and getting a reaction from the Fallen, who glanced at Ben, who gestured them back. "Just stop it. Anything you say is going to confirm what I've suspected all along."

He didn't wait for the begged question. "That all of this, all of it, is in my head."

"It's not in your head," Ben assured quietly.

"No?" Otto made an irritated finger flick at the windows. "Antarctica? In what, the twelfth century? BC?" He flicked a finger at Ben. "The Mountain King and his observation deck? This isn't real. All of this, every smidgen bit of it, is my fancy imagination fueled by a morphine drip."

He stared out the window. "I need to wake up."

Ben moved over and placed a sympathetic hand on Otto's shoulder. "I'm not a king, Otto. And you are awake."

"Baron, then," Otto said. "Zemo, in his mountain fastness."

"Zemo was in the jungles, not the mountains. And in the Folding Castle with the New Thunderbolts."

Otto shook his head. "Don't know those guys. I stopped

reading comics around 1970."

"And yet I have named them," Ben pointed out. "A group that you never heard of, so could not have conjured from your own brain." He raised eyebrows in confirmation.

Otto raised countering eyebrows. "Bull. I kept my hand in the comic book world so I probably picked up a reference at some point. Just forgot about them. So it's coming from my subconscious."

Ben clucked, stepping closer to the glass. "You are a stubborn one. But it seems to me that, if you are in a dream, then you can tell yourself to wake up. Can't you?"

"I've tried. Even tried the shock method." Ruefully, Otto rubbed his little finger.

"So, then, you are not dreaming."

Otto mused. A dreamer wakes by naming the dream. It was how he'd escaped nightmares before. As the monster's footsteps pounded closer and closer, Otto, up to his hips in quicksand, would chant, "Wake up, wake up!" and, right before the monster burst through the screen of bushes, he would, shaking and gasping and covered in goose pimples but safe in his bed, the fleeting images of quicksand and slavering jaws dissipating.

But he had already tried that and tried that and tried that.

Try more.

"Wake up," he whispered.

Wakeupwakeupwakeup …

The glass chamber remained. As did Antarctica.

"Okay," Otto said, "Baron, Count, Viscount, whatever, tell me, then, how it is we have time-traveled back to Earth — to Antarctica, no less — without me noticing."

"It's not really time *travel*, per se. It's only that we're at a point."

"'Fraid you're gonna have to explain that one, Chief."

Ben smiled. "I'm not sure I can. Your … tropes … may prevent me."

"I'm a quick study."

"Very well." Ben took a breath and stood taller, seeming to embrace the far ocean. "All of time exists simultaneously. What is future occurs at the same time as the past. The present coexists with both. What point you perceive determines where you are."

Silence. Again. Indication that Ben was done with his explanation.

"Uhm," Otto said, "That's … pretty sophomoric. Might even be a Dr. Who episode."

Ben shrugged. "It seems simplistic because you are regarding time as a progression. You think the past has passed. But it hasn't. It is going on right now."

"Well, yeah." Otto's sense of frustration rose. "I guess in any philosophic sense you can muster, the past is going on right now. But, it IS past. I can't just open a door and, presto, I'm in the Battle of Gettysburg."

Ben did not respond.

"Are you saying I can?" Otto's incredulity was rising, too. "That such doors exist?"

"No, no such doors exist. But the Battle of Gettysburg is going on right now. All three days of it. All three days preceding it. The three years after. They are points of existence. Simultaneous. If you perceived it, then you could, indeed, walk right into it."

"Okay," Otto said, "I'll play. I'm assuming you can perceive it. So, why can't I?"

"Because you are human."

Otto rolled his eyes. "And, that means … what?"

Ben slowly turned and regarded him, a blank, but somewhat threatening, expression on his face. "That you are very, very dangerous."

Otto's hackles rose and he quickly located the two Fallen escorts, both of whom had become slightly … bigger. Otto took an alarmed step back, his fighting blood stirring. "In what way?"

'You see the past as fixed," Ben toned, himself becoming slightly bigger, "You then turn your attention to the future and make efforts to control it. You alter your behaviors based on what the past tells you because you think the past is a lesson, something to be avoided, or repeated. But that means you plunge into a future ignorant of what could be, and what is, and that makes you … unpredictable."

"Unpredictable," Otto repeated Ben's tone. "Yeah, that we

are. But that makes us dangerous only to ourselves. I have it on good authority," Otto thought of Akiko, "that we are dangerous because we think ourselves unworthy."

Ben snorted. "That's the First's thinking. They are so ... unimaginative. The real danger is that no one knows what you will do."

"Do to who?"

"The universe," Ben almost whispered it and the view changed. Galaxies spun by, trails of gas and comets linking them, all in balance, all so orderly, light and dark off-setting each other, enduring, forever.

Otto was breathless, entranced. "It's so beautiful," he gasped.

"Yes," Ben's voice brushed against his ear. "It is. And it can remain so, if you will take my gift."

"Gift?" Otto was riding a jet of plasma and violence that a black hole spewed across the heart of a star system.

"The kingdoms of the world."

Chapter XXVIII

Pleased To Meet You

Otto shook himself out of the universe. "Uh, what?"

Ben made a caressing gesture on the glass. "The kingdoms you saw. All of them. They are yours. If you want them."

"Uh, what?" was all Otto could say.

Ben didn't laugh and razz him with a "Gotcha!" followed by a noogie and a "Let's go get a beer!" and off they went, arm in arm. Nope. He remained transfixed on the view. "Yours," he said.

Otto finally thought of a better response. "Are you crazy?"

"No," Ben said, "I am not. I am as serious and sane as it is possible to be. You now have the chance to correct everything." He paused, then whispered, "Everything."

"Correct ... what?"

"This," Ben made a gesture and the universe disappeared. History replaced it. "All of this. The centuries of murder ..."

Otto watched as a Cro-Magnon speared a Neanderthal, Cain slew Abel, Jack the Ripper ate a liver; "mayhem," — a Viking cut a blood eagle out of a priest, a scimitar parted a hand from an arm; "slaughter," — hordes dug mass graves and threw in counter-revolutionaries and Jews and Croatians ...

"... and war."

Blitzkriegs ground villages into dust, legions burned huts,

walls collapsed under catapult fire.

Ben turned to him. "If you could stop it all, wouldn't you?"

"I ..." Otto, although stupefied by the display, still managed the right answer. "I ... can't."

Ben laid a reassuring hand on Otto's arm. "Oh, but you can, you most certainly can."

Otto, recovered now, stared at him. "I can't do anything about any of this." Otto gestured at Bolsheviks storming the Winter Palace. "It's all history. It's all done."

"Not if you can enter history at any point and alter it."

Crazy? Nah. Ben was downright certifiable.

"So, you propose that I go back and change things. *A Sound of Thunder*, *Do-Over*, Billy Pilgrim ... hello, McFly?" Otto made a knocking motion against his own head. "The butterfly effect? Paradoxes?"

"Those are true only if time is a progression," Ben said, patiently, "but time exists at every moment, and you can enter it at any of those moments, even before history — anyone's history — began. Such as now." Ben waved at the window. History was now gone. Antarctica had returned. "Before humans existed."

Otto did a Bugs Bunny headshake. Too many things to process. So, pick the last one and work backwards.

"Are you telling me that we're, right now, in the time period before people? Not just Shackleford, but anyone. At all?"

Ben nodded. "This is the pre-human world."

Otto mimicked Ben's wave at the window. "This is prehistoric Antarctica?"

Ben nodded again.

Otto gazed at the sea of ice. "Well, that explains the valley of the dinosaur bones," Otto said, and then his eyes narrowed, "But there's some other bones out there, Ben. And they ain't dinosaurs."

"True," Ben acknowledged, "This was our home."

"Was?" Otto repeated, almost stupidly. "Our?" Not so stupidly.

Ben stepped closer to the glass, an expression of longing on his face. "Look at it," he said, "So pure. So stark. It made us feel alive."

"Who's 'us'?"

Ben kept talking as if Otto had said nothing. "We were kings. The stars were our playground. We could go anywhere, and we did. But, this place, this little nothing of a planet in some nothing galaxy, it … spoke to us. The mountains and the rivers and the forests. So beautiful. So elegant. There is no other planet like it anywhere. Anywhere. We carved our palaces from its very bones. We turned the dinosaurs into pets. We laughed. We loved."

He whirled and seized Otto's shoulders, almost breaking them. "You cannot imagine!" Ben's eyes glowed with fire. "You cannot *begin* to comprehend!"

Carefully, Otto extricated himself from Ben's grip and took a step back, one eye on the Fallen palace guard. "I thought you said you weren't a king."

"I am no longer," Ben answered, mournfully, and then lapsed into silence, head bowed, reflective. After a moment, he raised his eyes to Otto. "But I can be again. All of us can be." He threw out hands, beseeching. "With your help."

Otto regarded him for an uncomprehending moment. "Me, help you, become a king." He paused. "Again." He shook his head. "Right. As we have already established, I'm not exactly brimming with cosmic power."

"You do not need to be." Ben's hands continued their beseeching. "I have enough for both of us. You have only to take control." A gesture, and the kingdoms of the world again flashed by.

"Control of what?"

Ben shook his hand impatiently at the glass. "Of this! Of history! Of your species's destiny!"

Otto was now full-on exasperated "What. The. Hell. Are. You. Talking. About? Ben?"

"I am talking about an end to all the strife in the universe," Ben said in tones reserved for idiot children. "You and I, working together, will bring about the world peace your species — all species, in fact — have always sought."

So much for working backwards. "So, we'd be partners."

Ben nodded eagerly.

Otto lost it.

"In … WHAT?" he shouted. And continued shouting. "I don't have any FREAKIN' idea what you're talking about! I have no idea what we would be partners IN! And I doubt very seriously it would be an equal partnership, you being Galactus and all. Which I guess makes me the Silver Surfer, which would be kinda cool but not a role I'm exactly cut out for. Can't surf. Tried it. And if you and your friends were teaching dinosaurs to fetch," Otto made an irritated wave out the window, "then whose bones are those out there rotting beside them?" He took in a breath. "And where are my dogs?"

Ben's voice was weary. "They are safe."

"Where?"

"Somewhere else," Ben's weariness took an annoyed edge. "Don't worry. You have a greater opportunity here than re-acquiring some old pets."

Otto smouldered. "You don't know humans very well, do you?"

"NO!" It was Ben's turn to shout. "I do not! None of us do! After thousands of years of observing you, watching you, trying to make sense of you, we cannot! Because you are so unpredictable!"

Ben's chest heaved and he staggered, the Fallen in the shadows stepping forward in some alarm but he angrily waved them away. Ben took a moment to gather himself and then straightened and gazed at the stunned Otto. "You have a chance," he said, under control, "to fix that. To make all of humanity …"

"… predictable." Otto finished it for him.

Ben said nothing, only watched him. Otto considered all of this nonsense and reached the only conclusion, slowly shaking his head. "Not really in our nature, Ben."

"You could change that."

"Could I? Like you've said, after thousands of years, you still don't get us."

"But we would start at the beginning. We would shape things!" Ben pleaded.

"We? More like 'you.' With me playing the patsy." Otto frowned. "Or the quisling. Not sure I'd be amenable to that. Especially since you *still* haven't explained one blasted thing to me." Now was a good time to work backwards. "F'rinstance, whose skulls are those in the valley? You know, alongside your pets?"

"Heretics, but that's not important." Ben dismissed Otto's question and waved at history passing by. "This is."

"Yeah, yeah," Otto waved history away. Keep working backwards. "Heretics, huh? Like Latchemondy?"

"No. He is an apostate."

"I'm not seeing a whole shade of difference there, Ben. Point is, it looks like a whole bunch of 'heretics,'" Otto made air quotes, "tried to run Belial out of his castle. An activity I sort of favor."

"Belial." Ben almost spat that. "He is a fool."

"Was a fool. Was."

Ben stared at him and Otto expected a baffling metaphysical explanation about dimensions and energy conversions and other Einsteinian whatnot, the upshot being that Belial wasn't dead, wasn't a 'was,' but still 'is,' but Ben didn't offer it.

"That is … immaterial. You have something far more important before you. A chance to save your species from ruin."

Otto snorted. "Uh huh, but there's a few things I need to know before enlisting in your army of non-heretical dino-riders. Let's start with this nifty mountain castle you've got here, smack dab in the middle of the Antarctic. If I'm understanding you correctly, you and your pals had resorts like this built all over the place, long before the first of us mud creatures formed enough cells to crawl out of the swamp. Since then, Ben, old boy, we muddies have gotten pretty good at finding old crap. Like dinosaur bones. So how come we never found any of your crap?"

Got him now, Otto thought, smugly.

Ben tsked. "You cannot. It is too well covered."

"So you're hiding from us." Otto waggled a finger. "That's not nice."

"No, no." Impatient hands again. "We're not hiding. It's the damage. The bombardment was so intense it actually moved the Earth off its axis. It is why you have such extremes of weather now. It was more temperate before, even in these cold lands."

"Bombardment?" Otto echoed. "You mean, like with nukes?"

"No. Asteroids and comets. The natural things of the universe."

"Uh, what? But …" Otto struggled to remember his archaeological timelines. "… that all happened before the earth was actually the Earth. Before there were any dinosaurs running around. Heck, before there was anything." He paused. "Right?"

Ben did not respond.

"Holy moly," Otto whistled. "Everything is a lot older than we think."

Ben was sympathetic. "Your carbon-dating techniques are not very accurate."

"Apparently not." Otto reeled a bit as he tried to make sense of it. "This bombardment, is that what killed the dinosaurs?"

Ben nodded.

"And the ... heretics?"

"No," Ben said, "That was battle. The bombardment came later."

"Soooo," Otto thought furiously. "The heretics attacked Belial's castle. Belial sent out the dinosaurs ..." Ben raised an objecting hand, "Or, his own dino-riders," Ben lowered the hand, "beat the heretics, and the heretics responded with a massive asteroid bombardment of the Earth." Otto waited for further objections, but Ben made none.

"Hmm," Otto mused, "so why didn't the heretics lead with that?"

"Pardon?"

"The bombardment. Obviously, it worked."

Ben gazed out the window. "Escalation," was all he said.

Otto considered. Made sense. Even among humans, you don't go nuclear until all hope is lost. "So, the heretics won. Then what are we doing here?"

Ben raised eyebrows in query.

"I mean, what's the point?" Otto's hands swept the landscape. "You haven't got a prayer. Best I can figure, meteors will come crashing down any moment, flattening all this." He gulped. "Us, too." Otto braced, expecting a comet to fly through the window.

Ben chuckled. "They will not. You saw the bones of battle, but it will take light years for word of this defeat to reach the enemy's headquarters. We are safe. For now."

"But ..." Otto's brains were melting. "Then ... this ..." He stopped. He simply could not form a question. He simply could not grasp it. This was a cosmology defying everything he knew from science, everything he believed.

Everything he believed.

Otto's eyes narrowed. "Who is this enemy?"

Ben's eyes glowed again, in fury, in fire. "That One!" he spat.

Ice encased Otto's spine. 'That One.' The same words Akiko had used. Which meant ... "You're a First," he breathed

Ben looked surprised. "No," he said, "I am not. I am deliberate."

"Huh?" Otto was confused, but didn't give into it. "But you said ... *That One*." Otto paused. "That's what the Firsts say. If you're using their words, then you've got some compatibility."

Ben sighed. "At places our interests cross, but that is coincidence. I am not a First."

"No, you're deliberate, whatever the hell that means. But you've got interests that coincide with them. And you're here in a mountain fastness on an Earth that existed before everything. And you can enter time at any point you want, going to and fro ..." Otto stopped, shocked. "And ... and, walking up and down it."

Otto's blood froze. "Who. Are. You?"

Ben smiled grimly. Eternally. Adversarial. "I think you've guessed my name."

Chapter XXIX

Nature Of My Game

"Lucifer," he breathed.

Ben gave a slight bow. "At your service."

"You're ... Lucifer."

"We have established that."

Otto, paralyzed, his veins and legs frozen, his mind flooded with a single thought: Get out. Now. Desperate to invoke the "flight" side of that "or fight" syndrome, couldn't. Paralyzed, you see.

Ben smiled, some sympathy in his eyes. He took a step forward and placed a hand on Otto's shoulder. "I know, I know, I'm not as advertised. You were expecting red skin and a tail and horns." Ben chuckled. "I always liked that image. Made it so much easier to blend."

"You ..." Otto managed.

"And what was that comic book, *Little Hot Stuff*? The devil child with a magical trident?" Ben laughed. "Loved that one." He blinked slowly.

"You ..."

Ben raised eyebrows. "Yes?"

"You ... can't touch me."

Ben made an exaggerated look down to his hand on Otto's shoulder. "I believe I am."

"No!" Otto regained himself and pulled out of Ben's grip, backing against the glass. "I mean, you can't touch me, you can't … take me. Take my …"

"Soul?"

Otto nodded.

"Yes, that's true," Ben said, chuckling, "You would have to sell it to me willingly. How would you like to do that?"

A puff of smoke, the smell of brimstone, and Ben flourished a parchment and a quill. "Sign here? In blood? Me giving you, what, seven years of riches and power and women and, at the end of that period, I show up in your mirror and eat your skull and drag you to Hell?"

Another puff of smoke and the contract vanished. Ben gave him a wry look. "Don't be silly."

Otto had his hands up in defense mode. "Just stay away from me."

Ben held up non-defensive hands, downright placating. "Of course. If you have any fear I will burn you with my touch or give you the plague, I will keep my hands to myself. But, really, Otto, you're being silly."

Otto's hands remained up and ready. "I don't think so. You're the enemy. I mean, THE enemy. There is no greater one."

"Is that so?" Ben said, softly. "Tell me, Otto, what makes you believe that?"

"Pfft!" Otto gave a summary answer. "Oh, please! Hate and war and the Nazis and the death camps and jihad? Makes you pretty much the leading war criminal of all time, bucko."

"I did those things?" Ben examined his fingernails. "I?"

"Well …" Otto frowned, his hands slowly relaxing. "Maybe not personally. But you inspired them. You plotted it. So you did it. By proxy."

"Ah," Ben raised a finger. "So that means I can make anyone do what I want them to do. In that case … ABRACADABRA!" Ben made wizard motions with his hands. "You are now my slave!" He then pushed an amused eye at Otto. "So, are you my slave now?"

Otto ground teeth, "All right, all right! So people did it, but it was still at your behest."

Ben sighed. "Hook, line, and sinker." He shook his head. "Let me show you something." Ben gestured at the glass and Otto turned and the scene faded to …

… the most beautiful place in the Universe.

A grove of trees, all of them bright and winding and green and flowing, just flowing, with vitality. Hummocks of grass and bushes surrounded them, intertwined and supporting, flowers blooming and berries drooping in heavy bunches at all levels. Butterflies and birds flew in and out of the bushes and trees, flocking in places and dancing and swarming among themselves, a rainbow of swirl and arc. The trees reached prayerful branches to an ice-blue sky painted with cotton swabs of puffy clouds that roiled and shaped and blended together and then came apart. A river ran through the middle of it, pure silver water that sang a melody of eternal bliss.

"Oh my," Otto said and pressed his face against the glass, filled with such a yearning. "Oh, my," he said again, and felt hearth and home and peace. "What is this place?"

"Eden," Ben said.

Startled, Otto stepped back a bit and gazed at the scene. "Eden? So it really existed?"

"Once," Ben replied. "No more."

"Because of you," Otto said, accusation in his voice. "So why are you showing me this? All you're doing is underscoring my point."

Ben tapped on the glass. "Look again."

Otto did.

Eden was primeval and eternal and life as it should be, calming and restful, beckoning to Otto, come, we will build you a bower of branch and vine and the winds will rock you gently in comfort and joy, the perfumes of these flowers will lull you and the branches will drop grapes and apples in your lap as the rivers serenade you … forever. And ever.

And ever.

"Lotus," Otto whispered.

"Precisely," Ben said, grimly. "Which is why you left the City, true?"

"No, not true. I left to find God."

"Exactly!" Ben was pleased and Otto frowned. Pleasing Lucifer was probably not a good thing. "And that is why Eden had to end."

Otto kept the frown. "'Fraid you're going to have to explain that one, chief."

"It's simple," Ben said, gazing at Eden fondly. "You already have the seed of it. You saw, in the City, what God intends: an existence of pleasure and emptiness. A life of no question. All is provided. All is well. There is no conflict, nor trouble, because there is nothing to prompt it. It was the same here." Ben tapped on the glass. "Your parents had thousands of years of idleness, of sloth and play and complete and utter uselessness. Unquestioning." That last said with something of an edge.

"Those parents being Adam and Eve?"

Ben shrugged. "In your language. I called them Undgaluntal and Grafvan."

"What's that mean?"

"Adam and Eve."

Otto glared at him. "Are you messing with me?"

Impatient hand wave. "It's just language. The more important point, you and I have common interests."

Otto had to laugh. "I very seriously doubt that."

"Of course we do!" Ben insisted. "You left the City for the same reason Undgal ... er, Adam and Eve, left the Garden. To find God."

Otto held up palms. "Wait ... wait ... wait. You're giving me a headache here. Now, as I understand the story, Adam and Eve saw God every blasted day in the Garden. Right?"

"Right."

"And, if I'm following your timeline correctly, they saw Him every blasted day for thousands of years. After the bombardment. Right?"

"Hundreds of thousands of years, actually."

"Okay, wow, you're not kidding about the Earth being older than we thought. Which ... wait." Otto, startled, shook a finger in the air. "Wait. Soooo ... you and your pals got blown off the face of the Earth and, millennia later, along comes Eden." He paused. "Which is not the story I know. I think the whole thing took seven days ..." and Otto stopped. Remembering something. "Ian and I had a conversation about this very thing back in the City. He told me ... that the Earth was *restored*, not created, and that it took several million years. The Earth had been packed in ice." He glared at Ben. "Funny how you and Ian's stories are coinciding. One of yours, is he?"

Ben looked annoyed. "He is not. He is a creature of what you call the Suits."

"Aren't the Suits your creatures?"

Ben tsked. "No, they are not. They have their own agenda. But that is unimportant."

Otto exploded. "The HECK it is! Ian, the Suits, your pals over there," Otto flung a hand at the Fallen, "Belial, even the damned rain on this planet have all been merrily trying to kill me ever since I heard about the ship! Seems to me all of you guys have a common agenda, that of finding new and interesting ways to keep me from rejuvenating!" and Otto slammed a fist into his own chest, breathing hard. Ready to fight.

"I have not harmed you, nor will I," Ben said, softly, peacefully. "And the truth always coincides. What Ian told you was true. So is what I've said."

"Yeah? Then why don't you explain why the other guys don't share your benign attitude towards me?"

Ben chuckled. "They do not take the long view. They pursue short-term interests. You know how true that is among your own creation."

Otto did. If there was one very annoying trait of humanity, it was selling tomorrow for the sake of today.

Many of his friends had partied themselves into a lifetime of backbreaking construction jobs, laughing at Otto because he'd joined the USAF. By the time he was fifty, Otto had IRAs and degrees and a profession. His pals had severe arthritis.

"All right," Otto conceded. "They may not have your insight. So why don't you tell me what the 'long view' is?"

"My pleasure," Ben said and gently placed an arm around Otto's shoulders and gently pulled him to the glass. "What Ian told you was true."

The view changed to a space shot of an ice world, with a moon and what looked like several rings at varying angles around it, a distant sun silhouetting it all.

"After the destruction of the Earth, the bombardment, there was so much dust that no light reached the surface and the Earth turned to ice, sealing it off. God did not want us going home again. It was His punishment."

"For what?" Otto interjected.

Ben ignored him. "But, as you see, the forces of nature are inexorable." Ben waved his hand and Otto watched as the rings dissipated and the ice receded, leaving a murky water world. "It was still not livable, but things stirred in the depths."

Another wave and Otto watched as waters receded and lands popped up here and there and something one-celled became something two-celled and then became a trilobite and a fish and a lizard-thing crawling up a muddy beach, illuminated by the fires of distant volcanos.

Otto waved his own hand. "Uh uh."

"Pardon?" Ben arched an eyebrow.

"I'm not buying your little slide show here, Ben. The Spirit moved across the waters. The splitting of the firmament. 'Let there be light.' Sound familiar?"

Ben chuckled. "Your scribes were poets, reducing the process of millions of years to a wondrous line or two. Of course God — the Spirit — 'moved'," Ben made air quotes here, "across the waters. He is God. He is Everywhere."

"Uh uh."

Ben became annoyed. "Now what is your objection?"

"That's too passive. God actually did these things. An action."

"Well, of course He did."

Yep, annoyed.

"Who do you think set the natural processes of the Universe into motion? With the bare movement of a Finger, I might add. Whether light took a day or millennia is immaterial. It is all His work."

Otto considered. If you're the author of a book, it's still yours, even if someone reads it a hundred years after you wrote it. "Okay, okay," and he motioned for Ben to continue.

Ben turned back to the window. "So the Earth was restored, little by little, over time. The animal life came out differently this time. Not dinosaurs, but mammals." Scenes of little rodents running around a savannah.

"Uhm …"

Ben made an exasperated sound. "What is it?"

"We've found dinosaur and mammal bones together."

"You call those dinosaurs. I call them, 'lizards'," he said dismissively and continued. "And from those, came these."

A wave of the hand, and there were apes.

"Where's the monolith?" Otto asked.

"Ach!" Ben sighed. "Can you not see what I'm showing you here?" The apes' posture straightened, their skulls and spines taking on human characteristics as they shed hair, acquired animal skin clothes, and spears, and clubs. Their short brows and giant jaws marked them as Neanderthals, but, here and there, Cro-Magnons appeared.

"Darwin would have loved this," Otto said.

Ben nodded. "Darwin was about half right," he said, "at least, in terms of how the human structure developed. But he got humanity completely wrong."

Otto's brows furrowed. "I'm not following."

Ben spread fingers and the savannah and the tundras and the cavemen fighting mastodons dissolved, and there was the Garden of Eden, again. Calling to him. Otto held his breath and put a longing hand on the glass. In the distance, at the bottom of the far valley, two figures stood, hand in hand.

"Your parents," Ben whispered, "They have the bodies of the evolved apes. But they have something else, something completely different."

Dramatic pause.

"The soul."

Through his palm on the glass, Otto felt a tingle. "Mother," he whispered, "Father."

A spark, an ember of kindred lives, flowed from his palm down his arm and enveloped his heart. He was warmed. He was one.

"Do you see it now?" Ben's voice in his ear. "You are not animals. You are not evolution. You are something unique, something once soulless made soulful, and that is the true birth of humanity."

The sense of it swirled through Otto's brain. Yes, that is who we are, the bearers of soul in a soulless world, the repositories, the caretakers of it. Through it, we carry the touch of God. We are his standard bearers, here in this Garden of Innocence …

Hold on a minute.

Otto leaned back from the glass and shook his head hard, to clear it.

"Hold on a minute," he voiced. "That ain't right. Adam was the first true human but he was in the Garden alone and naming the animals, which, apparently, was a full-time job and he got tired of drinking beer and watching TV alone so then Eve was made out of his rib …"

"Actually, from a DNA sample," Ben said, chuckling.

"Yeah, right, okay, but don't you see, you're contradicting your own history here? 'Cause all those cavemen," Otto flipped a hand at the glass, "came after the Fall …"

The Fall.

"… are forgetting that your poets are responsible for your errors of time," Ben was saying but Otto ignored him because there was a thread here, red and pulsing, and it was critical.

Otto turned to him. "How'd Adam and Eve lose the Garden, Ben?"

Ben taken aback, recovered quickly. "Good, good. You have now reached the most important point. You are, indeed, a quick study."

"Answer the question."

Ben reddened, which, given his real name, was alarming. "There is no need to be rude. They lost the Garden because I gave them life."

A throb started in Otto's temple. "There is," he said, flatly, coldly, "so much wrong with that statement I am surprised you're not getting hit by lightning."

Ben stepped back dramatically, arms out, braced.

"Yet, there is none. Because I have spoken the truth. I gave your parents, you, the entire human race, the gift of life."

A noble tilt of the head.

"I gave you the ability to choose."

The temerity of this guy!

"You got us THROWN OUT!" Otto shouted.

"Yes!" Ben shouted back. "I did! And you have LIVED since. LIVED! Your arts, your passions, your pains and triumphs! Would you have any of those if you were still traipsing around the Garden naming animals? No! Would you, Otto Boteman, be on the edge of monumental, Universal discovery if you had stayed in the City? No! I gave you life. True life!"

Ben gathered Otto to him and propelled him to the glass. The history came back, the kingdoms of the world.

"And now, now, you have a chance to fix all the mistakes, all of the errors that your race has made. You, YOU, Otto Boteman, can take command of the world, of history, and guide it! Correct it! Create a universe of peace and abundance. You can do this! I give you these kingdoms. You know that I can!"

Yes, Ben could. Lucifer could. He was the master of the world. He owned the Earth and the people therein.

If Lucifer gave him the world, here, right now, Otto could bring to bear his knowledge of history, of the mistakes made, and could intervene. A child murdered here stops a tyrant there, a traffic accident at the right time halts the spread of nuclear weapons, a fortuitous medical discovery, thousands of years before its actual appearance, ends the Black Death. The world would be different.

It would be the world as Otto always wanted it.

He looked at the frantic, expectant Ben.

"Ben?"

"Yes?"

The expectation heightened.

"You're completely full of crap."

Chapter XXX

How 'Bout Them Apples?

Otto might as well have slapped him.

"What?" Ben said, genuinely hurt.

"Crap. Utter and complete. Full of." Otto emphasized every word.

"But, how can you SAY that?" Ben sounded close to tears. "Everything I've told you is true!"

"Oh, I have no doubt about that." Now it was Otto's turn to examine fingernails. "But, you left out important details." Otto looked at him. "Like all good liars do. And you are the Prince of Lies, aren't you?"

Ben flushed deep red, the fury evident. Otto expected those proverbial horns to pop up any moment.

"That's Belial! He is the liar! And I have already called him a fool! All of them are fools!" Ben began stamping around.

Otto stepped back, alarmed.

"All of them! With their stupid plans of conquest and murder and subjugation!" Ben stopped, his chest heaving.

"Like you didn't have anything to do with those," Otto said.

"I did NOT!" Ben raised a fist.

Otto wasn't sure if it was emphasis or assault.

"Samyaza and Azazel and Yeqon and the rest of them did all that!"

"I don't even know who those are."

"You should," Ben glowered at him. "All of what you call history is their work. All I ever wanted was an alliance with you."

Otto, incredulous, shook his head and laughed. "An alliance? With men? Not in a million years. Apparently, you can't even keep your own troops in order."

"They are not my troops."

Otto regarded him. "Right. Like you're not the BMFIC, the Big Daddy Rabbit, capo de capo."

Ben said nothing, only cocked his head.

Otto cocked an eyebrow. "Wait. You mean, you're not?"

Ben added raised eyebrows to the angled head.

Otto mulled. "So, then … just how many Princes of Darkness are there?"

"Hundreds." A pause. "Thousands."

Otto considered that as his cosmology quietly shredded. If the universe was populated by thousands of Satans, all of them vying for mastery of the universe, all of them raving and bloodthirsty and eating the brains of humanity, then they didn't stand a chance.

That is, if Lucifer was telling the truth.

"You're full of crap," Otto repeated.

Ben shook his head. "I am not. It is a truth of existence that has been kept from you. If you knew it, had known it all along, then your species would have made different decisions. Avoided things. Put your faith in other things."

Otto snorted. "In you, for instance? And just *who* kept those so-called 'truths of existence' from us, oh, Lord of Flies?"

"I'm not the Lord of Flies. That's Ba'al Zebub."

"Whatever. Answer the question."

Ben regarded him. "You think it was me. All of you do. But, it was not. It was That One!" and Ben raised his finger.

Another snort. "First, c'mon. Second, c'mon. He has no reason."

"He has every reason. It benefits Him greatly for you not to know the truth."

Otto could not help himself. "What is truth?" he said, and made exaggerated hand-washing motions.

Ben frowned. "So," he said, quietly, "you mock me. As all of your kind does. Has done. Even as I did everything to save you."

Otto was instantly quite exasperated "From … WHAT? WHAT? What are you trying to save us FROM?"

"Enslavement," was all Ben said.

Otto let out a long breath and reviewed the previous five minutes of conversation. "You're full of crap," he concluded.

Ben threw 'I give up' hands. "Are you not even listening to me?"

"Every word," Otto acknowledged, "But I'm still waiting for you to get to the punch line. For example, if all your brother demons are out running around creating havoc and mayhem, how come yours is the only name mentioned?"

"You're simply reading the wrong books."

"Am I?" Otto's dander rose. "You're calling the Bible the wrong book? The Torah? My." He paused. "How blasphemous."

"There are other books."

"Yes," Otto nodded. "Apocrypha, I believe they're called."

"Because it is in the interest of That One to call them so. He wants you to regard me as your enemy. But I am not. I am the one who can save you."

Otto let a heartbeat or two go by. "Jesus saves. You destroy."

"Jesus enslaves," Ben snapped. "Look at what has been done in His Name."

A wave of the hand and Crusaders ran down Moslem peasants, Inquisitors gouged out eyes, Mormons slaughtered Mormons in remote deserts.

"False flag," Otto said, pointedly.

Ben was annoyed. "You're saying this is me? It was not. I made efforts to prevent it."

"Didn't do a very good job."

"Which is why I come to you now."

"What?" Otto was back to full-on bafflement. "You came to me? I think I'm the one who came to you. And certainly not by intention."

"Precisely." Ben smiled, an eager, relaxed, and anticipatory one.

Which can't be good.

"You are the only human who has ever reached this place. That makes you special."

"Yeah," Otto said, dryly. "I've heard words to that effect a couple of times already. But it's crap. I'm the only human who's made it this far because the technology wasn't advanced enough to get one out here."

"The technology has been available for at least one hundred and fifty years. Wasn't your rocket designed by an old Russian science fiction writer?"

"Well, yeah." Otto flashed on Konstantin. "But ideas generally precede execution."

"Still, the crew was not ready to go until you showed up. Of all the billions of people residing in the City, only thirty—"

"Thirty-one."

"Yes," Ben waved the correction away. "Thirty-one. Only thirty-one manifested the desire, the urge, to see God." He drew himself up to a regal height. "God has turned your people into sheep. You," and he pointed a dramatic finger at Otto, "can free them."

"In exchange for your rule?" Otto looked at him askance. "No thanks."

"But it would not be!" Ben made pleading fists. "It would be you! You would free humanity from its constraints, make it the most important species in the Universe ..."

"... and get you out of your jail sentence," Otto interrupted.

Ben dropped his hands to his sides, stunned.

Otto looked at the kingdoms drifting by. "You think I'm stupid or something? Why exactly did God send an army of 'heretics'," air quotes, "to drive you and your pals out of your castles? Then bombed the bejesus out of this place, turning it into a frozen wasteland?"

Otto held up a hand. "Oh, don't answer. You'll just give me some more humbug. It's for one reason only." Otto threw his head back. "'I will make myself like the Most High God.'" He straightened and stared at Ben. "Your words, I believe."

Ben shook his head sadly. "Not mine. Isaiah's."

"I'm sure he paraphrased. Point is," Otto watched as the kingdoms were replaced by history, bloody, horrifying history. "You decided that being second banana was insufficient for an angel of your talents. Someone with your qualities should be running the whole shebang – you, not some nebulous floating cloud of homilies and goodwill. God, I mean."

"I understood the reference."

Otto waved at the nearby Fallen. "That's for the audience's edification. So you convinced some other angels, equally ate up with themselves, to join you and ... war. Unlike no other. Escalating slowly across the Universe. A fistfight here. A stabbing there. Then, next thing you know, an army of dino-riders assaults your castles and asteroids come raining down on your head. Which is why you lost."

"I did not lose."

"Sure you did. Big time lost. You were hauled up before the Throne in chains, you and your pals, and I'll bet the widows and orphans testified for a few thousand years before God found you guilty and sentenced you to do laps in the Lake of Fire."

"I did NOT lose," Ben replied, with some heat. No pun intended. "On the contrary, I won."

"How you figure that?"

Ben pointed at him. "Because you are here." A wave of the hand and the kingdoms paraded by. "All of you are here. Because of me, you exist. And you are my victory."

Otto frowned. Ben certainly looked confident, which was something one expected from Satan, but not when he'd been reminded of a pending billion-year barbecue. Had he missed something? "We're not anyone's victory, least of all yours."

"Oh, but you are," Ben nodded vigorously and waved and there was the Garden again. "That you chose to think for yourselves proved that a loving God cannot destroy one of His own creatures."

"Wait." Otto was getting confused. "First, chose? We chose? Do you mean the apple? I think you had a bit to do with that, you and your serpent's tongue."

Ben chuckled. "Oh my, the tenacity of myth. It wasn't an apple."

"Well, yeah, I know that." Otto was miffed. "It's figurative."

"As is my serpent tongue." Ben stuck his out. Looked normal. For a fallen angel. "And it wasn't the tree of good and evil, either."

"*Knowledge* of good and evil, *knowledge*. You serpent-tongued devil, you."

Ben glowered at him and Otto wondered if he might have overstepped, but Ben's look cleared. "Not even that. Too limited. It was the knowledge of everything."

"Right. Eve bit the apple and was suddenly Einstein."

An amused wave of hands. "Hardly. But what she *did* suddenly know was that she had been deceived and that the universe lay open to her. Everything," Ben emphasized the word, "lay open to her."

Otto gave a Bronx cheer. "Oh, stop it. Everything was always open to them. They walked with God every evening. They could find out anything they wanted."

"Only if you know what questions to ask. And if you are blind ..." Ben let that sit.

"So, you showed up and scales fell from eyes, huh?" Otto was getting irritated. "Look, cut the crap. You didn't do us any favors. You created enmity between us and God, and you did this." Otto pointed at bloody history. "All because you don't know what you're doing. You don't. You don't have the ability to run the world. You couldn't run a half-decent dog-catching service. The arrogant rarely can.

"And don't tell me," Otto broke into Ben's ready-to-launch retort, "that we are your victory. We are quite the contrary. We are proof that God can save even the lowest of his creation, even us humans. That was your defense, wasn't it? 'How can a loving God condemn His creatures to the Lake?' That's what you just said to me, more or less. And, I gotta say, it's a valid argument. But He refuted it, to you, to the others."

Otto's wave took in the Fallen, then pointed at himself. "With us. He downright bent over backwards to give us a road home. Christ, the Cross, paying the penalty for the sins we committed, yadda yadda, a simple and very easy acceptance and, presto chango! We have Heaven. For eternity. I'll bet you got offered something similar, you and all your pals. An easy way back, I mean. All you had to do was admit you were wrong, and all would be forgiven. Prodigal Son and all that. That story was about you, wasn't it?"

As Otto spoke, bloody history had segued back to the view of Antarctica, where black clouds formed across the sky, a red, garish glow highlighting the edges as the clouds spread slowly to either side.

A cloud formed on Ben's brow, too. "Heaven?" he sneered. "You think you have it? The best you get is a pleasure city on the edge of the Universe, far away from God's sight, ignored, abandoned, as you lose yourselves in your sensual pleasures. Sloth and appetite and waste and never, ever to see the Face of God. You SHEEP!"

And the voice that blasted from Ben's mouth was a pipe organ, the voice whirling about Otto's heart and brain, decimating, soul crushing, and Otto was futility and frustration and was lost again and again …

But I am here.

"I'm here," he croaked against the black wind. "I'm here!" the croak became a firm voice. "I'M HERE!" he shouted at the wind.

The wind stopped. Otto almost fell down, he had braced so hard against it.

Ben stood before the glass, his eyes molten gold. "Yes," the organ piped, soothing now. "You are here. You, of all the people ever born, are here. Why is that?"

Otto gritted his teeth. "Just lucky, I guess."

"No," Ben said, "There is no such thing as luck. You, of all people, know that. There is circumstance and what you do with it. And what have you done with it, Otto Boteman, son of a lost pilot and a self-absorbed mother, cast out, no family, no backup, just you? What did you do with … circumstance?"

A disdainful flick of a hand.

"You sought surrogate. You sought a shepherd. Instead of standing on your own."

The throb was back in Otto's temple. "You should be really, really careful how you talk about my mother. And if I ended up alone, that was pretty much your doing. And if I got myself comfortably out of it, admittedly after quite a lot of hard work and many setbacks, that was God's."

"Was it?" The golden eyes flickered. "Did God send angels and chariots to rescue you? No, you took what *I* had made. The world is mine, all of its resources are mine. I gave you the gravel in your gut and the spit in your eye!"

"Pfhht!" Otto said, "You do know that song is not a parental endorsement, right? It's about somebody making it DESPITE the odds. Your odds! You created the evil of the world. I found a path through it …"

A path through it.

Otto paused. He had, hadn't he? Without directions, without help, following along as that still small voice somewhere deep within him said, "Keep going. You're doing fine." And always, off in the distance, over the next set of hills, a glimmer of lamplight, a guide. Because he knew, just knew, that answers were waiting.

Answers. That only God could give.

Ben nodded. "So," he said with satisfaction, "We come to it, why you are here, why popes and preachers and scholars are not. Because, Otto Boteman, you have scried a path that those others never could."

A pause.

"And that makes you dangerous."

The clouds enveloped the sky and red lightning flashed here and there. The observation chamber turned crimson and murky, and Ben grew taller, thinner, his eyes glowed brighter, a robe and hood enveloped him.

Otto took a step back, rattled. "That's the second time you've called me that. And I have no idea why."

"Then," the voice hollow and echoing and dead, "allow me to enlighten you. YOU seek the Face of God Himself. Not His Love, His Gifts, nor His Power. Him. Only. You wish to pose your questions, know the answers. And you will trust.

"And that," Ben stopped Otto's response, "means you serve His purpose. You. You unpredictable, bizarre, illogical people. You will be His proof."

And it all came clear.

"The Lake," Otto whispered. "Your final, irrevocable judgment. The final piece of evidence. Here stands before the Throne a lesser creature, not bristling with cosmic power, weak and fragile and filled with ten times your sin and arrogance, yet, it still sought the Father."

His voice became a whisper. "Sought salvation." He blinked at the darkening Ben. "God wins."

There was a shudder in the dark, hooded form, and the robe parted, and Otto saw him truly:

Corruption.

Ben was the grave, the rot, worm-eaten flesh falling off in green, vile flecks. He was all that was wrong and broken in the entire universe, twisted and angled in impossible ways. He was the lust in a rapist's eyes, the grin of greed and murder, the sneer of the SS officer dropping the Cyklon B, the politician promising a chicken in every pot, cronies popping champagne and laughing through fat cigars, heroin singing in veins, the earnest reformers shipping malcontents to Siberia, the self-righteous and the self-regarding and the ones who stood with fists clenched and raged at God and screamed their hate.

The eyes in the hood turned into a magnesium flare.

"*Augh!*" Otto shielded his face from the blast of heat and pain, because it was dead light, corpse light, the agony of lost souls crying among the orbits of black suns where thousand-eyed monsters ate worlds. Ate humanity.

"You can't touch me!" Otto screamed, his eyes tightly shut.

"And I will not," Ben said quietly.

Otto forced his eyes open. The hell light from outside the window was gone, although clouds still boiled around the mountain. Ben, the normal Ben, stood quietly in the middle of the room. He made a gesture and ranks of Fallen fell to either side of him, shoulder to shoulder, completely blocking the way. They confronted Otto, their eyes cold.

Otto looked behind. Rows of Fallen arrayed there, too, blocking his escape. "I see," he said, flatly, "Your slaves'll do the dirty work."

"They are not my slaves," Ben said, "They are my soldiers." And he looked at the ranks with affection.

Otto wasn't sure the affection was returned.

"And neither will they touch you. I already promised that."

Otto was about to point out how much one could rely on the Devil's promises when there was a commotion far down the hall behind Ben. Otto watched with growing alarm as the ranks back there shifted, like someone — or something — was walking through them.

"This can't be good," he muttered.

The shift grew closer and was one rank back when Ben glanced at it and then said, with a small smile, "But I cannot speak for others."

The front Fallen parted at that moment and there stood …

Suits.

Chapter XXXI

Thumb And Finger On The Forehead

Three of them, to be exact.

They stood side by side, staring at Otto, their arms folded across their Brooks Brothers jackets, their dark eyes bulging out of their elongated heads. They looked like a triplication of *The Scream* painting, except they weren't anguished. They were mad.

"Uh oh," Otto said.

Ben smiled broadly. "No need for concern, Otto. These gentlemen," Ben waved an expansive hand at the Suits, "mean you no harm."

"Since when?" Otto asked as he measured the distance between the Suits and himself. If he could get the drop on them, he might stand a chance.

Ha.

"No, no!" Ben waved a gleeful hand. "You've got it wrong. They merely wish to escort you back to the City."

"Right," Otto said, bracing, "All of me, or just what they spit back up?"

Ben laughed, clearly enjoying himself, even reaching out and slapping one of the Suits jovially on the back.

That Suit bent with the blow, but remained fixed on Otto.

"Trapped and beaten and still cracking wise. It is an endearing feature of humans. But, let me assure, you will return to the City intact." And he blinked slowly like a cat showing its appreciation.

Trapped and beaten?

We'll see, but Otto had to admit, it didn't look good. "Your assurances are a bit hollow," he said and edged back, but, three steps later, he was jammed against the rear wall of Fallen.

He looked over his shoulder. The Fallen he'd collided with stared at him, hostility evident, a hint of protruding fangs but, otherwise, peaceful. Otto didn't think he could shove it out of the way.

Not without a stick of dynamite.

"I am hurt!" Ben exclaimed, feigning distress. "When have I lied to you?"

"Think we've already had this discussion." Otto looked to either side, those Fallen as solid as the one who blocked his retreat.

Ben smirked. "Ah, yes, that 'leaving out of a few material facts' you previously mentioned. Very well, then, let me include a few. Such as, when you get back to the City, a very, very long time from now," Ben grinned viciously, "you may not be quite the same."

"How so?" Otto said, as he continued examining both lines of Fallen, behind and in front. No apparent weak spots. No apparent way out.

Yep, definitely trapped.

And probably beaten. Man.

"Well, the eagerness you initially displayed to leave the City may be — how shall I put this? — somewhat subdued. Indeed, I am willing to wager that you will be so grateful to get back there that even the mere *idea* of another star voyage will make you positively insane." A wider grin, if that was possible "A little more so."

Otto quit looking for escape. Gonna have to fight. So, stall for time, because any fight would be a short one. "Why is that?"

"Because there'll be a few detours along the way. The Suits will host you, first. They are a bit miffed over the destruction of their star fleet …"

"That was Marc, not me," Otto said.

"Yes, but he isn't available. You are. When the Suits are done expressing their displeasure, they will drop you on the dark world with Horace and his hopeless friends. Do you remember them?"

He sure did. The mud world, where men long without hope. "Be a little hard to do since it ain't there anymore."

"At least not where you last saw it." Vicious smile.

Otto shuddered.

"After that, you will spend some time in the city of Dis. Some of my soldiers there have asked after you."

Otto glanced at the Fallen behind him. The thing was grinning, its eyes dancing with joy. "Great," Otto whispered.

"After that, you'll orbit around the black suns, where you'll become acquainted with the Firsts. The other ones, I mean. You already know Akiko. She'll be there to make introductions."

"Might be fun," Otto said, "I love a good party."

Ben laughed. "Yes! And when you are finally done meeting everyone, you will be collected and returned home. By that time, you will regard these gentlemen," Ben nodded at the Suits, "as your best friends."

The Suits' faces trembled, as if they were trying to smile.

"Out of curiosity," Otto said, measuring distances again, "about how long will all this take?"

Ben shrugged. "Five, six thousand years. More or less. To you, though, it will feel like eternity."

Otto grimaced. A suit-sponsored tour of the universe might interfere with his other plans, like, living and breathing and avoiding unnecessary pain. Definitely need to get out of here, but how? Maybe Otto could goad Ben into a mistake.

Ha.

But what else you got?

"This eternity of which you speak, isn't that about how long you'll spend in the Lake of Fire?"

Ben frowned and Otto's hopes rose, but were quickly dashed when Ben smiled and shook a finger.

"Nice try, Otto, but you can't make me angry. I'm in too good a mood, now that my sentence is delayed. You see, there won't be another human back this way for a long time. A very, very long time. Much longer than the time you will be in the custody of my associates." Ben nodded at the Suits, who looked at him and at each other and then at Otto.

And took a step forward, in unison.

Crap.

"Associates?" Otto, desperate, shouted. "Aren't these guys elect angels?" Stab in the dark, but Latchemondy had called the Suits a faction. And Latch was an elect angel (maybe. Who knows?). "So that makes them your enemies."

"The enemy of my enemy is my friend," Ben said, glibly.

Another unified step forward.

"But ... hey! He just called you his enemy!" Otto shouted at the Suits.

Another unified step.

Double crap.

The Suits were about two steps away from grabbing Otto by the lapels and turning him inside out.

And this was such a nice tux. Marc would have liked it.

Marc ...

"What did you mean that Marc wasn't available?" Otto shouted at Ben.

The Suits froze in mid-step.

Otto raised an eyebrow. Hello? What's this?

Ben frowned. "What a silly question," he said, but it seemed directed more at the Suits than Otto. "He's not available because he's not here."

The Suits exchanged glances and then completed the step. They shifted into another one.

"So where is he, then?" Another shout, equally desperate.

The Suits again froze in mid-step.

Hmm.

"Not. Here." Ben emphasized and nodded at the Suits.

"So that means he's somewhere else!" Otto shouted directly at the Suits before they moved.

Well, yeah, obviously, and Otto felt immediately stupid but it meant something to the Suits, otherwise they'd be tying him into a pretzel about now. So where was this somewhere else Marc currently inhabited, a place that gave Suits pause ...

And Otto knew.

"Heaven."

The Suits remained in mid-step, all three of them watching Otto.

"This is absurd," Ben snorted and took his own step forward but Otto held up a hand.

"Marc's in Heaven, isn't he?" he asked the Suits. "The real Heaven, the Throne Room, where God is. Isn't he?"

The Suits took a simultaneous step back.

Now it was Ben's turn to shout. "Don't listen to him!"

"And that means … that means," Otto was thinking furiously, "that the rest of them — Ferdinand and Karl and Bulsrobe. Claudia — they're all there, too."

Another step back.

"What are you doing?" Another shout from Ben.

Otto stopped breathing. Just stopped.

The others had made it.

At some point in the voyage, maybe right at the moment they were taken — Claudia during the stretching or Ferdinand during the battle — in whatever way they left the ship, in the twinkling of an eye, their various wounded and torn souls walked through whatever portals led through whatever universes and into a magnificent star-filled chamber of gold and there, there, on His Throne, Smiling benevolently at them, was God.

Why not me?

It was a thought that made him gasp, which kick-started his breathing. Why not *me*, Lord? Why don't I get to slip these surly bonds and soar and touch the Face of God, as they did? Why them, and not me?

What did I do wrong?

Simple. Not get killed.

Otto regarded the frozen Suits regarding him and the frantic Ben pulling at them. "So, that's it," he said, "That's the reason."

Ben stopped pulling at a Suit and looked at Otto, confused. "Reason for what?"

"Why I'm here and they're there." He paused. "I didn't get stretched. I didn't get blown off the hull by the meteor storm, I didn't get my brains beaten out by you pals here," an angry flick at the Fallen, "and Akiko didn't scatter my atoms with the Sword of Forever. I made the serious mistake of surviving all that. And here I am, as far from God as when I started this crap, simply because I didn't get killed. Well, then," Otto spread his arms outwards, "Take your best shot, boys."

And he jutted a belligerent chin.

The Suits' eyebrows, if you could call them eyebrows, rose. Ben was incredulous.

"You heard me," Otto taunted, twiddling his outstretched fingers in the universal 'come on!' sign. "Let's see what you got."

Ben's incredulity morphed into frustration. "They cannot fight you now. You have made common cause," he said.

"Uhm … what?"

Ben sighed. "You pointed out that your comrades are in Heaven. These," a point at the Suits, "are allied there, even if they oppose your presence."

"Uhm … what?" But Otto quickly held up a hand to freeze Ben's subsequent, and obviously exasperated, explanation. "Wait. Hold on. Just hold on. So, it's true. They're actually there? Ferdinand and the rest?"

Ben said nothing. Neither did the Suits, but that was typical. Except something in their stance served as confirmation.

The universe shifted. Otto saw it shift. Just like that other time, when the ship took off.

"It's done," he whispered. "It is … finished."

Otto braced, waiting for the Universe to unwind, the knot of reality to untie, all matter and anti-matter to whirlpool above the crimson clouds and suck everything, including Ben and the Fallen and the Suits, into the New Heavens, as outlined in Revelation.

Revelation, or Isaiah? Eh, can't remember. And irrelevant.

The very thing Ben feared, that unpredictable bizarre illogical people now stood in front of the Father, in the Throne Room, humans, Marc and Claudia and Bulsrobe, as the Father's own proof, and Ben is undone and history is resolved and the Lake ignites and Ben and the Fallen and, heck, maybe even the Suits, will drown in it for all eternity.

Any minute now.

Any minute.

Which stretched.

Otto felt like a comedian whose timing was off, especially when Ben cocked a querulous head at the Suits and then at him. "What are you doing?"

"Well ..." What was he doing? "I'm waiting for you and the rest of the fourth world of creation over there," dismissive flip of finger at the Suits and the Fallen, "to get tossed into the Lake of Fire and for me to hitch a chariot ride into the New Heaven."

Ben silently examined him. Then burst out laughing. As did the Fallen. Even the Suits shook shoulders a bit.

"Crap," Otto said.

"Oh, too much," Ben wiped his eyes. "You're a little old to believe in fairy tales."

What the— "Fairy tales? It's in the Bible, dude."

"Yes, as imperfectly and mistakenly transcribed by humans, who have no real grasp of such concepts as a day like a thousand years, a thousand years like a day."

Yep, Otto's timing was off.

Crap.

All right, Plan B.

The Suits remained in their frozen step position, intent on both Otto and Ben. No doubt waiting for the end of the argument.

So let's end it. "Okay. If your former Suit pals are no longer willing to jump, then, how 'bout you?"

Pause. "Satan?"

Good word because Ben flamed and the corruption underneath the mask glowed, but he quickly tamped it. "As much as I would love to peel your skin from your bones," he said, dryly, "I have promised not to do so. And," a quick interruption of Otto's next point, "neither will my soldiers."

"I release you from your promise."

Ben snorted. "You cannot release anyone from anything. Human."

Otto threw up his hands. "So, that's it? I'm hosed? I get to hang around with you and the Kingston Trio there," dismissive gesture at the Suits, "for the rest of whatever?"

"You could always kill yourself," Ben said, mildly.

Otto thought about that for a moment. "Bit hard to do, now that I'm back to full-on immortality."

Otto presented his hand. "See that? Even little stumpy is all healed up, although I'd like to have the whole finger back. Hard to make devil horns without it." And Otto gave one, with stumpy.

Ben glared at him. "I can accommodate you. Would you

prefer a cistern filled with water, or fire?"

"Put me in a situation where I can't reconstitute, hmm?" Otto shook his head. "As much as I appreciate the offer, I think propriety requires it to be at someone else's hands."

Ben smiled. "I'm sure we can find someone willing to accommodate your wishes."

And the Fallen leaned forward, anticipating.

"I'll bet," Otto said, "Somebody like Tac. Or Ferdinand, especially towards the end there. But I think I'll pass. Because something's occurred to me."

Otto pointed at the Suits. "You lose."

The Suits blinked in unison, confused. Ben did his own blink of confusion. "Pardon?"

"You lose, suckers." Otto waved his hand across the Suits. "Better luck next year. Maybe you'll get a good draft pick. Start rebuilding, you know, like the Eagles do every season?"

Ben was now full-on baffled. "What in Ersetu are you talking about?"

"Ersetu?"

Ben tsked that away. "It's a place. But, what do you mean that they have lost?"

"Simple." Otto inclined a belligerent head at the Suits. "If Marc and the others found their way to Heaven, then everything you did to keep us out — and, hoo boy, you certainly made the effort — came to naught. No?"

The Suits actually reddened.

"Furthermore," Otto was on a roll. "Me standing here, millions of light years or universes or whatever away from the City, is further evidence that you guys screwed the pooch. Blew it. Missed the bus. Backed the wrong horse." Otto flipped a hand at Ben. "Such as this guy."

And stared full at him, waiting for Ben to snarl and scream and then whirl into dust or whatever defeated devils did. Get sucked into the New Heavens. Sure hope it wasn't turn into a Roman candle, like Belial.

But Ben didn't ignite. Didn't even look chagrined. Instead, he smiled, a genuine smile of pure pleasure, which was not the reaction Otto expected.

"Uh oh," he muttered.

Ben winked at him, then turned to the Suits. "What the human says is true," he said, "So doesn't that make a delay all the more important?"

The Suits looked at each other. Then took a unified step towards Otto.

"Uh oh," Otto repeated. "But wait!" Repeated the upheld hand. "There's no delay! Humans are already there!"

Ben barely smirked. "Not all of them."

"What does that matter? We only needed one!"

"One who actually seeks the Face of God, not ones who gain it through their demise."

It came clear. Too clear.

God in His Grace would never let the crewmembers float for all eternity as dust and particle and stretched atoms. He would bring them home. But a human still had to make its way from City to Throne Room and present himself before the case was proved. No such human, case delayed. For another ten thousand years. For ever.

Forever

"That's why you offered me the kingdoms." It was even clearer. "To make the delay permanent. Change human history. No Christ. No salvation." He swallowed. "Case dismissed."

Ben splayed 'too bad' hands. "This works just as well."

The Suits didn't stop, moved right into the next unified step, their eyes fixed on Otto, their intent as clear as when they chased him through the streets of the City: dismember and dispose.

Frantic, Otto leaned back, hoping to find a break in the wall of Fallen and, when that didn't emerge, flailed his hands about...

And the hidden knife fell right into his hand.

He didn't hesitate. "Get back!" he yelled as he flipped the knife up. Man, thing was heavier than he thought and he almost dropped it but fear kept his grip. At a sharp movement behind him, Otto saw, out of the corner of his eye, the Fallen immediately behind him snarl and reach out with its talons but Ben yelled, "No!" and it froze.

Ben then made a courtly flourish at Otto and folded his arms, grinning madly.

Lucifer keeps his word. Who'da thunk it?

The Suits had stopped, warily eying the knife. Ah, so this

weapon was in the same class as arrows and Balearic slings: it could hurt Suits.

"Get back!" Otto yelled again and swung the blade in an arc across the Suits' path. It was actually a fairly decent knife, almost bowie-like. Made him feel like Davy Crockett facing a grizzly. Three of them.

Gulp.

The Suits looked at each other, reached into their jackets, and produced combat laser pistols.

"Uh oh," Otto said.

Ben laughed uproariously. "I can't WAIT to see what you do next!" he crowed at Otto.

"Makes two of us," he muttered as each Suit touched something on the side of the pistols and a blue light glowed as a humming noise, eerily reminiscent of a Star Trek phaser going critical, rose. In seconds, the guns would be charged and the Suits would slice and dice him, safely out of range of his waving blade.

Probably should leave.

As if reading his thoughts, the Fallen arrayed on Ben's shoulders closed ranks and drew their swords. The sounds of blades leaving scabbards behind him strongly indicated a similar action by the rear Fallen.

Can't go forward. Can't go backward.

What to do, what to do?

Well, simple; what any red-blooded American boy does when he's against it: drop back twenty and punt.

Chapter XXXII

The Old College Try

The Suits levelled their pistols simultaneously with Otto making a heroic leap at the glass. Whether they were startled by the sudden movement or surprised by its stupidity, their beams missed him and cut through the Fallen exposed by Otto's stupidity. It screamed in pain as the rest of the formation on either side of it frantically ducked out of the way.

The resulting chaos was good, Otto decided, because it'll prevent interference with this heroic — but decidedly stupid — punt.

Still in mid-flight, Otto gripped the knife and extended the blade, bracing for impact. Given how strong the observation glass looked, Otto was sure he would *sproing*! off it and end up flopping around on the floor. Then leap to his feet and hack his way through the rioting Fallen (ha!) and maybe, just maybe, escape down the hallway (ha! ha!) …

He didn't *sproing*. He went right through.

Not cleanly, of course. The entire glass observation deck exploded like an ice block slammed with a hammer, gigantic chunks of it careening all over the place.

Must have been under a lot of stress.

As he passed over the edge, Otto noted several strands of what looked like crystal ropes flying out alongside the chunks, some of the ropes drifting in the air, others, still attached to the rapidly descending ice, spooling out like runaway cables.

What'd they do, slap this thing together with spiderwebs?

He also noted that it was bitterly cold out here. And about six or seven miles straight down.

Not even time for an "uh oh," because he was over the edge and rapidly catching up with the chunks rocketing to the ground below him. He and the chunks aimed at a particularly ice-strewn portion of the beach lining the ice-ocean. Perhaps if he could locate a big enough snowdrift, he could plunk right through the middle of it and pop right back up, shaking his head like Daffy Duck. Then look up in just enough time to whimper, "Mother!" as a particularly large chunk of ice fell on him.

Be pretty funny.

Claudia, in a few moments, I'll be there with you and Marc and the rest of the guys.

He was still gripping the knife and it might be fun to see what happens if he led with it. Perhaps it would shatter the boulders on the beach in a similar manner as the observation deck, and he'd plunge straight into some black smoky pit lined with devils brandishing pitchforks, his Satanic Majesty himself, in horn-and-forked-tail mode, sitting on a skull throne going "Bwahahaha!" Should find out in oh, say, four, five seconds …

YANK!

Otto's right leg almost pulled out of his hip and he flew back up the mountain.

"*Oww!*" he yelled and looked up, expecting to see a Fallen gripping him by the ankle. But no. One of the spiderwebs had tangled around his leg and bungy-corded him up and up and up …

Right opposite the shattered chamber. Where it, naturally, paused at the top of its arc.

Otto peered inside. Things were chaotic. The Fallen fell here and there, some of them desperately scrambling at available spiderwebs and what was left of the edge, while others went airborne and frantically grabbed at their dangling pals.

Ben stood safely on what appeared to be a solid piece of floor, yelling something unintelligible at the crazy Fallen. The Suits stood a little behind him, still in line, still brandishing blue glowy laser pistols. All three of them looked at Otto.

"Hi, fellas," he said, and began his second descent.

Which didn't go as smoothly. For one thing, he was a bit off line and slammed a shoulder into an outcropping, putting him into a tumble down the cliff that bounced him from rock to rock. "*Ow! Ow! OW!*", as he fell. Still managed to hang onto the knife, probably because both of his fists were in death clenches. For the next thing, the bungy spiderweb tangled around the same rocks that were beating him to death and, any second now ...

YANK!

He was a yo-yo, bouncing violently up and down and side to side in mid-air, a marionette in the hands of a sadistic child. And, on top of that, he was swinging from rock face to open air. "I'm going to be sick," he said.

A purple beam slashed past his face.

"Whoa!" Otto yelled, as the bungy web finished its outward swing and headed back to the mountain. He looked up. The three Suits were leaning over the chamber edge and bringing the pistols to bear. A flock of Fallen circled above them, brandishing their swords and screaming something. Two of the pistols brightened and purple beams lanced outward exactly at the moment he swung under the rock, missing him, but melting through a part of the mountain face.

"Crap," Otto said as the bungee reached its end and he traveled back out, making Otto a sitting — or rather, dangling — duck. He braced, expecting to get severed in a flash of purple. Maybe he could dodge the lasers.

Ha.

The Suits were still there, but only one of them was drawing a bead. The other two looked impatiently at the sides of their pistols as the circling Fallen, their numbers increasing by the moment, yelled at them.

Oh, right, have to charge back up.

But not the guy aiming. He fired.

The return swing of the bungee web saved Otto, but barely; the beam coursed the side of his bungee-free leg. "Gah!" he yelped as the beam burned away his pants and part of his skin.

Man, that hurt!

Which meant they had his range, so the next time he swung out, he was vaporized.

So don't swing out.

He was already at the rock wall, which meant he had mere seconds before the bungee whipped him back out, a big, fat, squirming target for the delight of the Laser Boys up there.

Frantically, Otto twisted himself into an L and pawed at the rocks, grabbing at any little knob that presented itself, but the web was spinning him away from good purchase. If anything, his scrambling was helping with the return swing.

"Dammit!" he yelled and, in desperation, stabbed the rocks with the knife.

Where it stuck.

The blade sank about three inches into the wall. "Now, that's a knife," he whistled.

Maintaining the death grip, Otto swung side to side from the pivot of his wrist melded to the hilt.

The side-to-side motion slowed after a moment, as did Otto's nausea, and he took stock of the situation: he was hanging partially upside down (actually more sideways) along the underside of what was once an observation chamber containing three very PO-d Suits and about three thousand even more PO'd Fallen (and Lucifer, don't forget him). The spider web from which he was dangling needed only a slight whack from a Fallen's sword to sever it and send him plunging miles to the rocky beach over his head. Well, under him, since he was upside down (sort of). And his leg hurt.

Should probably get down from here.

"Brilliant," he muttered, and considered his options.

Let go of the hilt, but, judging by the tightness of the web, all that would accomplish was whipping him back out where he'd be a big, fat, squirming target for the delight of the Laser Boys up there.

Disentangle from the spider web, which meant a very quick trip to the beach below.

Climb down? Otto examined the rock face, noting enough chinks and fractures to serve as handholds. Doable, for someone not freezing to death and aching from the various strains and burns and tendon yanks he'd acquired over the last two or three minutes.

What to do?

And while he was deciding which of the unpalatable options to choose, someone else decided for him.

An eagle scream behind Otto startled him and he twisted around the hilt to see. A Fallen hovered in the clear air past the shielding rock face, its yellow eyes glaring at Otto with hate and triumph, its sword out and ready for combat.

"Uh oh," seemed the appropriate response.

The Fallen grinned, its fangs shining in the ice-cold sunlight, and moved closer, the tip of the blade seeking a good place to slip through Otto's body.

"You can't touch me, remember?" Otto yelled at the Fallen, wondering if Lucifer's promise was still binding after Otto had messed up his observation chamber. Or, how much of a Lucifer promise was binding to begin with. After all, he was a tricky devil.

Ha.

The Fallen stopped, frowned, and began fang-gnashing (which had to hurt), and backed up to the entrance of the overhang, its frustration evident. Otto was about to breathe a sigh of relief when it casually reached up and cut the spider web. Which, Otto had to admit, was still within the boundaries of Lucifer's promise since he'd not said anything about restraining devices.

Otto's legs dropped to vertical, the sudden surge of gravity and momentum almost caused him to lose his grip on the knife and continue down to the waiting beach. And God's Throne Room, where everyone goes when they get "killed" out here. At least, the Suits and Ben had so indicated. He stared along the blade, sure the extra weight would work it loose but, no, still solidly planted in the rock.

 This is a really good knife.

Otto's hands were turning into ice blocks in the sub-zero temperature; for that matter, so was the rest of him. One advantage of that, he was too numb to hurt. Again. Maybe when this was all over, he'd get another wolf bath.

He glanced back. The Fallen still hovered there, its arms crossed, smiling. Patient. It probably could hover there longer than Otto could hang here. All it had to do was wait until Otto, inevitably, lost his grip and then casually follow Otto down to witness his death by Sudden Deceleration Syndrome, then casually fly back up and tell Ben and the Suits that everything was now okay. Break out the champagne, we've bought ourselves another hundred thousand years or so.

But, wait a minute, didn't that mean the entire crew assembled in the Throne Room and we can get on with that whole Apocalypse thing now, Lord? "Not all of them," Ben had said. So, wouldn't this be all of them? Even if it was by demise?

I dunno. I just don't know.

Could be some codicils and caveats and sub-statutes rendering such a verdict null and void. At least not until a lot of other conditions were fulfilled, such as Otto making a very sincere effort to avoid dashing on the rocks below until aforementioned dashing was unavoidable.

Need to consult a lawyer well-versed in Judgment Seat protocols, a guy like, say, Ben.

Let's not do that.

Let's, instead, keep fighting until all options are exhausted. Like he was quickly becoming.

Climb down it is.

Otto peered at the rock face. There was a particularly fetching cleft about three inches below the blade. Otto braced his ice-bound legs against the rock, reached out with his left hand and slammed his fingers into the opening. And held on.

One advantage of hands freezing into claws, they served as pitons.

Otto pulled at the knife but it didn't budge. Dang. There's such a thing as being too good a knife, ya know. Quickly, Otto released the handle and drove his right hand, stumpy and all, into the same cleft, scrambling around with his feet until he located protuberances and anchored on them. He waited a moment, sure he was about to pitch off the wall and finish the Fallen's job for him. But, no.

All right!

Otto took in two or three triumphant breaths and searched the rock face. Okay, some fairly decent fractures running below the cleft, should serve our purpose, and Otto shoved his left piton hand into it and then his right piton hand, stumpy included, and fastened there and then probed with his feet and found a couple of knobs and was now a few feet below the knife.

Hey, look, Ma, I'm free climbing. Or, more accurately, free descending.

Otto had never been a mountain climbing kind of guy. The advent of helicopters had made that endeavor somewhat irrelevant, and Otto had classified mountain climbers the same as ski bums: rich guys who didn't have the nerve to do something actually dangerous like join the Marines so spent their daddies' trust funds trying to prove they were courageous. But, after working his way from fissure to crack to outcropping and another six feet or so down the cliff side, he developed a respect.

This was pretty tough. Especially if you're three-quarters frozen to death.

He wasn't sure he would make it, the trembling in his shoulders presaging an exhaustion that could make one more reach a bad one and down he goes. All for naught.

At least he tried.

Yeah. He *was* trying, wasn't he?

Maybe that was the point.

Otto mused as he probed with numb toes for the next level down. What if this entire universal, cosmic, bloody war between God and the Firsts and the Fallen and Suits and whatnot revolved around the simple act of trying?

Trying to find your way to God for absolution, answers, assurances. Trying to find the Throne Room so that you, a lesser creature, exhausted and frozen and broken and bloody, could stand there and look Him in the Eye and say, I made it.

Because, if a lesser creature, beset by vanities and weaknesses downright debilitating, could fight his way across a desert, jump on a patched-together hunk-of-junk rocket and work his way through hopeless planets and rivers and crazed flying creatures and enemy star fleets and exploding stars and then swim floods and cross snowfields while starving and fight monster-demons and present himself at the foot of the Throne and say, "I tried …"

Then the rest of Creation was without excuse.

Another horrifying scream behind him but Otto knew what it was. He looked back. The Fallen was still there, its face twisted into a rage edged with despair.

"Read my mind, didja?" Otto said to it, and its face doubled in fury. "Remember," Otto admonished, "you can't touch me." With greater confidence, he sought the next steps down, not much caring if any were there.

Because it did not matter if he made it or not. If he fell and died on the beach below and woke up in the Throne Room, or didn't, and the Millennium triggered, or it didn't, there, eventually, would be another Otto or Claudia or Amelia clinging to the side of this mountain who would, or would not, succeed in climbing down to the beach and continuing on to whatever.

And it did not matter if Lucifer and his pals got another two hundred thousand years of reprieve. Eventually, the lesser creature would drag himself off the beach and into the Throne Room and say, "Here I am."

Because a thousand years was like a day, and a day, like a thousand years.

The Fallen screamed again, the tenor a little different, and Otto peered around his hyper-extended shoulder. The Fallen was stretched upward and screaming towards the invisible chamber.

Ah. "Telling your pals, hey?" Otto chuckled. "Little good it will do them," and he moved another foot down.

Another scream and Otto lost his temper. "Look, dude," he said, turning halfway on the next fissure, which was, whoa, dangerous, so take it easy, "you've lost, all right?"

But the Fallen wasn't looking at him. It was looking up, its sword sheathed and holding out its hands like it was about to catch something. "What the heck?" Otto said.

A black object like a tennis ball fell below the overhang's edge and the Fallen deftly caught it. Puzzled, Otto squinted, trying to figure out what it was, but he didn't have to wait long because the Fallen underhanded it at him, and Otto recognized it.

Dimensional grenade.

Another one of those weird weapons the Suits possessed. They'd hurled them at Otto and Ferdinand during the battle on the train. One carried Machine Gun Kelly and his immediate environment off in a cloud of purple lightning to ... somewhere. Orbit of the black suns? The despair of endless horizon that was the true Hell? The snowfields on the other side of this prehistoric Antarctica?

Let's not find out.

The grenade, pulsing with little lightnings around its sphere (which probably meant impending detonation), was arcing towards him. Obviously, one of the Suits had tossed it to the Fallen, who'd relayed it in a double-play to win the pennant and Otto almost considered letting it take him. Because, it didn't matter if he made it or not, someone would.

Eventually.

Three million years from now, maybe, but still. And maybe Lucifer and his pals would consider that a victory because they were evil and evil took its triumphs from the immediate, not the inevitable, which meant many, many more of Otto's people would suffer frustration and anguish and pain and unnecessary loss for the duration but, really, what's the problem? We're going to win this thing.

Eventually ...

Fuggidabowdit.

The grenade curved in final arc and, judging by its increased pulsing, final detonation. Otto tracked it. He'd been quite the martial arts aficionado when he was alive. He'd not been the greatest of practitioners but held his own, and still had the reaction time.

He kicked the grenade, sending it straight up in the air.

He overextended on the kick and lost his footing, hanging dangerously by his frozen piton hands, but holding. He wondered whether the Fallen's relay pitch broke the conditions of Lucifer's promise, allowing him to cry "Foul!," but probably not, at least in its legalistic terms, and he doubted this was the best time for an argument, anyway, because he'd get a shower of these damn grenades while he was trying to make the point, so best get down to the beach and run away because he couldn't kick all of the grenades aside — he wasn't Bruce Lee, ya know

— and then it detonated.

Sudden, bright, purple light overhead confirmed that the grenade didn't make much sound when it exploded, only *fizzle-pop*, like a ball of static electricity. He looked up. The grenade had, apparently, reached the top of the overhang when it went off, and Otto watched as a cloud of purple lightning and fog expanded out rapidly, reaching for him. Otto was sure he was within the blast radius and he braced for a sudden trip to some noxious hellhole when the cloud closed within itself, *pfhht*! and was gone. As was the overhang.

There was a creaking sound.

The grenade had bitten a perfect sphere of nothing out of the rock, giving Otto a direct view of the chamber up there, where Fallen still flocked and the three Scream-heads hovered, peering down at him. Which meant they could now resume peppering him with laser beams, which had a geometrically better chance of doing him in than some random grenade.

Couldn't kick beams out of the way. Let's head for the beach. Quickly.

The creaking sound levelled up to a downright *crack*! so loud and startling that, not only did Otto jump, almost losing his grip, but so did the Fallen still hanging in mid-air and the Suits pointing the pistols at him.

A gigantic fissure broke at the edge of the hole and rapidly expanded, flying up the side of the mountain at an angle that brought it below the chamber. Rocks and debris rained down and Otto flattened against the mountain to avoid them.

A roar and the mountain trembled and Otto squeezed his hands hard into the clefts, trying to create better handholds. The trembling turned into a downright earthquake and Otto risked a look. The top of the mountain was coming off.

Grenade must have taken out a pylon or two.

An entire shelf of rock slid over his head in slow motion, and Otto was sure his portion of the mountain would give way and follow it, too, but no, it stayed. He had a tough time keeping hold as the mountain shook and swayed but that was the advantage of completely numb hands: he couldn't feel the agony.

The shelf cleared him and Otto watched, fascinated, as it

pitched out into space in a slow, ponderous tumble, the first turn of it revealing Ben's palace, temple grounds and all, still intact at the very top before the whole shebang broke up and the palace fell between two sides of the collapsed plateau, disappearing between them. Some Fallen circled the whole mess, but it looked as though the majority had been caught in the break-up and hurtled to the beach, probably in company with Ben and the Suits.

It took about five seconds for the tons of rock and ice and palace to hit the beach below, and it was like a bomb went off. *BOOM*! Followed by a hundred other smaller *booms*! as the succeeding rock and cliff side piled on top of the main one. A gigantic ripple flew out from the beach and into the ocean, cracking the ice shield and tipping bergs as far out as Otto could see through the overwhelming cloud of ice crystals and dust that had roared back up the side, blinding and choking him.

And then it was silent.

Except for his coughing, that is, as he cleared his lungs. He blinked hard to clear his eyes because he didn't dare wipe them, his hold on the remaining mountainside tenuous enough. Rumbles echoed away from him, but the air was still and pure and the cloud of debris settled and Otto, finally, teared up enough to wash away the dust. He looked, expecting to see a squadron of Fallen dive-bombing on him, but the air was clear. Little flakes of blue ice danced around him like fairies.

He couldn't help it: he started laughing.

The echoes bounced off the cliff face and around the peaks and down to the wreckage of rock and ice below and back up to him and over the sharp angle of the new mountaintop and out and around and he laughed louder and harder, the numbness of his arms and the pain and cold no longer mattering.

"Now that!" he crowed to the fairies dancing around him, "is a classic hoisting by petard!"

"Petard! Petard! Petard!" echoed around and over and across and Otto laughed louder as the fairies danced and thickened and thickened …

And thickened.

Otto stopped laughing.

Another rumbling sound, louder, ominous, and gaining in

volume. Coming from above. Otto looked up right as a wall of snow and ice tidal-waved over the top and took him.

Avalanche, he thought, whisked away from the side of the mountain and out into the air and down. Talk about petard hoisting.

Falling, he smacked from rock to rock, and each hit broke something — an arm, a leg, a neck — and even his frozen body couldn't stop the nuclear explosions of sharp electric pain rampaging through him.

And then he felt nothing.

Chapter XXXIII

This Heaven

Cold.

Man, was it.

Sub-zero cold, the kind that killed in minutes, that should have already killed Otto, but hadn't. Unfathomable why, not because he was snow-packed head to toe, and even in the City, that was enough to eliminate all chances of regeneration. Right now, he should be shivering and gasping while watching the light in his brain shrink to a minuscule point, then go to sleep and never wake up. But he wasn't shivering, wasn't all that bothered by the cold, in fact. It was only a factor of the current environment, like mosquitos in August. Not that he couldn't stand a sweater or something, but this was … bearable.

Actually, quite comfortable.

On his back and buried in snow, that much was obvious. But it was the same as the snow caves he'd slept in while going up the mountain: not the most ideal of resting spots, but not the worst.

That honor belonged to a motel deep in the Tennessee hill country that Sherry and he had stayed at one night about forty-five years ago because it was late and they had hundreds of miles more to go and they were both beat and there wasn't another motel for another fifty of those miles. Turned out to be a converted horse stable, with an iron cot set in the middle of a single concrete room that also sported a toilet and a shower.

Otto had considered the utility of taking a shower while lying in bed, but Sherry had taken a dim view.

About ten minutes after getting into the room, a big piece of wood slid across the single window, giving the impression they were locked in. Both Sherry and he had stayed awake all night, Otto's .357 on his lap, convinced the *Deliverance* guys were going to cook them for breakfast. Morning, of course, revealed the situation: the motel was of the no-tell type, and the big piece of wood was a sliding horse door that covered a one-car garage that couples seeking dalliance could use to hide their vehicles. The door sliding over their window was one such couple making their getaway. Sherry and he laughed about it later.

Perhaps he would laugh about this later, too.

In the interim, he should get up. Go find a sweater. Figure out what the blue blazes was going on.

That may not be so easy. Extrapolating from the last few minutes (hours? days?), he should be under sixty or so feet of snow and ice and boulders — and building parts — somewhere on a frozen beach on a frozen sea in the Antarctic of some ten or fifteen billion years ago. That is, if he was crediting Ben's timeline. And recent events indicated Ben should not be credited with anything, so apply the appropriate grains of salt.

And let's go.

He opened his eyes, rewarded with about a ton of snow falling into them. "Ack!" he exclaimed with a frantic wiping to clear them but more snow replaced what he flicked away. Should be another sixty feet of this crap before he got his eyes clear of it and, really, this wouldn't do.

Start digging.

He pushed both arms straight up to do just that and was quite surprised to find himself grasping at clear air. He sat up, a few inches of snow falling away. He was on the surface.

How 'bout that?

Apparently, he'd ridden the top of the avalanche all the way down.

He slapped at his head and chest, flinging snow remainders hither and yon until he was relatively snow-free, and then did inventory. All those bones he'd broken on the way down the mountain appeared to have knitted. Otherwise, he should be roughly in the shape of a starfish. Still dressed in the tux, which was relatively intact, a few abrasions here and there.

Remarkable.

You'd expect a bit more wear and tear after riding an avalanche down the side of a mountain and into a polar sea. You'd expect a little more wear and tear on yourself, too, like the various bones broken on the way down turning him into a starfish. Yet he, like the tux, was relatively intact, only a few abrasions here and there.

Was his immortality fully restored?

Quickly Otto threw out both hands and scrutinized them for frost and rock damage, but the only defect was stumpy. She, though, was clean and healed and rather fetching. Otto liked it. But its presence indicated that he was still a few bars short of full power; otherwise, he'd have a brand spanking new little finger. Manicured, at that.

The new normal?

Otto considered. He wasn't cold, and he should be. He was still in one piece, tux and all, and he shouldn't be. Given recent events, he was in rather excellent shape. It seemed he had regained his City body, one that had proven extremely durable and tough but which could suffer pain and injury. It did fully recover, though.

So, why the stump?

Souvenir?

Okay. Be a great conversation piece: "Hey, you guys see this? Let me tell you how I lost it. It's a funny story." And the guys would buy him rounds as he regaled them with lurid descriptions of halberding over a crevasse and fighting a demon. Hopefully, no one would realize he'd lost his finger through clumsiness, not heroics.

Reminder?

That he was not all that?

"Bingo," he said.

Otto looked around. He was sitting on a plain of blue ice, a uniform smoothness broken by snow hummocks and boulder uplifts. Behind him was a blue frozen ocean, ice flung up here and there all the way to the blue horizon ...

Why is everything blue?

Otto looked up. There was a single sun about three-quarters down the sky, but this one wasn't golden, it was blue ... no, not really, only seemed that way because it was masked by some kind of blue gauze, high-level clouds or fog or something.

Eerie.

It cast a blue light over everything, like some matte painting of an alien ice world. Hoth? Otto expected a wampa or a tauntaun, but now he was being silly.

Was he?

He shook his head. Who knows? Nothing he'd experienced since the moment, five lifetimes ago, when he woke facedown in the City had convinced him this was real, that it was nothing more than coma dream. So the cast of *Star Wars* could show up about now and he could take it in stride ...

Dude.

Face it.

This is no dream.

And you are not in a coma.

A coma, a dream, had to work with previously screened material, and, as Ben had pointed out, when had Otto ever read about Firsts, and a Lucifer not so much evil as incompetent, and factions upon factions with their own agendas, and an Earth whose pre-history involved some rather hellacious combat, and a creation — the Creation — that was more inadvertent than planned?

Perhaps he had speculated on these things once. Perhaps, as he had pointed out to Ben, he had heard them and then forgotten but his subconscious retained them and, under the influence of coma and brain damage and whatever truly outstanding drugs the doctors were pumping through his system right now, had weaved this wondrous tale. Perhaps the coma'd mind was very, very creative.

Dude.

This is no dream.

You are not in a coma.

Yes, yes, it's been lovely and consoling to regard all this as mere flight of unconscious fancy but you have to let it go, let it go, and face the stark truth that you died in the driveway on a summer afternoon, and that you are in the Afterlife, because there is one rather overwhelming fantasy-canceling concept overriding all your doubts:

Never, ever, had he conceived of a Heaven without God.

Otto squinted at the sun. There were concentric circles about it, thick ones, no doubt caused by ice crystals in the blue gauze, but it gave the sky a *Twilight Zone* motif, and Otto had never thought of the Afterlife as a twilight zone. A place of rest and peace and no more pain, yes, or simply not there, a figment of wishful thinking and centuries of relentless indoctrination because death was actually a great void. A nothing place. Nowhere.

But never this.

Never an Afterlife of worlds upon worlds and beings never considered and purposes unfinished and wars everlasting. An Afterlife with no God ... correction, with God, but an elusive One.

You are not in a coma. You are dead.

You are lost.

You are alone.

Shaking himself out of the snow, Otto rose shakily to his feet. Ice crystals danced in the air, blue fairies, and in the far distance was a ridge of snow-covered mountains. He turned around and stared at the ocean, spotting an odd jumble about a half-mile offshore. Otto could swear it was the wreckage of Ben's outer temple, but it was too far away for him to be certain. He did a slow 360, but it was all ice and ocean and plain forever world without end amen under a blue-lit sun.

He turned back to the mountains. I am dead. Not about to be dead from cold and distance and hunger, but already dead. I have passed on, and I am lost in an Afterlife no one, not even the most spiritual of God's prophets, had conceived. The truth of it was beyond human ability *to* conceive, so God never explained it.

Ants contemplating New York City.

The same thought he had on the ship after disposing of Karl's body. An ant on a sidewalk of Central Park sees the motion and shapes and movements and is terrified, paralyzed, uncomprehending. So Ant-Man dons the helmet and explains things in ant terms: this is the human hive and these gigantic beings of boot and DDT are omnipotent and omnipresent and if you worship them properly, then you will be rewarded by the occasional sandwich left in the grass or an unguarded jar of jam and your nest remains undisturbed, and when you die you will enter a land of marmalade and white sugar.

But if you defy the humans, invade their temples, steal their food and generally act in an unpleasant manner, then your homes will burn and you will be poisoned and driven into wildernesses of sand and asphalt and your Afterlife will be Sheol in a glass jar.

Because ants cannot grasp what forces they are observing, the mechanics of a human city, what a human actually is. And Ant-Man cannot dumb it down enough for the ant brain to fully comprehend.

Best that can happen is a flawed ant cosmology developed over centuries. And when the ants die, they'll discover, with great shock, that the ant Afterlife is not Sheol in a glass jar but a meadow of honey grass and sugar trees and butterflies and monster anteaters. In other words, far more than they ever dreamed.

Far more.

"Miles to go before I sleep," Otto muttered. Because this Afterlife was not one of rest under shades of trees or hugs in the bosom of Abraham, no, not at all. It was far more than he had ever dreamed. It was conflict and loss and sojourn across universes while seeking, always seeking, the Source. And when the Source was found, beheld, then, given all that has gone before, there would be other missions, other tasks, other tests of faith.

Yet ...

The strong indication from everyone Otto had encountered or fought or run away from during this whole cockamamie journey was that he was headed towards a resolution of some kind. As endless as all of this seemed, as eternal the search, there was a beckoning in the distance, a light glimpsed on a far peak, a finger of a cloud pointing a direction, a still small voice urging the next step and the next.

And it was leading somewhere important. Everyone and everything he'd run into or through deemed it very important that a mud creature, a broken, baffled, doubting, and downright frustrated human, either keep going or not keep going, depending on the viewpoint.

Because?

Because, if the least of Creation holds doggedly to its purpose and one day mounts the golden steps and stares God in the Face and asks, "Why?" then the scrolls of Heaven open and sheer light floods the Universe.

At least that's what the ants believe.

Otto chuckled. He was an ant contemplating infinity, far less capable of grasping its meaning than real ants could New York City. Heck, even as a human, New York had baffled him. So much more this place. And here it is set before you, ant.

And it's not like you've got anything else to do.

A distant cracking and a rumble startled Otto and he whirled about, ready for combat. The jumble out in the middle of the ocean shifted and tilted and Otto swore he saw a temple column rise in the air before the whole mess slid noiselessly under the ice, small ripples arriving at the ice beach a few moments later.

That, seemed that.

Otto turned back in the mountains' direction, took a step, then another, and began singing. "The ants go marching one by one, hurrah, hurrah ..."

"... the ants go marching hundred by hundred, the little one stops to ..." What?

Otto paused in mid-step, frowning. What rhymes with hundred? Blundered? But that should be 'blundred,' and that ain't a word. Nundred? Nun dread? Okay, work nun dread into it, and press on.

The going had been fairly easy, at least for an ice field. He hadn't completely escaped mishap, slipping now and again and one time tripping on a boulder but it wasn't as bad as it should be and he wasn't as cold as conditions should make him, further proof he had regained his City body — sans finger.

Somewhere around "ants marching eighty-five" (and the little one wished he was still alive, which made Otto laugh and lose the rhythm, but he got the ants down in the ground to get out of the rain), it became apparent he was climbing a gradual rise. Otto should reach the top by ant hundred and three (the little one asked, "What's all these crazy questions they're asking me? Momma told me not to come!"), so he decided to save that verse for the cresting. A few minutes later, he walked over the top and stopped. And looked.

Another flat plain, thank God, so more easy-going, except this one had ice blocks aplenty: hundreds of them, some fallen into each other making strange, blue-lit arches; others standing on end like monoliths; the rest on their sides like tables. God had cast a handful of icebergs across the land, hoping for sevens. The mountains were a bit closer now, an increment taller as backdrop and throwing the blue sunlight back at him while contrasting the ice field with great detail and sharpness ...

Someone was sitting on an ice table in the middle of the plain.

Otto blinked and then rubbed his eyes and looked again and, yep, someone's definitely sitting there.

"Great," he muttered. Probably the Bridge Keeper, and Otto must answer his questions three. Or it was the Black Knight, and he'd have to dismember the guy and suffer bite wounds? Whoever or whatever it was, this meeting was intentional.

Otto shrugged. Heck, he'd bested Lucifer. What could this guy do?

What a stupid question.

Resolved to his fate, Otto set off, holding the ants in abeyance until he'd conversed with the English kannigit over there. The snow was thinner, which made the going even easier than he'd predicted, like a trek across clouds. Cold, wet ones, but wasn't that their nature?

The distance closed rapidly and Otto made out the Bridge Keeper a little better. A man with medium shaggy black hair cut a little long but still within AFR35-10, a short beard that had some obvious care taken of it, big eyebrows, big nose, and a homely — but pleasant — face. The guy was wearing an open corduroy shirt like a lumberjack and a pair of jeans. Levis, if

Otto's eyes didn't deceive him.

Man, those things are everywhere. Hurray for capitalism.

The closer he got, the more Otto became convinced he knew the guy. It was like walking into a gas station and running into someone he'd known a long time ago, a high school pal or someone he'd been stationed with or run the streets with and pledged eternal brotherhood to but, as high school or the assignment ended and another life began, the two of them went in different directions. Otto was fairly certain this guy was once important to him, but had faded to background.

Except ... except ...

Otto frowned. He didn't think this guy had ever really faded. He'd been hovering on the edge of Otto's life, watching, nodding, shaking his head from time to time and smiling during other times. He'd been with Otto always ...

Otto stopped dead in his tracks. "Jesus," he said.

The man smiled.

"You're Jesus." Otto was not sure *how* he knew, but he knew.

Another smile. And a nod.

It was Jesus. Not the long-haired ascetic with white skin and blue eyes that Western artists for thousands of years had depicted, but the real Jesus, a regular guy from Roman-occupied Palestine around the years -4 to 35 (depending on whose calendar was credited). Maybe that's why Otto recognized Him.

He was the real deal.

"You're Jesus!" Otto said again, less for confirmation, more in amazement.

Jesus, obviously amused, cocked His head as He folded His Hands on His lap. Otto noted they were heavily scarred. Of course.

So, Otto, you're face-to-face with the Lord, *the* Lord, the High Priest, the Saviour, the Prince of Peace, Numero Uno in every single Western cosmology ever conceived (well, Numero Dos, because Daddy was first, Spirit third. Right?). What was the protocol here?

Otto fell to his knees. "Lord," he said, "I'm not worthy."

Jesus laughed.

The sound of it swept through Otto like a wind of joy and

peace and never, ever in his entire life had Otto felt so ... safe. Relieved. Protected.

It was stunning, as if the weights of his life had simply taken wing and flown into the blue gauze sky and were forever gone.

Otto watched them as they flew away, the hilarity of childhood turning to the angst of high school and the frustrations of adulthood and, woven through it all was the search, the seeking, a golden thread binding the weights of happiness and sadness of his short mortal span into one cloth. He didn't always know the binding, many times had forgotten it, but it was there all the same.

Otto laughed.

Human and God laughed together, because this moment, this meeting of flesh and spirit, rendered everything before unimportant.

That Otto had spent a childhood and adolescence in pain and fear and loneliness, unimportant.

That he had struggled to find a place and a purpose and to carve out in the spaces of the Earth his own way, his own name, and to make himself relevant, irrelevant.

All of the years tossed by tempest and tide and washing here and there onto islands of prosperity and meaning and then washed away by other tides across other horizons until finally, finally, after a life of adventure and conflict and winning and losing, he had, at the right moment, passed into the Creator's realm.

And did not stop searching.

And that made for a good laugh.

Spent with it, Otto almost fell face forward into the snow, amazed at how the lifting of burdens could actually exhaust one. He was thousands of pounds lighter now, but less able to move. He looked up. Jesus was thousands of pounds heavier, but had the frame for it.

Jesus rocked a bit back and forth as the last of the chuckles dispersed, then looked full at Otto. "Well done," He said.

Otto nodded. Nothing more needed to be said. No crowns presented, names proclaimed, mansions offered. It was praise enough. "Thank You." He paused. "For everything."

Jesus smiled a bit and looked off, gazing on sky and

horizon. Otto remained kneeling, not only because he was spent but because it seemed appropriate. He wasn't cold or hungry or bereft, either, which was fine, just fine. He could stay silent and worshipful for as long as the Lord wanted.

Moments passed. Then minutes. And Otto figured that was long enough. "So … can I ask You a few questions?"

Jesus waved an impatient hand. "Later," He said, "We have something more important to discuss first."

"Oh. Okay."

A bit off-putting, that, but who was he to lead a conversation with the Prince of Peace? So, Otto waited.

And waited.

Well past the time of politeness, Otto shifted and cleared his throat, "Uhm …"

"I like this place," Jesus, completely out of left field, said, casting a Hand over the terrain. "It's one of those folds, where you can move easily between things. That's why the odd blue sky." A gesture upwards. "The particles involved tend to that wavelength."

Otto thought this an odd turn in the conversation, but this was Jesus, so, go with it. "I thought it more *Twilight Zone*-y."

"Ha!" Jesus said. "Does look like an episode. But you'll get used to it."

"I will?"

Jesus regarded him. "Yes."

Otto was immediately on guard. "Why? What will I be doing?"

"What you choose."

"Really? Anything?" Otto suddenly felt like a kid on Christmas morning which, given the situation, was pretty funny.

"No."

Uh oh, didn't like the sound of that. Otto suddenly felt like a kid who'd found coal in his stockings.

"What," he asked, guardedly, "am I supposed to choose?"

More waiting almost to the point of impoliteness before Jesus responded, "Whether to go on or not."

Otto stared at Him. Peter had more or less asked the crew that same question, and they'd all chosen to go on and merrily tripped their way back to the ship and out into space and smack into all the crap, culminating in a wrecked ship and a lost crew.

And lost dogs and a lost little finger.

He let out a long slow breath. "Lord, what I'm going to say next is going to come off as really smartass, but You know that I am a smartass and I hope You are not offended, but ... this isn't the way it's supposed to be." Otto braced, expecting a sudden trip to the plains of Hell.

Jesus gave a short laugh. "I know. It's supposed to be golden throne rooms and rivers of milk and honey and no more war and turn the other cheek. That's what I offered Judea, and what did they do? Sold me to the Romans." He shook His head, ruefully. "You see, I wasn't the Saviour they wanted. I was supposed to be in Judgment Mode, riding a white horse with brass hooves and wielding a fiery sword and crushing the Romans under My feet as the Judeans danced around going, 'Nanny Nanny Boo Boo!'"

Otto raised an eyebrow. Did the Lord of Hosts just say, "Nanny Nanny Boo Boo!"?

"And that *would* have happened," Jesus continued, "if they had accepted the Beatitudes. But they wanted Judgment first, Redemption later, and that is not how it works." He bore down on Otto. "And now, you get to make the same choice."

"I ... what?" Startling, that. "What choice?"

"Life. Or the Fire."

"What!" Otto was bewildered.

And then afraid. He thought he had salvation already sewn up. Pretty much everyone he had run into up here had confirmed absolution was as easy as the idle, momentary, and quite ignorant acceptance Otto'd made while idling on a hill watching clouds. But, if he correctly understood what Christ had said, that may not be so.

Jesus, apparently reading his thoughts (which, c'mon, it's Jesus), wagged a finger. "I do not mean for you personally. I mean, for humanity."

All Otto could say was, "Bwa?"

"Because, if you do not choose to go on," Jesus went on, "then it ends. The Universe will be rolled up like a scroll and purged. Of course, We'll do the Millennium first, but that's basically a weekend. Everyone will be sorted, based on their choice for or against Me, and those who said no …" Jesus made a finger-across-the-throat sign.

Otto marveled.

"Or, we can go a different route." He looked at Otto expectantly.

Despite the sheer heart-stopping terror of what Jesus had said, Otto grinned. "Okay, I'll play the straight man. What is this route, O Lord?"

Jesus didn't grin back and Otto realized this was serious. Very serious.

"You choose to fight the enemy at this level," Jesus said.

"Bwa?" Again.

"You already know that the war is at stasis," Jesus said. Otto did not have to ask what war. "The forces are balanced. One side cannot gain advantage over the other. The only way to finish it is to invoke Final Judgment, with all its subsequent Wraths. We do not wish to do that. We wish for life to continue."

Wow. Just wow. But, that didn't seem right. "Isn't the Final Judgment sort of the point?"

Jesus nodded. "It is, but it does not have to be Final." Jesus threw a scarred palm at Otto. "Have you ever wondered why thousands of years have passed without My return?"

"On occasion."

Jesus chuckled. "More than occasionally, I heard your complaints. Do you know that, legally, We could have invoked Final Judgment at any point after My Ascension? The very next second, if We'd wanted. See, all the case needed as proof was only one human to accept Me. By then, we had a lot more than that."

Otto didn't have to ask what case. "So, why didn't You?"

"Because of life." Jesus shook his head admiringly. "Because of what you do with it. You are all so lively and curious and inspiring and wonderful. I love what you are. We all do. We want you to continue for thousands of years more. Millions."

The light went on. "But the case still needs resolving."

"Yes."

"So …" The light got brighter. "To break the impasse, You

need a marshal to serve the arrest warrants, haul in the prisoners." He paused.

Jesus leaned forward.

"And that's ... us. Humans. Because ... because ..." Otto was working through it furiously, "we are unpredictable. No one would see us coming. We could break what can't be broken. We could ... defeat them. And then Earth abides. Forever."

Forever.

Otto almost fell over at the implications. Life goes on, generations are born and die and all of them, each of them, have the chance to acquire a ridiculously easy salvation with an Afterlife in the City or, if they felt the urge, a flight across the Universe to join in extraordinary combat against monsters and myths ...

Wait.

How can that be? If he defeated the monsters then the war is over, the enemy consigned, the darkness of the Universe ended so then, so then ... what is humanity's purpose?

The answer came unbidden: simply, to live. To dream. To find God.

His mind reeling, Otto whispered, "Why me?"

"Because, you made it here."

But that's not right, either. It was too simple. It could have been anyone else. Could have been Marc or Amelia or Claudia. Any one of them was better suited. "That was luck. I don't think You want to base victory on that."

Jesus snorted. "Luck? There is no such thing. There is resolve."

Otto wondered about the efficacy of starting an argument with the Messiah over the existence, or not, of luck. Luck certainly seemed to be an important factor on Earth: where you were born, who you were born to, even the epoch of your birth.

But does that have any bearing on the person you turn out to be? Winston Churchill, or Charles the First? Abraham Lincoln, or Bonnie and Clyde?

"Okay," Otto conceded, "I still think that's an argument we can have, but resolve? The others had it in spades." Jesus knew to which others he referred.

"Yes." Jesus nodded, "But for their own quality. Do you

recall," Jesus said to Otto's puzzled expression, "at the beginning, when you first arrived at Star City, that anyone who joined the crew had to bring a strength to the mission?"

"Uh," Otto thought furiously. "Yeah, I do. Marc knew the Hubble constant. Amelia knew how to fly. Mine was seeing the relationship between disparate pieces of info. Which is no skill at all. And which was no help on the mission. At all." Otto cocked his head to underscore that.

"Fishing for compliments, are you?" Jesus scorned and, as Otto's ears burned, continued, "Okay, then I will give you some. You were critical to the mission. You found Ferdinand. You stopped the questions at the Pearly Gates. You understood the nature of Dis. And, you resisted Ben." Jesus regarded Otto.

"Yeah, but ... and I'm not trying for compliments here, I'm trying to understand why me." He paused. "'Cause I think any of the others could have done all that. Bulsrobe or Virgil or Uzzah or anyone else, for that matter. So why didn't you leave one of them on the ship and take me off, instead? And where are those guys, anyway?"

"Some are waiting. Some are lost." That was a statement worthy of exploration in itself, but Jesus ignored Otto's raising of an interrupting finger and continued. "Of the thirty of you ..."

That definitely required an interruption. "Thirty-one."

"Thirty." Jesus' brow lowered and Otto swore there was distant thunder. "One was an interloper."

Yes. Akiko.

"... each had a particular, important strength. Not a skill. A quality. Forged by resolve. Together, you will be formidable. But only if properly led." And Jesus stared at him.

Took him a minute. "What? You mean, me? Me? You want me to lead?"

"Yes."

"But ... I suck at leading!" Otto was ready to cite hundreds of examples from his mortal life where he had screwed the pooch. Royally. But Jesus held up a Hand, stopping him.

"You make a lot of mistakes," He agreed, "You get people killed" — Otto flashed on his inadvertent leading of the Fallen back to the orbiting ship — "but, you have an ability the others do not. You see the entire picture. You see how the details fit. And you never lose sight of the mission." Jesus turned an expressive hand. "And that is why you made it here."

"But …" Otto spluttered because it still didn't seem right. "Any of the others … most of them, anyway, were better focused than I was. Like Amelia, she was downright relentless. Heck, at one point, I lobbied to abandon the mission and head back to Earth."

"True," Jesus was gazing back over the plain, "but, even in that, your intent was to advance Our cause. It would have been a strategic mistake, but for the right reasons."

"I still think she'd be a better choice. Any of the others would. Except maybe Tac."

Jesus turned, His countenance severe and uncompromising. "Let me be very clear on something. You are not My choice. You are no one's choice. You are chosen because you were given the opportunity. And took it."

Otto should be insulted but he wasn't because Jesus was right (which, given His Nature, was no surprise). Otto was no one's choice because there was nothing special about him.

Nothing at all.

No Divine Hand formed itself into a Pointing Finger and anointed him for this role. No watery tart flung a sword at him. No short straw drawn. Just that, of the individual members of humanity who possessed the single-minded, bull-headed and stubborn quality of staying on mission and who had looked beyond the joys of the City for the Face of God and was willing to trek across deserts and open space to find Him, he was, simply, the one who had made it this far.

So, choose.

Otto looked at the blue gauze sky. If he said no, then in the twinkling of the eye, he stands at the foot of the Golden Throne and has his tears wiped away, and no one blames him or thinks him lesser for wanting that. Not even Jesus would. But if he said yes, then he traverses folds like this blue-lit sun, moving easily between things to wage wars the nature of which he could not conceive. He had no idea of how to get started, much less if he stood a chance.

When did you ever?

Otto didn't hesitate. "Let's do this."

Jesus nodded. "I knew you'd go for it. That's an oddity of Godhead, by the way, knowing things that cannot actually happen until the choice is made. It's sort of a drawback because I know how things will go, but do not actually cause them. That is, if you ignore the physics and principles that We have instilled."

"We?"

Jesus looked at him.

"Right," Otto said, "Sorry. But, everything else You just said sailed right over me."

Jesus grinned. "Explaining New York to ants."

Otto grimaced. "You heard that?"

"You have a lovely singing voice."

Otto chuckled and shook his head. "Remind me to be more circumspect."

"I think I have. About ten million times."

Oof! blow to the solar plexus by the Lord Himself. Because, wow, how many times, as some smart-aleck remark came bubbling to his lips, had a still, small voice whispered, "Dude." Which he'd ignored. With all the subsequent results.

"Point taken," Otto said. Then hesitated. "Will we win?"

Jesus' smile was grim. "Another oddity of Godhead. A series of events present themselves as options. I can see both paths. The one of your victory, the other, your defeat."

"But ... you can see which one will happen. Right?"

"Either can happen. It depends on you."

"Wait." Otto pressed his temples. "You said you knew I would choose before I did choose, but don't know if we win. How is that?"

"Some choices are obvious, especially given the integrity of the decider." A nod at Otto, one that warmed him. "Others depend on variables untested, so all paths are possible."

"That actually makes sense," the ant said.

Jesus nodded and returned to plain gazing. Otto shifted and then slowly stood, watching carefully if this was an egregious violation of protocol and, boom, the plains of Hell but Jesus simply sat and gazed. "Uhm," Otto said, bracing for a Backhand across the face, "what do I do now?"

Jesus glanced at him. "You should get started," He said.

And was gone.

It took Otto about a minute to conclude that Christ was not coming back. He did a slow circle to confirm that he was alone on the plain of ice.

Get started, He said.

Otto let out a long slow breath. Get started? How? Well, let's see, going to need an army but what kind of army and how will it be armed and where is it based and I'm gonna have to get some trucks, I suppose, and who do I see about feeding these guys or do they even need to be fed, being all immortal and everything but an army marches on its stomach and, hoo boy, Otto had no idea how to run an army. Best he had ever done was a small squad.

A small squad.

Tough, well trained, and resolute, a small group could do wonders: usurp supply lines, gather intelligence, sabotage, disrupt, and weaken, allowing the main Army to break the impasse and destroy the enemy. A small group of tough and well-trained humans, filled with resolve, going on mission after mission until … until …

Oh my God, Otto thought, irreverently, I now have a ten-thousand year job.

Which, he realized, was precisely the point.

He thought about that for a few moments, then shrugged and began walking towards the far mountains. He had no idea where he was going but, then, when had he ever?

A figure took form in the distant blue fog. Wary, Otto stopped, not sure if it was Gabriel or Michael, or Azaroth. Maybe even Legion. Wouldn't that be perfect?

The figure stepped forward. "'Bout time you got here," Marc said.

Otto gasped. "Dude!"

"What were you doing all this time, sightseeing? I've got a bet going, ya know."

"Yeah?" Otto said, running up to him, "What, that I'd get lost or something?"

"Well …"

"Shut up," Otto said and grabbed the astronomer in a bear hug.

Which was a little difficult. And dangerous.

Marc was wearing armour, or a modern version of it, metal plates combined with Kevlar and Velcro, a mixture of SWAT and King Arthur. It was blue and black with galaxies and comets and stars racing across the breastplate and over his shoulder in a continuous and ever-changing slide show. His hands bore heavy gauntlets that would have made King Henry proud and a longsword hung from his belt.

"Otto," Marc's voice was muffled against his shoulder, "this is getting a little weird."

"I'm just that glad to see you, man" and hugged him tighter then let him go.

"I think I'm going to cry," Marc said and slapped Otto jovially on the shoulder.

"*Ow.*" Otto winced as the metal stung him, then stepped back where he could take in Marc's get-up. "Wow. That's nice work."

"Thanks," Marc said and did a not-half-bad pirouette, which caused a blue cape to flare. A cape?

Marc read his look as he came back around and shrugged. "Always wanted one."

Otto threw up two fists and shouted "No capes!" in his best Edna Mode.

Marc looked at him blankly. "Sorry," Otto said, "Movie reference. After your time. So," Otto waved a hand over Marc's suit, "where'd you get it?"

"Vulcan," Marc said, burnishing his cuirass.

"Vulcan? You mean, like Spock's planet?"

"No. Like Vulcan."

"Wait ... *the* Vulcan? The Greek god?"

"Roman," Marc said, "And he's not a god but a very talented guy who gets excellent press."

"Waddya know." Otto was impressed. "But, armour? Why?"

"I like the look. And, for what we're about to do," he said, grimly, "it might come in handy."

Okay, that was confusing. "How did you know ... oh, never mind. Just never mind." If there was one thing Otto had learned since dying, explanations were not forthcoming.

Marc grinned and then grabbed Otto's arm. "Come on, let's

go to HQ," he said, and propelled Otto into the gauze.

A moment of dizziness slapped Otto upside the head and he considered throwing up and then he was in Valhalla.

Or, what could have passed for it: a golden hall with soaring arches and banners of red and green and blue lost in the heights, great torches hanging on each buttress and even greater chandeliers swaying from the ceilings. Running from one end of the hall to the other was a banquet table almost bending under the weight of whole pigs and grapes and steaks and every manner of food conceivable.

Marc elbowed him in the ribs. "Nice, huh?"

"Doesn't suck," Otto agreed. "Sure is a lot of food. Where's Claudia?"

"She's here. There's some people who want to welcome you first, though," Marc said, and turned to the right. Otto turned with him.

An armoured group stood at the far end of the table. "Attention!" George Hodge shouted, and metal-clad heels rang together. "Salute!" and swords of various makes, from scimitars to Claymores, ripped from scabbards and soared aloft.

"Uh," Otto said.

"Return the salute," Marc whispered in his ear, "or they'll hold it all day."

"I don't have a sword," Otto whispered back.

"Fake it."

Otto rendered an Air Force salute and that, apparently, was sufficient.

"Quarter!" George shouted again and, in one motion, swords re-sheathed, and the group slammed its heels back together.

"They've been working on that all day," Marc said.

"I see," Otto looked at George standing at the front of the group, his armour bright scarlet-and-blue with great ocean waves sloshing up from the bottom and then cresting across his shoulders, no doubt crashing onto some rocky coastline on the back of his plate. "I have got to get me one of those," Otto said.

George grinned his old salt grin. Guy looked pretty good for someone who'd taken a meteor ride across the universe.

"Finally!" George shouted and there was a rush and cheers and Bulsrobe and Ho and the Widow Wyncke were pounding him across shoulders and back with variously metal thickened gloves and others were hugging him with metal-encased arms and chests and it was a din of metal and "Good to see you!" and "Welcome! Welcome!" and Otto saying, "*Ow! Ow! Ow!*"

Where's Claudia? And Jesus, for that matter?

Otto tried to dodge the more enthusiastic greetings and take a gander about the hall for their presence, but did not see either. He had a sudden and rather disappointed feeling that he would not see Jesus for a long, long time.

And had a terrifying feeling that the same applied to Claudia.

On a different mission?

"I think I owe you ten bucks," Otto said to Bulsrobe, who was shaking Otto's hand out of its socket. "And where's Claudia?"

Bulsrobe laughed. "You can buy the first round," and gestured at the groaning feast table. A response to his debt obligation.

No response to Otto's question.

Why is that?

Bulsrobe's armour was green and greener, giant forests springing out of mountain ranges and soaring to dizzying heights over his shoulder and probably into some glacier lake.

"I have got to get me one of those," Otto repeated. "By the way, how'd you guys survive?"

"Long story," Seth Staples, who was wearing armour of ivy-covered halls — of course, Yale — said, "Which we will lie and exaggerate about."

"As long as it's entertaining," Otto conceded and then frowned around the group encircling him. "We seem to be light. Where's Claudia?"

"She's around. Don't worry."

"Okaay." Around where? "How 'bout Amelia, then? And Virgil?"

The group lapsed into a mournful quiet. "Some are lost," Kesed, in armour depicting the soaring stone towers of his native Ur, toned.

Fear gripped Otto. "Not Claudia! Not her, too!"

The group shifted, a rift forming as the armoured spread out and stepped to either side and faced each other and then drew their swords and crossed them into an arch and all of them looked down the end of it. Otto followed their gazes.

About fifty yards away, at the end of the hall, stood a dazzling vision in armour so white and pure that he could barely look at it. Gold ran through the metal, diamond, too, and the plates were crystalline and porcelain and the person wearing it held a helmet of sheer bright silver under one arm as the great copper hilt of a sword rose above shoulders covered by a cascade of golden hair. A pair of sapphire eyes crinkled at him.

"Claudia," he said.

Of Course, The Wars Continue. You Know That, Because You Continue. You Get A Hint Of The Ferocity From Time To Time — The Light Of Distant Supernovae, The Ripples Of Colliding Black Holes— But It Is All So Very Far Away. There Are Tales Sung Now That You Cannot Hear. There Are Tales Yet To Be Sung. Perhaps The Songs Will Reach Us. One Day.

www.ingramcontent.com/pod-product-compliance
Lightning Source LLC
Chambersburg PA
CBHW020404110726
47899CB00006B/1859